# Just in Time.

# Harry Buckle.

# Just In Time.   By Harry Buckle.

Published by - MarosaJokato Media.
This edition published under licence from MarosaJokato Dublin.
www.MarosaJokato.com
Email: MarosaJokatoMail@Yahoo.com

Paperback:  ISBN: 978-0-9935576-3-7
Kindle eBook:  ISBN: 978-0-9935576-4-4

**The book cover design is by Sam Buckle of
DesignAndFilmCornwall.co.uk.**

**Editorial Advisor Wayne Deakin.
Wayne@FarEastEditorial.com**

*Generally speaking this is a work of fiction, but I should confirm that the overall potential danger referred to in the plot, reflects rather accurately a serious and real problem facing our world today.*

Neither nations nor trader's hold much in the way of reserve stocks as these days 'Just in Time,' is the global business model.

*Any break in the supply chain is potentially very serious.*

Consequently there is a reality to the phrases I have used to show the situation as it really is. *I know, I know, it says all this on the cover-both front and back!-but I find most of my friends-indeed most of us- totally underestimate our reliance on imports.*

*'No Milk Today,' is a song...'No food Today, 'in truth or rumour is a family or even a nationally threatening situation.*

Not only that but, as has been shown in several western nations over the past few years the 'empty shelves 'situations referred to herein could speedily cause general unrest to erupt onto our streets.

With fact and rumour spread equally, at digital speeds these days, such problems, real or rumoured, could cause wider spread local or even national breakdown of law and order in just a few hours.

This is not scare mongering, but a simple truth caused by the almost total reliance of most modern societies on 'Just in Time' delivery of all that is vital to our daily life.

In past years the ships delivering your imports were many and quite small. Now a single ship can carry almost 20,000 containers. That's 20,000 truck loads of- something-anything-everything.

*It takes about 45 trucks to fill the shelves of the average superstore.*
*So there is both good news and bad news there.*

Stop the flow of freight and there's a widespread problem...but when your very big ship does come in, it fixes a lot of problems....

*....Provided of course that all those waiting, have stood quietly in line, for a few days. Likely with no fuel for bus or car, having walked there and waited in the dark, waiting for their daily bread.*
*Then what?*

---

4

*It is also for the many thousands of maritime workers of all kinds and with varied skills, who, despite all the oceans and the weather can throw at them, labour to bring us all we need.....
Just in Time.*

It is worth considering the skill and bravery shown by mariners- ancient and modern. The ancients, explored and then pioneered, from the buccaneering days of sail, the trade routes that still today enable and enrich our lives.

The moderns, unseen and usually unremarked on by the global majority, often now working, high above the seas on a 600 feet long leviathan  still face the daily and very real dangers of the seas and oceans.

Even the most sophisticated of weather tracking navigational devices cannot always avoid hurricanes, typhoons, cyclones, tropical and arctic storms, and the infrequent- but always possible rogue waves.

Waves that have been known to tower above the tallest ship and  to deposit thousands of tons of angry foaming salty water on to the decks and cargo.  Waves that have the power to bend steel, tear deck fittings from their sturdy moorings.

Waves that on occasion, rip apart bolts holding containers in place and then- taking the freed flotsam overboard pour still angrily, back into the ocean. This all leaving even the mightiest ship shaking -like a family dog on the riverbank- waiting for  yet another torrential assault. Or in the case of the family dog, another thrown stick.

Regardless of the waves that follow, then the ordinary seaman and deck crew - oceanic labourers all-will have to venture out on deck, climb high on the swaying and pitching load.  Clinging on and braving the next onslaught of often icy water, they will have to try to secure the cargo.

A cargo perhaps of Banana's from the Caribbean, a Leg of Lamb from New Zealand,  Apples from Southern Africa, Furniture from Ikealand, or from almost anywhere in Asia, a TV, a T shirt or a Telephone.

Who'd have thought, who does think, that many such items have followed in the, sometimes stormy, ocean wakes of those brave mariners - both ancient and modern.

**So this book is for all those men and women. Seafarers All.**

## *Names.*

Famous authors these days, are admirably able to raise money for charities by 'auctioning' the  names to be used as characters in their books. Obviously I have not yet reached that elevated position, but it does raise an interesting point about names in novels.

 The process of choosing names for a novel is not simple.

Allocating the name of, say, a well known politician, sportsman or pop star to be a villain, killer or lothario in one's novel, stretches the imagination and creative thought of both reader and writer in overcoming' the existing image of the 'real name.'

I have real friends called, Paul McCartney, Davy Jones, Daniel Craig, Charlie Brown, Brian Pern, even a George Clooney and a Siri.

All of them christened or at least named, long before their *namesakes'* became globally familiar. For them, the daily process of explanation can on occasions become more than a little wearing.

So I owe a considerable debt of thanks to the following friends who allowed me to 'borrow', without payment, their names.

I hope they enjoy their characters.

**Katie Stanton, Calle 'Charlie' and Amelie Haeggqvist, Magnus Sorensen, Joel and Betts Williams, Paul Isted, Barry Purchase, Matt Button, Alan Whaley,  Rewan Trelawney, Brian Pern, Dal Booth,  Andy Keeling, Andy Allister, Susie and Chris Todd.**

Of course should someone ever make a film or TV series based on this book, their lives will change. Each and every time they check into a hotel, order something over the phone, or just call to make a booking for a restaurant they may rue the day they agreed to become a 'paper' spy, a ships captain, a hero or even a multi millionaire...

**So to them- thanks:**

**Page.**  **Time Line and Events.**

**63. Monday June 20th. 8.30 am.TrePolPen Security Co. Central Singapore:** *Tennis. Don't bet on it!*

**72. Tuesday June 21st. 8.30 am.Marina Bay. Singapore:** *Save the world. No problem, but after last nights excesses, breakfast first.*

**75. Wednesday. June 22nd. 4.00 pm. Inbound towards Heathrow Airport. London. England:** *The actual need for, provision of, and use of, security, is directly relative to the level of threats; perceived or real.*

**87. Wednesday June 22nd. A bright summer's morning.At Rudesheim am Rhine.Germany. River boat moorings:** *Sightseeing time.*

**90. Wednesday June 22nd. Later, on a now cloudy day.Near Rudesheim am Rhine:** *Surprise and sudden fear can redesign your life plan in less than thirty seconds.*

**94. Thursday. June 23rd. 9.00am. An Old Mill and Farmstead. South West France:** *Terror stopped sleep, but eventually exhaustion won.*

**99. Thursday June 23rd. 2.00 pm. Heathrow Airport. London. Again, but this time: Outbound:** *Competent control?....'What's it all about?'*

**110. A long Thursday. June 23rd.Over Eastern US. Elapsed fly time 8 hours:** *Losing a very live A- bomb, even decades ago, must surely only be a bad movie plot, or possibly I supposed the work of complete morons,and in reality nothing to do with my current assignment.*

**115. Still a long Thursday. June 23rd. Sunset. On a US Navy Airbase. Near Fallon.Nevada:** *The US Navy shower provided plenty of water born power- a bit like their navy itself.*

**126. Friday June 24th. Mid Morning.Windsor. 20 miles West of London. England:** *The only problem with having children, is that eventually, they aren't.*

**128. Friday. June 24th. 06.00 am U.S. Pacific time. Navy Airbase. Near Fallon. Nevada:** *Free, with a cold San Miguel beer, an enticing smile, and numerical clarity with Filipino kalendaryo wisdom.*

**140. At 9 hours ahead of Fallon Nevada it was early evening. But still Friday June 24. in Rotterdam. Europe:** *At Calvettioni Ship Control.Hopefully more, 'Ready all the Time' than 'Just in Time.'*

**144. Friday June 24th. Lunchtime. U.S. Pacific time. US Navy Air base near Fallon Nevada.USA:** *More from the Presidents Club. International branch.*

**150. Friday June 24th. 2.00 pm. PST. Outbound.Ex. Fallon. Nevada.USA:** *"You'll arrive rested, relaxed and in stress free style in our latest version executive business jet."*

**158.Saturday June 25th.6.00 pm local. Central Taipei. Taiwan:** *Fear of the unknown is invariably worse than fear of the known.*

**164. Sunday. June 26th. 6.00 am. Central Taipei.Taiwan:** *One of those long, getting nowhere slowly, frustrating days when even the slightest hum from the aircon drives you crazy.*

**173. Sunday. June 26 the Morning. The Old Mill In the Sun. South Western France:** *Quite nice. But not really their choice for a holiday.*

**175. Sunday June 26th. 7.30 pm. Faro Airport. Algarve. Southern Portugal:** *"We have just landed at Faro, Portugal, where the local time is..."*

**182. Monday June 27th. 5.00 am. Central Taipei. Taiwan:** *Fans come in various modes. Wild and enthusiastic, as in music or football crazy,or slow and languid, as in 'Asian tropical cooling' necessity. Rotating or old style 'punka-flip flap', mode optional.*

**190. Monday June 27th Early afternoon. Marrakesh, Morocco, and Venice, Italy:** *Just a one centimeter break in a digital chain.*

**195. Monday June 27th. 7.00 pm. Offices of TrePolPen Vence. Near Nice. France:** *"Hello. It's me."*

**200.Tuesday June 28th.10.30 am.Inbound.From Italy. Copenhagen Airport. Denmark:** *The loneliness of the long distance abductor.*

**205. Tuesday June 28th. 6.00 am. TrePolPen Office. Vence. Near Nice. France:** *A perfect summer morning, Vence. Alpes Maritime.*

**214. Wednesday. June 29th. Too bloody early. TrePolPen Office Vence. South of France:** *The Germans usually call mobile/cell phones- 'handy's.'.. Maybe, just may be, this one was.*

**222. Wednesday June 29th. 11.00 am.In the street outside the TrePolPen office Vence. France:** *In the heat, my run took 35 minutes not the usual 20.*

**225. Wednesday. June 29th.Windsor. Around 20 miles west of London. England:** *River Thames, Castle, Near Ascot Racecourse, nice open countryside... No wonder the Queen lives there for much of the year.*

**228. Wednesday June 29th. Lunchtime. TrePolPen offices. Vence. France:** *All a bit of 'un Montagne Russe. 'Which, I am hopefully reliably informed, is, or should be the French slang for, 'Roller Coaster'.*

**230. Wednesday June 29th 5.30 pm. Geneva Airport. Switzerland. But in the real world...:** *For us arriving at Geneva, the peace and serenity of 'chocolate box' pretty Switzerland belied the turmoil of the unknown.*
*For the Swedish women and children it was ten days since they were kidnapped.*
*For the Asian girls and Brigitte, seven days.*
*For the Parents- an endless nightmare.*
*For us, intent on safe rescue with or without payment of ransom, too bloody long. So long, I wondered if we were starting to grasp at straws and rumour.*

**241. Wednesday. June 29th. 9.00 pm. Sun setting behind the mountains. A lakeside Hotel. Geneva. Switzerland:** *'Well we may be traditionally and peacefully neutral, but we sure as hell aren't neutered.'*

**248. Thursday June 30th. 07.30 am.Inbound.Montpellier Airport. Southern France:** *How they sought some good news, or actually <u>any</u> news, from Vence to Aix En Provence - or actually, Carcassonne.*

**255. Thursday June 30th. 4.00 pm. TrePolPen.S.Co. office Vence. France:** *Miles of smiles.*

**259. Friday July 1st. Good and early. With positive news, perceptions of early starts change. Montpellier Airport. Again. Waiting for inbound:** *If the necklaces had been designed to control by fear, the effect was more wide spread than the than the kidnappers probably assumed. Or may be they had been planning for all contingencies...*

**269. Friday July 1st. 5.00 pm. A horses field near Carcassonne. South West France:** *So near and yet.........*

**277. Friday July 1st. 8.00 pm. On the Canal du Midi. Just South of Toulouse city suburbs:** *The Accidental Millionaires. Part two.*

**282. Saturday July 2nd.06.30 am. A Vacation Villa Carcassonne. South West France. Sun coming up behind the house:** *Armies may, 'march on their stomachs', but they survive and win on planning. Planning is good. Unknown, is not good.*

**285. Saturday July 2nd. 2.00 pm. Marseilles. France. Marignane Airport. Freight area:** *One of the most evocative, and almost forgotten movie themes of all times is 'Borsalino'. A great movie, set in the intrigue of the criminal underworld of Marseille.*

**288. Saturday July 2nd. Dusk .On the banks of the Canal du Midi, a few hundred meters from the Old Mill in the Sun:** *TXT. Oleg: Departed MRS. Est. Arr NKC with Gold 9.00 pm local.*

**290. Saturday July 2nd. Evening. Boeing 737. SF Freighter. Over North Africa.Landing ETA- 9.00 pm Dahkla. Western Sahara:** *Globally, at any one time, 1,037.021 people are allegedly waiting for the pizza man.*

**292. Saturday July 2nd. Around 10 pm.Behind Le Vieux Moulin au Soleil. Between Carcassonne and Toulouse. France:** *There may well be, more relaxing ways to spend a Saturday night.*

**294. Saturday. July 2nd. 10.00 pm. Airside. Dahkla Airport. Western Sahara:** *Surfing was not why he was here this time, but maybe, ducking and diving could deliver a result.*

**301. Castelnaudary France. Around midnight July 2nd- early on the 3rd. Tears on the parade ground:** *No words can describe...*

**305. Meanwhile: Sunday July 3rd. 1.00 am. All is quiet in Dahkla town. Western Sahara. Dark:** *All that glitters....*

**320. End September. A meeting room, in a business hotel near Toulouse Airport:***Almost 12 weeks had elapsed since the parents of the two kidnapped Swedish mothers with their three children, and those of three teenage girls, had gathered in this very room to await the outcome of a bid to rescue their kidnapped offspring.*

**326. Castelnaudary. The first of three days at the end of September:** *Both of Andy and Faye-Lin's hotel barges were tied up alongside each other in the Castelnaudary canal basin, a broad expanse of water on the canal near the town center.*

**336. Castelnaudary.A second nice September morning:** *By 8.30 on a bright and sunny morning the smell of coffee permeated even the sleepiest of cabins.*

**341. September.The third morning in Castelnaudary Probably: That's as in. Probably the third.Probably Castelnaudary. Probably morning:** *The party, increasingly rowdy, had continued on the boats late into the night.*

**Four years ago:** *Accidental Millionaire: A prologue or perhaps more, an enticing travelogue.*

Andy Allister hadn't realistically expected to become a millionaire. Neither had he expected to become a gold bullion robber or a national hero in parts of Scandinavia and Asia.

Like most 'occurrences' in his life a woman was to blame.Generally considered by girls as irresistible when sober and outrageous when happily drunk. From his surfing days working on a Portuguese beach to his time at University he was either attached, unattached, getting attached or on the run from a variety of beautiful girls.

He was good fun company and was one of those guys who men generally didn't view as threat, except perhaps to their daughters. Andy had, by his early forties settled down somewhat. Settled down in fact as the owner skipper of a *'péniche'*.

A peniche in this case being a luxury hotel barge that, for much of the year, usually fully booked with guests, made its way in stately fashion along the gentle sun kissed waterways of The Canal du Midi in southern France.

The Canal, winding its way between the vineyards of the Languedoc or Aquitaine basically joins The Atlantic Ocean with the Mediterranean.

Cutting right across France, parallel with the Pyrenees and completing a navigable channel from the Atlantic coast of the River Garonne at Bordeaux to the Mediterranean at the salt pans,'etangs' and marshes that extend through the Camargue towards the bustling port city of Marseille.

Shaded by tall trees along most banks, the passage of huge old converted wine or general cargo barges like Andy's beloved 'Lady Faye' through sun baked villages is an idyllic and peaceful journey interrupted now and again by the bustle of an 'Ecluse' or lock.

Conforming to the laws of basic physics that require water to remain 'level', canals are essentially flat. Over distance, their routes however often require them to climb or descend hills. This is achieved with a series of gated, water filled steps or locks, 'Ecluse', to the French.

At these locks the controlled inflow or out flow of water into the dock area between the two sets of gates raises or lowers the boats to the level of the next stretch of water in the canal. Like filling or emptying a bath, albeit on a somewhat larger scale.

The only difference being that the drained out water gets re-used in the next section of the canal. The operations of the locks, lifting or lowering large boats majestically are one of the attractions of Canal life especially in South West France, although of course the region's famed wine and food probably has something to do with it!

Incredibly, Paul Riquet's vision of linking the two seas, opened for business just over 500 years ago. As Andy would later tell his guests-'that's almost 400 kilometers of hand dug channel, that coincidently makes Spain and Portugal an island.

For hundreds of years it was an enduring success, it hauled anything and everything- albeit slowly. Then came the 1950's, and as elsewhere, trucks started to dominate the freight business- faster and mostly 'door to door', and soon, in fact to become, 'just in time.'

The canal looked doomed. But in the early sixties the very leisurely nature of the journey, with some vision, surprisingly mainly from English holiday companies, made the canal busy again.

Self-drive boats, accommodating 4 or more were the thing, and the English, Scandinavians and eventually travelers from around the world, happy as ever to seek the sun, fell in love with the peaceful canal side villages. Their attractive granite or sandstone baking in the Aquitaine or Languedoc sun, surrounded by miles of vineyards.

They loved the simple canal side restaurants and cafes, and of course finding local wine's to sample and buy at the point of production.

The old tow paths along the Canal banks, originally for the horses that pulled the barges, those days made and still make perfect bike routes. Ideal for popping out to get some provisions, fresh breads for breakfast, some local cheese and fruit and of course a bottle or two for the evening.

Such cycling made easier by the fact that canals and their paths have that advantage of not going up or down hill. Except of course now and again at those locks.

As truck freight and general road traffic became the norm nationwide the French constructed an extensive modern network of toll roads, 'AutoRoute's'.

It was no co-incidence that the engineers of the AutoRoute system pretty much chose the same route as figured out five hundred years earlier for the canal by men on horseback, with not much more than some chain measures and experienced eyes.

So the AutoRoute 'entre Deux Mers', starting in Bordeaux, on the Atlantic coast ,was usually within five kilometers, and on occasions within a few meters of the canal as it also threaded it's way past Toulouse and then castled cities Bezier, Carcassonne and on through the vineyards, as the name stated, 'between the two seas' to the Mediterranean coast at Narbonne.

Andy Allister had been in the maritime oil prospecting and surveying business, which paid well enough, but months at sea confined on oil rigs or surveying vessels, had eventually made him think of making a lifestyle change.

In 2009 he had been flipping channels on his TV, when he saw a soon to be familiar sight. It was lock full of boats on the Canal Du Midi.

He watched on, and observed a famous and much liked British chef, Rick Stein, on a very luxury 'péniche' cooking and extolling the virtues of local produce, markets, restaurants and of course the wines, as the boat with its luxury cabins, and ambiance to match, made its leisurely way from Bordeaux down to the Med.

There and then, as he viewed the program he announced, to the shock of his work mates, friends and family, "I'm going to go and live on a boat."

Given that he'd spent the previous few years saying exactly the opposite. "I've got to do something else, I can't stand being on these bloody boats any more." No one took any notice.

No one took much notice either when Andy spent all his leave time travelling in his old car the length of the French canal system searching for a boat to buy or convert.

He learned as he researched, that the season on the canal Du Midi was one of the longest in France. It started quite early for international holidaymakers in April and finished in October as the days closed in and the autumn mists and cold morning dews enveloped the vineyards.

Andy also learned that many 'peniche' projects had over the years failed. Mostly as they were created by underfunded dreamers.

Many were now used as cheap engineless accommodation and most of them were in a sorry state. Especially as places to drag the boats out of the water and perform necessary maintenance were few and far between- and expensive. So wooden hulls rotted and iron ones rusted.

Then along came Rick Stein with the global appeal of his TV show which, coupled with the advent of the internet, had more easily enabled specialist holiday companies to be discovered and bookings to be made. Suddenly Luxury Barging Holidays on the canal had become big business. Of course, this had doubled or trebled the selling price of all available boats – even those barely holding water and sitting on a muddy canal bottom.

After almost a year Andy was on the verge of consigning his dream to the deep oceans on which he seemed to spend most of his life. Bored and annoyed, back at work ,as he scrolled through his mass of mostly spam emails in his account, he almost missed the one that would change his life.

Delete, delete, delete, he almost clicked delete on one from a company for whom he had previously worked. He didn't have very good memories of them.

Ten years earlier the company always seemed to have money troubles, and after one three month surveying trip, they had paid him in company shares-instead of cash.

On trying to sell the shares he discovered pretty damn quick that shares indeed do 'go down as well as up'. and his three months pay was pretty worthless. So he stuffed the shares in a drawer and forgot all about them. Until, a good few years later he opened that email...

*Att: Mr. A Allister. Formal offer. Further to our earlier mails. Regarding your shareholding.*

*This is to confirm that the takeover of our company by Marinfactus Surveys International is proceeding forthwith. Under UK company law (See note 341) We intend to exercise our option and compulsorily purchase your shareholding.*

*The price paid will be US $14 per share and thus after costs and we will remit to you in the UK £39,825. Subject to exchange rate on day of settlement. Please forward to us your share certificates. If the certificates are not available please complete the attached affidavit bla,bla bla..*

The last parts of the emailed letter were indeed a bla, bla, blur-but the amount offered doubled his available cash to buy a peniche, and wasn't bad for three months work all those years ago.

Back in the UK, on taking advice he discovered that indeed, 'what was offered was what he could get', and that the shares had to be sold. But he also found that due to his extended working time abroad, little tax was payable on the amount that was credited to his account in surprisingly quick time.

Once back in France- Easy Jet to Montpellier- and renting a car, he made straight for a small canal side boatyard. The faded and rusted old sign had seen better days, it probably read, '*Bateaux Construits et pour les Vendre, ou a Louer*'. The yard with rotting and rusting old boats of all kinds wasn't much better.

Even the dog and the owner looked like they had seen better days, although over time Andy would discover that was a bit of a hasty judgement of both dog and owner, and not a considered evaluation as a professional surveyor like him should make.

Much to his relief the reasons for his visit were still there, amongst some sad looking rental boats, there were two barges. One floating low in the water was surrounded by reeds and tall grasses. The other was on a slipway half out of the water, half way through a serious maintenance attack on it. An attack, beaten back by the sad demise of the owner.

The boatyard owner, a wily old gent called Jean-Baptiste was keen to see the back of the boats. But he was also keen to get paid for work and rent already in hand.

So he greeted Andy amiably. In pretty quick time, despite some hesitation by the owner's widow, the fact that the boats had failed to sell for more than three years, and with a threat from the boatyard to re-possess one in lieu of outstanding fees, she accepted Andy's basic offer.

Within 8 weeks, also quick, by French standards at least, Andy became the owner of two rusting hulks at much less than he had offered for one a year before.

The boatyard owner, on seeing the years rent in cash, in a plastic bag said, "Mai Oui, Andy could install an old shipping container on the quayside and convert it to live in, at no extra charge, *but he would have to feed the guard dog.*"

Within a few months Andy, now with shower and toilet installed in the trailer, and gas barbecue outside under an awning was learning new skills as a boat builder. Or more strictly a boat converter.

He employed two carpenters, Carlos and Joao, both Portuguese, who it turned out did have boat building skills and were delighted to work with Andy. A boss who didn't mind getting his hands dirty- and as it happened who spoke good Portuguese.

Within one month more, as spring approached a small flower garden and a veggie patch appeared around the converted trailer. A tablecloth graced the outside table.

When some remarkable underwear appeared on the washing line it became clear to the boat yard owner, who only came in occasionally, that either Andy had feminine side to him or a ladies influence was at hand.

Even the rough, tough and generally red wine coloured and fueled Jean-Baptiste was surprised and then entranced when a diminutive and extremely beautiful Asian lady appeared from the bowels of the Peniche with tools in hand and a smudge of dirt on her face.

"Bonjour Monsieur," she smiled.

It transpired that Faye-Lin was a second generation Vietnamese. Her parents lived in Paris and had a small café near Place Pigalle. She had followed some 'university romance to Narbonne', and after that failed she had got a job working on the cash checkout of a hypermarket near Montpellier where she had met Andy.

Several shopping trips by Andy, 'do you really need more fromage, sir, that's the third lot this week.' Eventually, discretely, as invitations from customers were somewhat frowned on by management, she had enjoyed a laughing and wine filled evening in a nearby Pizzeria.

A few more evening pizzas, and some Vietnamese food in Narbonne and suddenly Andy's trailer was home to two. Her cooking skills were great. Not only Vietnamese style, but somewhere she had mastered the legendary Portuguese Caldo Verde, a vegetable soup with spicy sausage. Even more surprising, she was a dab hand at Fejoada ,the great Brazilian black bean dish.

She explained. "Well there were thousands of Portuguese guest workers in Paris and in the Pigalle Area rather a lot of Brazilian guest workers also. In the Portuguese case, they were mostly builders, and in the Brazilian, many were mostly ladies or 'almost ladies' whose working hours were somewhat nocturnal."

Her mother had figured out that 'Pho', the legendary Vietnamese soup could be adjusted quite happily to suit both sets of local customers. The Parisian Brazilians and the Portuguese had reciprocated by developing regular taste also for spring rolls and spicy noodles. Ducks feet and crispy beaks, optional.

So it was a happy and well fed team that worked on through a hotter and hotter summer. Even the guard dog was getting fat.

Andy's budget held up well- helped by the Portuguese guys sense of economy, and the fact that they could see two or three years work ahead if Andy did manage to start work on the second peniche the following year.

Additionally the Portuguese building mafia seemed to produce amazing results. Carlos and Andy were for ever travelling in Andy's beaten up old van to boatyards as far away as Marseille, where for just a few euros they bought old style ceramic basins, old brass boat fittings and on one memorable expedition a whole truck full of engine parts for the Peniche's yet to run diesel. The bargain that really impressed was a load of reclaimed teak deck planks. More than enough for both boats, rescued from a demolition site's burn pile, all for the price of a case of wine.

As the autumn approached, Andy was approached by one of his previous employers to take on a month's very well paid consultancy work with one of their old clients.

He was loath to leave, but the Portuguese guys and Faye-Lin said, "It's crazy not to take it. The month's fee almost covers the rent for next year to Jean-Baptiste."

Six weeks later Faye-Lin picked Andy up at Toulouse airport in their old Citroen 2cv. En route back to the boat she moaned and moaned about the Portuguese. "The bastardo's," (Brazilian influence I think).

"For the last two weeks I never see them on the bloody boat. Never. They never put their foot on the boat one time."

Andy was seething by the time they pulled into the yard, and some shouts and banging on the hull of the Peniche produced no one. " Bastards. You're right." he said.

As he spoke, what sounded like a machine gun or series of explosions came from the old boat builders shed, and a cloud of smoke billowed out of the door.

As he ran towards the scene, out through the smoke came his two Portuguese workers beaming- coughing a bit –but beaming.

"You lazy good for nothings, call yourselves boat builders. Lazy bastards." Then having considered to whom he was talking, he stopped and then repeated his words in Portuguese.

The two Portuguese just stood there grinning- eventually Carlos said, "Hello Andy, welcome back. Let me speak."

Walking back into the boat shed through the smoke he said, "Come with me, look, you are right we are not boat builders. Now we are engineers." There belching smoke- but actually and amazingly running, was the Peniche engine."

"Now you have fired us we can get better jobs as engineers."

With a lot of back slapping and laughter- they adjourned to the autumn shade of the trailer where a welcome home feast was prepared. "We even remembered to stir the fejoada as well," said Carlos, "We make the plan with Faye-Lin to make you really pissed off. She work well I think."

They proposed a variety of toasts in the good local wine—and with some drawing on napkins they explained how they had managed to get the engine out of the boat. Andy had been worrying about the cost of renting a crane to do this  knowing he'd have to rent twice, once to get the engine out and if it could be salvaged, once again to put it back in.

It turned out that with pulleys, chains and an 'A frame,' borrowed from 'more Portuguese friends' on a Sunday, "the boss their firm not even miss it for a few hours," and with help from Faye-Lin they had achieved the impossible.

The plan the next day was to pull the now lighter boat right out of the water on the boatyard ramp. They had wanted to do it before, but when they did the whole boat started to creak, and Jean-Baptiste suggested they wait, until the engine was out.

Andy also learned that there was a plan for the re-installation of the engine-when the boat was floating, but before that, it, the engine needed a lot of work.

The Autumn passed quickly, and even longish spells of rain didn't interrupt work too much as they were fitting out the inside. The whole cargo hold, with a slightly raised roof allowing good windows and headroom, became five luxury cabins with En-suite shower rooms and toilets, and a stateroom/dining area.

In the stern they had a wheelhouse, a decent size kitchen galley and a smallish bedroom with a double bunk. On top of the cabin, they planned a sundeck with recliners and chairs.

Having installed the reclaimed teak deck timbers-and covered them in plastic to keep them clean, they were fitting the first of the deck rails on the top of that roof when fortunately Jean-Baptiste came by.

He had developed quite a taste Friday's Fejoada.

"Stop, Stop," or actually, "Arret Arret," he said. "Those rails will be too high for the round arch of the bridge at Capestang or even Carcassonne Ecluse." Andy looked panic stricken, having a luxurious and safe deck area was crucial.

"Wait. Attend," said Old J-B and he stomped off into the boat shed, calling Carlos to come with him, "vite, vite. "Some minutes later they appeared dragging some old style railings behind them.

He spoke, "They all have deck slots with a hinge into which you place them. You screw the base pieces in the deck and when you near those bridges you lie down the rails."

"The chairs you put on the fore deck, the passengers come and sit with you at the wheel. They love the adventure, provided you not forget of course." J-P continued, "I know those rails would be good for something one day. I give them to you - my cadeau- a gift for your bateau."

"Actuellement," he said, removing his dusty old beret, and revealing a surprisingly pink head, and bowing to Faye- Lin. "Non, actuellement, I give them to you, You feed me well all this year and you always smile at these bad boys."

All of which resulted in another early Friday finish for the team.

By the end of December the engine was re-installed - now completely re built by a local specialist- Jean-Baptiste's advice again. "You did well mon braves to get her out- but- she need the complete re-build. Because if she fail when you 'ave the customers then you 'ave the big sh*t."

Of course he was right. He usually was and it now ran very silently and smoothly.

The engineer said, "it's been well treated, once we cleaned out the rust and crap we found it to be good and oily underneath."

" These are really sea boat engines where they work hard, but because they were on the canal they usually only ran quite slow. Being in fresh water, not salt, helps and so now they should be good for years."

So Rick Stein was a hero again. With considerable appreciation of the food, and for the Canal scenes, even Jean-Baptiste had watched the TV series on dvd with a commentary in French by Faye-Lin.

January came and with their web site up and running the first of their bookings were confirmed for the last week of May.

In early April, it was the Easter holidays and a whole flock of Andy and Faye-Lin's friends and family came down to get the boat finished. Including his parents and hers. Her's making their first trip to visit her outside Paris.

Curtains were made, plumbing connected, final coats of paint applied. Faye-Lin, her Thai friend Mali and Faye-Lin's parents fed everyone wonderfully, with a mix of French, Thai, Brazilian and Vietnamese cooking. Andy remarking that, " They were geared up to feed guests of all nations once they started in business."

Jean-Baptiste became a favourite with all, as did Joao and Carlos's wives who had also come over for the final weeks work.

On the Friday , together, Andy's and Faye-Lin's mums smashed a bottle of champagne over the bows , and the 'Lady Faye' made her maiden voyage from J-B's boat yard along the canal and through the first lock from the yard.

There was, in fact, a good reason for going through the lock, just past it the canal widened out into a small lake, or 'etang'. At almost 30 meters long ,there were a limited number of places on the canal where she could be turned without getting a lot of mud and weeds around the propeller.

As the week's working party wound down on the Saturday night, by popular vote it was decided that the second Peniche, when funds allowed it to be finished should be named, 'Lady Mali.'

On Monday, the boat yard seemed somewhat deserted as the Portuguese guys packed up tents, chairs and tables borrowed from the campsite across the canal. Andy was nervous, today was the day of the fire and safety inspection, without a certificate for which they couldn't trade.

J-P's old van was the first to arrive and as well as J-P, a lady of indeterminate age got out of the passenger side. Somewhat shocked, for the first time they met Mrs. J-P.

A flood of French between Faye-Lin and Mrs. J-P produced the news that, "She had sat next to the mother of the fire inspector at school, and she had many times changed the little boys diapers. Any signs of trouble from him and there would be hell to pay."

Fortunately for Andy and Faye-Lin, and most probably for the fire inspector, there had been no corners or costs cut with the fire and safety work. Apart from a change of position for a fire extinguisher and a bigger sign on the emergency exit all was well.

That night for the first time, Andy and Faye-Lin planned to sleep in their cabin on the boat having moored up just a hundred meters or so from the boat yard.

They sat on the deck with a glass of wine, and agreed it had been a hell of an effort- but they were pretty much ready for their first paying passengers. The pickup point, Castelnaudary, was about 150 kilometers up the canal with about 62 locks to navigate first.

All good practice they decided, and blew out the candle lanterns.

## 2. 'Just in Time.'

*'No Milk Today', is a song.*

*'No Food Today,' in your supermarket or local store is a family threatening situation, likely leading to a rapid breakdown of law and order.*

A sunny morning on the Canal Du Midi. South Western France. Delighting, after a years hard work, in waking on their now completed barge, in fact so complete and luxurious that, 'barge' seemed a bit of a misnomer, Andy and Faye-Lin had a leisurely start to the day. Eventually Faye-Lin unloaded a bicycle from the davits on the back of the boat and set off along the – flat - towpath to buy fresh morning bread.

Andy roused himself, and relaxed in the sun on the deck for a while thinking about all the efforts of the past year, he had the urge to stay relaxed on deck, soaking up the sun and enjoying the morning.

But duty called and he decided that he should try and connect up the satellite TV system that they had installed for the use of guests who perhaps , despite the promise of, 'a vacation away from it all,' couldn't quite disconnect from the real world.

Much to his relief it connected very simply, and the first pictures that flashed and then steadied on the screen were from a 24 hour news channel showing huge container ships, tug boats, harbours, cranes.

In fact all the world that he hoped he had left behind. Never the less, he couldn't resist turning up the audio and listening as well as watching.

The sincere and, very serious, TV news presenter, of course these days, wearing a regulation life jacket, was balancing on a smallish boat with a selection of huge container ships in the background.The choice of pictures shown on screen now varied to fit with the sincere, very serious and now also uber dramatic voiceover:

*"Just in Time. You go out to buy something. In a market, a stall, a store, a village shop, a massive supermarket , a gas station. Whatever. Wherever...You pick up what you want, need, must have or can afford...Food for your family, a phone, clothes, medicines, furniture or a furry toy."*

*" Maybe some manufacturing parts, equipment to purify the nation's drinking water, fuel to keep us warm or different fuel to deliver unto us what we need, want or can afford."*

With extra emphasis the presenter-now looking a little wind blown, but very concerned, continued:

*"These days almost all of what you buy, need, or covet is imported or relying on imports in some vital way."*

Presenter makes dramatic pause...

*"Even if locally produced, it's probably manufactured, harvested or processed and then delivered, using imported machinery or parts."*

*"You wander the malls or high streets of the world gazing at the well stocked window's, or look at online shopping catalogues. Make comparisons and choices, your goods are instantly available."*

**"But find a gap, something out of stock and not on the shelf or in the catalogue, a missing display, a rack with one item not there, not your size...the empty space is like a missing tooth."**

**"Very annoying...but unlike your missing tooth, the space in the store, the gap on the shelf, out of stock items are mysteriously filled or replaced overnight...as if by magic.. Someone's boat has come in."**

*" In some cases, the now available goods are vital to, or even save, lives. Drugs, surgeon's tools, hospital equipment, fire trucks, phones, they all arrive. Just in time. Life continues. Just in time."*

**"The old and new worlds now live by: 'Just in Time'. And 85% of everything, everywhere, to fulfil that magic, travels by ship across the oceans and then by truck in those containers. With almost 20,000 containers on some ships, that's a lot of trucks needed ."**

The TV pictures showed enormous automated container ports, huge cranes plucking containers from massive ships, and accurately placing them down onto waiting trucks.

**" Most of our daily essential foods, fruits, fish, meats and more, everything, all arrive in those big boxes every day and very few reserves are held in stock by your local supermarket, corner store or those who supply them."**

The presenter, still looking deadly serious, but still balancing on a small boat as he delivered his words to camera...

**" Note this. Again. Even if we grow it or harvest it locally, as in much of Europe, it's very likely that the machines needed to plant and then reap that harvest, process, transport, sell and deliver our vital foodstuffs all rely on imported parts. "**

*"In the geographically larger USA, despite the benefits of them having some regional storage, the supply will be equally affected, as they have a longer 'supply chain', with more links at risk of breaking."*

*"Stop the flow of goods : and it's like turning off the life support of a nation or nations."*

*"But as has been shown many times, there is nothing more likely to produce an instant break down in law and order than empty supermarket shelves."*

The presenter stood, and even more unsteadily delivered, what Andy assumed was his closing lines:

*'No milk today,' is a song. No food today with empty supermarket shelves , is a street riot."*

But there was more, and now Andy, who had been somewhat converted by the facts presented, listened carefully:

*"If Just in Time isn't in time....If for some reason the boat doesn't come in"..*

*.. Then very quickly, spreading like wildfire, with both the reality and the rumour, of empty shelves in the food shops, the unthinkable will happen. Our peaceful society, as we in most western countries have known it for many years of plenty since the 1950's will break down. Very quickly."*

The camera cut away to fairly recent dark and blurred pictures , complete with dramatic music, of street riots and looting in North London and parts of the USA...long pause...and the voiceover came back, in slightly ironic tones:

*"But hey, relax. When we need more, of anything and everything, it's on the way, from somewhere, it always is.*

*It'll all be here tomorrow. Surely, 'Just in Time' the last minute magic will happen...... Won't it?"*

Long silence, and the TV screen cut to logo's and credits.

In Andy's case, he was still sitting, somewhat concerned by what he had seen, when Faye-Lin returned with bread and chocolate croissants.....

*Just in time.*

### 3. One Day in May. New Zealand.

*No one expects problems to come out of New Zealand. Unless you're an opposing rugby team that is.*

Just a couple of years back, the town council of Cubert, South Island, New Zealand were more than a little relieved when after some months of uncertainty a company stepped in to take over their soon to close meat processing and export plant.

Local farmers relied on it to buy their beef and lamb as it was the only processing plant for several hundred miles. Despite a little, as was expected, bad mouthing from the local labour union over the fact that the new owners were apparently a Japanese or Chinese company, the investment was a welcome relief.

Regardless of where the money came from, jobs were jobs.

For the farmers, a sale was a sale. No sale, was a still hungry sheep and an equally hungry farmers family.

When the new owners announced a speedy plan to upgrade the facility, relief turned to smiles. They needed to respond to increasing global demand from supermarkets for 'ready to cook meals'.

Having carried out market research, they intended to add a range of prepared meats and frozen dishes to their range of products.

Not only that but apparently they also had a demand from Japan for organic, line caught fish. Another bonus for a specialised small business in which New Zealand excels.

So the plan for a new laboratory and processing lines with some new jobs was positively beamed at, and quickly approved at local planning meetings, and warranted a small civic reception complete with pictures in the local paper and a decent write up in the farming press.

New Zealand with its purity of location and produce has long had a worldwide reputation for its excellent meat, fish and dairy products. *So indeed, no one expects problems to come out of New Zealand- unless you're an opposing Rugby team that is.*

Really, no one expect problems of any kind from New Zealand, and so although highly professional, as the shipping companies demanded, security was usually at a basic minimum in the *'reefer'* filling section of the meat processing plant.

*Reefers are the shipping term for refrigerated containers, a special type of those big truck sized metal freight boxes that you see everywhere.*

Both *frozen and chilled* shipments left this particular plant in containers every week. Storage life of frozen meat can be many months.

For *'deep chilled but fresh'* , shipping lines have to organise ship routings to deliver to markets within about 60 days.

At the processing plant the big steel containers are steam cleaned, disinfected and reversed up to the loading docks, connected to air blowers emitting a stream of cold air. Depending on the planned reefer temperature, the already chilled or frozen, plastic shrink wrapped meats are loaded in huge open sided plastic crates.

Various temperature probes throughout the container are then plugged into load condition recording units through the front wall of the container. The doors closed and sealed.

Paperwork, certificates of origin, health, and hygiene with bar codes and customer destination details are recorded on computers and paper copies inserted in the docket box located by the refrigerators built into each container.

The reefer container, relies on its own refrigeration unit, powered at first by the truck carrying it and then by a network of special connectors on the container ship, is good to go.

Once on the ships, information regarding each refrigerated container or 'reefer", it's 'load condition,' i.e. temperature, origin and destination is fed to the shippers and customers agents, every few hours. Data originally sent via the power cables to the ships bridge where it was sent on by satellite.

*More modern containers systems incorporate a satellite data phone on every container.*

This not only sends data reports direct in real time from anywhere in the world, but also allows the shipper or content owner to make remote adjustments to temperature, humidity and such, directly to each container whilst it's still thousands of miles away from its destination.

So as to be ready, *'just in time,'* for onward shipment to supermarkets and their customers, some importers chose to remotely start the defrost or final ripening processes before the ship even arrives at the final destination port.

Container ships with reefers of perishable produce are mostly routed East out of New Zealand direct to the West Coast ports and markets of Canada and Long Beach USA .Some go through the Panama Canal and into the East Coast ports of the US or straight across the Atlantic to Europe.

Others via transshipping docks in Asia, then via the Suez Canal bound for Italy, France, and Spain or right round northern France to U.K., Rotterdam, Hamburg or Scandinavia. At the recently renamed, 'Cubert Meat and Fish Supply Company' over the next two years business went well. Around December last, a new manager was appointed by the Japanese owners.

The plant already had an exemplary safety record and his new product ideas, re-packaging and an investment in ultra modern temperature control reporting systems, looked set to win them even more business from a global market increasingly obsessed with food hygiene and traceability.

So it was, that over a three week period in May that around 75 reefer containers were loaded, with pre-certified frozen meats and ready meals, and loaded with other containers on various ships, with a further 45 following a two weeks later.

Some were destined for the USA, East and West. Some for various locations in Europe. Other shipments, with most containers, were bound for a container port in China, where the containers were transshipped into different vessels going to a variety of destinations.

At the container port in China, as in other similar facilities worldwide security was tight and professional. Fear of terrorist action and of course smuggling, meant that the destination nations demanded it.

In the vast transhipping area, with its huge gantry cranes, trucks and railcars - inspections were routine, but professional and efficient. Inspectors even inspected the inspectors.

Inspection mainly consisted of comparing loading dockets with the e mailed bills of lading with contents listed. Most containers had some kind of radiation scan (Bizarrely containers full of cat toilet sand, regularly set off the alarms).

Special investigators with sniffers, sniffing for explosives sampled a few air vents. With 15,000 containers going through the loading and unloading docks that day, there wasn't much time for each sniff.

A really full physical inspection could take hours per container and with soon to be 20,000 containers on some of the biggest ships and 10,000 on most, *so sniffing was a key* 'routine'.

Origin 'New Zealand', shipments qualified as of slightly less concern than certain smaller ports elsewhere.

In conventional non reefer containers, perfumes, scented candles, floral air fresheners, and many of the adhesives used in furnishings also made the sniffers react. Strangely enough fireworks, of which the Chinese export many, did not.

So the routine was:

Sniff, check.

Get a sniffer alarm ,

Check the manifest.

Check the docket on the container, ready meals. OK. Origin New Zealand.

So, NZ. Good.

Push the OK button.

Move on...... the next container was waiting and the next, as were the cranes, the supervisors, the ship, and somewhere, the customers.

So it was that no one noticed any problems with number of containers packed with boxes of frozen 'ready to carve' processed meats. Shrunk wrapped extremely airtight in double plastic.

Special temperature recording cables plugged into a sensor recording unit (new improved model, direct connection to Sat phone) mounted in the fridge bay on the end of each of the reefer containers.

No one noticed either, in the usual pressured environment that about ten of the ships, with general mixed container loads, all with some full reefers on board had a number of crew changes before departure. There were always crews coming and going, the majority Filipino. On leave, changing ship, fired from what is after all a tough job, re-joining after sick leave or a rare visit home to family.

New crews employed or retained by agencies known to the shipping lines, joined and left at many ports.

'Papers in order? Check.

'Passport'? Check.

'Health Certificate? ' Check.

"Mariners transit visa?" Check.

'Mariners passbooks'? Check.

'Marine security pass'? Scan. Check.

All fine. "The bus will take you to loading berth 14. Have a good trip, see you in a month or so."

## 4. One day in May. Manila City. Philippines:

*Beware of Gringo's bearing ideas and offers....Or not.*

With it's much needed and regularly rain filled open storm drains, choked with rubbish, block built houses patched up with pressed steel sheets, old plastic advertising signs. And everywhere, that, seen worldwide, blue and white tarp stuff, the little side street looked very much like many other Philippine city suburbs.

Or slum, to most westerners passing in a cab or Jeepney.

Despite its run down appearance, to the nine families who lived there, it was not only home, but unlike many of the shanty towns and flood refuges that surrounded many of the key cities in the Philippines, and more to the point, the families owned the land it was built on.

And they had the papers to prove it lodged in city hall.

Or they thought they had.

The families in Pele Montinez Rd had formed an association and bought the land ten years before from a hard up builder who needed cash. He was stuck with this little parcel of land.

It was just bad luck for him that an ever expanding supermarket chain had taken over the main site, thus almost cutting his little parcel of land off from the main road, with the exception of a small narrow track.

With some effort, the purchase price was manageable for the Ortegas, the Lopez's, the Los Valamos and the widow Simonez and the others. Nine families all related over a couple of generations one way or another by marriage, or by parenthood of various kids.

They had the money to buy the land as twenty of the men folk and five of the women were employed at sea by various cruise and freight shipping lines. Although regarded as being poorly paid by international standards, their wages were good and regular by local Philippine standards.

The fact that they had any savings was down to some strong women and one particular 'grand mama.' The women regularly intercepted incoming remittances and cash before their 'boys', spent it in bars and karaoke's when they came home on their rare breaks from sea.

Most Filipinos working at sea are doing so to support their families and are rightly proud of their children's progress in society.

With 450,000 registered mariners working around the world there's hardly a ship in afloat, except for Indian and Chinese ones, that doesn't have some, *'Pinoy',' Philipino', 'Filipino'* crew.

The much quoted Captains joke is, 'They're the only people in the world with about ten spellings for their name.' But shipping companies, and indeed Captains love them.

They mostly speak reasonable English, at least to their officers and customers, amongst themselves local Tagalog or Filipino Bisaya dialects unite the various styles of the mainland cities and islands.

On cruise ships , they appear neat and smiling to passengers when serving food or servicing the cabins. And they are cheap. Not quite as cheap as the Chinese, Indians and Bangladeshi's, but cheap.

On almost every freight delivery ship, piled high with containers, you'll find Filipino sailors. Some skilled watching charts , dials and computer screens in, depending on latitude and routing, the air-con cool or warmth of the control room high above the oceans. Looking out over 600 feet (200 meters) of ship carrying boxes, boxes, boxes.

Most Filipinos in fact, are on board 'labourers'. 'Ordinary', despite their skills, not even really 'Able'- seamen. Hunched, clinging on for dear life, high above the water on top of a container stack in salty sticky coats, in all weathers, checking clips and bolts that hold those thousands of boxes firmly on to each other and the ship. At 6 or 8 to a container that's a lot of clips.

All to preserve goods that must at least look fresh on the supermarket shelf, even if in reality the apples and other fruits and vegetables were harvested far away, many months before. So with valuable and sensitive cargo's that's a lot of checking.

But generally speaking, with better pay, regular meals, the job is way better than seasonal work in the rice or sugar cane fields. So there are lines of Filipino's waiting to get jobs at sea. There's also quite a local trade in forged qualifications and documents.

About 200,000 Filipinos also work for the cruise lines- not such dangerous work as on the container ships but hard work, long hours, and away from home for 9 months or more at a time.

Somehow the Filipinos legendary 'Tagalog telegraph,' keeps families well informed both at sea and in the shanty towns at home.

Back in Pele Montinez Road the five families observed the gringo's arrival immediately he eased himself out of the three wheel, 'tuk tuk' that had managed to, just about, squeeze down the narrow path to their homes.

It had been just four weeks since the well connected, and thus all powerful, supermarket company had announced they, not the families actually owned the little parcel of land.

With most of the men folk away at sea for months or years, the women were not without resolve. Sadly, despite meeting lawyers and the smooth suits at city hall, right up to the mayor, they got nowhere.

They and their local Catholic priest Father Ignatius, tried to interest the local TV channel. They usually liked stories of injustice such as this. But nada. The Big Supermarket company were big advertisers on that TV channel.

Same non story at the Newspapers.

Like thousands of innocents before them they had been well and truly stitched up by big business. They had lost. The families had three months to get out.

So right now visitors of any kind, particularly unknown Gringos, were greeted with considerable distrust.

He smiled and said. "I understand your problem I am here to help." He started to speak first in English. The women nodded but understood little. But one older lady hushed the others and hustled some children into collecting chairs, and a bottle of water and took a seat herself.

As was usual with many Filipino women of a certain age, unless they've worked in a bar or indeed on a cruise ship in the past she had little English, so she said, in local style Manila Tagalog dialect to her daughter in law, " Ask him what he wants."

Rather to her surprise the Gringo broke into Filipino mixed with Tagalog as well, a little bit 'Manila Yankee,' but good enough. The women glanced at each other.

He had a proposal.

The head office of the shipping line that most of their menfolk worked for, a mix of American and Scandinavian finance  had heard about their problem.

And they had a plan.

The women looked at each other scornfully and some put their hands on their-mostly rather ample- hips as if to say 'Now buster-what game are you playing.'

But in another surprise for the grey haired matriarch of the group, and all the ladies and few men gathered round, the plan he had was interesting.

Unusual and a surprise, but interesting.

May be -just maybe.

Gringos with plans needed watching.

He explained that the shipping company had many business activities in and around the world and indeed in the Philippines. Now however the shipping line had a new plan.

They were the operators of cruise ships as well as freighters. For many years their cruise ships had cruised the Caribbean, just off the coasts of Florida in America. Some of their families worked on those ships.

The ladies nodded, they were aware of that, obviously. They had never been there, but they and their children had the t shirts and had seen the pictures.

The gringo went on. More and more cruise ship business was starting around the South China seas. Moneyed Thai's, Taiwanese, Koreans, Singaporeans and indeed huge numbers of Chinese themselves wanted to experience cruises. So much potential business, that the shipping company was bringing in some new ships to work exclusively in the Asian region.

The ladies nodded.

The Gringo continued. In the Caribbean, near America, various cruise lines, had each bought several small sandy islands, planted extra palm trees and installed some of their own facilities on them.

Now their ships stopped at these, their own islands, to offer their cruise ship customers. '*The complete luxury-desert island experience'*. With clean sands, snorkeling and of course beach barbecues, cocktails with umbrellas and (plastic) palm trees.

All in lifeguarded safety for their cruise guests, and all with, 'American style', sanitized toilets and safe food. Guaranteed clean ice with every coke, beer, wine cooler. All of course, bringing more money directly into the cruise company.

The gringo explained, The Shipping Company that their men worked for, had now bought an island in the Philippines. The island was previously a diving resort in a fairly remote location, badly damaged a few years back in a typhoon.

All of this was rather beyond most of the ladies, who apart from a few trips back to distant villages had rarely been beyond their enclaves in the outskirts of Cebu or Manila.

But the grey haired lady nodded. " Why you tell us all this? "

The gringo, taking a sip from his water bottle explained. Their plan was to '*refurbish the facilities on the island*', and to open it exclusively, *in the same style as in the Caribbean, t*o visits from their own ships cruising in the region in about six months time.

They needed staff. Housekeepers, cooks, waiters. With the island being similar to a ship they also needed electricians, maintenance men. Generator, air-con, refrigeration engineers, laundry staff, even musicians.

As they already employed men and some women from most of the families here, they planned to start their recruiting campaign with them.

There would be good accommodation -free good water, they had to pay for their electrics. There was a school thirty minutes away on the mainland, with a guaranteed ferry service.

The pay would be good, about the same as their men and women earned at sea. After all being on an island was bit like being on a ship.

He explained that the contract would be for three years....and would start in three weeks. If they wanted to do this, they had three weeks to pack up and they would be collected in trucks and buses.

But there was one very serious condition. *'This had to completely secret'.* They wanted to do this before their rival cruise lines woke up to the plan.

If one word- just one word-got out, it was all off.

"I mean one word out there, and it's all off."

" That's why we started with you, as we know and we know your families value their jobs with the shipping line." So a strong and very thinly veiled threat. 'Take the job, but keep it secret.'

It was up to the women. No gossip, no stories, no phone calls, and so for three weeks for the men, beer and rum at home only, not in the corner bar with all those young girls listening.

The grey haired lady spoke. "Go away gringo, and come back tonight, we will talk with you then. But first we have much to discuss here. If you come back tonight, bring some beer, we will feed you well."

She looked around at the other women and fixed her strong brown eyes on the five men sitting on some boxes listening.

"We will all be here- and there won't be any talk to the young puta's in the corner bar.....will there Jorge, will there Juan. We are all here except for Maria who is at the hospital with her youngest, but she will be back tonight I hope."

She stood and shook hands with the gringo and shoed the kids away to "go and find this man a 'tuk tuk' ."

Although this needed thought and discussion, it was such a miracle that could hold the family together, that, despite it being a secret she would immediately walk over to St Rosas and give thanks to God and The Virgin for this Miracle.

If the priest was there ,she'd ask him what to do, secret or no secret. 'The Virgin' would advise, or Papa' through Father Ignatius.

### 5. One Day in early May. South Western France.
*Real Estate Agents. 'They would say that, wouldn't they.'*

From the 'Franglaise' wording on the real estate company web site, the property of course, sounded great.

' *Le Vieux Moulin au Soleil* '—'The Old Mill in the Sun.'

'An idyllic retreat for today's business man and his family. A small farm house with collection of converted farm buildings around a swimming pool. Set in 125  hectares of old vineyards and pastureland (some let locally )these stone buildings are nestled at the end of a 500 meters private driveway with gatehouse. All in quiet secluded countryside.

Not overlooked and with all main services connected (private water and drainage)'. 'A haven of peace in the Midi sun, and yet just about equidistant from Montpellier and Toulouse airport. (Auto route entry 15KM)'.

The photos on the real estate company web site, indeed looked idyllic and as for the description- 'well they would say that wouldn't they.' As it happens, if anything, the usual flowery salesmanship was, in this case, remarkably accurate.

Almost 50 years ago the same ex farmstead had been described as 'a place (au soleil) to free your creative soul in the peace of the countryside and chill out.'

Converted from an old  mill and farm it was a successful residential recording studio. By the late sixties, the rock and roll business had become a huge and lucrative global business. Technological advances had made studio recording equipment both more complex and more transportable.

Music companies were increasingly professional with schedules, budgets and voracious demands for new recordings to sell.  Pressure to deliver new success, did not always sit well on the shoulders of many musicians and creative types, for whom budgets and planning schedules, were a world from which their music had allowed them to escape.

With help from managers who understood the 'softly softly' approach more than the accountants at demanding music companies, successful musicians, with their own funds, or a decent record company budget advanced to them, freed themselves from the pressured city environment and set themselves up in the country.

In just a few years, state of the art rural recording studios were created high in the Swiss Alps and Rocky Mountains. In upstate rural New York -in fact in upstate almost everywhere. On Jamaica and several other Caribbean Islands. In French Chateaux. Even in small villages in Cornwall England or the Highlands and Islands of Scotland and Scandinavia.

Some studios were even installed on old wooden sailing vessels.

The best were booked for months on end by bands and solo musicians, intent on, 'getting away from it all'. To be 'chilled out and totally creative man'.

Some musicians installed their families, friends and hangers on in their rural idyll and in many cases, apparently included in their retinue the suppliers of recreational but illegal narcotics.

Creativity bloomed but productivity tended to slow. Some enduring masterpieces were indeed produced, but over time musicians, trends and music companies (with their budgets) moved on.

The world echoed to sounds with an urban electronic edge to them. 'Industrial' became the new 'in.'

Over time many of these idyllically rural studios reverted to being just collections of rural residential buildings. Out of fashion and favour, empty, outdated remnants of a gentler analogue age and now for sale.

Thus it was, that after an exchange of some detailed online communications, that two real estate agents were driving slowly through some narrow 'D' roads way out in the country of South Western France.

Followed by their clients, whom they had just met at an agreed rendezvous in a busy auto route gas station stop on the A61 AutoRoute 'Deux Mers.' They pulled into a driveway and stopped at some impressive, if a bit rusted gates. An elderly man, walked slowly across to them and looked in at the window. Having recognised the real estate agents, with a 'bonjour' he opened the gates  and waved them through.

After negotiating the pot holed driveway and going up a slight incline the agents parked in the shade of some huge old plane trees, as did their clients. Perhaps potential clients was a more accurate description.

The agents had been trying to sell or even rent out 'Le Moulin Vieux au Soleil',for three years since the unfortunate death of the owner in a jet ski accident in Thailand.  Even before his death it had been many years since the studios, and indeed the owner had created successful music there.

The agents were under now instructions from his widow to 'do a deal at any price.'

Apart from her desire to sever all connections with the establishment that had eaten all her husband's cash, the land and building taxes together with basic  maintenance costs were now eating her available cash.

To cap it all, the wife of the old man at the gate, had recently fallen off some small steps whilst cleaning one of the cottages. She was in hospital with a smashed hip. The repair of which was expected to take many months.

So the gate keeper who was also the gardener, maintenance man, guardian and now only resident had decided, with his wife to take the 'industrial injury' insurance money and depart.

With some of the generous 'unfit to work allowance' paid to his wife they had taken a small apartment in a Toulouse suburb near their daughter. So to add to the owner's problems the guardian wanted to 'allez a demain'--- 'go sooner' rather than later.

The agents also wanted a client as they usually had problems in collecting their monthly management fees from the owner's widow.

Their clients, with negligible French language skills, one perhaps English and the other, wearing a baseball cap, maybe American Asian were very cool in demeanour. All of those characteristics were very much, 'le normal' in today's France.

Foreigners renting properties both long term and for vacations had for many years made up the majority of real estate work in that area of rural France. So both agents spoke a some English.

Having opened the second gateway in the chain link fence that surrounded the buildings, they walked between the old buildings into a courtyard.

The old Farm House formed the top end of a courtyard.

Old farm buildings had created four cottages.

A modern but stone covered building at the rear of the courtyard housed the now defunct studio and control room, extra toilet facilities and a kitchen.

In the center of the old stone paved courtyard- was a swimming pool and to the side an impressive barbecue area. The pool, almost violent blue in the clear hot sun of the Languedoc morning

"The pool is serviced weekly." the agents said reassuringly.

The house and grounds were surrounded by a surprisingly high chain link fence, and beyond that were hectares of farm land and an area of woodland.

An agent explained the high fence, "the previous owner wanted to keep the buildings and studio secure due to value of the equipment, now mostly removed." "Or keep out the drug police," his associate murmured.

"The farmland used to be let, but is no longer. We have just agreed that a neighbouring farmer can come in sometime in the early autumn to cut and remove the long grass. Otherwise no one comes here or is allowed to come here. The mailbox, electric meter and other services are all down at the gate."

Throughout the tour the potential clients showed no enthusiasm, no emotion and the prognosis looked somewhat bleak.

But a little later, standing under the trees by their cars, to the surprise of the agents, the eventual delight of the owner, and the old guardian, a deal for a one year rental with options to extend was made.   Not only that, but the clients agreed to pay six month's rent in advance.

Also 'naturellement', to lodge a security of 5000 euro's with the agency from which the agents could also pay the insurance, land and property taxes and the electricity costs.   No they didn't need the phone, everything was cell phones these days.

If the paperwork was ready they would come to the offices tomorrow in Carcassonne and pay the deposit. To the delight of the agents they enquired if cash would be OK for the deposit.

They would make a bank transfer for six months rental when they had the paperwork the next day. Oh- yes they would like to occupy in two weeks. 'Mais Oui, Messieurs.'

"'Oh yes', if the agency had a team of cleaners perhaps they could give everywhere a good clean."

Indeed the agency did have such a team as they managed many vacation rental properties in the area. They would agree the price for the cleaning the following day.'

They discussed maintenance and it appeared that the buildings were in good condition thanks to work by the previous 'guardien.'

The agents having agreed the deal then mentioned one more thing. There are a couple of horses that graze in the very large field behind the farm house. "The horses, they get water from the little river . We'll work on getting them moved, but it may take a little time. No one come's to ride them or anything like that."

The renters were fine with that, and the agents made a small joke about free grass cutting.

Everyone was happy, except for the pool company who lost a client, the renters informing the agency that they would have a maintenance man living in the gatehouse.

He knew all about pools, and, yes of course he'd keep an eye on the horses and call if he saw they had any problem.

Within the allotted time- contracts were signed, no one bothered too much with references of the new tenants as they had paid a large cash deposit and indeed six months in advance.

They also paid cash for the cleaning.

When the rental money had been transferred to the agent's bank, as arranged, keys and copy documents were sent to a Paris address by FedEx.

The clients also made polite noises about possibly, 'buying the property in their next financial year if the price was right.'

So taking into account the good rental and amount paid in advance , removal of all overheads and even a possible sale the 'difficult owner' relaxed somewhat, and went on holiday to her sister in Narbonne.

The agents went and celebrated with a good lunch.

**6. Wednesday. June 15th. Late afternoon. 10 Hours drive from Manila. Philippines.** *On a Jeepney, a ferry, and a prayer.*

In the oppressive heat of a Philippine afternoon, a rag tag collection of overloaded pickup trucks, Jeepney, and four mini buses waited in the loading line at a small ferry dock about 10 hours from the outskirts of metro Manila. They were in sight of their destination, a small island about two or three kilometres off shore.

The passengers, about 45 assorted women of all ages, about 20 men and teenage boys plus smaller children were tired after hours on the road, several ferry journeys and considerable En route roadside maintenance to the various vehicles.

But they were all very cheerful. Not the least of reasons being that as they left, at the first gas station truck stop the 'Gringo' of whom they had been so suspicious a week or so before, had paid them their moving expenses and first weeks wages.

They all had bank accounts, as in most cases they had at least one family member working aboard a ship somewhere around the world.

The nine families, En route to new jobs, and possibly a new 'life,' this time actually on shore, had between them a further 25 or so relatives, husbands, wives, mothers or grown children working at sea. Somewhere. Most worked for the 'The Company.' as they called 'the gringos' employer.

Before they had agreed to accept the job, and the move, the old lady had checked the wages and the costs and they were reasonable. Father Ignatius was suspiciously concerned at the coincidence, but happy if it was fact.

So an agreement was made, a timetable set, old suitcases, cartons, plastic bags and bundles (various) were packed. Many reminders were issued and mostly heeded about secrecy and now here they were.

Whilst she waited for the ferry the old lady sat in the shade and considered the overall situation. The new job opportunity for the families had arrived at just the right time. The coincidence was concerning, but jobs were jobs, and these seemed real enough.

Even though they had packed up and moved with all their worldly belongings- including most of their flimsily built houses, Father Ignatius, with a local workers rights organisation was going to continue the fight for them to retain or get paid for the city land.

Before she had left their home in Manila there was one matter the old lady needed to settle.

There were no, or certainly very few activities entered into by her extended clan and her neighbours about which she didn't know. She had been brooding for a while about something she had recently learned in the market.

Four Filipino seafarers, not actually from her family, had, in far off South America, Brazil actually, where ever that may be, come into a serious sum of money.

She knew full well that serious sums of money didn't just arrive by good fortune, hence her deep suspicions when the gringo had arrived with 'good news of future jobs.'

Drug smugglers were the usual source of potential 'extra income.' There were and still are hundreds of thousands of Filipino seafarers, on deck and exposed to the elements or working on various types of ship for long hours as cleaners, cooks, laundry staff and the like who are not very well paid.

So the temptations were always there, always being offered, and of course sometimes taken. Their own extended family had three previous breadwinners incarcerated in the USA with long sentences received for their part in attempts to smuggle something illegal into the States.

So the stories had concerned her greatly.

Then, just before they left their homes, for what she assumed may be the last time, if all went well that is, the newly enriched sailors suddenly returned. The market was abuzz with stories and rumours.

Flash with cash, the men had had flown from somewhere, wearing smart clothes, bearing gifts, toys, i phones and all sorts of items that the old lady didn't really understand, and certainly couldn't work. There were rumours of deposits being paid for pick up trucks and more.

There were even rumours of quite a few more sailors having the same luck promised over the next months, but of course, communities such as theirs lived as much on rumour as on fact.

She knew better than to ask directly about their lucky fortune. In any event she hated to waste her time considering untrue stories and yet more rumours. So she bided her time, and of course as she had expected, within a couple of days one of the bar girls at the now extra busy karaoke bar across the street from their homes had the full story.

Some years before, the mother of this girl had fallen very sick back in her village, advice and help from the old lady had most likely saved the woman's life. The old lady didn't disapprove of girls who chose to work in bars, she just didn't approve of her menfolk spending all - repeat all, their cash in those bars. Others could do what they wanted and good luck to the girls who earned the cash.

So over cup of sweet coffee the bar girl had revealed all. Or rather over a sweet coffee and as usual where the old lady was involved, sweet coffee and a bowl of chicken rice, "Come on now Conchita, you're looking very thin, let's see you eat this whilst you tell me what's happened."

It seemed, according to Conchita, that the each of the four miscreant Filipinos had been paid several thousand US dollars to 'take a holiday' and let someone else take over their jobs. They had been in a port in somewhere loading beefs and bananas.

Quite liking the sound of getting three months wages, and a ticket home for nothing they had reported in sick, and then gone straight to the airport.

The old lady decided this did not sound good. So despite the hustle of packing up her life, she found the men concerned and demanded to know more.

This produced stupid stories, which made her fume. When she asked if there were still other Filipinos on the ships they had left and the answer was," Yes of course, many." she ignited. Explosion more than ignition was uppermost in her mind.

She had no idea how big a bomb was- or exactly what it could do but "What if those people want to do bombs on the ships. What if people were hurt, what if the ships sink, what then?"

When the men just, 'shrugged' instead of answering back, actually out of deference to the respected old lady and not daring to lie, they looked at the ground and looked guilty, but shrugged all the same. She crossed herself and walked away muttering.

After two sleepless nights and with just three days to go before she and the clan embarked on their great adventure she made up her mind. She got her daughter to call another gringo.

A Mr. Paul, that she knew and trusted. He was a newspaper and TV man from Hong Kong. He had tried to help them with the story about the seizing of their land, staying for a while nearby to film the families and report on the situation.

The old lady had liked him a lot, very sincere good man. Too much beer, but a good man never the less. She thought he was American. In fact he was English and he lived in Taipei, but no matter. It seemed he was in England at that time, which was why he had called her back at his expense.

"Yes, he remembered her".

In a mix of Tagalog and Manila Filipino, and some English from her daughter, she told him about the problem. "Someone is paying money to replace Filipino sailors on certain ships."

" She hears stories of a lot of ships but knows for sure about two or maybe four. She worries for all the crews on the ships, you know, may be, can be a 'bomba'."

"No, she didn't know the name of the ships but she would find out."
Which she did, and the following day her daughter sent the names of two
of the vessels to Mr. Paul, wherever he was, by sms/ text.

A rumour from a bar girl, via a grandmother in a slum looking
collection of shacks was not going to make front page news, or even a
paragraph on an inside page. Having considered the matter for an hour or
so, Paul had called me in Singapore.

With security of ships and shipping being pretty much my main concern
I knew him well, and we regularly worked together exchanging leads and
tips.

Having given me the relatively scanty detail that he had, he concluded,
"Daniel, you're the man on the spot, and you know all the shipping tycoons,
who sails what and where. Remember where you got this from if this
stands up as a story," and he was gone.

I looked at my watch. Pub opening time in the UK no wonder he'd been
brief.

As far as the old lady was concerned that was that. She had done the
right thing and so she didn't even trouble Father Ignatius with her
concerns. In three days they'd be moving everyone and everything and
there was much to be done, and there was. But it all got packed and now
here they were, waiting for the ferry to a new life.

The small ferry took several trips to get everyone out to their new homes
and their new place of employment.

There they found the accommodation simple, clean as promised.
Things were looking good or as the old lady said. 'Good so far.' and after
thanking the heavens above –directly this time- not via Father Ignatius,
she slept well.

## 7. **Thursday 16th June. Late afternoon.Narita Airport. Tokyo. Japan:***In the Land of the Rising Daughter.*

As their chauffeured Mercedes eased from the Narita exit road into the main Tokyo bound traffic, Yamada Hiroshi- or Hiroshi Yamada – to his international friends, patted his wife's knee fondly.

"Tamiko - she will be OK - but it's still hard to keep smiling every time she goes off to school in Switzerland. Even though she's seventeen now I still think of her as our little girl."

His wife nodded and replied quietly - still always conscious of the chauffeur even if he was the other side of a panel of glass.

"I think the worst was the first few terrible months when she used to call home all the time. But you were right she soon made friends.  Now this year she has even chosen to go back for the extra summer school activities. They start with the history cruise on the River Rhine and the concerts most evenings."

Hiroshi-san patted his wife's knee fondly again and said. "She's been looking forward to that- and to see her horse again."

"In fact sometimes I think she thinks more of that horse than me - every time I go to her room she's had live web cam pictures of the horse on her laptop. With us being in Japan and the horse in Switzerland I hope she's right about that Skype thing being free."

It was his wife's turn to squeeze his hand, and say,  "At least now we know she's meeting May at Singapore Airport and they'll be rooming together again for the trip and the semester."

His wife continued, "I like May she's very sensible - who'd have thought that our old Japanese family would have such close friendship with a Taiwanese family."

" I think the fact that they both study cello and are in the orchestra together helps. Oh yes and they both like the horses."

Hiroshi smiled. "All those years ago when I ordered that first Taiwan made ship there was a real outcry here in the press, but the fuss soon died away when I ordered four more from Japanese yards."

"May's father said to me once, that just as with Japan surviving after the Second World War - Taiwan also had real need to develop quickly to survive after they broke free from mainland China. Their heavy industry and their electronics have rivalled ours for a long time."

" Once we had the same problems - as countries and as companies. Now we are becoming friends, at least in business, or in our case as families.

May's father is a good man- and was very supportive to me when Japan hit hard times in the eighties. "

" But I didn't know him that well and knew nothing of him having also chosen the International College of the Alpes for his daughter. Then, when the girls really bonded, that was good for both families."

"Mind you I was surprised when we went to the prize giving and met Mister Calvettioni there also. Tamiko had spoken about her friend Brigitte and her horse but I never picked up on her second name. With his being one the most aggressive Europe owned shipping companies he's pretty much our main rival for some Euro-Asia freight. "

"So that's three children from big shipping companies at the same school."

His wife responded, "Well you know, with the cost of these special international colleges there's only some who can pay the fees. I know from the parents association that the daughters of both of Japan's biggest rival electronic companies are also there."

Her husband started to say - "These days, not like when I was young, there's now a place in industry and management for girls...at last here in Japan as well as abroad. Maybe at some time in the future when our girl has taken over from her dad".....he tailed off as his wife glared at him.

"OK, OK let's wish together she stays our little girl for a few more years. But horses not boys."

They squeezed hands fondly, but whilst loving and close, their thoughts were slightly different. His leaning towards 'maybe she will like ships as well as boys,' and his wife's were perhaps a little more traditional or conventional.

## 8. Thursday June 16th. 11.00 am.New Hudson View Hotel. Weehawken. 'Noo Joisey.'USA:*"See you in a week or ten days.Love to the kids."*

Just across the Hudson River from the magical skyline of New York, Magnus Sorensen was leaving his hotel room in Weehawken, New Jersey when his mobile phone rang. Glancing at the incoming number he touched one of the buttons and on hearing his wife's greeting responded with, " Hey Honey that's a nice surprise.

"Where are you, this is a great phone signal?"

He was surprised as he hadn't been expecting the call, as he knew his wife and young daughters were not at their Malmo Sweden home but in their holiday villa in Southern Portugal. And at that villa there was little or no phone signal.

The villa was in the Monchique Hills just back from the Algarve coast. Although they had quite a few neighbours, a fold in the hills meant that to get a decent voice connection and even reliably receive or send  messages required a trip down the valley to a more open space.

His wife explained that, earlier that day, with their children she had driven down in the morning and picked up her sister with her daughter from her father's house on the Vilamoura golf course. Then they had all been to 'Slide and Splash' - a remarkably good water park just outside the old Portuguese sardine fishing port of Portemao.

She went on, "I just wanted to say 'bon voyage' and we'll see you here in about a week or ten days or so."

" The phone signal's extra good because, we're having  sardines and then ice creams by the beach. Anna and Liv are staying up at our house for a few days to keep me company, and the children love it together."

"Send me a text when you get to Europe and we'll pick you up at Faro Airport. By the way I'm looking at the sea now and it's very calm."

Smiling to himself, he resisted the temptation to say that a lot of weather and changes in sea conditions could happen in 1000 meters let alone three thousand kilometers across the Atlantic, and having sent hugs and kisses to his two daughters as well as to his wife he closed the call.

He checked around the room one more time, and clad in work boots, jeans, denim shirt, and big padded jacket instead of his usual rather smarter office gear he went down to check out.

Smiling again, as he remembered Britt his wife, suggesting he looked like a band member from seventies gay disco music icons, 'Village People.'

He was the chief training officer for B.O.S.N. forlags. Or as it was listed in most formal documents, The Baltic and Orient Steam Navigation

Company. Founded by his father in law's family in the late 1860's with steam ships mostly constructed in England.

The company was still mainly family owned with old man Calle Haeggqvist, known globally as 'Charlie', the company chairman. Chairman may-be but a very hands on one. Mostly carrying passengers back then in the 1800's , the company now was one of the worlds largest freight carriers.

Magnus was mostly office bound, 'teaching the teachers', company policy however dictated that twice a year he experienced the real world of the offshore working environment. It was a policy that had been dictated by his wife's grandfather and carried on now by her father.

This meant even on their largest container ships - trying to operate his laptop whilst it - or rather she, even container ships were 'she'- was pitching and rolling across the oceans of the world.

But he had to agree with the old man's 'hands on' concept. He could observe the daily work realities and practicalities of the crew as they went about their various tasks.

Some doing skilled navigating, noting radar, depth gauges, GPS, currents and weather. Others fine tuning engines for economy in a warm and dry wheelhouse or noisy engine room.  Others for many long hours exposed to the elements doing vital daily checking and maintenance on deck.

As the man responsible for, 'training and safety at work', across their fleet of around 1200 – most owned and some operated or chartered, many of his recommendations had indeed improved daily life for the ordinary seamen.

Just as with thousands of other ships around the world the company employed many Russians, some Ukrainians, quite a few Poles, some Indians but mostly Filipino's. Captains and senior officers tended to be Scandinavian, Dutch, German or French with quite a few Brits and Americans.

For the crew a month or more at sea was routine ,but this was a quick trip for all of them - Newark to Rotterdam . So in just over a week he would be enjoying some vacation sunshine of Portugal, and probably a few rounds of golf with his father in law.

Magnus hailed a taxi. The driver, having seen a hotel guest exiting with luggage was happily planning a lucrative Airport run all the way to JFK or La Guardia. He wasn't best pleased to have to find his way through the mountains of containers piled high at part of nearby Newark's huge and sprawling sea freight terminal. The taxi driver glanced at the usual array of names painted on the side of the big steel boxes, major and respected companies but names meaningless to most; Cosco, Hapag,Maersk and many more.

The cab took a left at a red light and continued,the road making it's way between between thousands more containers; IDF, BOSN, F.I.C., TOPS, Nippon-TOFCO. He recognised FEDEX and UPS as being familiar from their thousands of local delivery vans.

Mostly though, to the taxi guy they were just mysterious boxes, glimsed every day stacked in factory yards, or driven past- with content unknown.

From somewhere, going somewhere.

To his passenger however, each big steel container, or 'box' in the trade was owned leased,  licensed or transported by someone.

All those 'someone's' keeping the world of commerce moving. In fact they kept the whole world moving. If the boxes stopped then so would much of life as we know it. Those boxes paid his wages- and indirectly in this case, today they paid the cab guy.

Having indeed paid, Magnus shouldered his two bags and passing through some rather serious, and not very friendly US style security, was escorted to the dock where the 200 meter long, 65 meter wide  ship was loading the last of its containers.

This being the penultimate leg of its regular Far East-East Coast US-Europe-Far East routing, the containers were mostly empty, or full of items for re-cycling, returning back to Asia. There to be re-filled, and to start their regular global transit once again.

All scheduled services, as reliable as your neighborhood bus or train service. Or in the, usually rather jaded opinions of regular train and bus commuters in most countries- a lot more regular.

## 9. Friday June 17th. 4.00 pm.On the Bund. Shanghai. China:

*"It took more than one man to change my name to Shanghai Lily."*
*Marlene Dietrich in the 1932 film, 'Shanghai Express'.*

'Shanghai.' Just the name is an exotic cliché for most Westerners, conjuring up images of a bygone era of dimly lit, misty riverside wharves, secret agents and smugglers ,intrigues and espionage, slinky ladies, bars and dens (various).

One's thoughts almost revert to flickery black and white with a slightly crackly soundtrack. All, as I said, clichés, but I suppose my thoughts these days should be more cell phone than celluloid.

I have been in the security business for around twenty years. In U.K. Government service for the first ten with M.I.6, and the latest ten with my own company, mainly based in Asia.

With most of my clients now being in the ships and shipping business, I deal daily with a varied repertoire of threats, some real, many angry, amateur and opportunist.

With my researchers we try to head off, the modern world of smuggling, terrorist and extortion threats, and old style piracy, not to mention scams and fraud.

Information is key to what we do and it was a suggestion that I could learn something of use that had taken me to Shanghai.

Security relies on the securer having a good reputation. Thanks to my predecessor and my current team we are both well respected and also well connected.

But even I was surprised when, at the appointed time I responded to the tap on my hotel room to admit my visitor. Not the once predictable slinky oriental cliché in slit skirt, cigarette smouldering in a long holder and husky voice, but a damned close descendant.

I suspect I stammered, as I greeted and shook the proffered hand of Liu Qiang the chief of China's MSSS. Their all powerful Ministry of State Security organisation.

The Chinese equivalent of the CIA / MI5 /MI6/ Homeland Security / NSA all rolled into one.

He spoke, perfect English, English. No US inflection. "Daniel, good to meet you, thanks for coming over."

That's when I suspect the stammer crept in. "No problem, only a short hop from Singapore."..

His response. "Oh yes of course, I was thinking London, how stupid."

I offered, "Coffee, tea, something stronger?"

In almost BBC English tones he refused all, with thanks, and said, "No, I've got a meeting with some of my political masters in Beijing later, so just a quick word."

He glanced around the room and said, "I suppose we are reasonably secure here."

I started to say, " Well, if," and then thought better of it, then again what the hell, so I continued, "Well if anyone knows if this room is clean of listening bugs I have a feeling it should be you."

He laughed, not a knowing chuckle or conspiratorial smile, a real laugh.

"Good point. Actually no one knows I am here officially, and even if they do unofficially, what I have to say will very soon become State business for the general benefit of both the Western nations and ourselves. So it needs to be said, and then sorted."

I sat forward. "I'm not sure, that me being in private practice these days as they say, that I have much influence in 'sorting' the British or any other nation."

Again the laugh, I listened carefully as he went on. "I am aware, of course that our old friends at Vauxhall Cross pay little attention to you private contractors these days. The Americans are much more open minded to sub-contracting , but of course that's mainly to avoid direct political blame when things go wrong."

The laugh again, this time more of a, 'just between us,' chuckle really. I figured, despite, these days, the Vauxhall Cross HQ of the British Secret Service, being now well known, film famous even, that this was a rather unique moment. To hear the name uttered by the one individual whose statements, actions and motives occupied the thoughts and concerns of more analysts in that very building than almost anyone else.

He leaned forward and adopted a serious tone. "I am here simply because I am receiving suggestions of a planned attack or multiple actions designed to cause serious disruption to global shipping. By shipping, of course I mean, container freight. Our fear is that many ships could be affected."

I nodded, all ears.

"Of course all of us professionals, are plagued these days with internet rumour and sorting out the on line fantasy from the real, or the genuine from the deliberately dis-informative keeps us all busy. But what I am hearing seems to be based on fact, and more concerning than the usual."

Whilst I was recovering from being included in the 'us professionals', not in as much as I am not, but to be lumped in with the immense resources of the Chinese MSS. was a new one on me. Correct in reality about the annoyance of rumour though, but never the less, a surprise.

He continued, still leaning forward, talking very directly to me. "As I don't need to tell you, we need those exports and imports to maintain and sustain China Limited. Also, almost all nations in the West cannot survive without imports or in many cases without exporting raw materials. So shipping keeps the wheels of life turning for us all."

"We have seen before several times, that any serious problem in one place these days quickly hurts the world. And what hurts the world of shipping probably hurts China even more Why do I approach you and ask you to be the bearer of news from East to West?"

"Simply because this matter is urgent and me getting approval for a formal 'Nation to Nation' approach takes too long. Months usually are required to get State policy approved or even worse, changed, to suit diplomacy."

"Also of course, you have an exemplary reputation and you are a specialist in both shipping and the region. Unlike your old employers and indeed those of the US security services, you have your feet on the ground here. They, the US, have been stung before by losing touch with real information."

I nodded again, almost in a state of shock considering who was talking. The laugh again. He continued, "Of course, maybe I am showing my age and the length of my service, when I say I prefer real information to online stories."

He stressed real and online. "Certainly the upcoming fans of all things online in our ranks think so." He continued, "I am sure we in China have some effective online activity. The politicians and the press in the USA certainly tell me this is to be the case. Although I wonder how many of those outraged US warnings are based more on local budgeting and political concerns."

He went on, "However we are short of time, so fact not conjecture is the need today. Although I would be happy to accept your offer of a drink sometime to continue my lecturing to such an astute and polite listener."

This time it was my turn to laugh, or at least smile. "That would be an honour and pleasure sir."

Liu said. " I do not know from where these attacks will come or even their style or precise target. We have information of something happening on 6/25 and again on 1/27. That's all we know."

" This is not to be taken as a threat from us. We also have rumours of someone seeking to set up and engage an entire ships crew. I don't need to tell you of the potential blockages or damage to vital port and canal infrastructure that could be created by a ship manned by a rogue crew."

"The perpetrators, or at this time plotters, may be Chinese, they may be Western, Middle Eastern, even Russian. As we all value and appreciate our own national interests I doubt they are government sponsored, so extremists or criminals of various persuasions is the most likely."

" I only know that my information, although not much more than a rumour is from a usually reliable source."

I said. "Well we too have heard rumours, and in the past three weeks there's been an increase in the number of unexplained fires in containers. Two other items that stand out amongst the usual. Nothing confirmed, but we also have heard of someone recruiting a complete 'ghost crew' for a container ship or ships, so that is indeed a concern".

"The other story that seems to have more fact to it is that someone has paid several Filipinos to leave their ship and be replaced on board. They have paid them well, several month's wages. Cash like that usually suggests drugs smuggling of some kind. Bad but not unusual. We haven't found out much yet."

"Although neither of the two ships named so far belongs to any of my clients I am still keen to know more." I wrote down the names of those two ships and gave them to him. With scarcely a glance at the note he slipped it into his pocket.

"The man who knows most about this got back from Europe this week. He's checking to see what else he can learn. He can't have uncovered much yet as otherwise he would have called. He only ever calls with facts or news, rarely for a chat."

I continued, "With the down turn in hijacks off the coast of Somalia, thanks to the international Navy presence there, maybe the pirates are looking for new ideas. But most of that problem was relatively local in structure, not a global crime gang."

" Rumours of a container crew needed, suggests we're talking big ships, not the coastal piracy still going on around Nigeria and just south of Thailand. I went on, "We all live everyday with the possibility of a Panama or Suez blockade. That for sure would be political. But for a crime, I am not sure. It's hard to move let alone hide container ships!"

Liu laughed and said, "I agree it's not easy to conceal ships of that size. If I had more detail than I have, I would pass it on and indeed, will pass on, when and if I hear anything. We have noticed Isted's work, and whilst not always to our liking, it is always fair and objective. Particularly for the victims of injustice or inclement weather. "

"By the way," he continued, "I meant it when I said, I like my hard information to come from, 'shoes or feet on the ground. I note that these days in American and English the old 'boots on the ground' phrase has been hi-jacked these days to mean soldiers in place."

He stood and with his hand out to shake mine, he stepped towards the door. Then with that smile again said, "Two things more."

"When you have a private opportunity, please send my regards to Miss Stanton your old boss. Not only an honourable and clever woman, but also very attractive."

I almost stuttered again at his totally unexpected words.

"Certainly, sir, and the second point."

"Oh yes. Apologies for the very short notice in inviting you here, but I my schedule's a bit tight and I only recently realised you were fully booked with your American visitor from next week. Feel free to share our concerns with him."

I asked for a way to contact him. " Of course," he said. "I forgot, my email is on this card. I do get them, although when the system plays up at home I have to enlist the help of my son."

We shook hands and he was gone.

Or rather he wasn't. Minutes later, a tap on the door, I opened it again. He said, "On considering the matter, sadly I think it better if you don't pass on my words to Miss Stanton, or they will start to read all sorts of nuances and coded messages in them."

He smiled and went on, " It's better, like your Lord Nelson, they spend their time to think about their fleet of ships and any attack on them." The door closed. He was probably right about focus.

With my Singapore based security business having some of Asia's largest shipping companies as key clients, his warning about ships, trade and those wishing to disrupt same should also be my priority. Recovering slowly from the shock of whom had walked in my door, I realised I was hungry, and Shanghai had a gastronomic reputation to live up to.

But throughout a solo dinner in the hotel restaurant and a sleepless night my mind was filled with extra questions.

As ever it seems Shanghai has lost none of its ability to invoke intrigue and create confusion. Liu's Miss Stanton comments, his comments about 'official policy changes' and how did he know about my 'Americans' impending visit, after all it had only been fixed two days before.

'The American' was Barry Purchase , who worked on maritime security for Matchless Security Consulting , a major Washington based US security company. Our paths had crossed some years before when I had resolved a problem for one of his clients. We got on well, and Barry had fed my company with various decent bits of business over the years.

We had one of our regular 'catch up meetings' scheduled for Singapore the following week, and I was looking forward to seeing him again, if not relishing the inevitable hangover that was sure to ensue.

Despite my continuous recycling of today's meeting, that evenings dinner was great. The hotel restaurant was brilliant and certainly maintained Shanghai's gastronomic claims to fame, even if accompanied only by my thoughts and not a sultry companion with smouldering cigarette in a long holder,

Being China, there was however enough smoke from the other diners and sizzling platters not to miss that aspect of the occasion.

I decided that although there's no smoke without fire, that a few more real facts were needed, and to await the arrival of 'American Barry 'before passing on any warnings to the UK.

It was only later as I was dropping off to sleep that I realised he had connected Paul Isted's name with my two leads. I certainly hadn't mentioned it. Intrigue, as ever in Shanghai.

**10. Saturday. June 18th. Morning.Pudong Airport. Shanghai. China. Outbound:***'Informed Security works. Routine security gets lucky. But only sometimes'.*

Despite those words being both somewhat accurate, and also rather unfortunate for someone in my line of work, I didn't let that worry me as I queued for my flight back to Singapore from Shanghai. My mind was occupied enough pondering the previous days meet.

In the world of container freight there are hundreds of ports, thousands of ships, and hundreds of thousands...no millions, of containers. There are of course, at any one time, even more millions of rumours, conspiracies, jealousies, stories, and on occasions, crimes involving all of the above.

As ever, rumour being both the time consuming blight and key sustenance of security organisations worldwide.

With my information regarding at least two named ships coming from Paul Isted, I trusted it enough to pay serious attention.

Paul was one of our best contacts, and an expert at sorting the real from the imagined, or as he put it somewhat graphically, 'sorting the balls from the b*llocks', or in mixed company, using a cricketing metaphor, 'sorting the bails from the bowlers'.

We had inherited Paul's ongoing advice when I bought the company. With his background we were back in Asia, land of cliché's again. He was a semi-retired newspaper man.

Veteran of not only the Vietnam conflict, where his graphic writing had gained front pages in respected broadsheets around the world, but also a good few years as a CNN or BBC stringer, expert, correspondent. Appearing on screens and in print from dusty desert conflicts, from the chill of the Afghan mountains and up to his neck in a deluge of flood stories in myriad locations.

He described himself as a dying breed, and given the passing of years since the Vietnam and some other conflicts he was probably right about that. A cliché in both life and style.

Paul would be the first to say that, 'despite clichés usually resonating truth, critics and these days, non tabloid editors, are the enemy of the cliché.'

But old traditions do hang on out here in Asia. The mostly excellent, FCC's, Foreign Correspondents Clubs, clichéd indeed legends of a pre digital age, and others of varying age, style purpose and reputation still just about exist in Hong Kong, Bangkok, K.L. Singapore and many other places.

Paul lived, in a village just outside the sprawl of Taipei.

He said, "*I like to live where I can see rice in fields, not listen to it in my breakfast cereal.*" We liked that quote, even though we had heard it repeated on many a late night.

Remarkably well connected throughout the region, we had him on an annual retainer. 'Just keep your ears open.' His years of experience, meant that he rarely wasted our time with nonstarters or pointless gossip.

He was also great company, and was welcomed everywhere we ever went, particularly in bars and clubs where 'non-smoking' rules were unenforceable and closing time. 'last call for alcohol,' was never heard.

I had called him the previous afternoon shortly after Liu Qiang had left. His long suffering housekeeper had answered and said, slightly hesitantly, "Hang on Daniel san, I try."

Eventually the sound of footsteps and some interesting Anglo Saxon words got louder and louder as he approached the phone.

No greeting straight into the business. "Nothing to report, but the face who was making the offers to recruit an entire crew is allegedly coming to town in a couple of days. I'm on a flight to Manila tomorrow. "

"One mystery is that I can't contact the original lady who called me with the warning. Her phone is dead, but I'll get a cab and see if I can find her."

I mentioned the approach from Liu Qiang. His response." Nosey bugger,ears everywhere, but interesting." He clicked off with what may have been a smokers cough or a fond, for him, farewell.

As my flight continued its path to Singapore, I was trying to envisage scenario's that could involve multiple ships, and prolonged problems.

Mostly I came back to the usual list of potential threats, usually, and thankfully, threatened by amateur and unskilled opportunists, with an axe to grind or a wallet to fill.

Multiple sabotage on a major scale. Unlikely and hard to set up.

Threats of spreading notifiable infections such as chicken flu, SAR's or even the Camel infection, MER's,seemed also unlikely.

Counter-measures were in place and well rehearsed. I forced myself not think about how people got infections from Camels and stayed focused on, 'things that might stop the freight fleet.'

Radio-active spills could be a long term concern. Nasty too.

But took quite some skill and planning.

Bomb and booby trap threats. We were used to them all too regularly, but thankfully, usually more 'bluster' than actual 'bang.'

Beating the existing security systems.

Despite the processes being overloaded, beating the security systems in multiple ports seemed to involve massive planning and some luck. For sure container ports were sprawling expanses, once open to massive crime of many kinds. Modern security systems had resolved most petty crime...but of course the content of the containers was not always what it said on on the label!.

Back to recruiting 'a whole crew'. Doesn't make sense. Agents get requests for an engineer if someone's gone sick or leaving. A cook, even a captain, but rarely a whole crew.

Obviously a new boat needs a whole new crew, but the owners or operators usually move up a selection of skilled crew from other ships. A new boat is promotion and they want the best on board, and to encourage ambition with the rest. Even a lower deck Pinoy crewman knows how to find jobs online, or has a mate who'll help him.

So I came back again to Terrorism? Always possible.

Piracy? More difficult these days.

Crime. Narcotics or other smuggling? More likely, in fact given the profit margins, the most likely. But not *affecting more than the usual number of individual ships.*

Ten days earlier when Paul had first called me with the tip off and then the names from his Filipino grand mama contact I had checked through the register of shipping and instantly found that the ships referred to were medium size. Both appeared to have been in Brazil loading beef and bananas.

It was matter of moments to establish that one ship was en route and nearing the USA at Newark New Jersey, and the other Folkestone UK. Both appeared to have about five days to run.

I had carefully composed an e mail to Barry Purchase and the various owners, agents, port security companies giving them details of what we knew. We all regularly exchanged data, tip offs, warnings and we all did our best to filter out the opportunistic, the amateur and the vindictive.

To Barry I had added, *'look forward to seeing you next week.'*

Arriving in back in Singapore, for once I had a relaxing weekend planned. Except of course for my nagging concern about the message I had received from the boss of the Chinese MSSS.

**11. Sunday June 19th.Early evening.A Villa in the Monchique Hills. Algarve. Southern Portugal:**_Control.It's all about control, Controlling fear,or using fear, to control._

With their three children asleep upstairs, fed, showered 'but mum we've been in the pool all day'.  A nonstop play filled day in the heat of a southern Portuguese summer, even in and out of the pool, is more than enough to exhaust the most boisterous of 5 and 6 year old girls, and their mums.

The mums, Britt-Marie and Anna,  the two Swedish daughters of shipping line  owner Charlie Haeggqvist relaxed over a second, or perhaps a third, ice cold glass of fresh, slightly tingly Portuguese Vino Verde.

 Today had been their third outing in two weeks to Slide and Splash, the water park Britt had mentioned to her husband Magnus.

Slightly frazzled by the sun, they had popped in their fathers house to collect clean laundry. As ever, his maid Ermalinda had fed the kids, and then treated them to her special home made Portuguese cakes, Pastel de Nata.

"It hardly seems possible it's only a week till Magnus gets back, we've been so busy. The girls really want to do Slide and Splash yet again but I'd rather keep that for when he's back." said Britt Marie Sorenson the older of the two sisters and mother of two of the children sleeping soundly upstairs.

Anna responded, "How about tomorrow ,if we nip down to Lagos and go out dolphin watching, the kids love that and I'm sure Magnus and dad will have had enough of boats when they get here "

Anna poured another glass of the moreish Vino Verde into both their glasses. They were after all on holiday.  No irresponsible parents these, with Vino Verde being generally low in alcohol they were alert and busy making plans for the following day.

 Alert, but not alert enough to hear a mini bus pull up outside the house. Definitely not alert enough to notice the two intruders coming quietly round the side of the house with hand guns.

Glasses were nearly dropped, hearts jumped and available hands flew to open mouths when a male voice - very close - said. "Keep still ladies, and you or the kids won't get hurt, keep your hands on the table and away from you or your phones."

"What do you want - if it's money you want we can show you where it's kept. Then go"?

It was Anna. Always the strong and impetuous one of the family. Probably too strong willed said her friends, that's why she lost two husbands.

"Sit quiet and listen. This is about money, but not that money. This is about your husband and your father and the ships. It's not about your kids either but if you make any move whatsoever. Look."

He held up a plastic trash bag- put a bottle of water from the table into the bag and dropped it into the pool. It bubbled slightly and sunk slowly to the bottom, where it rested, a small trail of bubbles escaping still.

"That's what will happen to your kids if you try anything. It will be a slow way to die. I know that from experience. I bought the bag with me in case you had a bloody dog- they die silently in water." The women shuddered and sat frozen in fear.

The man went on. "You can do this the easy way or the difficult way. We're going on a trip, a journey - quite a few hours in the car."

"The easy way is that one of you goes upstairs, collects together some clothes for you and the kids. Some toys if you like. Any medicines you or they need. You do it quietly and come down without touching anything else."

"The not easy way is that I go upstairs with this , he showed them a big roll of sticky box tape, I tape up the kids mouths and arms and sling 'em in the trunk of the car which won't be fun for ten hours. I think there's enough air in there but I can't be sure."

Britt Marie, " We'll do what you say- just don't hurt the kids."

The other replied. "Look, let's be real, we need those kids fit and well to force your dad to make a deal with us."

" So bring food for the journey. Toys, spare bedding anything that makes this easy because we don't really need you two mums."

Britt stood up. The first guy spoke again. "Before you move 'put this on." He placed a cable around her neck necklace style, and fiddled with some kind of lock at the back. It looked like a cheap bicycle lock with cable.

He fitted one on Anna's neck also. Each 'necklace,' had a small soft pouch on the front-about the size of a matchbox.

"Listen carefully. There's a small bomb in each of those. "

"Small but big enough to blow your throat open- and take off your head. Not a nice way to die and not a nice way for your children to see you die." Britt sat again suddenly looking pale.

The guy continued. " Listen very carefully to this part. They are safe, the kids can bash them, you can shower or swim in them. But if you try to take them off, or if you go too far from this. "

He held up a device with the flashing lights. "Then boom. Not only do you go boom splat everywhere but so does the other one." Anna sat and threw up on the floor...Fear is a great controller.

"Quietly now- you've got ten minutes. If the kids wake up just tell them you're tidying up."

After several trips around the house bringing down a growing pile of bedding, toys, clothes Britt assembled most of it into a couple of sports bags. She also handed over their passports, although Anna didn't have hers.One of the guys said. " Give me your phones." One of the men removed batteries, sim cards from the devices, saying as he did so. "I assume there's trackers in these."

The four of them loaded the bus outside and the men said, "OK now get your kids and let's go. It's a good ten hours drive. We'll stop so the kids can pee."

"Like we said- let's do this the easy way and no one gets hurt- it's all about the money...and by the way it won't be your old man's money. It'll be insured."

"Oh yes, neither him or me are going to put our hands in your pants, or those of the kids. But there's a lot worse can happen and like that movie says 'dead men tell no tales,'- or in this case, dead mums."

"If we get stopped by the police- we're just coming home from holidays. Got it. Right, use the toilets and we go."

And they did. With sleepy children's questions being hushed as they drove down from the hills and east along the old 125 road toward Albufeira. Then Faro and the Spanish border at Tavira.

Being within the European Community , no one on the Portuguese or Spanish side checked their passports or papers.

As they eased through the narrow border crossing, video cameras presumably recorded the numbers of the bus and presumably checked automatically against a data base of wanted vehicles.

With several stops for fuel, and several times having left the main road for quiet side roads so that the ladies and children could pee in various fields, after about eleven hours they had traversed all of Spain and were almost at the border with France.

As the highway wound up through the Pyrenees at around eight in the morning they passed through the Spanish French border, just one of a huge number of regular commuters. No passports, no conversation- but again probably cameras and number plate recognition. Probably.

Soon after the border they made rendezvous with another mini bus with French license plates  and transferred the passengers and all their belongings. The children sleepy and complaining.

One new driver guard. One of the originals remaining with the first bus. The new driver was quite friendly- and said in English. "Not long now kids.

Soon be there and you can have a swim." He didn't quite 'get' why the two women shuddered and cuddled their very frazzled and bored children.

Late morning they turned into a gateway under and old stone arch. Negotiated a potholed driveway, entered a second high wire gate and parked under some trees.

One of the guys said,"I'll bring the stuff, you follow him."

The women holding their children close nervously did just that and entered a pleasant courtyard- with swimming pool.

As Pete - as he said they should call him- showed them two cottages he said; "This is where you're staying."

The children rushed around and came back very excited and said, "look there's lots of toys in the bedrooms". Pete smiled and said to the two women who were standing there with tired drawn faces.

"Like the other guys said. This can be hard or this can be easy. There's a lot of stuff here for all of you. Just no TV or phones."

" The food cupboards are full and if you give us a shopping list we'll do our best to get stuff for you, especially stuff the kids like. In that large building there's freezers full of stuff."

" There's even wine. There's a pool table, table tennis and even horses that look over the fence. But before you unpack first come and look at this." He showed them across to a large and rather overgrown vegetable garden behind one of the houses.

On the wall at the end, by a high chain-link fence, were three large water melons. He showed one of the children what looked like a car key, two buttons but no key. Look he said, "watch the end melon, it's fruit fireworks."

Under his guidance Annika pushed the button and the melon exploded rather dramatically- spraying red fruit flesh everywhere, " Me next!" said Lisa ,and the same thing happened as it did when Liv did the same to the third one.  Pete spoke quietly to the two mothers who had rather guessed what he would say. "Just to show you what happens if you stray too far or get the necklace off."

"You must stay inside the wire fence otherwise you can go anywhere, do anything. Keep whatever hours you want. There's knives and barbecue tools in the kitchen but don't go getting any ideas about jumping one of us guys.  Someone has to re-set the proximity sender at regular intervals. Remember- this may take weeks. "

He drove out of the high gates, and shut them behind him.

## 12. Monday June 20th. 8.30 am.TrePolPen Security Co. Central Singapore:*Tennis. Don't bet on it!*

Apart organising my research team to keep looking for clues on Paul Isted's tips and those leads suggested and cogitating about the approach from my new best friend, Liu Qiang, my relaxing weekend had been exactly that.

I also got some time on the tennis court. Much to the satisfaction of my opponents, on both Saturday and Sunday, I lost. Twice. So the drinks were on me. Twice.

Monday morning, and I was waiting in the office for Barry Purchase's arrival when Susie, known to all as 'Squeeze', my long-time PA , and now our company operations manager, reminded me it was exactly ten years since I had left my previous employers, having been with them since university. I had left to become the owner operator of my own small security company.

By chance, leaving the secure career path of employment with the U.K's Secret Intelligence Service, SIS or MI 6 as it still called by many, had turned out to be surprisingly simple.

I'd been posted for six months or so to Kuala Lumpur, Bangkok, and Jakarta keeping a weather eye out on the after effects of the search for the Bali bombers. Also trying to learn a little of the serious or not Muslim skirmishes on the Thai Malaysian, and also the Northern Burma, now Myanmar, borders with various countries.

Although serious with some excitements, the work wasn't too routine, and the Asian lifestyle suited me. In the UK I had recently split from a long time relationship. She had blamed, 'lack of commitment', I suggested the cause was the usual security operatives well documented, 'unplannable mix of working and leisure hours'.

The work in Asia bought me into contact with a long time expat Brit. cricket mad, with the traditionally Cornish name of Rewan Trelawney. He owned and ran a private security business, TrePolPen Global Security Consulting, that functioned across the region.

It was pretty obvious what I, as the extra 'military attaché' was doing at the various UK embassies. So over time we had shared a few hire cars, flights , bars and beers together and, with professional care on both sides, some useful information.

Most of his clients were major shipping companies, keen to keep a lid on pilferage and other scams. Many a ship's captain, purser or land agent has paid for spares and repairs that never happened, for fuel not all delivered. Many an insurance company has paid out on claims for missing goods that no one saw disappear.

With increasing terrorism and other security concerns, as well as the daily routine, his office had also started work on preventative and defensive plans for agents, ships, port authorities and the like.

One evening, over a few too many beers in the Moonlight Bar on Rawaii Beach in Phuket Thailand, there had been much talk about insurance companies. I had been moaning about, "too many new work and safety rules and regulations that 'stupid prats from London', are sent out to teach me. I think all that new rules stuff is all insurance driven."

" Most of these prats are spotty kids straight out of training collage. They wouldn't know the first thing about operating in the field if it hit them, let alone making risk assessments."

"Their preoccupation this month was; '*only rent a motor bike if you are satisfied the outlet is properly insured, the bike regularly serviced and the helmet meets international standards'*. Given the old smoking wrecks we normally end up with from most village locations they can forget their new bloody rules."

Rewan sipped his beer and grinned, "I thought for a moment that old smoking wrecks was going to be a wind up about me...or my car. Don't let 'em get you down boy. Or leave and become your own boss."

I think I looked startled, "Right now I'd quite like to, but I've got no funding."

Rewan leant over, and putting his hand on my arm said, quietly "Daniel, listen I'm pulling out of the game here. You could take over my business and a young bloke like you who knows which knife and fork to use, and rides a clean motorbike could build it up well."

"But don't ditch the insurance companies completely. More and more it's those insurance bleeders who are demanding that clients at least take steps to learn how to take care of themselves and their business."

Having pointed out that I really had no cash, he explained that his wife was very sick. "Now those same 'bloody insurers' say we're running out of health cover here so I'm moving back to the UK where at least we can get free medical care."

" I kept a property there, my son was living in it and as I've also got an Irish passport the UK lot haven't really noticed I've been gone for twenty years."

He went on," I've got some pension plans, and if you pay me a retainer or something over the years that'll be a bonus for me. If you don't pay then one day the Asian bogey men will get you."

He grinned, and we cracked our bottles together. An idea had been born that would change my life forever.

The folks at Vauxhall Cross SIS H.Q. were not best pleased when I gave in my notice to leave, but when I explained what I was doing they, 'grudgingly wished me well,' and within a surprisingly short time my 'access most areas' pass stopped working.  I received a P45 (leaving employment slip) and a worryingly small amount of money and I was on my own.

So it was, that about six months later, ten years ago now,  Rewan, having introduced me to all his clients, most of whom stayed, at least for a test period, and I was my own boss.

With help from an old schoolmate who was international manager for a huge freight company I was allowed a years working residence permit in Singapore. I was registered as a safety and security consultant/ advisor.

"For God's sake keep your nose clean here," he instructed. "The Singaporeans are very keen to keep out of any messy politics especially theirs, or anyone else's for that matter.  Business is what they want, and business is what they do. So they will tolerate you helping keep the reputation of the whole shipping business clean around here."

Just as when employed by my government, but in a more relaxed way, I became quite used to deflecting enquiries about what I did. 'Security consultant, you know helping companies avoid computer hacking and that stuff, all a bit nerdy really', was usually enough to deflect questions.

At worst, those who enquired then asked for advice on protecting their own laptops. In response I simply recommended the usual well known list of  sold systems: McAfee, Symantec, MS Defender, Norton, Kaspersky and others.

All excellent in their way. Mind you when Mr. McAfee appeared somewhat disheveled looking, apparently wanted for interview by police in various parts of South American I did wonder a bit, even though he had been long gone from the excellent company that bore his name.

Ditto, when Kaspersky, still a deservedly respected security favourite of many established banks, had  a bit of drama  when Mr. Kaspersky's son was apparently kidnapped by some  Russian underworld characters. I have to say I pondered the safety of my pin numbers. But his reputation and business still flourished I even kept seeing them as sponsors on some red 'Formula 1' racing cars.

My clients viewed me as Mr. Dependable - or a 'lovable and reliable tower of strength', as the wife of one long term client put it. Strictly business, but on occasions wives and girlfriends were useful allies when trying to persuade a powerful man not used to taking orders, that a change of route, routine or even restaurant may be a sensible precaution. Right now I had enough going on to occupy every waking moment.

*As reportage of terrorism and threats perceived or otherwise boomed, so did our business. Or rather our function was to defuse problems, before there was any destructive boom - actual or imagined.*

Our clients were mixed in nationality and business. We had some old 'Far East' trading companies. Originally British and Scots owned and based in Hong Kong. These days their true financial bases were more likely Singapore , Switzerland, Ireland or the Dutch Antilles, but for many, their main operations hubs were still in good old 'Honkers'.

Some other business we inherited from Rewan, was with two old established ship owning families, one, Chinese in Taiwan and the other Japanese in Tokyo.

The Chinese connections continued into the mainland China. Obviously there our operations were somewhat limited and we had to take care not to step beyond certain defined areas of activity.

Having said that, as I had just had confirmed, ever pragmatic, the Chinese, as the world's foremost traders and always mindful of business opportunities, were extremely keen to ensure smooth running of all they did. Where ever they did it.

In particular, for years they had been  investing hugely throughout Africa. So on their behalf there we also now represented a couple of African heads of state.

We had some newer UK companies as clients. They were venturing into Asian business for the first time, or seeking to ensure safety for their supplies and suppliers.

Most  were very surprised to find the Asian world of big business was surprisingly old established and remarkably well financially endowed: Rather more old money, Switzerland style than the new money of the Caribbean or even Luxembourg.

With anti terrorism, hi-jack and piracy prevention training much now insisted on by those same insurance companies that had annoyed me ten years ago, we had set up a ships officer training center in Europe.

Located in the South of France it was starting to attract reasonable business from European shipping companies as well as our core Asian business.

My regular team, some inherited from Rewan , were freelance in attitude and style, but in reality exclusively retained. They were mostly ex Government or special forces security professionals from a variety of national organisations. South African, Israeli, a Swede, a Czech, some Brits and crucially several from Hong Kong and mainland China.

In the not so distant past, the Hong Kong element would have been British ex Hong Kong Police, but my two were Chinese nationals - one from the mainland and the other HK born.

My mainland China man was an ex toy exporter which created plenty of opportunities for a good ribbing from his western colleagues in our multi skilled team.

We carried out a lot of our own research. This research was used a lot - at least to make ongoing risk assessments.

In the case of two of our African clients that included our concerns on power likely to be grabbed and national assets likely to be stripped and moved to banks based in cooler, often mountain pastures.

Those research files were chivvied, collected , collated, and interpreted by an unlikely duo, Jacko and Suki. Jacko, a truly multilingual Venezuelan who had exiled himself from the troubled economic and political world of his homeland.

His partner, Suki, a slightly manic, very beautiful and very intense Japanese girl whom he had met online in a WikiLeaks crusade. They had been together for ten years, which given the volatility of both was quite surprising.  As Chuck Berry sings, 'It just goes to show you never can tell'.

My awaited visitor, Barry Purchase ,ex CIA, was a senior manager with Matchless Security Consultants . A company, way bigger than us, based in the US. Their discretion and skill belied the more usual gung-ho blare of 'good old boy' ex US Special forces.

Traditionally most US operations units were always 'bigger, better, stronger, fitter, better trained, better armed, more fearsome and so on'. Matchless were a little different - more reserved almost in 'True Brit' style really.

Although on occasions they too suffered at the boastful and extravagant claims of some of their wealthier private clients. 'I really need those guys -- and boy are they the best and so on.'

Mostly, such bragging came from newly and usually quite suddenly enriched traders of one kind and another. A client with real security needs, was usually smart enough to realise that, the lower their profile the safer they were, at least from copy cat crazies.

Regarding 'copycat crazies'. It was the view of most experienced diplomats and indeed security experts, that much terrorism, *was driven by an urge for fame and personal publicity* around their crime or supposed martyrdom.

Our view was, and still is, that America, would help themselves if they chose to pay attention to the Iron Lady, Mrs. Thatcher. She, Britain's steely Prime Minister from the 70's whose maxim was for such matters was, *'deny them the ozone of publicity'*.

The US news networks seem to overdramatize and endlessly repeat all terrorist activities. In their constant search for increased viewing figures they mostly focused on, 'what if, and could have been' theories more than waiting for 'hard facts and real news'.

This, in our opinion creating great satisfaction, exactly the 'they made the TV news' glory amongst the very terrorists they are seeking to defeat. Such TV coverage making even relatively minor terrorists-heroes in their village or gang.

Mrs. T. wasn't really my choice of politician, but the point she made, about 'bad creates more bad' has been proven time and time again. Her views it seemed were also privately shared by a number of US politicians, diplomats and military men. Privately? I had enquired of several, their response, "We don't dare upset the almighty power of TV news networks."

Barry and I went way back to when I first went solo without the team at Vauxhall Cross taking care of me. He maintains that I saved 'his company butt' in a messy oil tanker hijack case where he represented the cargo, a lot of very valuable oil, and I represented the ship's owner.

The oil tanker named 'The New Reliability of Valetta', whilst not a megaship by the standards of today was big enough, but years of trading in illegal Libyan oil shipments had left her tired and badly maintained. Nevertheless both she and the cargo were insured by increasingly anxious insurers from London and Tokyo.

Essentially she been hi jacked, not with guns but with a spurious 'pollution and damages to the dock facilities' claim by the local authorities in a scuzzy little harbour less than a few days steaming from Panama.

Held to ransom by a local judge who had attached various legal warrants to the ship- which meant she couldn't sail until a bundle of cash released the vessel from this paperwork.

Guarded by some marine bailiffs and gun toting local police, all of whom were very aware that every day she remained tied to their crumbling old dock facility it was costing the various owners of cargo and ship thousands of dollars.

It's an old trick in dodgy harbours, but an overheating engine bearing and a fault in the hydraulic pumps that operated the winches, lifting gear and the steering hadn't given the master much choice other than to dock at the old Anglo Noriama jetty.

More modern and better maintained ships have multiple backup systems but the now 'Not New and Unreliable of Valetta', was well past her sail by date.

Matchless Consulting's insurers got all excited about weeks of expensive legal work to convince the judge and free the ship. Of course the reality was the South American politicians, lawyers and police chief were all family or long time friends of the judge. All of them were on the take.

After a quiet word from Barry, with a couple of my guys we extracted the boat one dark night using a few dollars petty cash to open a couple of locked gates - and a local tug boat hi-jacked with cash, by ourselves in a similar smiley way.

The now 'Almost Reliable' captain, with his steering and engine all repaired was able to make way, surprisingly quickly as soon as he was pointed in the right direction by the tug boat, and the assisting vessel then went off for an already well paid day's fishing.

As mine was a new start up business and needing almost any work we could get, we were on a minimal fee from the 'Unreliable's rust bucket tanker's Maltese owners.

Worse still, there was some doubt we would even be able to extract the fee from them. In fact they would probably have been happier to lose the ship which they had doubtless over insured.

Matchless Security with more power and more bargaining reputation were on a massive results bonus from the oil company insurers, but only if they actually did the job!

It was Barry who well understood that the oil company insurers small print actually suggested that if the ship's cargo was freed by 'action from third parties' i.e. not by Matchless Consulting that the insurers substantial bonus fee went unpaid.

It was Barry, who quietly produced a sheaf of instructions from him to me to carry out the re-hijack, confirming in fact, 'our quiet word,' and it was Barry who wrote into that paper that we would share the bonus.

Matchless Consulting were happy having been rewarded substantially for not much more than a few phone calls.

As the, 'we', in those days was pretty much just 'me', it was essentially Barry who gave me enough working capital to build a decent client base and business.

So almost eight years on, it was a pleasure to welcome him again to our office in Singapore. Brushing the water bottle condensation from his Hawaiian shirt, big Barry flexed his hands, cracked his knuckles.

I hate that. Large Americans, even of Irish extraction, and diminutive slim Thai ladies always make that flexi noisy joint cracking action, and I really really hate it.

"I think we have a problem mate," he said in an appalling English accent, worse even than that of Dick Van Dyke in Mary Poppins. He upended his water bottle, and as was his way, came directly to the point.

" Two of our clients and we suspect some of yours have been or are being set up in a nasty scenario or more likely a scam. I can tell you, we've put everything we can into this but we haven't a clue who the bad boys are...not even a whisper or a sniff of who, where or why".

I interrupted. "I've got an add on for that. Three days ago I was urgently asked to go to a meeting in Shanghai with a promise of some useful info. I dutifully went. To my surprise the meeting turned out to be with Liu Qiang."

Barry looked suitably surprised, or to use the English English only phrase, gob smacked. I continued, "Liu told me that he had heard of plans for, as he put ' a major and possible multiple assault on global shipping.' "

"He wanted to me to be aware and to let London know that if there was anything to be done he was there to help." I continued, "Liu also told me I could share the word with you also, as he obviously he knew you were coming here."

Barry raised his eyebrows, "No surprise, I guess."

I continued. "Well, all a bit of a shock. I had time to say that any contacts I still had with London were informal, and that was that."

"You know the Chinese. Very hard to read. Bit unusual to say the least, but I held off doing anything till we met. I did talk to him about rumours of a complete ghost crew being recruited."

"The only new thing I have to add is this, overnight my two researchers J&S picked up an odd one. A report from this morning's Japanese media, in Japanese and now English, suggesting a ' damaging fire attack on global shipping underway .Hard to confirm origin of story. Looks like a plant of some kind."

I passed him a printout.

Memo from Jacko attached : this is the exact quote copied, mistakes and all:

*A number of important super big (sic) cargo ships have been fire bombed at sea over the last 48 hours.*

*Those ships and now others have been ordered to stay out of harbours and deck (sic) areas until matters resolved. More attacks are threatened for 25/6 and 27/1.*

*Shipping delays to world freight transport can create <u>highlyest</u> (sic)*
*damage to world trade.*

*<u>Imports</u> (sic)prices can go up if products delayed or spoiled on*
*<u>voyaging</u>. (sic) . ends*

J&S made some more comments, noting: *<u>Italics</u>* are our insert, showing errors in language. Could be someone using old version of an auto translate or similar. Usually national variations in language teaching show up and reveal origin of translation.

Our gut feeling for us is Japanese influence. Note this feeling based on style of mistakes in English, not the source of the quote.

Barry said, "For sure nothing major has happened out there that between us we wouldn't know about. Given the dates in that report are the same as you got in Shanghai it also kind of makes you wonder about Liu Qiang, maybe he is playing a game".

He and I talked on through that afternoon and then more quietly whilst out and about for some of a slightly less professional and alcohol fueled evening.

I am not sure which hour or which bar we were at when, back in the world of oriental cliché's, jet lag and too much alcohol plied by diminutive Thai and Chinese ladies caught up with mighty Barry. We decided that saving the world would have to wait until the following day.

## 13. Tuesday June 21st. 8.30 am.Marina Bay. Singapore:

*Save the world. No problem, but after last nights excesses, breakfast first.*

Following our 'boozy' night it was an overly bright morning when I arrived at a more than multi star hotel to continue our meeting.      I found Barry tucking into a serious stack of pancakes with bacon and maple syrup in the coffee shop about 50 stories above Marina bay.

He smiled a greeting and indicated the kit to make a cup of English Breakfast tea. "I have always that the height is conducive to a good mornings work," he said somewhat indistinctly, wiping crumbs from his mouth.

I studied the spectacular view of the Singapore Harbour Straits with hundreds of freighters of all kinds at anchor, mostly waiting for world trade to pick up.  So a still life of world shipping from this height, but a very impressive one.

I responded, "At school we were always told that rooms with little or no view produced more focused studies".

He frowned at this old style opinion, and then glancing out of the window at the extraordinary view, as if for the first time, and said, "actually I was referring to the height of a good stack of breakfast pancakes."

"Sets you up for the day. I always have a breakfast special at the IHOP. near my office on way in to work."

He wiped some crumbs from his mouth and continued. "Mind you given the hours we keep sometimes it's lucky it's a 24 hour joint."

Having taken Barry's comments on board, I said "I am not sure that the Michelin starred chef of this illustrious hotel restaurant would be too flattered by your comparison to the many franchises of IHOP. The International House Of Pancakes. Excellent though their product is with both real maple syrup and real pig related bacon."

Both in need of fresh air we moved out onto the rooftop pool area and installed ourselves at a reasonably isolated table. Between the terrace railing and a loud splashing fountain we figured we were secure enough there.

500 feet or so in the air with a lots of background noise seemed reasonably safe from listeners, although we were very aware it wasn't 100%, but it seemed neither was my office despite all our checking.

Barry said. "I think we agree the situation is as follows:  Rumours suggest that the global shipping industry, or ships, some of them likely to be  our clients, may be at more than usual risk from something. Political gesture, terrorism, some scam, hijack, piracy, pilferage at sea we don't know. Yet. You've even had a heads up from Chinese state security. Strikes me that, on this we probably are on the same side as the Chinese. But with them you never know everything."

"This week in the Japanese media there's been a bizarre story of a non event involving freight ships. But nothing apparent yet."

"Suspects: One : Terrorism. Always the first question, particularly from the USA. Although sadly usually asked to cover someone's back, 'just in case' and needing real facts. And in this case indeed, we have no real facts. But to be fair a ship with a bomb on it makes most security organisations and Governments lose sleep."

"Suspects: Two: Criminal. Commercial fraud, insurance scam or robbery. Nothing known, yet."

Suspects: Three : Political. Two thoughts:

"A. Serious 'Look at us- and be warned.' The kind of thing that has a North Korea connection written all over it."

" They like to aggravate the US. Also consider, they have again been jamming local GPS on shipping. But anything major, more than aggravation unlikely, and surprising if they dare upset the Chinese."

" B. Still serious. Demo's Greenpeace, Sea Shepherd. Other whaling concerns .Stop global warming. Suspects. Many. Mostly admirable causes but  annoyance and cost factors considerable."

"So in addition to our need to protect our clients, business, ships and staff, the real concern for governments is that any of these events could create major uncertainty for international trade" .

"That in turn creates volatility in the markets of the world, which apart from hurting global business stability and growth can be manipulated for financial advantage. Anything that hurts global trade - really – hurts our clients."

I said. "All agreed and the conclusions are?"

Barry cracked his fingers again.  I winced as he went on. "Firstly all governments know that 'empty shelves in supermarkets mean a rapid and serious breakdown in law and order. They fear that as much, if not more than a bomb in a box on a ship."

"Problems on one ship aren't going to stop the world, or even empty the shelves. So it's really just 'potential' trouble as usual. Except for the unusual heads up from the Chinese, them being concerned or suspecting, that more than one boat is at risk"

I repeated. "And the conclusions are?"

" One. In addition to the steps we have taken we need to redouble our own efforts to source the real facts."

"Two. See if one or more of our operatives could get signed up, by whoever was recruiting this ghost crew."

He paused, "And three. Because of the Chinese approach, and in case there was indeed a North Korean or other national aspect to this, we should indeed probably inform our previous employers. They may deign to share some information with us. Unlikely, but would be useful, if of course they actually know anything."

" Oh yes, four, we should add the warning dates he gave us. 6/25 , June 25 and 1/27, January 27. Especially as June 25 is next week."

After some further discussion of the pro's and con's of alerting our former employers we agreed to at least give them the basics. The 'pro's' taking into account -it could be a,' nation' V 'nation' situation developing...at least on a political level. The 'con's' being that we both found London and Washington leaked 'secure 'information like sieves.

Considering that any message was apparently, despite ,our up to date sweeping for listening bugs, just as likely to be intercepted from my office as from where we were, using our Blackberry's, we reported  then and there, discretely, to our respective countries.

I did say to Barry, "If they could see us now as we send the reports, eating Caesar salads high over Marina Bay, I think they would even more likely to file our reports in the nearest rubbish bin. Or in your case, garbage can."

So it was rather a surprise when, later that evening I was summoned by txt/sms to the UK, and like the alligator sandwich, 'make it snappy'. The first 'snappy' direct flight available for me was at 7.00 am the following morning.

Despite good intentions, knowing we both had early starts, it still ended up being both late and with too much alcohol.

At dawn we shared a cab to Changi Airport. We were actually in the spotlessly clean cab, driving along spotlessly clean flower lined streets, this was after all spotlessly clean Singapore, that Barry got a similar 'Be here ASAP. ' from Washington.

Looks like we've touched a nerve with someone' he said.

With a 'See you, speak you" we departed.

Him 20 hours, Eastbound and me, 12 hours, Westbound.

**14.  Wednesday. June 22nd. 4.00 pm.Inbound towards Heathrow Airport. London. England:** *The actual need for, provision of, and use of, security, is directly relative to the level of threats; perceived or real.*

I relaxed and dozed - as much as one can after twelve hours confined, even in the luxury of a business seat, of a Singapore Air 380S. Despite having the impression I was awake, I roused with a start as the Captain announced we had started our descent into London's Heathrow Airport.

Notwithstanding the millions spent by Airbus on ergonomic seat design, better ventilation, life enhancing lighting, even the smiles and ever attentive professionalism of the 'Singapore Girl,' crew didn't really make up for the need for some personal space, real fresh air and a brisk walk.

With eyes closed again, half sleeping, half planning, I considered the immediate next few days schedule and my report to be made to my old employers. The melody for 'On the Road Again,' playing in my mind whilst I pondered.

Although we happened to have our office in Singapore, central to most of my clients in the shipping business in the rest of Asia, even in this electronic communications era, I was almost more familiar with transits through the two airports, Changi and for the private flyer, Selator, than my office.

Asia was still great after ten years, and had become the business and trading center of the world. That must be true, because even legendary investment guru Warren Buffet had said so several times over the years. If anything, the focus on Asia was even stronger now. Others wrote that Singapore was within a five hour flight of fifty percent of the worlds middle class, by spending power.

On occasions, in that most brilliant place to live, the cost of actually living there made me wonder if it they should have written, it was the top fifty percent by spending power that actually lived in Singapore.

 Globally the security business generally was pretty busy-including mine. *The actual need for, provision of, and use of security is directly relative to threats real or perceived.*

In the case of democratic nations, that risk or threat should be based on real and potential dangers to the nation.

In reality the level of security provided is more usually based around budgetary considerations, and the need for local politicians to produce highly publicised activity for electoral situations or personal ambition.

In the case of nations controlled, shall we say, 'rather less then democratically, 'retaining power for the current incumbent of the Presidential Palace, usually at any cost', is the key motivation driving their use of private contracted security companies.

For individuals and companies the need for, engagement of and indeed payment for such security *is based on the fear level of the client.*

*That fear of potential danger or threat is often promoted by the very people engaged to protect against threat.*

A quick look online will show many adverts from old established and reputable insurance companies offering:

*'Insurance cover for personal and family kidnap, terrorism, and protection against those attempting to hold brand reputations to ransom'.*

The contents of their brochures look like pages from a movie script or James Bond novel. A different world.

Needless to say, <u>*specialist subsidiaries of those very insurance companies,*</u> or their contracted partners just happen to also provide protection services against such risks. Such services, mostly advertised as, 'being staffed and operated by former special services officers'.

Use of such services often being mandatory for getting the insurance cover-and sold as, 'enhancing your security whilst reducing your insurance premium costs'.

*The way they subtly promote both, the fear, and their solution,* is a classic lesson in doublespeak marketing.

Their brochures for special forces investigation and protection present very different images from the soft focus TV adverts for the same insurance companies, where the reassuring, benign face and voice of an actor - complete with calming music - presents pension, health and life assurance plans.

I stress again, *from those same insurance companies as being,* 'From an age old, reliable, safe, secure and well established company with family values'.

It's comforting to know that family values these days may include the need to hire someone with a range of covert gun skills or even a spot of 'water boarding'.

Of course only when absolutely necessary, and doubtless all with a calming soundtrack and a fluffy towel afterwards.

All of which some say is a bit, 'chicken and egg' , which came first, the fear or the fear of fear ?

But hey, as Rewan Trelawney had said a few years back, I mustn't bite the hand that feeds me. Essentially we also provide 'enhanced security' and as it happens many of my team in my private security company are actually ex special forces.

To be fair, the origins of some of those old established insurance companies and their preventative protection squads go back centuries. Back to the days of when they hired men with lanterns and stout sticks to patrol the Castle Keeps in which were stored plundered gold and silver bullion delivered across the oceans on wooden sailing ships.

Ships crewed and captained by privateers or even pirates, also skilled with pistols, tough interrogation and even then presenting an ultimatum involving a board and water.

In that case, the victim was walking on the board, the water far below was salty. Sharks were optional. Not much changes really then: Just a bit of updating.

My client list, was mostly wealthy ship owning families, where we worked at first with the companies and increasingly, in this troubled world directly with those high net worth families.

It was a collection of possible threats to several of those shipping clients that brought me hot seated to London and to my first formal meeting in five years or so with my old employers.

Possible threats? Always.

Probable threats? Increasingly likely.

We landed with a slight bump, 'welcome to London Heathrow' and instantly the inevitable tedium of the voyage was replaced by an urge to get up and get out. Unfortunately that same urge was shared by 400 or so others- many of whom seemed to be even more anxious to get off than I.

I was looking forward to a decent shower, a snack and a big sleep in readiness for a pressured next morning. Any urge to win the race to disembark was tempered by the thought of then waiting and shuffling slowly through immigration.

Why did I always choose the line, where in older airports those in front had not yet filled in the little landing card or in newer terminals, where the auto eye recognition machine was confused by someone with new contact lenses or shaved eyebrows.

So I shuffled, bag in hand towards the airplane door. I had had two fairly boozy and late nights in Singapore with my US colleague Barry Purchase. So, fit as I am, I was almost hungover sleepwalking in the airless, and 'follow me to the terminal tube', stuffed with my fellow travelers.

Consequently I almost missed the guy in a suit holding up a discrete card with my company name on it. 'TrePolPen S. Co.'

I shook hands with my 'meeter greeter' and he showed me onto a waiting golf cart. Then, with those usually annoying, but in this case welcome 'get out of the way' beeps and clicky sounds from the cart, we made quickish progress to the main terminal.

As we drove he proffered some i.d. and remarked. "I was just starting to wonder if I'd missed you in the scrum at the gate -- there's a lot of people on those 380's. I didn't want to attract attention by putting a call out for your name."

At this mention of my name, as usual I reacted a tad quickly and glanced at him sharply, but he continued "Still need to do immigration sir, but we'll be first in line over there at the desk marked closed. Whilst you do that I'll call up the car so it's ready out front."

Minutes later as we walked down the steps and through customs I said, " Best not ask how you knew I was coming out of the business exit from the plane or even how you figured which flight."

Meeter greeter just grinned and guided me across some taxi lanes to a black windowed Range Rover waiting at the kerb. "That's me done - the driver knows where you're staying. You may want to turn on your phone sir, I think the boss will be calling."

In my still hung over jet lagged blur I had forgotten to turn on my Blackberry. As I sat back in the car I gave some thoughts to the fact that I hadn't really checked the i.d. very carefully or even given much thought to the legitimacy or not of the meeter greeter.

The surprising urgency of the summons to London and the leaving of Singapore had been such a rush, that even with the entire world available on my phone, I had done little more than book a hotel room and order some stuff from Amazon U.K.

By the time my phone had discovered it was in England, we were out through the Airport tunnel and on the M4, nose to tail in the early evening town bound traffic. The boss or more correctly my ex boss had called or auto-dialed me three times.

This time I answered. It was actually the deputy chief, Sir Geoffery Barker. I listened. Crisp and to the point.

"Welcome Daniel, thanks for coming at such short notice. Team meeting tomorrow usual place at 09.30. Before that though, briefing at your hotel as soon as you get there."

If I needed anything call so and so. Oh yes. Hotel was paid, just any extras my responsibility.' I hardly had time to acknowledge, and he had clicked off.

The driver spoke almost for the first time. "You're now booked into the Savoy sir. Was there mail or anything needing to be collected from the hotel you had originally booked".

"Actually there is '" I said.' There should be some packages from Amazon waiting my arrival at the Kensington Hilton. We could swing by and collect them if we go left just after the Hammersmith flyover."

The driver responded, "If it's OK with you sir I'll get a colleague to do that. I believe there's a meeting scheduled at the Savoy."

I pondered ' a meeting scheduled at the Savoy.'

I had been gone from my old employers at SIS, still known to many Brits as MI6, for ten years now and I had hardly been back in the UK for ten minutes when they started to organise my life without so much as a 'please or thank you.'

I settled back in my seat, if they wanted to send a car to collect my Amazon packages, serve them right. If they checked the online shopping - actually they probably knew already, they'd find they contained a large pack of PG Tips tea bags and a couple of books.

You can buy anything in Singapore and indeed I usually did. But Andy Keeling ,one of my key employees claimed he could only function if regularly fueled with mugs of tea - and only 'real English bought PG Tips' would do. Not for him the ubiquitous and rather weak, Lipton's Yellow label more widely available throughout Asia.

Nor would he countenance as he put it 'those hoity toity titty boo,' fashionable little cotton bags of handpicked specially selected 'English Breakfast Tea' so loved and highly charged for these days by modern hotels and fashionable coffee shops.

At one of our company briefings the girls from the office gave him a gift of a box of 'Monkey Picked Tea.' I feared for his sanity when persuaded to drink some.

I feared the girls would explode ,as only we knew they had replaced the original very expensive tea content of the 'Monkey Picked Sachets ' with the last of the real PG Tips from my kitchen.

My man Andy had the last laugh, he sipped and immediately said, " Someone's taking the piss here boss,' long pause - barely suppressed hysterics from the girls- " You've been ripped off, someone's been putting PG Tips into these little bags and selling them for ten times the price."

Another long pause during which the girls collapsed. Andy looked at them and said in his still broad northern accent, "Fooking clever those monkeys." and polished off his mug with relish.

Thoughts of monkeys and more meant that we arrived at the Savoy driveway in seemingly quick time. "See you another time" - I thanked the driver.

Waiting was MG2, another meeter greeter- a vaguely familiar guy this time. He started with – "You're all checked in sir, I've got the key."

Following a flurry of top hats and smart long coats, all with no surprise shown at my lack of luggage, deck shoes and my wish to keep my hand luggage close to me - we were quickly in a plush carpeted and very silent elevator, brass gleaming.

A few steps and MG2 opened the door, "River suite here sir. It's 6.30 now and the DC will be here in about 30 minutes. So if you want to freshen up I'll wait here if that's OK with you "

Slightly jarred into wakefulness by all this action I asked him "I'm a bit jet lagged - where did we meet before?"

MG 2 beamed - "Indeed sir. I'm Johnnie Wells, joined the service just about as you were leaving. You were one of my assessors after we ran a test op trying to infiltrate one of the official government country residences at Dorney Woods sir."

It all came back to me. "I remember, and not only did you infiltrate but you caught a member of the British government with his pants down with his secretary."

He grinned - "That was us sir."

I went on "Didn't the boss - I mean Miss Stanton, who was in charge of recruiting then, give you some stick because you titled the report in what she said was an inappropriate way, what was it now?"

He grinned again- "She did- she was very angry. I had called it, 'I said take dictation Miss Jones - not take my dick.' "

I laughed out loud-- and he said " It was only your intervention that saved the day for me and my team."

I looked puzzled. "How the hell did I help you out of that one."

"In your report you wrote 'Thank God at least this is one minister who likes girls,' and gave us full marks."

His phone beeped with a message and he said "If you don't mind me saying, sir, the DC will indeed be here in under 30 minutes.'

I was still chuckling as I figured out which of the ten or so gleaming taps in the shower would deliver a much needed refreshing blast of water. Water apparently from their own artesian well deep under the hotel.

Refreshed and wearing a clean but slightly crumpled shirt I started to gather my thoughts as MG2 ordered up a welcome cup of tea.

This being the Savoy I assumed delivery would be by Flunkey not Monkey and indeed the trolley with tea flunky, another bearing my Amazon boxes from the Kensington Hilton and the D. C. all arrived at my door together.

Which meant that the DC's first greeting to me as we shook hands was, "So much for a discrete visit. I came straight from No 10. If you come along the river embankment road you can usually slip in the back door of the hotel without meeting too many people."

He continued. "I'll be brief- you'll be tired and I've got a train to catch. Of course we asked you here as a very serious situation seems to be developing and possibly gathering momentum. Subject to our discussion I've brought a detailed FYO backgrounder for you. "

I gestured at the impressive selection of bottles on the ornate table, no little mini bar here- "It's been a long day, for me at least, and assuming your work rate is the same as usual, a long day also for you, certainly by the time you get back to Surrey. Would you care for a dram."

He smiled and said to MG2 who had leapt to his feet and was poised near the bar. "I'll have a small Bushmills ,little bit of water, no ice'"

"You are right about long days- even when there's no 'flap on'. More reporting to more bosses has made the work load worse. On the other hand, since you left us we've become even more internet reliant, so I have indeed managed to keep living in Surrey at the old Chiddingfold house. Keeps the wife happy and doing a bit of gardening at weekend is very therapeutic for me  - even if the brain keeps ticking whilst I'm cutting the grass."

I explained that I used to see him occasionally on the train out of London's Waterloo station- although I alighted at Godalming- a few stops before his at Haslemere. I omitted pointing out that I was commuting home crammed and usually standing for the first part of the journey in an overly full third class carriage- whilst he was seated, in some space at least, in First Class.

He sipped his whiskey, me my gin and tonic,

"Right - let me update you."

MG2 turned on a machine that emitted a low and slightly intrusive 'hum.' and said a "Jumbler sir-mixes up our words and apparently protects our conversations a little against radio mikes."

I nodded, didn't bother to tell him that I could buy that very model of 'Jumbler' in most street markets throughout Asia. We didn't think they worked, and as it happened it also seemed the Chinese MSSS were listening in to my phone or office anyway.

The DC started. "Your e mail rang a few alarm bells. You've picked up some early stage rumblings of someone recruiting for a complete ship's crew that seems a bit worrying."

" It also seems that an earlier message of yours a few days ago, resulted in local security here this morning intercepting a container ship with fire bombs inside them. Burnt out the interiors of the containers, and destroyed most of the evidence. Forensics are working on it."

" Not high explosive thank god. In any case the fires were contained at sea. If they had ignited in port they could have closed parts of Felixstowe or London Gateway for a week whilst we figured it all out. Then you come up with a threat for, 'Something 'on June 25th and more after Christmas."

I said to him, " I've also got something else to report that I didn't want to send by open coms. Last week I was summoned to a meeting with Liu Qiang about these or other shipping threats."

He looked at me intently, "That's very interesting, fill me in after we get this out of the way. It's a little background stuff. Now don't yawn, I know they teach this one in school these days."

He continued, "In 1939 having concluded that construction of an Atomic bomb was now possible and reasonably likely, Albert Einstein wrote that famous letter on the 29th of August to US President Roosevelt."

" His letter said. '*A single bomb of this type, carried by boat and exploded in a port, might very well destroy the whole port together with some of the surrounding territory'.*"

The DC looked at me somewhat sternly and said, "But you knew all about that. But now let me quote US President Obama seventy five years later, in March 2014."

"*He said. 'I am less concerned about threats from any regional superpower than at the prospect of a nuclear weapon going off in Manhattan'.*"

"Before you can't hold back that yawn any longer and say to me, 'Not still the old bomb in a box problem, sir', whilst I agree it is, although it's hard for the politicos' to shout about it, we think there's a bigger and more troubling scenario."

"*We're now all so totally reliant on imported everything we now see disruption to trade as being as much, if not a more likely threat than 'the bomb in a box.*"

"As we see it, if or more likely, when, the boats don't come in, if the supermarket shelves are emptied, *or even just rumoured to be* emptying by shortages and panic buying, civil unrest follows on fast, on a huge scale, and it will spread like wildfires in a wind."

" Policing that threat, even on an island is bloody hard. If like the USA and most other countries, you have thousands of miles of coastline and thousands of possible of entry ports it's even harder. In the real world, very few of the so called 'initiatives' put in place here or elsewhere are comprehensive enough to be much use.

"A very small percentage of container freight is thoroughly inspected. Despite some loud PR about new initiatives it is not likely to be."

"A year or so back a senator from Florida called most mandatory port security passes, as being, 'About as much use as a library ticket'. Most still are. There's some very good practice here in the UK especially from the big port operating companies, but globally, out at sea or especially at container filling points, checking is still unreliable."

"More to the point our reliance on products and even parts made in the Far East is almost total. Even the US President's own most secure transport- their Flying White House in the event of a national emergency, 'Air Force One' apparently has more than five thousand component parts made abroad - many in China."

"We all know that each and every telephone in current use worldwide if not made in Asia, has Asian components. The switch gear that keeps all our power and health services and systems running have vital parts imported. The same applies to our latest jet fighters and other defence items, and almost all hospital equipment."

"Despite endless warnings from us, the military and other advisors the politicians in most western countries have lacked the will, support or balls to create any stocks of emergency goods, let alone food and fuel. The Germans and the Swiss have some but that's more weather related"

*"In short, any interruption to the just in time supply system and society as we know it breaks down. Any recovery, not only of law and order but also of society as we know it would be a long and difficult path."*

"When I tell you that The Chinese government and the Russians as well as us, the USA ,our mutual allies and most of our enemies are all agreed on this matter I think you can assume it's being taken very seriously."

I interjected. " That's exactly the message I have come to report."

I told him briefly the key points of my meeting just a week before with Liu Qiang.

DC Responded, " Well it's not the first time we've heard directly from them over the years on many subjects, but usually such mutually interesting items arrive via diplomats. Did he say why he chose you?"

My reporting Liu's 'need to move quick and shoes on the ground', made the DC say, "Well that just goes to show there a few of us old duffers out there who think the same way."

"When your warning came in, it touched more than a few nerves and rang a few alarm bells ,I can tell you, mainly because, the day after tomorrow we're at a meeting in about all this in the USA, and we have no firm or stand up-able facts."

"Despite our efforts, and I suspect those of the Americans, frankly we haven't a single clue. Let alone any hard evidence to sort the real from the rumour."

"Nothing."

"Then in quick time you've delivered a bullseye with the detailed info about those containers and now with your personal message from China it looks like you are 'the man in the know '."

"In many ways the service has become, 'Jack of all trades and master of none.' Mainly because we currently have to attend to so many areas of interest around the world."

" So your specialist shipping connections, your location and even before you delivered today's bad-fortune cookie message from your Chinese chum, it was your suggestion that one of your operatives may be near to getting himself recruited woke up a few people. That's why you're here."

"That's also why we'd like you to attend the final day wrap up of this weeks joint US-UK shipping security meeting the day after tomorrow as one of our UK representatives. You're American friend Mr.? "

He tailed off, glancing at his notes.

"Mr. Purchase," I suggested.

"That's it Purchase, I understand he'll be there. "

"Together with the CIA  The FBI, the NSA, ASIO, DHS. The whole bloody alphabet of US-UK  security. As it happens Miss Stanton is already out there with the PM at that conference . She feels they are all lacking real facts. That meeting coincides with a global oceans warming palaver, it was the timing of that meeting that set the schedule for the security update ."

"The security meeting is to try and make sure we're all on the same song sheet. The wrap up day, happens to be on June 24th so now there's talk of the team being in the right place at the right time. But frankly it could be a simple matter of us or them grasping at straws and relieved to have something new to report."

"Or it could be a co-incidence. Given the global implications of all this, some months ago we angled for the Chinese to be invited, the the Yanks didn't want to know. We suspect their new President will take a less kneejerk reaction, and it seems he's taking a close personal interest in all this. "

"We also think we need to plant some seeds in the US Military and Security to make a  more global approach to all this a reality."

"Miss Stanton asked me to tell you that she is looking forward to meeting you again, should you be available to attend. I also have to tell you that I came here direct from Downing Street, and the Foreign Secretary also feels we need to apply all available resources to this situation. So I hope you feel you can assist."

I nodded as the D.C. continued, " I realise that coming here rather than going directly to the USA is a bit of a bloody diversion but, obviously on something as delicate as this and with you being 'off the books', I felt it was better to speak to you directly rather than suggest anything to you over the line to Singapore. We'll get you to Nevada where they've scheduled the meeting on a direct flight in some exec jet or other."

"Before you reply," he went on.

"Despite you signing a whole sheaf of non disclosure papers when you left us - the powers that be would like you, they insist actually, to agree to some up-dates to those signed papers that we have on file."

He looked at his notes, "They want you to be 'contracted, retained staff. As a freelance ex employee you don't currently qualify to get updated info from all those attendees." He looked over glasses and grinned, "That's despite you bringing in more bloody info than they've managed to find in the past six months."

I agreed to sign whatever was needed which would apparently make me a, 'retained staff consultant.'

The Deputy Commander of my old employers rose. "Knowing the ministry I doubt the retainer will be up to much, but Queen and Country you know. Mind you these days I'm surprised the daft bastards didn't ask you to re-train as well as retain."

With a grin, he continued, "I wonder what their automated profiling system will make of your personal contacts with your Chinese chum. I'd like to be in that meeting. In any event I'll get Johnnie here to nip back to the office and let Miss Stanton know about the Shanghai rendezvous on a secure line."

Giving me a sealed folder containing a background briefing paper, he gathered up his own papers, and shaking hands said. "I knew you wouldn't let us down - anyone who played opening bat and got a ton against Hambledon Village must be good."

"Oh yes,"- he went on "I can't remember if it was in this hotel or the Ritz . In 1978 writer Graham Greene was interviewed by Gavin Young for the Observer Newspaper about his new book and his days in the service."

"Green suggested then to Young, that very simple sabotage of the Panama Canal would bugger up world trade for quite a while."

"Hope that's not an omen. Even then, the report of that in the Observer that Sunday caused a bit of a stink in the office on the Monday."

With a, "See you tomorrow," a brisk handshake, and taking MG2 with him he left.

Having been delivered of the news that Barry and I apparently had the survival of global society we know it in our hands , I poured myself a second stiff gin , and mulled over the legendary 'Our Man in Havana' author, Graham Greene's, Panama thoughts.

It had taken almost fifty years, some years to heed his warning , but recently at various bottlenecks they doubled the canal waterways, in both the Panama and Suez Canals.

It was claimed they needed more capacity, but the word in my world was, that in both cases it was simply to avoid closure if serious sabotage happened.

I opened the briefing papers and started to read but with eyes blurring after twenty four hours on the move, I opted for a wonderful Savoy bed, booked an early call, and decided to read in the morning when I could take it all in.

I also pondered at the old man remembering my scoring a hundred runs as the opening batsman for my village cricket team. In my reconstruction, I think I got as far as walking out to bat, and I was gone to the world.

**15. Wednesday June 22nd. A bright summer's morning at Rudesheim am Rhine. Germany. River boat moorings:**
*Sightseeing time.*

"Come on Tammy, we'll miss the taxi."  Tamiko and Brigitte were on the little terrace outside their riverboat cabin photographing each other with a background of the river and behind that some hills with lines of vines rising from the river.

Tamiko "Hang on I'm trying to send this to my Mama but the connection's very slow," she typed a caption for the pictures:    *'Having a great time. There's three schools on two boats. Tell Papa the river boat is 125 meters long and 150 of us on each boat. Here's me, and Brigitte.*

*Today we're going to see the riding academy and the walk around in the little town. Fireworks tonight and tomorrow lots of castles on the river. End of the week we get to Basle for the Concert in the Park. Love T.*

May, always organised and business-like as could be expected of her Chinese heritage, sat on an unmade bed and read the day's newsletter.

**> 'River of Castles , Romance and Music. Summer Tour'.**
**Day: June 22 Rudesheim am Rhine. Day at leisure.**
Girls may disembark anytime after breakfast.
(Note: You must wear your school/ship id bracelet at all times)
Some rain is expected in the afternoon.
The list of suggested sightseeing within walking distance has been discussed in yesterday's assembly.
Use of taxis and other transport is strictly forbidden, except for the shuttle bus or cable car up to the castle and the booked transport to the F.v.C.Fahrman Riding Academy. That will depart at 10.00 am from the taxi stand at the right end of the dock.
The Castle and the Cable car have special prices for students. Show your boat tour I.D. All Girls must be back on board by 6.30.
Buffet supper 7.30 pm. Fireworks over the river at 9.00pm.
NOTE. All GIRLS FROM THE COLLEGE OF THE ALPES ARE EXPECTED  TO MAKE THEIR BEDS AND LEAVE THEIR ROOMS /CABINS TIDY . THERE MAY BE A CABIN INSPECTION DURING THE DAY. NB.**You must remember to sign in at breakfast**.
HAVE A NICE DAY.<

Having been urged again to "hurry, come on," by May the three girls tidied the room straightened the beds and rushed out. Tamiko saying, "this internet's terrible, remind me to send my photos later."

The girls all eager to meet their show jumping idol F. v. C. Fahrman or actually more keen to meet his horses.  Photos of which adorned their study rooms back at college.

With girls from 23 countries at the college, most room decoration was a mixed selection of pop star posters reflecting both international and home country fame.

The three horse mad girls were nick named by their college friends  in a mix of languages, 'Les Trio Cowgirls' or even 'The  Samurai Girls Cavalry'.

Which was a bit unfair on Chinese May and Swiss-French Brigitte and actually also on the only Japanese, Tamiko. Not to mention the legend of the Samurai Warriors.

Although to be fair there are historical records of women Samurai warriors and the use of horses.

The two long river boats, low to get under the bridges of the Rhine and Danube, were moored alongside each other so the girls picked their way across the deck of the inner boat and joined the queue of chatting girls going down the only gangway.

There, under the watchful eye of a security guard in a small tent they swiped their id bracelets. The 'rfi' chips on each, registered their exit on the on-board computer. Just as, later in the evening it would confirm their re-boarding of the boat.

The system was excellent and given the importance of counting numbers of passengers in say, a fire or accident, ships pursers and captains liked its instant and accurate information.  Better than a manual count and signing in process. With just one gangway, even in this peaceful old wine town on the river, security was ever present.

They walked across the cobbled dock towards the taxis and as ever it was the organised May who spotted the driver holding up a brochure for the Riding Academy. The three girls even knew the name of Jack, the handsome horse pictured on in the cover.

The driver was smiling but asked. "There are three of you, yes? I had expected two." May (again in charge and expecting a scam or at least a price increase) "Sorry, is that problem ?"

"No no" said the driver opening the door." Just a little less room."

As May settled into the back of the taxi she said. "When I made the booking on Facebook I didn't know that Brigitte would be with us as well."

They continued with the driver listening to English language chatter. After just a few minutes they turned off the road, passing under a carved wood sign- that proclaimed : 'The F.v.C. Fahrman Equestrian Academy.'

May, "Stop stop- we must get a photo." The driver stopped and then had to operate three phones, two apples and a Samsung, as the happy trio posed under the sign.

They got back in the car and drove up the driveway between neat fences surrounding short scuffed cropped grass with many horses grazing.

The driver said. "Not much for them to eat in those fields."

As the girls started to explain, in some detail, of the health perils of too rich grass on some types of horses they arrived out side the stables. "I'll wait there under those trees." He said. "I now know more about horses than I have ever known before."

But he was speaking to an empty space as the excited girls had gone at a brisk trot through the massive double doors into the yard.

The driver pulled out his phone and after a seconds waiting spoke urgently. "There's bloody three of them not two."

He listened, and - "I don't bloody know - but she may be family for all I know- from what they were saying I think her dad's something to do with ships as well."

He listened again and," OK I'll call when we're leaving - you'd better be ready."

**16. Wednesday June 22nd. Later, on a still sunny morning.
Near Rudesheim am Rhine:** *Surprise and sudden fear can redesign
your life plan in less than thirty seconds.*

The three girls were laden down with shopping bags and chatting
animatedly when they eventually exited the riding stables.

"Look," said Tamiko, "We can just not go up to the monument in the
cable car, no one will know. As long as we're back at the boat by six." They
put their bags in the back of the cab and climbed in. "We'd like to go to the
center of Mainz town, please how long will it take ?"

The driver said, "From here ,about 45 minutes at this time".

"Great," said one of the girls," There's a shop we need there. How much
if we can go there. You please then wait for us . We'll grab something to eat
after the shop and then get back to the boat dock before six."

The driver thought a bit and said "total including this morning, 150
euros."

The girls all said, "50 each. That's fine," and they set off.

Having the found the store they wanted- more horse stuff- the driver
said, "Look there's no parking here" gave them his number and said, "Call
me, and I'll meet you by that little park there. We will need to be away
before 4.30 to be sure of getting back in time."

The girls were gone again in a medley of multilingual chatting.

The driver quickly dialed a number on his phone and said, "Bit of luck,
I've just taken them into Mainz. We'll get them in the place we agreed  on
the way from there.  This way they will be seen on loads of cameras and
probably use their credit cards in the town, so that will create more
confusion when the shit hits the fan. I'll call you when we leave."

Which he did soon after four.

With yet more shopping in the back of the car, the girls were excitedly
talking and hardly noticed when the car stopped in a secluded field gateway
with another car close behind them.

They certainly did notice when both doors were pulled open and two
men with guns said firmly." Out now, all of you and don't touch your bags
or your phones."

The noisy trio were now not.

"Listen, this is not about you, nothing bad is going to happen to you.
This is about the ships and money. We're going on a journey in that car.
You are not going to get hurt if you behave. You can have this the easy or
difficult way."

He took a large melon from the back of the other car and walked a good few meters away from the girls. They stared at him wide eyed. He took something from his pocket and sat it on top of the melon.

"Look carefully," he said- and holding out what looked like a mobile phone pushed a button and the melon exploded in a mess of orange pulp.

From a bag he took three necklaces, soft black plastic around the neck- with a small pouch on the front, about the size of a matchbox or small folding mobile phone, and gave one to each girl."

"Put them on. I'll lock the clips" which he did."

Now," he said." If any of you make any problem, if you go too far away from this, or if you go too far from each other," - he waved the phone thingy that had set off the melon bomb, "Then what happened to the melon will happen to your head. The explosive is in the pad at the front. You keep them on, and never take them off."

"We're going to drive for about ten hours. I'll stop when you need the toilet. If we get stopped by the police, say nothing except we're going on holiday. Remember at all times, and if we get stopped, it's a proximity bomb that's in the little bag on the front of that necklace. Lose me, lose your friend, and you lose your head."

The girls,all huddled together shuddered.

The gunman continued, "Like I said, this about the money. It's not about you-no one's going to mess with you. We need you well and happy so that your papa's will pay."

"Now give me your mobiles and I suspect that all three of you may have trackers in your bags as well as locators in your phones.."

The girls gave him their phones and indeed May and Tamiko did have small trackers in their bags. The trackers, each about half the size of a mobile phone  sent out a coded 'beep' with gps details every few minutes to a central office. "Now finally give me your ID bracelets for the boat."

"Let's go now, before someone comes to investigate exploding melons."

The girls climbed into the back seat of the other car. All their shopping bags were chucked into the trunk of the car and they left.  Their original driver carefully removed batteries and sims from the phones and trackers and drove back to the boat dock.

An hour or so later , it was lashing down with rain as the car, with the three girls in the back,  arrived at the German to France border and joined the line of cars slowly creeping past two smart looking but inattentive guards.

On the French side, for a second the driver was concerned as the French uniformed officer, waved him down. The driver lowered his window- the French guard peered in, saluted and waved him on.

It was also raining like hell back at the boat dock, when the taxi guy got back there. The bored security guard at the gangway to the two boats was only too pleased to discuss the weekend's football whilst trying to keep dry under the little tent and the taxi driver's umbrella.

In ones and twos the other girls returned, mostly huddled under plastic cagoules and umbrellas. A bunch of about ten girls rushed in together laughing. The guard didn't notice the cab driver brushing the three wrist bands concealed in his gloves across the receiver, as the group passed through the tent, still chattering.

The on board the computer blinked at three together, but when the totals were read later at 7 pm by the school organiser and the boats purser, all girls were apparently safely on board.

Later the clouds cleared- and 250 girls clustered around on the crowded decks taking photos of the fireworks. Or to be more accurate 247 girls were on deck. The missing three were well on their way westwards across Europe. Sitting wide eyed, silent, holding hands in the back of the car.

The taxi driver, whose name was Hans, didn't see the fireworks either, he was long gone. Having changed the registration number of his 'Taxi' and disposed of the stick on roof sign, he was driving South East across Germany, towards Linz , Austria and then following signs to 'Italia'.

In a shopping bag on the seat he had the three mobile phones and various other devices. Those phones weren't going to be missed until tomorrow evening or at the worst tomorrow late morning.

The other car travelling west, despite the late hour, found the roads were busy with families, eager to start their holidays. Bound for the cottages, gites, campsites, beaches and sunshine of South West France and Spain.

No one noticed yet another car with three very subdued girls in the back, nervously touching their locked on necklaces. The driver could see them in his mirror constantly touching the necklaces. "Don't worry about those. They will only explode if told to do so. You can bash them, hit them, twist them, shower and swim in them. They will be fine. But don't take them off, get used to it."

"Where we're going is quite nice. You won't be locked up or tied up. There's food, good beds even a pool. There's even a horse that looks over the gate."

Just as an early summer dawn was breaking, the girls dozing in the back when having left the busy auto route and driven for some time down smaller and smaller country lanes- so called 'D' routes in France he pulled in to a gateway.

Under the arch of the old stone gate house, he touched the sender that opened the gate and made his way up the potholed driveway and parked under the trees.

The girls followed him nervously and silently into the courtyard .

"This is your cottage" he said. "Loads of food in the fridge and in the big building there. There's nice people and kids in the houses on the other side of the pool."

" There's knives and all you need for cooking - but remember don't plan to knife one of us. Or to walk away from here, or from each other or many heads will be blown off. "

"The same thing will happen if you try to remove your necklace. So don't try. Clearing up a blown up head is worse than clearing up a melon, believe me, I know."

"Sleep well." He shut the door and they could hear him walking away. They collapsed onto each other in floods of tears and shaking with fear.

### 17. Thursday. June. 23rd. 9.00am. An Old Mill and Farmstead. South West France: *Terror stopped sleep, but eventually exhaustion won.*

An old Farmstead in Southern France, on a sunny morning with bougainvillea and other climbing flowers illuminating the warm stone walls should be a nice place to be in early summer.

Less so, for three teenage girls abducted at gunpoint in Germany with the threat of having their heads blown off if they removed the 'tag' necklaces their abductors have locked around their throats.

The three girls, still nervously fingering the, 'can explode at any time,' neckbands around their necks, peered gingerly around the door of the cottage where they had slept.

Terror had stopped sleep, but eventually exhaustion won.

In the morning sun across the stone courtyard they could see two blonde women clad in toweling robes - sitting on the edge of a clear blue swimming pool in which three young children splashed and played.

Nervous was not a strong enough word to describe Chinese May, Japanese Tamiko and French-Swiss Brigitte. Terrified and sick with fear was more appropriate. It was May, impetuous, inquiring as ever who stepped out first and stood silently gazing at the scene. The other two crept out behind her - holding each other.

One of the women- startled, by suddenly noticing May standing there, touched her companions arm and pointed in their direction. The women stood and as their robes slipped a little the girls noticed that they too were wearing the horrible things around their necks.

The women approached the girls, warily at first and then Anna spoke. "I think you may be have the same problem as us."

It was as if a switch had been turned and they all started to talk at once...the girls increasingly shrill and hysterical in a mix of languages. The other woman stepped forward, and putting her fingers to her lips said. "Careful please, please, we don't want to alarm the children, they don't understand there's a big problem. Do you speak English?"

May responded, putting her fingers to her lips also, and gesturing to the other two girls who were still shaking and still on the verge of hysterics. "Yes we do" " Come on Brigitte, Tammy listen to this lady. We must help her, those are little children, we must not alarm them."

Britt-Marie said, "Thank you, thank you. Seeing you was a shock. I heard a car in the night when it was still dark I guess that's when you came in."

Anna, pointing to a long table and chairs under two old and slightly tattered sun shades, and with the green leaves of an old vine invading and taking over the shade duties said. "Let's sit there and talk ,we can still watch the children are safe in the pool. I'll get some water."

The three girls still holding each other walked around the pool to the shady side of the courtyard and sat on a bench with their backs to the warm stone, and gazed around open eyed- almost in shock.

Britt- Marie, said "We know how you feel. They brought us here a few days ago. In the end, for the sake of children we had to get ourselves together."

Anna came out with a tray, loaded with water bottles, fruit and plastic glasses. She went into the building and came out again with yoghurts, some French bread, and a pile of plates.

She announced, "I'm making coffee'."

The girls were too shocked to eat but nervously took the offered water. "It's OK" said Britt, "I know how you feel. The water's OK, and you probably need to drink." She herself up ended a bottle and drank deep.

With the children still splashing in the pool, the five women talked. Introducing themselves hesitantly at first, followed by a flood of questions, with the words spilling out in nervous relief. Telling of their abductions, their journey and their arrival.

One of the children came over dripping water and asked, in Swedish, for a yoghurt which Anna opened for her. The little girl looked at the three new arrivals and spoke in Swedish, obviously a question.

May again the most confident, smiled and said in English, "I'm sorry, I don't speak Swedish. I'm May ,and I'm from China."

Without a moment's hesitation the little girl said, " That's nice, I'm from Sweden." and skipped back to the pool.

May to the ladies, "actually, I'm from Taiwan but with little kids sometimes ,'China' is easier at first." The group talked on, and urged on by Anna and Britt - Marie, the girls eventually shared some yoghurts, breads and Brigitte took a coffee.

The talk ranged from Sweden, School in Switzerland, Portugal but more about where they were. 'No they hadn't been hurt.' Britt and Anna confirmed that, 'it was well stocked with food.' One of the men had delivered fruit and bread the night before and had asked what they needed for today. 'Just write a shopping list'. They spoke about the necklaces- and shuddered together over the exploding melon demonstrations.

Then as their confidence grew they looked into each other's cottages, the children were now watching a dvd. " There's no tv signal but lots of dvds which yesterday we ignored but now we realised it can be good to get the kids out of the sun for a bit."

The girls did have some clean T shirts that they had bought at the German stables- and in their cottage they found several supermarket shopping bags with shorts, more shirts, swim clothes, even a selection of underwear.  In another bag they found toothbrushes, toothpaste soaps, shampoos, towels and sun cream.

" From the way they are equipped I think these are holiday rental cottages," said Anna.  The morning passed quickly, during which time the girls, urged by Britt went to shower, and put on clean clothes, "That will make you feel better. Don't forget the sun cream. You do that ,and I'll get some lunch together."

The three girls claimed not to be hungry, at which Anna spoke. Quite strongly. "I read a book once about some guys who were kidnapped in Beirut. Their food was terrible for months, but they always ate when they could as they wanted to stay strong. If they were strong they could win, if they were weak and sick they would lose. "

"So after our first day Britt and I decided we needed to win for the sake of the children, so please come and eat. At least a little at first." So after a weirdly normal lunch, the kids were sent to their room for a 'sun free' siesta, 'no more swimming until you've had a rest'. The five, more relaxed now started to talk again over coffee.

"If it wasn't for this,' said Anna, indicating her necklace, "I'd feel like I was on holiday."

Tamiko, gaining confidence said, "I can't stop worrying about my Mama, "at which a silence fell over the table.

"Where is she?" asked Britt. Tamiko explained that she was in Tokyo but that her father was probably in Taiwan as, 'May's dad had a new ship.'

At which Britt and Anna said." Ship, what ship?" and in a jumble of explanations they figured out who did what, where and as May pointed out. "'That's what those men said. It's not about you, it's about the ships and the money."

They fell silent when they heard a car stop outside. Two men in jeans and t shirts came in. "You all ok?" No answer. "Do you want any shopping- we're going to Carrefour and can get what you need. Make a list because we're not going there tomorrow. We're just going to check the swimming pool pump and filter so you've got a few minutes to do a shopping list."

Britt- Marie had a notebook on the table in which she had been writing down all their details. "I don't know why, but maybe it can be useful sometime. "

So a shopping list was compiled. Anna, "Put some wine on the list, and some ice cream." After some time a long list was compiled. Fish, chicken, fruits vegetables, salads, oils, vinegars. Bread. Washing powder, toilet paper.

Britt saw May and Tamiko whispering and asked what they wanted. After some more Japanese / Chinese talk, sanitary towels were added to the list.

"'Good idea," said Anna.

Tammy said," In my country men not like to buy them."

"Tough shit," said Anna. "In Sweden we have the men trained to collect anything." "Ask for some candles so we can sit outside, and mosquito spray and maybe some charcoal for that barbecue."

The men returned and said. "We've sorted the pool, it's fine to swim in." The younger man studied the list and queried the English or Britt's writing, and said he'd be back in a few hours. "You'll have to come and help me with the shopping bags when I'm back."

"'But what about this?" said Britt fingering her necklace.

The response. "That's safe. It's ok anywhere *inside* the wire fence. But for Christ's sake don't go outside there, and don't try and take them off."

" We really don't want you to get hurt. Jack and me both have kids so we want them to be OK as well. This is just a job for us, so if you make it easy for us we'll make it easy for you. Otherwise we lock the lot of you inside that big building there and after a few hot weeks of that you'll be crazy."

"I can tell you - the digital fuses on the necklaces are very strong. They use them on delayed action bombs that they drop from planes. They smash into the ground- but they'll never go off until they are told to. *So just don't go outside the fence or take them apart."*

"The kids can't unlock them and they won't harm in the pool or shower. We need you happy and fit so your families want you back. Tomorrow we're going to send them a picture of you all."

"See you later."

The girls sat in silence.

"I think I might go and lie down for a bit with the kids," said Britt. They agreed to meet 'later'.

The sun was low in the sky when the hooting of a car horn outside the courtyard gate roused them. A bit sleepily, but with more confidence the girls ventured out of their cottage. A cheerful shout from the gateway. "Come on girls, give us a hand there's bloody hundreds of bags."

Many hands later and the big table was soon covered with plastic bags which Britt and Anna started sorting through.

The younger of the two guys came in carrying a couple of heavy boxes. "'Wine,' don't drink it all at once." and dumped the boxes by their door.

"We'll be down in the gatehouse...don't forget don't try anything or the results won't be nice for any of us. Worse than melons," which made all the women shudder.

He walked towards to gate, and called back, "Oh yes, a couple more boxes here". May and Tamiko walked around the pool and soon returned with four big boxes. "It's Lego," said May.

Anna looked and said, "That's not only Lego that's the big new sets. It's so expensive I told the kids they'd have to wait until Christmas for them."

Britt said. "Quick girls, go and hide two of those boxes in your place and if we are here for a long while we can bring it out when the kids are really bored."

They worked together stowing shopping in fridges freezers etc. Wine in the fridge and even found the ice creams. "Last bag of course," said Anna- " but they're still quite hard, I'll put these out of sight as well or they'll all be gone in one go."

May returned from the other cottage and said- "Look it's the dvd of the Lego movie." The children who were wandering around demanding 'one last swim' were granted their wish, fed, and then grabbed the dvd and were gone.

Over supper. Wine for the Swedes but,' not for us' from the three girls, they all agreed. "If we take care, say together, help each other it seems that they won't hurt us."

Britt-Marie went on "Like you say, May, they need us to be ok or no one's going to pay for our release. You know, them being nice to the kids by bringing that Lego make me a bit less, frightened. Maybe I will sleep tonight. Apart from this bloody thing", she touched the explosive charge around her neck."

Eventually, exhausted by the strain of a dramatic 24 hours the girls started to doze and so made their way across to their cottage leaving the Swedish ladies finishing up their bottle of wine.

## 18. Thursday June 23rd. 3.00 pm.Heathrow Airport. London. Again, but this time: *Outbound:* *Competent control? 'What's it all about?'*

Outbound, just 24 hours after my arrival, or to be precise 23 hours, and I couldn't get a bloody song out of mind. 'What's it all about, Alfie?' When was it? 60's-70's, before my time and not my style of music, but somehow from somewhere ,it's popped up in my head and it won't go away, and who the hell was Alfie?

To my clients I apparently present a strong image of competent control with few weaknesses visible. Certainly not stressed by annoying songs, my name, or the more routine aspects of business travel.

Yet right now, yet again, I am annoyed that despite indeed being a fit, confident, solvent, experienced traveler of just over 40 years old, I still find myself fidgeting and extracting what is I hope the appropriate amount, to pay the cab driver, long before we have arrived at our destination.

As usual I am counting notes, as in money, not annoying songs, before we have even left the red tarmac taxi lane from the M4 highway into London's Heathrow Airport.

As usual, I am calculating how much more will likely tick up on the meter before we reach the terminal. Ridiculously, I usually have the money in hand, before we have even plunged into the gloomy strange orange light of the airport access tunnel.

No, 'as usual' tunnel today though, although still clasping my handful of cash I am instructing the cabbie to ease off left just before the tunnel and slalom his way around the Airport's Perimeter Track Road East, to the far side of the airport.

About half way round, the surprisingly still public road, cuts across the end of the active runway. There are huge gates and traffic lights for both cars and planes...that's as in planes already on the ground. Red lights stop the cars and allow planes access to the maintenance areas.

As we cross on the green lights, the cab shakes in the shadow of a huge plane 20 or 30 meters above our heads at it comes in to land on the main runway.

We're going just a little further, to the badly signed and relatively, these days, little used, private or 'general aviation' terminal as they are more usually labelled at airports worldwide. Back in the eighties, LHR London Heathrow became overly busy with commercial flights queuing nose to tail and wing tip to wing tip to land and take off.

Airline operating economics and air traffic control safety rules had to enforce a serious reduction in the number of small executive jets or general aviation as they were taking up too much time and airspace. This had resulted in almost all, 'general' or 'private ' jet traffic being re-routed south west to nearby Farnborough or south east to Biggin Hill.

This move pissed off a few mega bucks commuters with weekly season tickets to and from Moscow or Monaco, but proved a boon to the eager real estate salesmen in nearby leafy Surrey and Kent. Military and ministerial flights were routed via the diminutive Northolt just a few miles north of LHR.

On the rare occasion that foreign royalty or presidential power prevailed, the well defended and rather smarter  VIP suite on Heathrow Peri Track West was dusted off.

"Quite a while since I dropped here guvnor," said the cabbie as he eased between some rusting, concrete filled dump bins into a wire fenced compound and stopped outside a porta cabin.

The scruffy building looked just as it had about 10 years previously when I had last used it. In reality, it had probably seen better days, even before it reached its temporary location then. I agreed with him and then over tipped, slightly, rather than wait for change and get involved in further conversation.

I remembered always thinking way back then, that theoretically, private aviation users were the movers, shakers and super- achievers of the business world and here was a vile scruffy building that would be their first and last impressions of the UK.  All somewhat on a par with a 1950 British Rail waiting room, I feared then and now for the sandwiches and despaired at missing a final decent cup of English tea let alone a latte or other fashionable coffee.

A grubby glass window, set amongst a harvest of fading warning signs and notices on the once magnolia wall of the porta cabin ,slid open to release a blast of fetid heat and smoke. So much for the various pictures of cigarettes overlaid with a red crisscross no smoking logo. The fug cleared and revealed a bleary looking teenage security guard in an overlarge uniform jacket.

His badge, 'Bassett's All Square Security' was hanging from his shirt.

His i.something headphones, were hanging from his ear and still broadcasting a healthy bass beat. His mouth, hanging, somewhat vacantly, open. I had time to think that my 'observe', 'think', 'act' training was still functioning, possibly a bit hyperactively, before he spoke. Carefully and with effort, as if just awoken.

"You might want to keep that taxi, this place is all closed up now." His almost implanted headphones meant that his words were delivered at quite full volume and whilst very clear to me were equally clear to the cabbie some meters away despite the sound of a surprisingly near jet engine.

The cabbie, doubtless dreading the usual two hour wait in the cabbies compound for his turn to pick up a lucrative, return airport to city fare ,settled back and gazed at us impassively and I assumed, speculatively.

I showed our, 'Mr. Bassett's All Square', the 'Airport All Areas' pass that had been issued to me 'as a contracted staff consultant' less than two hours previously. Complete with non-smiley photo stamped with today's date.

I suggested politely to the face at the window that I was due to fly from this very place within about 30 minutes. The so far, bodiless face at the window looked somewhat dubious. "No one's told me anything, I'll have to make a call. Mostly this is all closed up and now the flights all go from the main buildings in the middle of the airport."

As he spoke (still shouting over his bass implants) a black Range Rover drove into the compound. Three people on board.

Right behind the Range Rover , a very non black, very bright blue yellow and red police car -with what appeared to be a surf board crammed in the back-swiftly entered the now crowded wire parking cage...making it impossible for the cab to actually exit.

All Squares face disappeared from the window, and reappeared at the door - this time with baggy uniformed body below it and with phone in hand.

Two of the suits from the Range Rover got out and showed photo i.d. to our hero of the day, which produced from Bassett's All Square a nod of acknowledgement. More than I got.

In what I assumed was probably a knee jerk reaction to a misspent youth All Square deferred to the only other uniform present and addressed the Police officers. "'You'll all have to wait out here whilst I check something."

The policemen (both) remarkably fit looking but with seriously bulky jackets and belts from which hung a variety of communications and other equipment both offensive and defensive, sighed and quietly suggested that, 'All Square did just that a bit pronto as there appeared to be a medium size jet just about to enter the rear doors of his cabin.'

I noticed with some interest on a chair just inside the door amongst the pile of newspapers and food wrappers a copy of 'The History of MI5'. All Square struggled to hear his phone over the sound of a now less surprising, but extremely close jet engine.

As the sound of the jet wined and wound down, the Range Rover gents checked my i.d. briefly.

One of them nodded at the figure crammed in the back of their car and said, "He's just on the dog and bone to the boss." Despite my more than ten years in Asia, even I could remember the Londonism, dog and bone, 'phone.'

A little further down the porta-cabin office a second door labelled, 'departures no smok....' opened, from which exited a tall smart young man, dark trousers, uniform style white shirt with pilot braid on the shoulders.

Having had a brief word with the Ranger Rovers and nodded to the two uniformed guys, ignoring All Square, he held out a hand to me and said.

"Names Rory. I'm your pilot for this one. If you don't mind the Met Police boys will just give your bags the once over. Even though it's your charter we have to keep to the usual Heathrow and UK systems. We need to get away pronto as we've got a take off slot and they're like bloody gold dust these days. According to my paperwork there's supposed to be two of you."

The Range Roverers nodded at the figure in the back of the Range Rover and said," We'll hustle him along."

With that Pilot Rory gathered up an armful of what looked like dossiers and maps from a Range Roverer and reversed back into the room, through the open door of which I could now see steps folded down from the door of a smallish jet.

The Met boys , that's 'Met' as in London Metropolitan Police, as opposed to London City, who are responsible for what's called 'The Square Mile,' or CBD as I guess it is in todays terms, lowered the Range Rover tailgate to use as a table. And with remarkable thoroughness checked my bag and briefcase , and also inserted a variety of sniffers and electronic wands over and into all its recesses and then  me.. Or at least all over my clothes.

All Square, having been ignored by all, eventually finished listening to instructions on his phone, and beaming and with seeming new found lively confidence said. "Welcome sir. You're good to go". A bit late, I mused, but officially approved at least.

One of the uniformed guys asked All Square to go and make sure no one else tried to drive into the crowded compound which he did with some alacrity stationing himself in the center of the gateway.

Range Roverer 1, spoke for the first time. "Indeed you're fine to go sir, and now he's out of the way" He nodded at All Squares back- and opened a bag that was very clearly filled with a variety of weapons and other rugged looking items.

"Regarding your bag, bit of red tape, might be new to you but as you're not weapons authorised for the UK any more we need to show that you're taking them with you. We doubt you're going to need them, certainly not where you're going. But if this develops it's easier these days to have some kit at least on the same continent."

" Regulations  say, I put them on the plane  after you get on board. If you could just sign here for this extra bag we'll take it and you to the plane."

I noticed the cabbie still there blocked in, and All Square's back.  I hesitated, a little concerned about a slight lack of discretion in what was supposed to be a rather low key departure.

I nodded at All Square, the cheerful cockney cabbie and the open bag. Range Roverer 1 responded. "Quite. Good point sir. That cab, that's one of ours sir, and Nicky has been with us for twenty years. He puts the fares and tips into the widows and orphans Christmas box at Vauxhall Cross HQ."

Nicky the cab driver smiled encouragingly.

I glanced over in the direction of All Sq. and the Range Roverer grinned. "He's not one of ours, sir. Just as well really."

As he spoke a young guy in beach clothes got out of the back of the Range Rover. Another youth, also with i.something headphones implanted- white cables dangling, I noted.

"Oh yes, let me introduce Oleg Tverskoy. He's coming with you. Don't worry about the Russki name he's one of us."

We shook hands. I said, "Good to meet you, I wasn't sure if I was picking up my minder here or at the destination."

He replied. "I was on a beach in Cornwall with no phone signal about four hours ago ,when these guys drove onto the sand flashing lights and all, they then drove like hell otherwise I don't think I would be here."

He grabbed a sports bag and a smarter looking business bag from the Range Rover and said, "I'll just get in there and change before we go," and he disappeared into the porta cabin.

Range Roverer 1 leant toward me and said quietly but loud enough over the airport noises, " You should know his clearance is 1AY, so with yours being a temporary re-instated 1AX ,whilst you're the boss he outranks you security wise."

Oleg reappeared, still casual but definitely not beach clothes. He thrust the sports bag at Ranger Roverer 1, and said, " Don't dink my new surfboard or I'll change all your home computer passwords without telling you what to do."

"Oleg, bugger off wherever you're going, and don't go showing Mr. Craig any of that smutty online stuff you keep finding. Oh yes, and good luck mate." Oleg walked off and boarded the plane.

Range Roverer 1 spoke again, quietly."Madams very keen on that one. She says he's the brightest online op. we've ever had - and unlike the other nerds uses his noggin. What we all like is that he can also explain in good clear English to humans what's going in deep in web world or cyberspace, wherever that may be. "

"I realise he's a new boy for you Sir, and a Russki name as well but he's been here in the UK since he was a kid. I must say all those who have had him assigned to their teams are keen as mustard about him...and I don't mean the bit that gets left on the plate."

"I hope this all helps a bit," he paused, "Jimmy here and I would both be happy to have that lad watching our backs, in the real world or the cyber one."

I nodded, shook hands and moved towards the door, "Thanks for the heads up, that's all good stuff, really is good to know."

A nod from the Met boys, a cheery cab style wave, well in character from Nicky, and after just about twenty paces and three steps up I was welcomed on board a sleek looking, *aren't they all*, exec jet.

As our first destination was a long haul to Nevada USA I was a little surprised to find the seating layout as 1-1 either side of the aisle. Longer range, 'pocket rockets' as the steely eyed pilots love to call them, were usually slightly larger and at least 2-1, as in the more usual long range Gulfstreams.

Oleg, was settled in to the back row and appeared to already be plugged in to a variety of pads, laptops and similar. This time he was wearing seriously large noise cancelling headphones, although I couldn't help wondering if he was still implanted with the i'devices under all that soft foam padding. His change to smarter jeans and sweat shirt from his beach kit seemed to have got him instantly back in work mode and he looked alertly busy and grinned with a thumbs up.

I settled into my seat and before I had a chance to start thinking about distances, routes, flight times, Pilot Rory was leaning around the cockpit door - and over the increasing whine of two engines running up - gave me what suffices for a safety briefing on private flights.

"Best to use the seat belt at the usual times sir. Check you can see the three emergency doors. Lifejacket under your seat. Toilet in the rear of the plane. Flight times about 10 hours nonstop. That's nonstop provided I manage to find the refueling funnel."

He paused, for effect I think, and went on. "Also provided the special relationship with the USA still extends to giving us credit for two tanks of av gas to be delivered at 35,000 feet as we enter US Airspace."

"I'm pretty familiar with small jets on a regular basis but mid air refueling is new one on me .I'm impressed." I said.

Rory grinned and said, "Well, sir, this indeed looks like your average 'Olibus', much beloved of Russian Oligarchs and their wives and mistresses but this is a slightly tweaked model. Much like some of the wives and mistresses actually."

" In this case it now includes longer range with that  re-fueling, some defensive and extra communications capabilities. It's French, very new and relatively secret, in the last stages of testing."

"That's testing by us as probable buyers, not as in, does it work-is it safe?  We were doing multiple tests at Farnborough so this longer trip suited us very well. That and a slight lack of instantly available Gulfstreams."

"The French are also developing a very short take off and landing version to land on the odd aircraft carrier or two. I guess that will be mostly French or American the carriers, as ours seem to live in Portsmouth, something to do with their cost per mile fuel bills I believe."

" It's thinking about the potential for future landing on carriers that explains why my co-pilot is from the Wavies."

We both smiled knowingly about both operational cost cutbacks and the well known general rivalry between the Air Force and the British Navy with its Fleet Air Arm.

He added, "Oh yes rather good coffee and sandwiches etc. in the galley sir, and even a bottle or two of wine. We don't see much of that in the service these days, so I guess that means they weren't telling me porkies when they said you were a civilian. I'll nudge you half an hour out from Nevada."

The door hissed and clunked shut and the jet started to move rather swiftly around the busy Heathrow taxiways.

Having decided that any thoughts or indignation about my ex employers enlisting me as a guinea pig passenger for aircraft testing was a bit late now, I  moved on to think about taxiing speeds.

The relative sense of greater speed one gets in an executive jet is more akin to a low slung sports car whereas  lumberingly slow,  high above the taxi ways, in a jumbo's is much like a mega truck.

Then with a flurry of headphone leads Oleg, launched himself into the seat across the aisle. With considerable skill he strapped himself in whilst handing me an open bottle of icy, 'Storm' Sauvignon Blanc and two glass glasses and a bag of nuts. No plastic glasses in private first class.

By the time I had filled his glass and mine we were punching our way through the gloom and low cloud into the always surprising brightness of an evening sunset.

"Nice wine "he said. "I never had this New Zealand one before." I smiled and started to ponder how it was that Miss Stanton and her team at Vauxhall Center had known this was my wine of choice these days. My musings meant that we were now already high above the clouds and levelling of, with a helpful lowering of engine noise, so we could converse across the aisle.

"Based on my curbside briefing I guess I could ask you how Ma'am knows about my preferred tipple."

Oleg grinned and responded, " Indeed you could but I have feeling that's an answer I am allowed to know and..." He tailed off looking a little embarrassed. In my most reassuring manner I smiled and said, " Sometimes the rules are indeed worth keeping to  Our Range Rover chums speak highly of you and suggest that unlike most of your breed you know when the rules need bending, but this is not one of them."

He looked a little disconcerted and possibly a little wounded. I plunged on possibly compounding the problem. " By breed I didn't mean Russian, I meant Nerd, although I may be digging my self in even deeper with that."

Visibly relaxed he smiled and held out his glass for a refill.

"Nerds fine by me. Actually it's a slightly wimpy label that suits me fine ...and it also provides a bit of a cover. My real interest is surfing."

I almost managed to avoid rolling my eyes, I raised an eyebrow and I nodded as if to say bloody obviously -- but he went on-- "No, not what you think, not on the computer. I am a surfer and a kite surfer and love big waves when I am lucky enough to find them. That's why I went to Uni. in Wales and then lived in Cornwall. "

"It's also why my three year accounting and computing course took six years! Today I was actually outback in some quite good surf, at Holywell Bay in Cornwall when I saw the police car on the beach flashing its lights. It was Holywell where they built the Korean Army camp for the surfing start of that Bond movie."

At the mention of Bond, my facial tic-ticked and my hand tightened on the stem of my glass glass, but young Oleg grinned with what I felt was sincere innocence, accepted a third  refill from the Storm bottle, studied the label and exited neatly rearwards saying, " Work to do for you before we arrive. Thanks for the wine sir."

I did my usual tick concealing yawn and relaxed my grip on the glass stem a little. My dry throat and the facial tick betrayed a side of me that I thought had gone for ever- but now it was of concern again. I'd only been back in service for half a day.

Originally when I first joined the service twenty years ago, British Special Intelligence Service, SIS, were supposed to be ultra secret. Even the existence of the service was hardly officially recognised then, and unlike these days, the name of the chief was a closely guarded secret.

Our trainers at various locations and then Vauxhall Cross HQ deemed it better, and less likely to cause family and personal stress if we were reasonably upfront and usually accurate to family and friends at least about any recent travels.

In what I always felt was throw back to Graham Greene, Len Deighton or Le Carre, they suggested our best cover whilst undertaking those travels and tasks was that we were *journalists, insurance assessors or advance NGO's bearing aid.*

Given that most of the regulars at the Cricketers pub, the cricket team. In fact the whole bloody village where I lived, seemed comprised of genuine journalists, insurance agents and would be Oxfam or UNICEF heroes the cover was hard to maintain.

So as the beers, and usually the wickets went down they started to deduce that I was being somewhat economical with the truth about my employment.

Having then once been seen exiting a train at Vauxhall Cross ,the ribbing became markedly worse. For sure, what I did for Queen and Country within SIS was reasonably confidential but not spectacularly so.

But no matter how hard I tried, 'Batsman 007's out for a duck, again' and 'Another pint of Skinners, shaken not stirred,' still produced a reaction.

That reaction was only a slight tick on my left cheek below my eye, a tightening of the throat and probably a touch of sweat glistening at the temples. At least I didn't flush or blush. Well I didn't think I did, but a pub mirror mainly covered with an arty promotion for the wonderful Skinners Real Ales wasn't the best place to check that out.

Although the reaction to such mild joking both annoyed and concerned me, I never raised the matter at any of our regular assessments with the ever present office psychologists and shrinks.

*I had concluded that the reaction was based on my deep seated concern over my probable conduct if I was ever captured and interrogated in any kind of aggressive way.*

That was a little unlikely to happen on the 7.45 morning commuter train from Godalming to Waterloo or Clapham Junction.

But later, on more and more frequent occasions my commute was on rather more rugged vehicles in the Hindu Kush, or with increasing frequency in downtown Lahore, Karachi, Kabul, Ramala and rather memorably Mogadishu.

However Piers Brosnan hung up his license to thrill around the same time that I left the service, and moved to the private security sector in the Gulf states and then to Singapore.

That's me to Singapore, not Piers Brosnan as far as I know.

For a while the whole 007- Bond crazy publicity world seemed to go quiet for a while....then when Barbara Broccoli the producer and part owner of the Bond franchise chose their new actor- it all got stupid.

For me at least.

Earlier that morning I had been standing across the street from the SIS office with a mug of tea in my hand, watching big red London buses go by filled with commuters.

I had forced myself awake at 5 am London time to read the briefing paper. Despite it's style being more readable than most, it had taken a while. All of which meant that I had forgone the doubtless excellence of a Savoy Hotel English Breakfast. Shame really.

Hence, standing on the pavement at Vauxhall Cross smelling bacon sarnies cooking. Suspecting that these days little cups of latte or chamomile tea and ghastly fluffy 'muffins' would be the norm in the modern offices across the way, I had stopped at a greasy spoon van for a decent mug of tea and a bacon sandwich.

Thus, I would be well sustained for what I expected to turn into a rather long session when I revealed all to the team in a hopefully secure room. Doubtlessly monitored - at least by the good guys.

Revealed all, would in reality mean, revealed as much as I wanted. With the full connivance of Barry, we had agreed a plan of action to hold some vital information back until we sussed out the likely political impact and likely action from our old employers.

Despite feeling that this matter was becoming dangerously reactive for just ourselves, and thus hoping for some official re enforcements, we both had concerns about the heavy footed and usually unzipped lips of The White House and London's 10 Downing Street.

So I stood on the pavement near the futuristic Vauxhall Cross tube station with bacon sandwich in one hand and tea mug steaming in the other. It occurred to me that any of my old instructors looking across the six lanes of traffic to my very visible breakfast would freak out, knowing that both defensive gun or knife hands were full of Sarnie and a Wet.

The fact that I no longer carried neither gun nor knife in the UK enabled me to enjoy one gastronomic part of the UK that I truly missed almost on a daily basis. Both hands occupied, did however mean that I was unable to answer the shrill ring of my mobile. With a heartfelt and very genuine, "Thanks mate" to the breakfast bar operative, I took my life in my hands - again - and set off across the six lanes of busy traffic.

As I approached the security gate with smiling, but probably very well trained guard, I felt my throat dry and the bloody tick started tick tick ticking again. Instantly dealing with those old deep seated 007 type problems came flooding back to me. In a cruel twist of coincidence involving my name, in the last 24 hours it had come back with avengance.

The guard held a clipboard.

"I have an appointment with Sir Geoffery Barker," I announced, delaying the tick tick moment.

" Certainly sir," was the response in a friendly west country burr, "and you are?"

" Craig " I said. "Daniel Craig", inwardly cursing the global re-emergence of the Bond franchise and the massive worldwide success of sodding Skyfall and bloody Spectre.

Even Daniel Craig, the brilliant actor quickly became pissed off with being identified too closely with the name, but in his case his ire was aimed at James Bond.

I tensed, waiting for the usual witty response, but all I got was a salute, a badge and an instruction to proceed to the main doors.

I thanked him, trying to control the bloody nervous tick and reached the conclusion that the guard had probably used up all his witticisms with his mates when preparing the badges earlier.

As I entered the main doors a familiar and friendly face awaited..."Daniel! Geoff. asked me to keep an eye out for you. Great to see you again. Polish Pete at the cafe gave me the nod when he heard your phone ringing."

I was indeed back in the world of Big Mother. I focused on the job in hand and the upcoming meeting. Now to save the real world, in probably slightly longer than a ninety minute movie. At least I wasn't called Johnnie English, or worse, Mr. Bean or even Basil Fawlty.

But thinking about all that, and still being on Singapore time meant that now in the real world at 10,000 meters above the Atlantic I dozed off.

## 19. A long Thursday. June 23rd.
## Over Eastern US.  Elapsed fly time 8 hours.

*Losing a very live H bomb, even decades ago, must surely only be a bad movie plot, or possibly I supposed the work of complete morons,and in reality nothing to do with my current assignment.*

The door between us and the pilots opened and our steely eyed pilot stepped out. "Be with you in a moment sir" I almost heard a brief few words between him and Oleg as he went back, presumably to use the toilet or to make a drink.

On his return he handed me a mug of tea, "Oleg says he believes it's no sugar and these should be some of your favourite biscuits."

He settled himself into the seat across the aisle from mine.

"Refueling in about 20 minutes. Of course with one of our new Gulfstream's we could do this nonstop, but as I explained this is what we had on standby today. I hope the pilot confirms to base who we are, when we're going inboard to certain US bases they like to keep an eye on us  from take off to landing. So, ex Heathrow, our original filed flight plan was via the US Air base at Moron, Spain."

I raised an eyebrow.  He continued, "Moron? That's that massive US - Spanish military air base in the South West of Spain. It's so large that it was one of the main space shuttle emergency landing diversion sites .It's still fully manned and I think gearing up to be an emergency lander for some of the new private and commercial trips into space."

" It's getting quite a lot of general aviation traffic these days so it's a good cover. It also means as we join air traffic control for Moron area, we then request a new flight plan from Mid Atlantic military air traffic control on Ascension Island or Tenerife."

He went on, "If it wasn't that people died in the accident I always thought that in January 1966 when the US lost those live H bombs on land and in the Mediterranean just off the Spanish coast it would have been quite appropriate if they'd come from a base called Moron."

I recalled meeting a a novelist once called Harry Buckle who had actually been enveloped in the dust cloud as the bombs hit the ground near Palomares on the Spanish Coast back in '66, but before I could respond, some radio coms from the flight deck had him on his feet and with a cheery, "Time to play insert the nozzle sir," and he was gone.

I peered out into a surprisingly bright sky but could see nothing noteworthy. Initially my thoughts returned to style of tea and the Marks and Spencer digestive biscuits, indeed my favourite.

In Singapore we referred to M&S as Marks and Spensive, but when it comes to biscuits and tea you have to have the real deal.

Oleg came up from the rear of the plane, and said, "Another cup of tea here. English breakfast from a sachet not a samovar." Even whilst my awaking brain was processing what was possibly a dream and what was reality I smiled at his Russian tea connection.

"After your tea, sir, it would be good to go through the key points of why we're here...or at least will soon be there...if you get what I mean."

I gave him the thumbs up with my tea free hand, and ten minutes later after a quick dash and wake up the face, splash, in the aft, 'rest room ' as I noticed it was labelled. I settled into my seat across the narrow aisle from Oleg who seemed to be equipped with a variety of pads and ultra books.

"First of all - let's get one thing straight. I am not 'sir'. I am Daniel or Dan and for what it's worth, those who call or refer to me as me as 'Danny' usually get the evil eye from me, and nervous glances from my staff who know me well."

Quite surprisingly we missed the 'OK Sir - I mean Daniel,' stage and Oleg steamed straight in with, "OK Dan, take a look at this." Obviously quick on the upload our Oleg.

He brought up on his screen the 'Backgrounder' that I had read yesterday. No, correct that, at dawn today sitting in London's Savoy Hotel. "I read that earlier.  The D.C. gave it to me last night. It's very clear."

"Thank you," said Oleg. "I wrote, or at least condensed most of it from our current situationers. Apparently at this week's meeting in the US, they circulated my report to all attendees as being the UK position. Quite frankly I am not looking forward to meeting all those heads of department that I identify as being unready."

I reassured him, or at least tried, "There's an overall impression amongst most Brits, both on the street and in the uniformed defence forces, and as it happens many of the people at Vauxhall Cross, that all American Generals are close descendants of  Dr. Strangelove. That's not true, although admittedly they are still using B 52 bombers, 50 years later."

"Some of the best and considered social, military and political thinking is coming out of the American forces. As ever the jury is still out over the real long term effects of Afghanistan. Ditto on Desert Storm and part two in Iraq."

" Over the years they also very visibly burnt their fingers in Vietnam, Korea, Mogadishu. Military might, in  every case, losing out to scattered stealth on the ground. The question is though, how much those US generals, with a more mature, globally informed and long term view are now being listened to?"

"Tabloid newspapers world wide love the image problems. Even if it's not Strangelove's, 'nuke 'em now,' the general impression is that, redneck drone jockeys are trigger happy cowboys trained on video games. All operating in the real world from the safety of bunkers under Texas. Targets mostly based on bad local intelligence."

Oleg said, "It always comes back to good intelligence."

I swallowed the urge to say, 'tell that to George Bush and Tony Blair' and just nodded and said, "I'll fill you in the details of my team, a bit later but you do need to know your key point of contact."

"My operations director for many years is Susie Todd, but everyone calls her Squeeze. Without getting too involved in rules from your employers about security levels, she is privy to 100% of our company activity, because most of my staff spend so much time out of the office as we need a fixed 24/7 contact and control point."

"I assume London gave you the full S.P. why Barry and I are at this meeting. I am not sure if the top floor told you that we had brought in some Asian and other shipping updates, or if they claimed credit and suggested we may be able to help. It seems that both the US and UK feel there's been rather a lack of facts at those freight security meetings. With some kind of wrap up happening for the President scheduled in Nevada after he's been to the Oceans Warming event in San Diego, that's where we come in, bringing, local knowledge and shipping expertise."

Oleg grinned, "Local expertise and indeed at least some facts is what London told me. But four days ago I was just setting off for a long weekend surfing. It appears that you and Mr. Purchase have better placed ears on the ground that we Brits do or even the mighty US with its multiple intelligence agencies with their global electronic reach."

I nodded, I was quite pleased at that last comment, with Oleg being a relatively unknown quantity to me I wasn't yet aware if he was purely a digital info man or had an open mind to old style,' *ear to the ground'* intel gathering.

Having thought that, I did momentarily consider that the last time my ear was actually on the ground the other ear was being firmly pressed by downwards by a size 12 boot of a swarthy gent armed to the teeth and who regularly spat some foul smelling tobacco, quat or betel juice to within an inch or so of my now sweaty and dusty face.

But back to the matter in hand. I continued. "What the top floor at VC want is for us find the source of the problem, as at the moment it seems to be Asian originated. Barry says the CIA and the US Government want the same." I looked at my watch, "I'm still on Singapore time, but I guess we'll be there soon enough."

Oleg glanced at his watch, an old Sekonda I noticed, and said, "Actually 'there' is very nearly 'here.' I make it that we'll be landing soon."

In fact not only did we land soon, but within minutes of that landing we were escorted across a few meters of taxi way baking in the desert sun and into one of a line of black SUV's ,engines idling to keep the air con running.

Before we moved off, a uniformed officer saluted in the American way and said," If you let me have your passports sirs, we'll get them processed by immigration and get them back to you in your accommodation. If I may also request no camera use. "

He continued, "Phones will reactivate within the accommodation. Usually we're instructed to hold guest phones until they leave but I understand you have special privileges."

With another salute he was gone. The accommodation block was a ten minute drive away through pretty featureless slightly hilly scrub land. I observed Oleg carefully noting distance and all turns.

"Escape committee?" I asked.

"Well last time I came to the States, it was as a tourist for a cousins wedding, and despite my British passport the Russian name rang auto bells and Homeland Security kept me waiting at immigration for six hours . So despite me being invited this time ,I figured that my presence on a top secret Air Force base may cause some excitement."

I stretched back in the seat and remarked I could, "Murder a gin and tonic before getting some shut eye."

As we entered the obviously well watered and manicured grounds of what looked like a decent 60's hotel I caught site of a sign. 'The US Navy proudly welcomes you to US Naval Air Station Desert Harbor.'

I pointed this out to Oleg wondering if the Navy would be more hospitable than the Air Force. His concern however was for me. "I understand  that unlike the British Royal Navy in the US Navy their ships are dry." .... I raised a quizzical eyebrow, he went on "That's dry as in to alcohol, not dry as out here in the desert ."

With a flurry of salutes, and, "That's OK we  can manage our bags," we were ushered inside the cool of the lobby. Where not only did we get handed keys, but also our passports, quick work by someone.

I noticed the visa stamps were on slips of paper folded into the pages instead of being stamped on the actual document.

Another smartly dressed officer- this time I paid a little more attention and realised he was Navy. "Welcome -- sir. You'll notice from the passports that you are not actually here- but do keep those slips of paper safe or you'll find it hard to leave. Communication instructions are in the rooms. Breakfast is from 5 am local, in the coffee shop or you'll find room service works well here."

"Your first meeting is 7.00 am. You'll be collected from your quarters which are just a few steps just down that that way at 06.45. Sir. If you need anything else? Sir?".

I declined. Oleg opened his mouth as if to speak but thought better of it and with another crisp salute we were on our own. Oleg muttered, "I was going to ask about the gin, but never mind."

We agreed to meet for breakfast -and we checked into our adjoining rooms. It had been a long day at the end of a long few days. My body clock seemed to suggest that 8 hours sleep was the next priority but first a shower.

Old habits die hard and I pulled the curtains tight shut having too often suffered too early wake ups from shafts of bright morning light. Then of course, as usual I had to blunder about in the pitch black figuring out which switch was the room lights.

Having succeeded, I was then able to locate the shower room.

Competent control ?

Not evident right now as I blunder around in the dark.

**20. Still a long Thursday. June 23rd. Early evening.pst. On a US Navy Airbase. Near Fallon. Nevada:** *The US Navy shower provided plenty of water born power- a bit like their navy itself.*

Showers are remarkably reviving. For once without igniting my ridiculous 007 sensitivities I recalled that the incomparable Ian Fleming had James Bond very specific about his shower power, temperature and of course his special lotions from I think a supplier in London's Jermyn St or at least St James.

I had to concede that the US Navy shower provided plenty of water born power- a bit like their navy itself. The desert water smelt very slightly of chlorine but hey' after a long flight - even in some comfort- it was most welcome.

I didn't have to check out their shower gel as I had my own. Rather more Marks and Spencer or supermarket than Bonds exclusive and expensive' Floris' or 'Trumper'.

My reviving reverie was broken when I realised I could hear the room phone ringing. The Naval issue towel wasn't quite up to fluff but there was a good  supply of them. I grabbed the phone and heard the familiar tones of Barry Purchase.

"I believe G&T is on the request list and if you come out on your terrace you'll see me just across the gardens. Young Oleg's on his way to join us, he had some concerns that considering your age and all that you may already be sleeping."

"Cheeky sod - I'll be there in five." I replied and scrabbled in my bag for clean clothes. I noticed that my mobile phone was still searching for a signal and wondered if that was desert isolation or the Navy version of homeland security."

Pondering why, considering the secure location, and using my usual code I stashed my wallet and passport into the pretty standard hotel style safety box and stepped out onto my terrace. In the fading evening light I could see Barry and Oleg under some trees. As I neared what looked like a rather nice barbecue area Barry was putting quite hefty logs on to the wrought iron 'fire-pit' which crackled and cast some dramatic shadows on the umbrellas, table and chairs.

As we shook hands a navel orderly arrived with glasses, ice, limes and tonic with reassuringly yellow labels.  Barry reached under the table and produced a brown bag from which he pulled a bottle of Gordons gin and a bottle of Jim Beam.

"Good to see you Dan. Oleg and I were just discussing that I recalled you telling me although the British Navy had put a stop to the traditional daily rum ration but that some alcohol is still permitted on board British ships."

"With this being a stone frigate- or shore based US Navy establishment I too wasn't sure if indeed all the US Navy is a dry as it's supposed to be -so I stopped at a bar just outside the entrance here and with some difficulty bought some booze for us."

As Barry dealt out ice, limes etc. and poured and Oleg stirred the fire I confirmed a little more of British Royal Navy wardroom (officers mess in US terms) traditions such as toasting the King or Queen of England. As we stood to propose a toast to 'The Queen'....a voice came from the shadows from the other side of the fire.

"You may want to include 'The President in that toast'.

I had observed Oleg standing somewhat open mouthed and looking startled. I had assumed he was bemused by our fascination with Royal Naval tradition and so as Barry and I turned we too probably looked equally amazed, as from the shadows stepped the more than familiar figures of the President of the USA and the British Prime Minister David Howells.

With them, my old boss Miss Stanton, and someone who turned out to be the head of the CIA, Dal Booth.

Having to hastily transfer my icy cold G and T glass from right hand to left meant that I returned the Presidents welcoming firm handshake with a somewhat wet grasp. I noted that Barry had the sense to wipe his hand first before greeting his President.

After a round of introductions and handshakes, Oleg and a naval orderly bustled around to bring up chairs around the fire.

I noticed Miss Stanton introduced Oleg to the President as, "One of our UK team, and the author of the shipping update we were discussing on the flight."

As we all sat Oleg leapt to his feet again and said, "Can I get you a drink sir?" The 'most powerful man in the world' glanced around and said, "Well given the time of day, the occasion and the fact that we're miles from prying eyes I'll have a small Bourbon - with one ice block please."

The British Prime Minister responded with a request for a G & T, "But easy on the gin young man please, I may need to talk sense with President Appleyard." The CIA chief and Miss Stanton also chose G&T.

When the drinks were poured Barry grinned and indeed toasted the President and 'your' Queen.

President Appleyard leant forward and addressed Oleg.

He went on," Now young man, I'm sure you are very up to date with the latest equipment in your trade. Although we're miles from anywhere here - do you think that those guys up there," he pointed skywards, "who follow my every little move ,can see through this umbrella to note my choice of drink?"

Without missing a beat Oleg replied, although with a glance towards his boss, "I'm sure they know you're here sir, but I think the heat radiating from this fire will have them confused about the details."

As the seven of us sipped our drinks, the glasses and ice catching the twinkling of the fire I ventured, "Talking about knowing where we are, Sir, I left the UK in such a rush that I was just going to ask Barry, where are we, apart from a Naval establishment somewhere in Nevada ?"

The President responded, "We're at an isolated part of US Navy Airbase Fallon about one hundred miles miles from Reno. I was telling Prime Minister Howells and Miss Stanton as we flew in. We're in Churchill County - it was named a hundred years or more ago after a member of that illustrious family, a certain Sylvester Churchill."

He went on. "You guys may be wondering why I am suddenly here. Of course" he smiled, "It would be good to tell you that we wanted to meet you so much that we flew here just for chat ,but sadly, Presidents are not allowed much down time, and in reality not much choice over their working time."

"Prime Minister Howells and I were both at the trade and security talks in Washington and we are both scheduled to be at tomorrow's Oceans meeting in San Diego, after which, I was anyway scheduled to call in here to pick up Dal and some of the others for the flight back to Washington.

Then my secretary learned that Dal needed to see me to update some shipping related security matters before tomorrow's meetings. She is an ex-Navy girl so her navigation skills are spot on, and she realised I'd be departing Washington and then overhead here at about the same time as Mr. Booth and Miss Stanton, but in separate planes. So it then seemed practical for us to travel together in both directions."

"So courtesy Air Force One we shared a ride, and got some decent time to talk. It is interesting to hear about the offer of co-operation from the Chinese from such a high up source, although we now have something to add to that."

"As President I obviously have to rely on daily briefing papers, but on occasions I am very happy to get a direct and personal feel for situations, especially when I have become personally involved."

"Also in this case my security people were  delighted we can park Air Force One in a secure place for an hour or so. They don't usually like sudden variations in my schedule but given this is now the main Top Gun Naval air base I guess they figured were we're secure enough to let me stop here."

"We'll get to San Diego a couple of hours late, but I'll know a little more, which may also be of background benefit when I am at the Oceans conference."  He sipped his drink slowly "Although I suspect the Mayor of San Diego and the Governor of California will be a bit miffed that their private dinner with me, got re-scheduled as a 'nightcap.' But we'll make it up to them. Of course current affairs of national security take precedence over most things including meeting the Mayor of San Diego."

" The bonus for me is some fresh air around a campfire barbecue with old and new friends. Now, despite the media being surprised I have to sleep sometimes-they seem equally surprised that I also have to eat. So I hope the kitchens here have been at action stations.  Having established that your arrivals were imminent we made a call from Air Force One and made some requests. I suspect a call from Air Force One will make even the Navy jump to it."

Raising a hand and his voice, he spoke to a uniformed figure standing close, but discretely out of earshot, and minutes later a flotilla of Naval personal arrived, and laid cloths, cutlery, condiments and sauces on the table and placed a large grill over the now gently smouldering logs.

Some men and women in whites and chefs hats also delivered a trolley laden with salads, breads, steaks and prawns, or shrimp as the Americans call them.

The steaks, shrimp and chefs looking ready to grill.

The President rose to his feet and dismissed the chefs saying, "This all looks great. Thank You. If it's OK with you gentlemen and ladies we're a little short of time so if we cook this ourselves we can talk business at the same time.  First though, I'll just come by the kitchens and thank your crew over there for their speedy service. In the meantime gentlemen, it seems we trust you with the security of our nations so I think can trust you to grill me a small steak...medium rare please."

He walked off at some speed closely followed by the chefs and the shadows of his security team.

Barry busied himself at the grill. Not only had the adrenaline of a surprise encounter with the President of the United States of America banished all signs of jet lag tiredness but  the smell of steaks sizzling soon made me think I was starving.

Dal remarked, "I've worked with a few presidents, and many like Ronald Reagan, and both the Bush's liked to 'ham up' the old style outdoorsman. But with President Appleyard what you see is what you get. I wasn't very enthused by his pre-election talking, all that, 'let's get some fresh eyes on America and find a new way forward', and suchlike. But he seems to have judged the situation right, the public like his cut the crap approach."

He paused, " So far at least."

I was just about to enquire about any conclusions from the New York trade talks when we were all somewhat surprised to note 'POTUS' as his security team refer to him ,walking carefully across the grass, kitchen gloves on either hand carrying a large and obviously hot tray of French Fries, and baked potatoes.

He smiled, "It's been a good while since I worked my way through college doing some restaurant waiting duties, but couldn't resist revisiting my skills. But I nearly had a disaster, there were so many flashes from the kitchen teams phone cameras that for the first few steps out into the darkness up to the grass here. I almost stumbled."

He went on, "One of my predecessors, an excellent President actually, stumbled once and was forever after known as the President who couldn't walk and chew gum at the same time. So although those Navy guys won't be able to share their pictures until they leave the base tomorrow, the media won't get yet more ammunition to diss their chief."

The President observed that several of his security detail, still on full alert had correctly approached rather close to the barbecue and were standing there somewhat poised.

"That's OK guys, thanks for your attention but I think it's unlikely that my friends and colleagues here are going to try and set up a new Presidential election by attacking me with the barbecue tools." The security detail stepped back, but only very slightly, as we sat and after some exchanges of sauces, salads, breads, started to eat.

The President, smiling at me said, "Here's the good bit for me. 'Executive privilege'. I can at least eat whilst you run through the latest you have for the team tomorrow. The Prime Minister and I want the full version,  of course we've been briefed but there's a lot at stake here. There's something going on that doesn't add up, and you guys seem to have found out more than our combined security services."  He glanced across at Dal, "With every respect Dal.'

I told him that Barry and I were very used to not over reacting to rumour. But we had both intercepted early stage information inferring possible hijack of or attack on a major merchant ship or worse merchant ships. There was a very faint suggestion of North Korean involvement.

Then I had also been summoned to Shanghai and been briefed by Liu Qiang the head of the Chinese State Security Service. They also had been tipped off about a 'shipboard event happening on the 25th,' and more in January.

Barry and I had talked it through and decided to share the information with London and Washington. Which seemed to arrive at a useful moment.

The President then said." Well Mr. Purchase, Mr. Craig, young man, he nodded at Oleg. "The Prime Minister, Miss Stanton and I each have something along those lines to report also. In reality it is this that also triggered my brief stop off here."

"Last evening at a function in Washington Prime Minister Howells, found himself approached by the Chinese Deputy President with a similar concerned conversation about threats to world shipping trade. At around the same time our Secretary of State for Foreign Affairs had pretty much the same one sided conversation with the Russian President at a function in Canada."

The President smiled. "It was at a youth games Ice Hockey match in Toronto. The US beat the Russians I'm sorry to tell you Oleg."

Oleg blushed and said, "Actually sir, from the age of 15 I lived and went to school in rainy but iceless England, so I'm more familiar with Rugby than Ice Hockey." The British PM, of Welsh origin and therefor with a Rugby background himself beamed encouragingly and helped himself to another G&T.

Somewhat to my surprise the President picked up my so far uneaten steak from my plate with the barbecue tongs and said, "OK whilst I put a bit of heat back into your steak, let's ask questions."

"Why is this situation different to the thousands of alarms, stories, rumours, exaggerations and deliberate miss-information that we and I am sure your people get deluged with every day .The stuff that Dal's and the Homeland Security staff have to spend much time investigating, 'just in case.'"

Barry took a sip from some iced water and replied as the President returned my steak to me- a little charred I noticed.

"Between Dan's in Asia and my employers in Washington, our two companies represent the owning families or holding companies that handle almost 50% of the world's container freight. Of course that focus and having feet on the ground in various shipping centres explains why we likely picked up information earlier than Dal's team. Of course much of the shipping business involves Asia."

The President exaggeratedly shrugged, and put his head in his hands and said. "Both me and Air force One put in a lot of air miles keeping up with the real world of business these days. Between you and me, it's lucky I can use chop sticks and like Asian food. Also, unlike one of my predecessors, so far I have managed to avoid throwing up all over my fellow diners."

I took up the baton. "As we know all too well most terrorist threats, imagined and real, come in waves. They are often copycat and clearly linked to fashionable stories on social media. Movies, TV shows and books can spark off copycat threats. The internet is always heaving with stuff."

President Appleyard leaned back in his chair and looking serious said, "We're all aware of the strain that sorting out the corn from the husks puts on our systems."

" In my case it also had another effect. Having my children living in the White House is tough enough on them. When there was suddenly a batch of movies showing their home being under attack, destroyed, or even invaded by aliens they were nervous and alarmed to say the least. Marion and I try and keep their schooling and life as 'normal' as possible, but after those movies none of their class mates wanted to come home with them to the White House even for birthday parties."

As he sighed, I glimpsed the very human side of America's most popular president for many years. He nodded to me, and I continued. " Barry and I are likely in the right place to be first to hear that someone somewhere is setting up something. We could bloody well do with finding out who, what, where, and when -- before something nasty happens. Excuse my language ,Sir."

The President stood and warmed his back to the fire: "So whilst we all agree we need facts, the Russians and the Chinese, who need world trade to remain calm for different reasons, have also picked up on something, and its worrying enough for both to pass it on."

"Or they, the Russians and Chinese are up to something." Dal Booth growled.

The President nodded. "Point taken Dal. Obviously it's not usual for me to be directly involved at such an early stage on intelligence matters just based on rumours.  But in addition to logistical sense of me coming by here with these guys " he nodded at Dal and Miss Stanton, "the very unusual direct personal approaches from the Chinese and Russians presidents that put me firmly in the firing line. Direct approaches at that level are very rare."

"When I was elected I discovered the existence of 'The Presidents Club'. This is when former US Presidents- even those who are perhaps somewhat less regarded by the public or at least voters, get together to guide the new occupant of the White House through some of the intricacies' of the world's most complicated job. Maybe we need to add the Chinese and Russian presidents to the team."

"Tomorrow you guys are briefing the CIA, The Homeland guys, SFA plus the Navy, Air Force and the rest .There's a lot of competition out there to be heroes but I hope everyone can work clearly together on this."

I am well known for not liking committees, as I find mostly they focus less on the problem and more to their own agenda."

He paused, and went on "A week ago I had the pleasure of having one of my regular dinners with Sam Charles."

Barry and I glanced at each other at the mention of the name of the now retired and apparently rather out of favour ex head of the CIA.

The President continued, "I rather like Sam Charles. He was an inspired choice to shake up the CIA. As a lawyer with an arty, well read, almost pacifist background and a huge Anglo and Europhile. Commentators in Washington feared the worst. As did the heads of our military. Then they found him also to be hugely well informed about the Middle East and Asia."

" That had two effects, it stopped our Five Stars and some of their close political allies trying to pull the wool over Sam's eyes , and those of the President at the time. Sam tells it like it is, when it comes to the defence of his country he has no time for local politics or politicians. His style is somewhat gone now in this internet age , but the way he tells it,' *there's no replacement for experienced ears on the ground'.*"

" It seems to me that you guys embody that spirit with your professional ears to the ground you are both in the right place and on to something. The direct messages from the Russians and Chinese mean something. Of course I agree with Dal that they may be up to something, but I have a hunch it's less likely, 'a something' where they are working together to cause mischief."

"Mind you, I don't envy you making your presentation of 'sorry so far it's only rumours, hi powered, but still rumours.' to the team tomorrow. But If they can raise their eyes from their 'i pads' than maybe they'll notice something" He smiled said, "But that's another thing none of you heard me say."

Miss Stanton said. "Years ago, I heard Sam Charles speak at a small gathering of European security chiefs. His main point then, much as we have been discussing is how to cut through rumour to get actionable facts. "

"Although," she paused and smiled at both President Appleyard and P.M. Howells, " he did finish by saying that, 'politicians had a habit of using intelligence, like a drunk uses a lamp post'….that is, for support, more than illumination."

The President laughed, and said, "It's a very old line but still a great line. If it wasn't such a serious matter I guess that could be applied to one of my predecessors and your Prime Minister Blair over their much then promoted and now criticised reasons to pursue direct action in Iraq, but again you didn't hear me say that."

"But as ever, the reality is exactly that, did they have a real problem with the veracity of the facts, and were some of those facts somewhat, over emphasised on their way to those two gentlemen."

"It's never easy. I can't, as they say, 'be everywhere,' but I do want you to keep me up to speed on this."

He glanced over at one of the alert looking  suits standing ready for his call. "We're stopping here tomorrow on the way back to Washington to pick up Dal, Miss Stanton and some of the other security chiefs, what time are we out of San Diego tomorrow?'

The 'suit' with the earpiece and the briefcase spoke. "Your keynote welcome speech is at a breakfast sir at 8.30 am and after various other meetings you have to be away from San Diego by 12.00 Lunchtime sir .We have a 45 minute pick up window scheduled here at about 1.00. That's so we can get back to Washington by 11.00 PM for you to show up at your wife's fundraiser for that children's charity."

The President pondered and spoke to the suit and to the rest of us, "Well Daniel, Barry, if there's anything new that comes up you can jump on Air Force One here and report briefly whilst the others board. Telling all those general's and the rest of them that you have to brief me personally tomorrow might just focus a few minds a little. Make them take the rumours a little more seriously."

He paused, "After all the new Chinese and Russian honorary members of the Presidents Club seem to be relying on me."

As he stood he said. "Oh yes there's one other point, about the Chinese. Sam Charles is a massive supporter of our friend Dal here, both publicly and in private. But he did say to me that when it came to China I could also rely on information from you Brits, particularly if it came from Miss Stanton here."

" I had the opportunity to speak to Miss Stanton about this on the flight here and I liked her answer a lot, although it nearly made Dal spill his coffee."

With handshakes all round he left, ushering the British Prime Minister head of him. Miss Stanton and Dal Booth left with a Naval orderly to check in to their rooms. As the President stepped off towards the main buildings with his security detail closing around him I noticed a somewhat red faced naval officer stand to attention and salute. "Great steaks you serve here, thank your team." Said the President and he was gone.

I rather collapsed into my chair and Oleg and Barry did the same. I glanced at my watch and realised that it was only just over an hour since the surprise arrival of both the President and indeed dinner.

I noticed that the President had touched hardly a drop of his bourbon but that the British prime minister had downed a few hefty G&T's. The Naval officer, whom it turned out was the somewhat shocked  commander of the base – hotfoot we learned from a family function 100 miles away in Reno - came and joined us.

Having introduced him self as Rick E Dugan, removing his cap and mopping his brow he said, "Next time the Commander in Chief comes to call, as the current commander of this base I would be happy get more than an hours notice. I got the message, but then the problem is all general mobile phone coverage is blocked within 20 miles and an hour of the President, his Limo or Air Force One."

The lack of a mobile connection was also ,it turned out to be why neither Barry,  nor Oleg or I were aware of the encoded texts alerting us to the impending visitors, and in Oleg's case to the arrival of his boss. Barry proffered the bottle of Jim Beam and our now introduced host accepted "just a jigger please, I'm driving".

As we discussed with some respect and indeed some awe 'what a great and very real' guy the President seemed to be, a chef appeared with a team to clear the tables.

The Navy commander, stood and thanked the chef for a job obviously well done. He remarked, "The President really liked the steaks, chef."

The Chef, pushing his hat back beamed at his superior and said, 'Just as well really sir, most of our Navy supply rations are good but not quite not that good.  Croftus here ran over to the restaurant just outside the main gates and got them from his friend the chef in their steak house."

The chef paused and with a grin continued, "It's good the President liked them, as we put them on your account there sir!"

A somewhat relieved base commander congratulated the chef and his team on their initiative and remarked, "Well, we may be competing with the damned Air Force and Army for dollars for our much needed new planes, but I think we can pay the bill for the Presidents steaks."

After a few more minutes in which I reminded Barry and Oleg that even during the darkest hours of the cold war the security services of the opposing nations had kept channels open between themselves at the highest level. So the Chinese and Russian approaches whilst arousing suspicions of self interest, could be based on genuine mutual concern.

I turned to Barry." I haven't had a chance to discuss this with you. Whilst I was in London I learned from my researchers that there's a more than usual amount of speculation out there on future hikes in commodity prices."

Barry cut in, "We have a similar situation here, I also agree it's more betting than what you and I would call investment, but it seems that many bets get laid off, some on prices rising, others on a fall. We've got a Texas based, billionaire client who has also made some serious, we are talking several billion trades that would pay off big time for him if there are any major variations in commodity or stock prices, caused by delivery problems with those commodities."

"Seems to me, and I'm not an expert that that was also the situation that's crashed the economy a few years back. No wonder the powers that be worry about major trade interruptions."

"Or the rumours of same.' interjected Oleg.

With that, we left the clean-up crew at work, and agreed to meet at the apparently unholy hour of 6.30 am.

Although as I entered my room my now fully connected Mobile phone reminded me that whilst it was 4 am in London it was only 9 P.M. local in Fallon. So for once I slept right through until the 6.00 am Fallon time alarm.

**21. Friday June 24th.Mid Morning.Windsor. 20 miles West of London. England:** *The only problem with having children, is that eventually, they aren't.*

"Mum it's all right. It's Glastonbury and everyone will be there and I'm going with Tiggs. Her mum said it's OK and she's taking us to the station".

Her mother gazed at her daughter, sitting on the living room floor stuffing a huge back pack with pants, shoes, bags, towels, makeup, phone charger and much more. It seemed these days you needed a lot of kit to attend England's legendary music festival weekend.

"Here mum try and pull this shut, and remember I am 16." They pushed and squashed to close the obviously overstuffed bag. In between gasps of exertion her mother said, "Look my girl, you are actually only 15 and a half and quite how your brother got you that ID card I don't know."

"Also as it happens I don't really know how you got the tickets. I thought no one ever got tickets for Glastonbury because they all sold out in seconds."

Her daughter sighed and said "I've explained, Tiggs won them and I've saved some spending money."

"Actually Melissa, I think you persuaded your long suffering and very generous grandmother to '*advance* ' you the money. You may think she will forget but I won't let her. I just wish you father was here this month. Anyway, promise me you'll all stick together and call me twice a day. Oh yes, for God's sake no drugs, and if you must drink, stick to wine or beer from bottles we don't want any funny business put in your drinks."

As her mother went to respond to a hammering on the front door Melissa grabbed some gaily painted waterproof boots, tied a few last items on to her backpack and struggled out of the living room door.

She heard her mother saying, "Tiggs, is your dad home yet ?" and Tiggs responding, "No Mrs. Brown, he was at sea somewhere, but now he's in Tokyo or Taipei or Thailand or somewhere taking delivery of a new ship. Mum can tell you -- she said she'd drop in for a coffee after she's left us at the station."

Joanna Brown made thumbs up and exaggerated coffee drinking mimes to Sue, her closest friend, Tiggs mum, who was in the car at the end of the short driveway, and continued, "Tiggs I really want Melissa to call me twice a day", and looked somewhat exasperated at Tiggs non stop response.

"Actually Mrs. Brown that may be tricky because Michael says it's nearly impossible to find charging places as there's 150,000 people there for the festival and there's always long lines and anyway the signals out in the country are  dodgy-- so don't worry if you don't hear—everyday."

" We'll be back on Tuesday 'cos on the Monday, we can get some money for helping with the clear up and the re-cycling. Then we can pay back our grand ma's."

Before her now frowning mother could respond to that, Melissa hugged her, as much as a huge back pack allowed, and went down the path to the waiting car.

Mrs.  Brown calling out as under the weight of her backpack her willful daughter staggered down the path , "Well at least all stay together and have a nice time. I'll look for you on telly. I just hope neither of your dads are getting a  TV signal wherever they are out at sea. If they see you on the screen they'll have a fit."

With a flurry of 'Bye Mrs. Brown,'

'See you on Tuesday'  and ' Bye Mum ,love you,' they were gone.

Blinking back tears , Joanna Brown started to tidy the now silent and rather empty living room and noticed that someone had rearranged some of the pictures on the side table.

Now at the front, was a framed photo of her, a wet bedraggled waif of a girl, standing with a burly guy in a sea of mud and rubbish. On the back was written, *'Jo and Steve. Hyde Park Festival. In the Rain. 1994. Pink Floyd.'*

She smiled and sighed and went to make the coffee.

**22. Friday. June 24th. 06.00 am U.S. local. US Navy Airbase. Near Fallon. Nevada:** *Free, with a cold San Miguel beer, an enticing smile, and numerical clarity with Filipino kalendaryo wisdom.*

Having avoided the jugs of insipid looking coffee, and found the tea, I loaded my plate with corned beef hash and collected a bowl of 'fresh fruit' salad. I joined Oleg at a corner table.

He was looking tired and troubled as he toyed with a plate of eggs (easy over) corned beef hash and frazzled strips of what the Americans call, 'Canadian bacon.'

"Problems Oleg?" I enquired.

" Eventually my computer connected to the world, I've been up for a while looking for facts or updates to the information we have  and I can find nothing. This leaves us still discussing 'rumours' with the most senior military and intelligence officials in the USA. I think they'll tear us apart for wasting their time."

Before I could respond there was a touch on my shoulder and with a smiled hello we were joined by Miss Stanton, my old boss and Oleg's current employer. Cup of Tea in one hand and a plate with yoghurt and an apple in the other.

She glanced at my and Oleg's plate and frowned slightly, "An apple is enough for me, but Corned Beef hash is something the Americans do really well."

Whilst she opened her yoghurt, I spoke, 'Oleg was just telling me that despite more research he cannot find any confirmations or facts to back up these new rumours of a global ship or trade attack. He is concerned that the US powers that be in the intelligence community will tear us apart for wasting their time."

Miss Stanton sipped her tea and in a considered way said," Well I sympathise with you Oleg, and actually also with them. But you and Barry have given early warning that something's going on, and it has apparently caught the attention of the Russian and Chinese high command, and now indeed that of us and the US President."

"They have also had the written version of Oleg's excellent resume on our view of the current situation, so I think I will save you from having to go over it again, and I'll cover the key points in what I say."

At this, Oleg cheered up visibly, and started to tuck in to his hash with some enthusiasm. Proceedings then stopped as a huge pile of waffles approached, behind which lurked our colleague and friend Barry Purchase.

"Good Morning Ma'am and folks." he beamed and with an atrocious faux ' country hic' accent. "I have three important bits of news. The first is that knowing you Europeans liking for a real coffee, I have traced an Espresso machine in the Officers Mess."

" Behind that door as we speak I think that our friendly host Commander Rick E Dugan of the US Navy is operating same on our behalf and will arrive imminently."

"Secondly my people have had a word with our client the Texas trader." He glanced at Miss Stanton, "Apologies, this came up after you had left last evening. Dan and I have been alerted to several very wealthy financial cowboys taking some extreme positions on commodities and suchlike. Our Texan client has bet several billion dollars that problems with global shipping means that parts of the commodities world will rise- shortly."

"He also claimed not to have facts or focused information or any detail at all. For him just speculation and rumour is enough to cause some pretty severe market swings the markets, so right now rumours are enough for what he is doing. "

"Essentially, he claims to have no further information. We've worked with him for quite a while, and my people say he seems genuine in this."

Miss Stanton smiled and said, "So there we have it, sometime rumours are enough ,even to risk serious money on."

Barry went on. "My third point is. Dan, that tip you sent in about suspicious crew changes on a banana boat. There have now been four more. US Coastguard intercepted the ship last night and found that it had suffered a mysterious series of electrical failures to about 30 reefer containers."

"Consequently the ship stank of rotting fruit. Once they sorted the gasses out, as the rotting fruit make the containers dangerous to enter, they expected to find a drugs shipment, but so far have found nothing. Two of the reefers had small but fierce fires in them. Again nothing known yet. They're planning to detain the crew when they dock. But no clue yet on whom to focus further enquiries."

Miss Stanton said, " I notice we've just had a similar incident a couple of days back in the UK, that involved some container fires, does that mean the information to act also came from you?"

With a mouth full of Corned Beef hash, I could only nod. Miss Stanton said. "Excellent, excellent."

Barry addressed himself to the important task of demolishing his stack of waffles  and looking at Oleg now tucking in to his corned beef hash, before saying." Sorry about this one, but I guess we can assume that the investigators were seeking a different kind of 'hash' under all those banana's."  As we all groaned, the base commander appeared. It's not often that you are delivered with a tray of coffees from a US Naval Commander in full uniform, which promoted Barry to remark.

" Things are changing in this world of secrets, firstly it's the President of the USA with trays of French Fries, and now it's the next Admiral of the US fleet with coffee."

The Commander smiled and said, "Admiral, I am not sure, but what I am sure of is that your audience awaits you in secure C Room 12. Also that I need you to be ready in the lobby for transportation at 12.30 prompt.  The report to the President will take place on Air Force One, on the tarmac I assume."

He led us through to a small conference room with rather odd metallic walls and a flurry of greeting, handshakes, introductions and hello's ensued.

The US contingent, 25 in all, were a mix of uniformed types, some looking rather traditional 'Five Star style'.  Some suits, and a team of fit looking short haired bright looking guys in chinos, polo shirts and penny loafers. Really to my eyes straight out of the Ralph Lauren or JC Crew catalogues.

A rather pale and slightly frowning Dal Booth took a place at the head of the table. Miss Stanton, Barry, Oleg and myself just a few places away.

As the chat died away Dal said. " Welcome, particular welcome to you Ma'am. I note Daniel you came in from Singapore via London." at which I spotted a glance in my direction from one of the Ralph Laurens.

He continued, with I thought a slightly condescending air, "Barry, many of you obviously recall." Barry gazed ahead impassively.

With a sotto voce sigh he stared straight at Oleg and remarked, "It's not often that we all get to welcome Russians in these meetings, even those with Brit passports, so welcome Oleg."

I saw 'Madam' stare meaningfully at Oleg.

He went on, "This is our usual quarterly meet, concerning effects of any attack on American shipping and supply lines." He stopped, glanced at Miss Stanton and said, "Sorry, Ma'am I should have said any attack on ships belonging to the USA ,or our Allies."

"In the past seven days we have received early day suggestions of a crew or crews being hired, possibly for such an attack on a merchant ship or ships. This *was raised in our priorities* by Barry and Daniel here, both specialists and advisors to some of the world's largest shipping concerns."

I glanced at Barry and noticed Miss Stanton smile as he mouthed, "neat get out Dal."

" Then three days ago, Daniel received a call from, and then had a meeting with Liu Qiang chief of the Chinese State Security service MSSS."

I saw a distinct shockwave go over those listening. "Liu Qiang had similar concerns, and suggested two problem dates, 6/25, being tomorrow, and 1/27, the latter at least giving us some breathing space. "

"Then two days back the British Prime Minister got a similar heads up from the Chinese deputy president who is in New York. At about the same time we had a similar 'warning', directly from the Russian president to our Secretary of State."

"So not much detail, but something is afoot. Information at such a high level is unusual and thus concerning. Something is in play now. Oh yes. The President is keen to learn more and I have to report to him personally by 13.00 hours today. So although this is all based on rumour, it's pretty darn high flying rumour."

"Dan and Barry both specialise in shipping security, and happened to be in the right place to receive this information.  So I want to get them to update you with some background, but first a word from Miss Stanton."

To Oleg's ongoing relief she ran through the key points of, 'concern as it appears to British eyes'. "What we have is not new but a resume of the current situation as seen over there. Of course, most of our focus here today is intercontinental shipping."

"I do also want to draw your attention to the fact that although the UK benefits from being an island we are daily dealing with many thousands of containers that have initially come overland not only from Europe but also from Eastern Europe, Russia and all it's old states, as well as Iran, Turkey, the Arabian peninsula and further East. People smuggling also continues to exercise our control systems."

I was up next,  knowing I lacked facts. " My company  tends to look at this from three fronts, and although they interact they are: Criminal, Political protest and Terrorist. Any one of those, if there is any reality, in even part of this,  could cause rather dramatic swings in global economic terms."

"Interestingly we know from various major investors that rumour  can be enough or possibly even better for serious investment in their manipulations and trading gambles. I hope we are not being 'used' to further their trading gambles. We're quite good at sniffing that stuff out, but so far we are not yet sure."

I went on, "For me this started three weeks ago when my people picked up these stories up in The Philippines and Taiwan of complete crews being hired in secret. Then I was privately fed the same story by Liu Qiang. Barry's people heard the same story amongst shipping employees in Florida and Longbeach."

At which point all the Five Stars and the 'be-chinoed', spooks all looked up. "One thing that struck us as being odd, was and is, in this case, apart from the usual daily crazies, there's almost nothing to be found anywhere on the internet."

I noted the Polo shirts looking at each other with raised eyebrows and barely concealed shrugs of disbelief. I suspected that was more about my 'failure to research the internet properly' than my meet with the head of MSSS.

"All of these high level approaches make the same simple point. Someone is planning to physically interrupt some or a lot of global container freight traffic. *Problems with one or two ship's is usual. Problems with a lot is a real concern."*

The small audience were definitely paying more attention now. As Barry started to confirm his end of the story, a phone on the table rang. Our host the Base Commander picked it up and stiffened considerably as he listened.

"Sir."......"Indeed yes Sir..... He is right here sir I'll put him on. It's the President for you."

That really got the attention of the entire audience who strained to hear as he handed the phone to Dal Booth, who after a greeting listened looking more and more serious and then rather shocked. He murmured, "Yes Sir. Indeed. I am confident that my people are already on that sir."......"Thank you sir. Goodbye."

Dal, "OK. Listen up. The main reason the President called is this. As he, was being shown around this morning at the Oceans conference in San Diego at about 09.00 local time here, most of the world's shipping vanished from the  global positioning screens that were on display."

"It seems it was not a glitch with the equipment, and obviously it doesn't mean that several thousand ships have sunk. It seems to be another cyber attack." The NSA chief started to speak, but sat back as the CIA man continued. "The President is keen for advice on what his response best be, as ever the media are baying at the door.  It seems to me that we need to take a short break to update ourselves on what happened. "

He turned to the base Commander and asked, "Could you enable all communications for the next forty five minutes or so ?"

"I can," was the response, "but just before I do ,I can just appraise you some detail about most people call the AIS and VDR systems. After 9/11 with some speed it was mandated that all ships, as with air planes, with very few exceptions, must carry transponders providing not only their location and headings, but also details on their cargo origins, destination and more. These provide information in real time. There are a number of service providers and access to the main basic details are reasonably freely available. "

"There have been suggestions that such tracking details could aid troublemakers, but on balance it has added not only to security for most nations but also increased safety at sea."

He, the Commander stepped out, I assumed to arrange to connect us to the real world. Barry and my old boss from MI 6 came over to me, and I remarked on the two changes to our status. "One, we are now colleagues and secondly, on other hand, still a condescending attitude with him referring to the need to find, facts."

Madam smiled and smiled again as Oleg rather loudly said, "At bloody last," as his laptop came to life. The next 30 minutes was a blur of clicking fingers as the 25 or so people hunched over their lap tops and pads and checked with their offices and checked for anything pertinent. All seemed to be a lot of high powered effort just to give the President a press statement.

We gathered again. The director of the CIA stood and said, "Let's do a quick run round the room. Anything to add."

The Director of Homeland Security stood. "My folks are drafting a response for the President regarding this mornings situation. On the bigger picture. I appreciate you folks coming all this way, and thanks you for the information regarding Europe overland. Here the maritime port security is I believe better than you suggest. But of course always room to improve."

" We have made major steps with both physical security and widened our global network of information gathering at point of shipping. Just today, based on information received we intercepted a vessel," he glanced at his notes, "nearing Newark with, it turns out some containers likely full of drugs, concealed in rotting Bananas. Some fires were set, likely to destroy evidence we assume." Miss Stanton raised her hand, and the HLS boss stopped in mid speech and said, "Ma'am."

Miss Stanton smiled sweetly and said, "A good job by the boarding crews, and in fact a day back, we also had a similar situation in the UK. "

She paused," We should acknowledge however that the very detailed tip off about *both* these shipments came in fact originally from Daniel and

Barry. Considering those shipments were ex Brazil it suggests that their sources of information are interesting and likely credible, to say the least."

The director of homeland security, who had been scrolling furiously through his i. pad, muttered, " Indeed, noted ,thank you."

Dal nodded at the uniformed Five Stars.

One responded with, "Nothing new yet on today's matters. But a threat to shipping on any scale is a huge danger to the United States. More so because relying as we do on 'Just in time' supplies, as we keep warning, at all these meetings, in reality, nationally we have very few reserve stocks."

"Our friends at Homeland Security have quite a job with X million containers crossing our borders .I don't envy them their task. But an offshore attack on multiple ships is a different matter, and I don't think that even our combined Naval resources could police all freighters on all the oceans of the world. We really have to focus on the ports and either ends of the supply chain"

" I am minded to think about the blockade of the Atlantic during World War Two maybe that's what caught the attention of our British friends, this seems to be potentially equally threatening."

Dal Booth, "It is natural for me to be suspicious of messengers particularly Chinese and Russian ones. But there may be some common ground behind the approaches from them. We do also have some good contacts with them particularly regarding terrorist threats to all of us. Lets go on record here that we must review the possibility of expanding that co-operation with invitations for them to attend more regular meetings such as this."

Now it was the turn of the entire US contingent to look at each other with raised eyebrows! Barry passed me a note, *'Looks like he has been listening to POTUS as well.'*

"More comments gentlemen, anything about this morning's ship locator blackout. Particularly as was obviously scheduled to occur exactly as the President was viewing the system." He looked at the Polo shirted team. A Ralph Lauren from head to toe reported, "Well sir, of course right now the internet is overloaded with, 'why's my ship tracker gone blank? "

" But that's to be expected. We are allocating resources to trace how the attack could be scheduled for exactly when the President was viewing the set up."

" Regarding the point raised earlier. My team and I find it hard to believe that we won't find some online links between these threats. At the NSA we find new codes in use hourly and so a quick look this morning is not yet a full answer. We will dig deeper."

The CIA director looked at us.

Barry spoke. "Firstly, I am not surprised Dan and I were first with information, factual and rumoured. We're in the right place, and our clients handle almost 60% of global sea freight, *and incidentally the majority of your US military freight shipping internationally."*

I saw the Five Stars shuffle in their chairs, as Barry continued, "My company does have some possible leads but nothing factual, and fully appreciating your dislike of rumour it's nothing that warrants reporting on further at this time. Of course, depending on what is decided here, I will keep you informed, but Daniel does have some factual updates for you."

I could see Miss Stanton raise her file to her face to conceal a broad smile at Barry's, ' Knowing your dislike of rumour.'

My turn. "I do have some information regarding both the current problem with ship ID's, and with the overall threat details. In fact my final point probably makes this whole journey worthwhile at least for Barry and myself."

I could see Miss Stanton flinch a little at that one.

"My people in the Philippine's and also my guys in our Singapore office have been searching through the local equivalents to Facebook, Twitter and the big Asian site 'Line' in various languages including local Tagalog, Cebuano and Mani-Filipino."

I saw frowns from the Polo's. "As you may know there is hardly a merchant or cruise ship on the ocean that doesn't have Filipinos in the crew. There are lively bars in the portside area of Cebu and Manila where they even project the global locations of ships on their big screens. That is when they are not showing sports or their beloved famous boxers."

"The word being shared around Asian social media right now, by the girls working in those red light bars, is that disconnection and reset will work for all ship locator units. But only after 6 am  their time."

"Regarding this being targeted for exactly when the President was viewing the system. Although the timing of his visit was well publicised in advance, I think we will find that midnight is the key."

"9.00 am, this morning the 24th in San Diego was midnight Philippine time. Given the time and date differences, I should also point out that, out there in Asia it became the 25th at that very moment. So possibly a part of the Liu Qiang rumour has become fact."

I paused and observed considerable shuffling around the table, also to my surprise, a slight grin from Dal Booth.  "Regarding the suggested timescale that will then allow a general re-boot of the ship ID system. With that information, about the ship locator systems reset time being after 6 am their time, also coming from very sleazy portside Girly bars, I can understand your likely disbelief. "

"However, based on more than ten years of local experience I will be not be surprised if the ship locators re-boot as suggested."

" So the remaining question now is. Today's info screen outage. Why, how and who? and I suspect that our friends here," I nodded at the Ralph Laurens, "with their online resources will soon trace some clues if not answers. It would be helpful to share in that information."

" The word in Lucky Lips and Girls 4 You and Me, on the Manila dock street is 'Blame the North Koreans'. "

"This North Korean rumour is rather predictable as many Filipinos have been on ships where the GPS regularly goes blank near N.K. In fact I understand it was constant GPS threats that has brought back celestial navigation-with sextants- not electronics, to US Naval training. I do have a final point to make. This one probably enough to warrant this whole meeting."

Around the table there was a general straightening in chairs. I let them settle and went on.

***The USA is the only country in the world to use M.D.Y. Month, Day, Year, when noting dates. "***

*"It took your 9/11 to make most of the world realise you have a different and almost unique system here."*

"The UK, Europe, Russia and many others use, DMY, Day, Month, Year."

I paused, observing that some were making notes on their yellow legal pads—so much for electronics there. But I guess they'd precis that into their systems later.

" China, Japan ,Korea ,Taiwan use YMD, Year Month Day. So there's a lot of opportunity out there for confusion."

" *But shipping agents and bar girls like to know when their ship is coming in.* To avoid error, most shipping and freight agents worldwide, and as it rather logically happens, girls in red light bars tend to use a different system. One that works worldwide. "

***"So they use week numbers."*** I paused to let that sink in around the table. "This refers to each week, and each day of each week, by number. First week of the year is week 1. Within that week 1, the day numbers start with 1 for Monday through to 7 for Sunday. Second week in the year is 'week 2'. Then again days 1 Monday through 7 Sunday. Repeat this system weekly as needed through to end December and week 52, day 7. Last day of the year."

I grinned and said, "I can see you all starting to lose the will to live, But stay with me. I think you will be interested in what follows."

"Using the week number system. *This week now in June* happens to be week number 25. So *tomorrow here*, happens to be *Saturday or day number 6 of week 25* .

But unusually, and <u>note this doesn't coincide every year,</u> tomorrow's date is the 25th in the sixth month, June."

" Just to re-iterate: *unusually this year--6/25 or 25/6 refers to the same day in either system.*"

I could see Dal starting to fidget with his paper. One of the Ralph Laurens yawned, which provoked a follow on yawn from one of the Five Stars. I ploughed on: " Then lets look at the warning for 1/27.

Some here, and elsewhere *figured that out as January 27th.* That would be breathing space, indeed. *But if you use the week number system instead it's:* **Day 1 of week 27."**

"As any girl or lady boy in an Asian dockside red light bar knows, waiting for that ship to come in: *Day 1, week 27-using week numbers: This year translates as The Fourth of July."*

I paused, slightly, for dramatic effect......

" So I think we have an interesting problem."

I paused again "*But of course you may prefer to consider it as just red light bar rumours."*

The reaction around the table was extreme, stunned silence, then a burst of comment, conversation and concern.

Dal stood up, and raised his hand, for silence. "The President and I had dinner last night with Barry, Dan and Oleg, and we found, as Miss Stanton had told me, her professional team indeed have excellent local knowledge."

Dal continued. "I think Dan has just given a clear and graphic example of that local expertise. July 4th does usually produce a spike in anti American rumour In this instance I think we take the warnings as fact not rumour. And I thank you Daniel for drawing it to our attention."

He continued "In general terms I don't have to re-iterate the need for handling this carefully and confidentially. Where do we go from here?"

"A. What are the immediate threats to the USA, and our allies ? Current attacks suggest some credibility for recent threats. But we all lacking facts. Investigation is a priority with extra consideration given to July 4."

"B. What are the Russians and Chinese up to ? For or against. That position needs to be open to rethinking."

C "Then we have the request for any update for the president as requested on The Ship Position outage?"

" I have a note here from the NSA, which will provide the President with an answer for today at least, they say: " As ever our experts are continuously monitoring and updating our systems worldwide, against cyber attack and other interferences. We are very aware of the latest situation'."

Dal looked at me and grinned and said, "I think we can add a line to that, 'Restoration of the systems is imminent. All US registered vessels have back up and alternative systems available to them at all time.'"

He put down his papers and said. "Right. I have a suggestion. As you all know well, quite often these days we have turned to private contractors to assist in various activities, and bring in specific expertise."

" The use of such parties whilst usually excellent, has also on occasions returned to bite us hard, usually as a result of overzealous actions by individuals. So the engagement of subcontractors is now days a very complicated and time consuming business."

The Five Stars nodded vigorously.

He went on. "But I would like to propose the following. *We need to act fast, and we need more specialist research. It is obvious that Barry's and Daniel's companies are well connected, locally well placed, and indeed well thought of. "*

"I propose that, we, the CIA simply extend the existing agreement we have with Mr. Purchase's company to include Mr. Craig's company as specialist advisors. Their specific mission to look further into mutual concerns for us and our British allies."

I saw my old boss nod in agreement to the plan, as did I.

Barry said, "That's fine by Dan and I, my company is indeed on the current list of approved contractors, and you're right, to avoid delay, we can bring in Dan and his company via our existing contract."

Dal said. "In conclusion, and I am shocked to hear myself speaking the following words. But if the Chinese and Russians think this is serious then I think we have to make damn sure we have the best team looking into it. "

" I know that the President also urges you all to provide both Mr. Craig and Mr. Purchase with all assistance that you can. Please report regularly to the action team in my office and they will of course keep all parties fully informed, including yourself Ma'am."

He approached Barry and I, all smiles and with outstretched hand. We shook hands and after some exchanging of contact details we were left alone. I looked at my old boss and said, "Does that work for you Ma'am?"

"Lovely," she said, " Absolutely lovely, I had spent half the meeting trying to figure out how I could find the budget to pay you!"

She smiled and said to Barry and I, "I have a feeling that Daniel's contract coming via you will perhaps be somewhat more generous than at UK rates. And of course as Dan told us earlier he has more than ten years personal experience of those dockside bars.  So rather Barry's people approving the expenses than me."

Which produced considerable smiles all round.  Barry remarked, "Dal Booth is a wily old operator, you'll have noted, 'he called the meeting' and we then gave 'extra input, with local skill'. "

"I think you, Dan gave him a big wake up call, especially given that there's around 250,000 US Military stationed in the Philippines.  Must include some spooks."

" What are they bloody doing all day. Maybe their mums, or bloody P.C rules don't let them go to Girly Bars."

He glanced across at Miss Stanton.  "Sorry Ma'am office politics is not my speciality."  She with another smile, "Quite Mr. Purchase, quite, I couldn't possibly comment on your view. But I am very glad we have you on board. Obviously I can rely on your, and Dan's experience to take care of young Oleg in those bars."

We laughed again.  She continued, "Today is a perfect example of how the expectation for Presidents and P. M.'s to instantly re-act to any and all 24/7 TV news upsets the routine and stops daily business. "

"There's enough people in all our offices to have looked into today's blackout of shipping. Without us wasting time on that we possibly would have achieved a lot more from the meeting, although as we all know we are lacking hard facts."

" Also for God's sake, all those generals and the rest talking their usual platitudes, 'World War Two' even. Well meant I know, but at least they are now following the 'keep it brief' rule. President Appleyard's probably right about committees and brevity".

She looked at Barry, "All a bit like your breakfast, mostly waffle."

Whilst we laughed again, she said, "On the other hand I think you Dan, with Barry on this are now properly regarded as useful team players."

"I am very pleased also that you, Dan, out of all the people here know how to tell the time and figure out the date properly."

" I'm glad we taught you something before you left our employ."

Before I had time to much more than smile, Barry said, "On the subject of time, we have just 20 minutes to get ourselves sorted, see you in the lobby."

**23. At 9 hours ahead of Fallon Nevada it was early evening, but still Friday June 24. In Rotterdam. Europe:** *At Calvettioni Ship Control. Rotterdam. Hopefully more, 'Ready all the Time' than 'Just in Time.'*

Operating twenty fours a day, control centres for shipping lines look much the same regardless of their location around the world. Indeed not only do they look similar but the equipment used and the origins of a lot of the data used are common to many.

Banks of flat screen monitors using a variety of systems show ship locations accurate to within a few meters. Proprietary or off the peg systems provide a constant flow of information, updating fuel consumption with least cost / time routing, factoring in existing sea conditions and weather projections.

The evening had been hectic. Earlier what was presumably a computer glitch blanked out half their screens. That had put a quick stop to any conversations about that evening's upcoming soccer match between Dutch team Ajax and their biggest rivals.

Back up locator systems cut in automatically and any relief at 'seeing' their ships again was short lived as a 'major alert' warning signal produced shock and at first more disbelief, than awe.

The operators punched keyboards, juggled mice and raised phones to call the IT department whom they immediately suspected of screwing things up, yet again.

The IT teams protested that it was not them, but a fault or a hack on the incoming data they were getting from the global positioning alert system. Grudgingly their colleagues across the desks concurred and concluded that it started to look like a malicious hack..

But then ,within minutes, further details: *four ships were reporting reefer problems.* Their locations, as shown on various back up systems, were each considerably offshore.

One in the Pacific destined for Long Beach California, One in the Indian Ocean destined for the Suez Canal and then Genoa Italy.

The third and fourth having come via the Panama Canal were En route, one for Newark ,East Coast USA. The other for Felixstowe in the UK was not far off the Azores Islands in Mid Atlantic.

The reports were similar. ....Reefer overheating.... Reefer smoking. Reefer lost contact.... and in one case orange coloured smoke appearing from a container stack.

Captains and deck officers reported that there appeared to be no immediate danger to the ships but were investigating and preparing to fight fires.

Unfortunately it was the middle of a dark and stormy night at the Indian Ocean location of the ship reporting smoke so there were no useful pictures, but the container by container sensors indeed reported some dangerous changes.

Whilst the various tech experts hovered, waited, instructed and consulted, the duty supervisor had called the manager of fleet operations. He calmly passed on a report of, ship locator systems gone down. Back ups starting up.

That manager, Alan Whaley ,happened to be in a car with the CEO of the company driving to Ajax football ground where they were to entertain clients in a directors box. He obviously explained the situation to the CEO Gerry McMullen or to give him his correct title Captain McMullen.

They had been discussing some budget requests that Whaley's people had put in for yet another monitoring system - this time to satisfy the latest American regulations for ships entering their coastal waters. Gerry smiled broadly and congratulated Alan on 'choosing exactly the right moment to draw attention to the budget request,' and returned to the more important matter in hand- that of the need for Ajax to beef up its team of strikers, "the existing ones are getting a bit old now- a bit like me." he joked.

About 60 seconds later he stopped smiling and joking when his secure, and definitely very private Blackberry delivered a text message. *CSC. To GMcM. Fires reported 4 (four) ships. Ends*

He showed the message to his number one man who paled and grabbed his own phone, after a brief conversation with operations control he said, " Boss, drop me here there's loads of taxis I'll get back to ops. centre. '

His boss, preparing to instruct the chauffeur to make a U turn listened as Alan went on, " It's probably another glitch or a hoax from vegetarians anonymous or similar. So it's better you take care of business as normal at the game, we don't want word getting out and bringing satisfaction to copycat hoaxers,"

Knowing this made sense they ordered the driver pull over, and Alan quickly found a cab and hurried back to the drab, featureless but very secure building that housed the ops centre.

There the calm and assured scene belied the situation. Before he could even ask, the duty manager said. "Nothing new. All four ships are going by the book. "

"Their masters, with no apparent terrorist threat in the vicinity have each slowed their vessels to the slowest speed appropriate to local sea conditions."

Fire trained crews were climbing and checking the containers where alarms had been triggered. Fires below decks were treated with halon and other fire suppressing gasses, but reefers tended to be installed above decks.

His phone rang ,it was Captain McMullen, in the background Alan could hear the roar of the Ajax fans. Alan reported it did seem to be genuine, but extraordinary problem. *Four ships with fires simultaneously was not co-incidence.* McMullen responded with a curt, "I'll be there in ten minutes."

The CEO was well respected not only by the masters and many of the officers who worked under his command, but also by the higher echelons of the whole industry.

Despite the best efforts of his wife and various tailors he remained, as the press and indeed his grandchildren used to refer to him, 'A grizzled old blue water seadog.' After years at sea he had wanted to be away from home less, and joined Calvettioni lines head office in the late eighties.

All they had then were some rather old and battered ships tramping mainly around the French controlled islands of which there are many scattered across the globe.

His seafaring knowledge was legendary, and his ships masters liked the fact that when needed, he would stand up for them- and their ordinary seamen in fights with 'the bloody bean counters' in his own head office.

His command of Tagalog, the locally varied dialect spoken by his Filipino crews gained him an enviable loyalty across the fleet and indeed the industry. Such was his presence and the respect that he generated, that on his return to the office even the most laid back and egalitarian Dutch staff stood when he entered the room, and there were several 'good evening Captain's,' as he rapidly made his way to the control desk.

"OK. Listen up. This at least, looks serious- time will show if it is real. But with four ships at once, get hold of Matchless Consulting we need them to look into this."

"Then: One: Confirm we have disabled all crew to public communication systems we don't need e mails and selfies floating round confusing the world at this time. They could slow down emergency response."

"Two: Let me see that list of all vessels nearest to ours, with eta's in case they need assistance."

"Three: Inform the masters of the four of the situation on the others."

"Four: Raise an alert- a standard one- to all other vessels in the fleet and send a general alert to the various agencies handling other ships at sea. Stress, standard, and not yet confirmed."

"Five: Tell the four masters we assume they preparing for an orderly disembarkation into lifeboats in case this necessary. All personal to take extra water and nutrition where they can. Note orderly disembarkation- not abandoning ship.

" Six Coloured smoke makes me nervous. I know jack- sh*t about Hazchem or bio stuff. Check the 'worst case 'situation files .

They are going to need some kind of specialist Hazchem suits. Find out all about them. The Navy and or salvage companies will have some. I am sure Smit Tak or what ever the hell they call them now, Crowley's, who ever, and everyone else in the ship rescue business will see something' s going on by now."

" If we can wait, but only if it's safe to wait, I'd rather contract for some specialists in Hazchem suits to do a job for us than have a full on salvage attempt, with all the 'we rescued your ship,' legal costs that implies. "

" Thinking about that, call Jens, the Rotterdam Harbour fire chief and ask him to come in here pronto to see me. He'll know all about that stuff."

"Seven. Tell the masters, taking into account potential Hazchem's, only if they feel confident about staying on board , to ask for volunteers to maintain a minimum crew on board for the ships safety and possibly to investigate more. And I mean, ASK I don't want them selecting people to volunteer."

"And Eight. He gestured at the room full of equipment, "Use all this stuff to find our estimable Chairman. I called Madame Calvettioni at home in Grenoble and the somewhat slurred response was, 'He's away until next week.' She knows not where."

" Oh yes- just in case the cat's out the bag already in this instant digital age- or if those who are threatening us have started to share their glory with the world when you get hold of Matchless Consulting get their press guy onto this; Pronto."

Commander McMullen sat back in his chair and closed his eyes, and after a moment or two said, – " Tell the four ships masters I'd like a word at a moment convenient to them."

**24. Friday June 24th.Lunchtime. PST. US Navy Air base near Fallon Nevada.USA:** *More from the Presidents Club. International branch.*

As I joined Barry and Oleg in the lobby, Barry showed me an incoming message from his office on his iPad.

*Flash. Matchless Consulting Control. B.P. Calvettioni ship control Rotterdam rprt's simultaneous container fires on four ships. Appear controllable. ends.'*

Barry said that Calvettioni's were clients of his for about the last ten years, with no out of the ordinary problems over that time. They were Rotterdam based. Mainly French financed.

Dal Booth joined us and obviously we started to discuss if there could be links with the  other two ships we already knew about, but we figured it would all take a while for us to be updated. Barry's office were on the case, with their client.

Transport was waiting , so having made the quick ride to the terminal buildings and been thoroughly security checked, and thus having our internet connections disabled, we stood just inside the terminal watching the big 747 that was Air Force One taxi to a stop.

A young military policeman from the frisking squad reminded us ultra politely. "No cameras or phones please gentlemen...ma'am. You'll need these pass slips to board." I studied the plane intently and speaking loudly above the noise remarked to Oleg, "There's no sign it's much different to a normal jumbo."

From right behind me Dal Booths voice cut in. "Believe me it is, but most of all it's a great working space in travel time. But it'll be around 30 years old by the time we get the new one. But as we all know, to get that built without all those those potentially insecure  international components in there is an interesting project."

He turned and started to speak with Miss Stanton. "It's good you and Barry will be coming East with us to Washington. I'm happy to have this chance to talk this through more. Quite frankly, right now I'm still a little unsure of the realities and thus the priorities, although this latest report from Barry is a concern."

Miss Stanton said," Indeed. One priority on which we're all agreed is that the sooner Dan can be back on station at the source of the rumours in the Far East the better. So he's going directly back there from here. Although it occurs to me standing here, that what's Far East for us Brits may be further west for you guys."

Even with a skilled team, it takes a little time to park a Jumbo jet and whilst we waited Dal continued, talking to us all but addressing the head of DHS-Department of Homeland Security.

" Mr. Pern, I have a little problem for you. Last night the President told us that Sam Charles strongly recommended we listen to our friends the Brits when it comes to China. In particular if Miss Stanton is involved. Perhaps you would share his reasons with us Miss Stanton."

With a broad grin my old, and Oleg's current boss, the UK's senior security officer smiled sweetly and said, "That's because when I was at a university doing my Mandarin and Cantonese studies one of my classmates was Liu Qiang, now head of their state security."

"He's an interesting man, from a poor farming family, not from one of China's elite, groomed for power from birth. He's progressed through work and ability. I liked him, very straight forward and far from being the archetypical 'inscrutable oriental' I could read him like an open book."

"I knew him pretty well. As good students at the time we even smoked and drunk too much beer together. That is at student parties with a lot of others I stress." She smiled sweetly again. If her story had amazed me and Oleg, it had stunned Brian Pern the head of DHS. Indeed far from any western version of ' inscrutable' he looked shocked, at her 'smoking and drinking' words I thought he'd explode.

Dal cut in, " Now Brian how are you going to square that with your profiling systems. We don't want Miss Stanton getting held up at airports every time she pops over the Atlantic for a cup of tea at the White House. "

"And by the by, before you start sending me memos about us sharing information with you, those gems about Miss Stanton weren't in our files either, I learned them on the flight here from Washington. I really I like Sam Charles, but he was a devil for keeping stuff to himself."

I figured, as Barry had pre-warned me, despite Dal's smiling demeanour there was always an agenda in there somewhere.

Possibly that agenda was revealed when Dal continued, "Whilst we're about it we'd better teach the system about young Oleg here, I see he nearly missed his cousins wedding in New York."

Before any of us could react we were called forward, a standard set of steps had been rolled into place to the front door - no red carpet and military guards of honour for us.

The door opened and an Air Force officer came down the steps at quite a speed and requested Commander Dugan to board first which he did also taking two steps at a time.

After a moments delay as we handed over our 'passed security slips', a bit like passengers on an old style group holiday and followed the officer up the steps.

As we entered the door we lost all the sound overload from the plane which was creaking in the sun with its APU unit in the tail making a huge hissing roar.

We seven entered the lobby just as the base commander was leaving -- massive beaming smile. " Had a photo op with the president, have good flight," to Barry and the rest, and he was gone.

We were shown along a fairly broad corridor to some fairly standard first class style seating. I noted seats for about 30. Before we could think about starting to sit the door opened and the President almost bounded into the room.

As is seems to be a tradition with US 'Commanders in Chief', he had been presented with some special travelling kit to use regularly on Air Force one. So he was wearing a sweat shirt with Air Force One in vintage baseball style lettering. Quite cool actually, and way better than President Bush's leather jackets. They had distinct Doctor Strangelove overtones about them.

He said, "We've got about fifteen minutes before they push back, so let's get started right away. "

He ushered Miss Stanton and we followed ,into a conference room. Biggish table with 10 airline style seats. He sat at the head of the table next to a woman whom he introduced as "this is Janet, my personal executive secretary."

"Firstly gentlemen," he nodded at the NSA,DHS and CIA side of the table,"With apologies, but this is obviously my first opportunity to inform you of this. In the past few minutes I have had further conversation with the President of China and our Ambassador in Moscow had a call from the President of Russia. "

"They had but one subject to talk about. The same one that we have been focused on for a few days. Their calls triggered by the white out on the ship ID systems. Potential shipping problems on a large scale. "

"In a nut shell they are as worried as we are. As we obviously all realise, in Russia's case they need trade of all kinds, including imported foodstuffs to sustain their recent lifestyle upgrades."

" In the case of China they need the smooth continuation of exports and employment to, as the President just put it to me, 'to keep the peace on his streets'. That's an interesting admission."

I obviously replied,' that we had contingency plans in place for any attacks on our shipping'. But he, the Chinese President continued to press the point. He also mentioned that apparently the during the blackout, some kind of incident has occurred on a number of ships." Barry, Dal and I nodded to each other.

"I have note here of what he said, I quote. 'Mr. President what you can do, is not always the same as your free press allows your people to believe what you can actually do. So I have no pleasure, no political game, only sadness in fearing also for your peaceful and delightful American streets'."

The President raised a hand." Gentlemen I share your suspicion and your concern as we have discussed over the past few days in various meetings. However I did feel that his comment was not said as a threat or even a veiled threat."

At this I thought the three CIA, DHS, NSA men would burst.

"I note your understandable re-action, I can assure you those who threaten our nation directly or indirectly will not find me an easy push over. I do however genuinely believe the Chinese President was talking out of concern - sorrow almost."

Dal Booth said," Just before we leave I should report that Dan and Barry have likely focused down one of the 'threat dates' from January 27 to July 4, which is of course both usual and a concern". He continued. " I guess we can will fill you in further with details of that and the incident the Chinese President was referring to  as we return to Washington."

The President stood and said "I guess we'd better push back and get flying."

I stood quickly. "Actually if you'll excuse me sir, before you order doors shut  Oleg and I are making haste back to Singapore to see if we can get a direct connection to the original sources of the rumours that started all this."

The President stood and with bone crushing handshakes said to both of us. " As we have discussed it's a rare privilege for me to meet 'The Ears on the ground and all that'."   I didn't dare look at the US security chiefs, but I did have to smile when the President went on, " Keep all my guys on their toes now."

His assistant, now known to me as Janet, gave Oleg and I a sheet of paper and said, "Catch up with this on your next flight. The back of this plane is now full of journalists so this explains why we stopped."

We were shown out - with a murmured 'good luck guys,' from Barry and Miss Stanton. Oleg and I both paused at the top of the steps, dazzled by the bright desert sun after the dim light on board.

As we made our way down the steps still blinking in the brightness Oleg said. "No wonder they always stop and wave a bit before they come down these steps, especially as we learned that US Presidents are never allowed to stumble or fall over."

We were hardly off the bottom step, when they were on the move, pushed by a team of navy men.

The base commander was waiting, with a smile. "Your kit's all been loaded on to that one there- pointing at a Gulfstream of some kind nearer the buildings. But you'll have to wait thirty minutes to take off until AF One and POTUS are out of the air-space."

" That applies to your wireless and phone coms as well. So there's just time for an all American hamburger-Navy style if you want."

We realised then that the Presidents news updates had meant no lunch and both Oleg and I were starving. The commander was great company, laughing heartily when Oleg taking a healthy bite of his meaty burger said, "I had wondered if a burger Navy style' was be fish'. "

The commander also said – "They transferred some interesting bags from the secure store room to your new people carrier, which is what the pilot boys round here call those GS650 ER's. With a good top speed and long range they are impressive birds even if they aren't Navy."

"Mind you the guys here have been itching to crawl all over the plane you came in on, and they tell me there's now a carrier friendly one on the way. I guess I'll be retired by the time we find the will to buy it or the cash for that, especially as it's French. You know what politics are like here."

"Getting back to your bags. I nearly had a major drama on my hands with them being in the vicinity of AF One. Luckily I was there when our X-ray guy spotted the contents, and he called me over to look. A bag of weapons like that is not what he's used to seeing, even here. You have to understand I'm working to the 'AF One on the ground at your base', manual and should have sounded the alarms."

But I realised AF1 was ready to start already pushing back, so we rolled your bags back into the X-Ray scanner for a second look."

I congratulated him on a 'brilliant Admiral Lord Nelson naval solution to an unwanted sight'. It was time to leave by the time I had explained to the US commander and to Oleg about Britain's foremost Admiral at the Battle of Copenhagen in 1801.

Admiral Nelson, who had lost an eye in an earlier battle with the French, on being told his superior had ordered him to withdraw as he was outnumbered- put his telescope to his blind eye- and said, "I see no signal.

"and proceeded to demolish the bigger enemy fleet.  His superior was recalled in disgrace and Nelson appointed Admiral of the British Fleet.

The commanders comment, " It's dammed hard to sail your own course these days."

With sincere, "Come and see us in London and Singapore's," we said good bye to the good commander and re-encountered pilot Rory Macleod at the top of the steps.

" I have to tell that apart from the usual pilot and  air traffic control stuff there's no general coms yet - but as soon as we're clear of Fallon you should find we're well connected to wherever you want. I'll come and give you the full SP when were 'up there'."

I sat back in the considerable luxury of the top of the range Gulfstream and whilst waiting for our on board communication systems to be allowed to function as Air Force One got further away  I realised I had the paper from the Presidents secretary in my pocket.  I read.

Executive office .6/25 Friday briefing: Oceans are Warming. Annex 1.
*"In the continuing process of using governmental and executive resources effectively AF1 stopped briefly directly at FNA on its scheduled route from San Diego to Washington. The 30 minute wheels down - no POTUS exit- was to enable the picking up of the Director of the CIA, DHS and various advisors who had been attending a routine security meeting at Fallon Naval Air Station Nevada. The President was returning to Washington from the "Oceans and Warming " meeting in San Diego. On arrival in Washington the President will be joining Mrs. Appleyard at the closing stages of the 'Unite for the Young of the World,' function." AF1. P.M. EST.*

I noted Oleg reading also, he waved the paper, smiled and asked me,  "Is there any surf in Singapore?"

**25. Friday June 24th. 2.00 pm. PST.Outbound. Ex. Fallon. Nevada.USA:** *"You'll arrive rested, relaxed and in stress free style in our latest version executive business jet."*

The above, a quote from the rather predictable air charter company leaflet in the seat pocket of our Singapore bound plane.

Indeed, good Commander Dugan had been very impressed both our all new, 'on test ultra capability' narrow body that we arrived on, and by our plane for the flight to Singapore. As he was by this, a Gulfstream GS650, an 18 seater, apparently the fastest on the market, with more than considerable style and comfort, greater range and I guessed, price.

I had noticed there were four crew. I assumed this was because we had a very long flight. We were hardly off the ground and high in the cruise when Capt. Rory appeared at my side. "Just to let you know. We can do Singapore with this light load nonstop, but we're going to do a touch and go in Seattle to drop off the two pilots from the delivery crew, and collect two more. I didn't get the full rest time after the hop from London, and it's a long way to Singapore."

"We'll also top up the fuel. It won't add more than few minutes to the 12 hour schedule, as actually having re-fueled we can then fly faster."

He looked at me "Our communication connections should liven up in fifteen minutes or so as we're flying away from AF One now."

" If you're sleeping as usual, I'll consider it a challenge to get down in Seattle in just over an hours time and off again without waking you," and with a smile he was gone.

I eased my seat back a degree or two and stretched out.

Indeed there's nothing like sitting back in an airplane seat and being able to take time reviewing the situation, past, current and future. Usually you do this in quietish solitude, forty thousand feet in the air being usually uninterrupted.

So a focused place to cogitate, and of course to remain rested and stress free. Despite their promise, a lack of communications was not aiding my stress levels as I was keen to hear more about the four new ship fires.

After a moment's thought I moved to sit at a table opposite Oleg who was studying his computer intently, also waiting for connections to be established.

"Whilst we wait to get connected to the real world shall we go through the past week. See what we might have missed. Also to give you a heads up of what we do in Singapore and who my people are."

"Good idea," said Oleg, "but hang on one sec."

He disappeared to the front of the plane and re- appeared from the galley a few minutes later with two large English Breakfast Teas, in bone china mugs no less. "It was EBT that got me through my university exams."

I had been making a few notes.

"Okay. Good tea by the way. Ten days ago it was business as usual in Singapore. As we're En route to the office I'd better give you some more details. I already mentioned Jacko and Suki, J & S, my researchers."

I continued. "I do have another couple who work for me. I told you my operations director is Susie Todd."

Oleg "That's Squeeze."

I nodded, "Her husband Chris, takes care of everything practical. From the office, the cars, logistics, office equipment and supplies. Meeting clients at the airport and stuff. The clients all love him and now ask for him if they come to town which is great. "

"Employing couples is usually risky, as problems with one means problems with two, but I think it works when they are thousands of miles away from their home base."

"Then we have twelve individual client or case officers, a mix of men and women, mostly assigned to particular clients. That's the main HQ team in Singapore. "

"We've also got a small training  office in the hills behind Nice. That's centrally located and so a great access for all Europe, including the Mediterranean East and West from there. Its run by a guy called Sam Barkshire.  I'll fill you in on others as we go along."

We talked on about the Fallon meetings and then still with no communications, true to my training mantra, 'Restore personal batteries at every opportunity', I reclined my seat and whilst running through the facts yet again in my head, dozed off.

I awoke with a start as we started our decent into Seattle.

Oleg saying as we touched down." Still no coms, but Rory say's there's a techie ready and waiting to fix it here."

The turnaround indeed took not much more than 30 minutes and as we climbed steeply away from the airport Oleg's  computer came to life.  He read out a message from his laptop.

" This from Barry an hour back but we were off air then.

*BP. 'Ship fires, under control, but need detailed investigation. So far only affected are Calvettioni Lines.  Barry end stop".*

Oleg said, "Shit, this looks more urgent-this in right now." he passed me his laptop.

The message was from Squeeze in my office:

*SQ. Marked Flash DC & OT only: You off air. Advise receipt.*

*Reports from Europe. Three teenage girls gone missing from River Rhine Germany schools cruise. We believe them to be May Lim, Tamiko Yamada, Brigitte Calvettioni.*

*Not confirmed yet. More will follow.*

*Ulrike aware. Believe School in contact with parents. End stop.*

Shit indeed. That woke me up.

The Lim's and Yamada's were two of the biggest ship owning families in the world and were my corporate and personal clients, and as of the past few hours the Calvettioni's were also on my radar.

As I explained the potential family connections to Oleg my lap top seemed to be taking forever to log on to the air coms.

Oleg confirmed the plane systems, now over the Pacific were talking to a different satellite. Having found the world, my laptop repeated the incoming messages as shown to me by Oleg.

I acknowledged receipt the messages and added to Squeeze.

*DC. Copy original report to B.P. and Miss Stanton, add words, Concerned copycat publicity, use this info with care. D.C.end stop.*

It was a moment later when the laptop beeped and I could read, what I figured, was the inimitable hand of Susie Todd.

*SQ. 'Unclear if girl's gone overboard, done a runner after boys / horses / parties/ joined a save the whales demo/ or been abducted.'*

*Local police report no signs struggle.*

*Nothing missing from cabins, as far as they can tell.*

*Passports, cash in place.*

*Ulrike Sommer En route to boat current location. ETA 1 hour. No contact yet Lim's or Yamada's.*

*Strongly suggest you divert Taipei as both families there now for naming ceremony of new ship. Advise. Squeeze. End stop*

Oleg who had been reading his copy on the other side of the table said, "What about Taipei?"

A touch on the call button produced, not a smiley air hostess but captain Rory. Or on this flight with crew being provided 'Acting Captain Rory.'

With broad grin. "At your service, sir."

We asked about the possibility to divert to Taipei and he said, "I'm sure that's easy, and actually looking at the weather ahead it may be better. Let me go and see."

In a few minutes he was back and said, "Diverted already. No problem. ETA eleven hours, plus. Quicker than Singapore, and we may well be able to improve on that arrival time....as it says in the Gulfstream sales brochures, thanks to it's Rolls Royce engines, 'this plane flirts with the supersonic'."

"Our insurance for this trip is 'all mainland Asia but Taiwan qualifies. Just one thing. The base commander at Fallon obviously gave me a heads about that bag of yours. I understand it's under diplomatic protection but you may need to amend that. They'll be shit hot in Taipei about such things."

Oleg said, "I'll email UK about that."

My laptop beeped.

*From Squeeze: SQ. Note you diverted to Taipei. Assuming you need usual hotel rooms. I will inform both sets parents you on the way. End stop.*

I mentioned this diversion being public knowledge, and Rory said, "It's a complete nightmare the amount of public tracking that goes on. Dangerous as well if you ask me. But of course in this case useful." With a cheerful ,"I'll go and see what we can do to avoid the rock n roll weather systems out there," he disappeared into the cockpit .

For the first of many times in what became a long night I speculated to to Oleg that kidnapping could be interpreted as an attack on world sea freight, but it smelled more of criminal extortion than politics. I wasn't sure why. It just did.

*From Barry Purchase: BP."Note diversion, Ship fires, Calvettioni  Fleet Control concerned  coloured smoke suggests Chemi or Bio attack. Factor in missing girls and this looks coordinated and nasty. First need to alert Lim/Yamada ships about  Calvettioni attack. Difficulties locating Mr.C. but are in contact Mrs. C. BP. End stop.*

This latest message got both Oleg and I wondering about the warnings from the Chinese and Russians. Surely bio and chemi attacks were terrorist, and thus rapidly became national defence and military issues, or at least until any ransoms demanded.

Kidnaps in the west were usually criminal, but the reasons, depended on the kidnapper's demands when received.

In Singapore all the team were exploring any and all links, suggestions, theories...however tenuous or far fetched.

Miss Stanton responded with a:

'*Agree use information with care, . Ends.*

Oleg was in contact with Squeeze getting a 'missing persons' folder together for his office. I filled him on a few personal details not already in his shipping files. David Lim  and his wife Peggy had built up a large and successful shipping business headquartered in Taipei on the island of Taiwan.

Despite the presence there of several other major shipping and transport companies that developed around the same time, David Lim's, 'Taiwan Ocean Pacific Shipping', labelled 'LIMTOPS' on many thousand shipping containers had become a major factor in the market. He had focused on sea freight and some of his rivals had diversified, also very successfully in fact, into air freight and passenger transportation.

Also well known in the global world of cargo shipping ,the name or acronym: 'NIPPON.TOFCO'. They referring to Hiroshi Yamada's Tokyo based- 'Nippon Tokyo Ocean Freight Company'.

A major player, with less ships than David Lim, but including a number of bulk ore carriers, whereas the Lims ships were mostly designed for containerised freight.

*I emailed Ulrike/Barry. DC. "May Lim and Tamiko Yamada have trackers in their phones. May Lim should also have crumb and trace tracker in her bag. Sure they will have phones with them, trackers maybe. Squeeze on the case with tracking company. DC.*

The hours of the long flight unwound desperately slowly.

Snacks, water, more bloody snacks, water .

Despite my reputation for snoozing on all flights, I was way too focused to doze.

So searching around the internet for clues. None found.

Minds and conversations between us churning over the various scenarios.

Six hours out from Taipei. My German staffer, Ulrika Sommer reported.

*Ulrike. Not much being given away here.*

*Press holding fire on promise of exclusives  later understanding police want to avoid copycat sighting calls.*

*Three girls horse mad. Had been on scheduled trip to local stables.*

*At the boat stop in Rudesheim am Rhine they had auto embark /disembark passenger counting  system (rfi-electronic wrist bands).*

*It showed them checking out just before 10 in the morning And back in together on time around 5.30. 'As  wrist band checker showed all present, they not missed until next day. It having been a regular day off for all the girls on the boat, which was moving upstream through the day as scheduled.*

*Local police not ruled out girls run off with some boys. But having said that have also put out all points border check.*

*Am going to previous stopping point. Ulrika. end stop.*

I was rapidly running out of useful scenarios and was thinking about border checks being a waste of time with the European Common Market original open borders policies.

Somewhere between our satellite system and the undersea cables of the world through which all internet traffic passes Ulrika's message had been delayed as a second one came in pretty quick...

....Five hours out from Taipei.

*Ulrika: Am back in Rudesheim am Rheine where they last seen, on the boat dock where boat left from. I know it quite well, I can see a video cam in the bank and another in a cake shop. They may show dock and gangplank. We are checking cake shop cam. Bank closed but security people En route.*

*Police asking about phone trackers and possible track and trace. Security guard boat dock 100% they didn't get off again. He can't confirm the electronic trace of their arrival against faces. There were hundreds of girls returning over a short period of about an hour as two boats were moored rafted outside each other on same gangplank. It was cold, wet and the girls all wearing coats, hoodies, scarves etc. end stop. End*

Two hours out from Taipei.

*Ulrika: Nothing obvious seen in fast scan of three hours video from both cake shop and bank. Can't recognise any girls as yes they all covered against rain. But have noticed two things.*

*1. I have counted returnees shown on video and the numbers don't add up. There are three less than they say got back on the boat. So that seems to confirm situation.*

*2. Guard at boat dock spends almost an hour chatting to a guy sheltering under their awning at gang plank entry. Says they just discussed football. The guy was a taxi driver but not known to the guard.*

*But can confirm guard doesn't leave his place and is obviously alert, that gangway only way on and off boat from the shore.*

*Trackers all stopped around 4.45 somewhere on road from Mainz to Rudesheim where the boat moored. That not really on the direct route from stables back to boat. I have feeling we ahead of police on this. Will go and see if they will trade if we help them. Rgds U. end.*

Oleg said. "I've got a mail confirming that someone will meet us at Taipei gate to seal and ensure diplomatic status our 'difficult bag."

After what seemed to be one of the longest flights of my life, despite the Gulfstream's speed we prepared to land at Taipei.

A final mail in from Squeeze in my Singapore office.

*SQ: Four adjoining rooms at Hotel. DC, OT, CT and meeting room. Toddy will arrive before you. I figured this was going to run for a bit. Remember after all the golf outings, Hiroshi and Lims like Chris a lot.*

*He's got back up coms, chargers, another lap top and a change of clothes for you. Toddy got them on his way to airport as I told him I wouldn't know how to choose the right size leopard skin thong for you.*

*J and S have nothing new to report.*

*Keep all receipts , except thong, as will need for rebilling Matchless! Squeeze. X.*

I could see Oleg chuckling at the e mail. 'Just wondering boss, if Miss Stanton knows about the leopard skin as well as your choice of wine."

My F*** O*** response was fortunately drowned by the sound of the two Rolls Royce engines doing their reverse thrust slowing us with the lights of Taipei airport flashing past the windows.

Taipei. A nice city but I didn't think we would be seeing much of it. After brief quick taxi from the runway to a very sophisticated 'general aviation ' terminal, complete with ramp tube to door. After a brief delay, the front door opened, and with a uniformed escort of some kind, a guy from the British embassy, known to me for years, stepped in.

Looking at me with some distain. "Mr. Craig. This is a very short notice call, I was engaged at a function. I don't think the ambassador is going to be too happy about this."

With some considerable style Oleg stepped forward and showed his ID. "As Mr. Craig is only a passenger on my flight I don't think he knows what you are speaking about Mr. Err ?"

The Brit. Dip. looked shocked. Introduced himself, as I knew full well 'Peregrine Molesworth. Assistant M.A. at the Brit Embassy.'

He looked even more shocked when Oleg asked to see his I.D. and then requested he step outside for a "quiet word."

I thanked Captain Macleod and exchanged business cards with him. When I exited Oleg was standing there grinning. "Hope I didn't blow it there sir."' as we walked up the jet way to the terminal.

I said, "I've told you Oleg, I am not sir, and no you didn't blow it. Where is the bumptious little shit."

"He's down there in the rain sealing the two bags to confirm their, ' no one can look in here diplomatic status '."

Probably because I was tired and grouchy from the flight I said, "He's an interfering pain in the arse, and has an insatiable ability to gossip and make trouble. We could do without any press coverage ."

I looked down out of the terminal window where indeed Molesworth. P. was half in half out of the little cargo hatch.

"Hang on a sec then," said Oleg and nipped down the air stairs and stood under the wing speaking to him, who even through a rainy window at some distance I could see looked completely shocked. He then nodded , and rather unwillingly shook Oleg's outstretched hand."

Oleg bounded up the air stair and reappeared on the jet way into the terminal. As we walked towards immigration and customs I asked Oleg what he had been up to.

Another big grin. "I showed him my 'laissez passez' from Miss S. and told him we'd just arrived from spending 'quality time' with the head of the CIA , the UK PM. Oh yes and that our dinner had been cooked for us by POTUS. If he went online he could see the President with our dinner in the kitchen at an airbase in USA."

" He went a bit quiet then. I followed it up with, 'there has never been a more top security rating than this op and the President of the US was setting up a smoke screen for it.' Oh yes and I was glad he, Molesworth was there."

I looked at Oleg, "Very diplomatic indeed, although I thought we were supposed to be a bit discrete about that President bit."

But Oleg said, "The pictures of the President carrying our French fries are all over social media from the Navy chefs and their families. As is the listing of who went the Fallon meeting ,I think that came from  that briefing paper they handed out to the press on Air force one. So I think we're fine."

I nodded my approval and worried a bit about Molesworth's heart rate. Not.

Immigration was standard and the cab to the hotel, was quick despite the rain, and waiting in reception, the inimitable sound of London welcoming us in the form of Chris Todd.

## 26. Saturday June 25th. 6.00 pm. Central Taipei. Taiwan.

*Fear of the unknown is invariably worse than fear of the known.*

Chris had already checked us in, so after introducing him to Oleg, our arrival was a quick and easy one. I have always suspected that it's the pressurisation of any airplane, including fancy exec jets, that make all flights, even short ones quite wearing.

Of course the flight from Fallon to Taipei was a longish overnight one and so despite the 'restful relaxing style,' as promised in the air plane brochure, it still took another cold shower to revive me enough for what was going to be a difficult evening.

There's nothing worse than having nothing to report to anxious clients. In a way, even bad news, to a degree is better than no news. Actually reconsidering that, in this case, reporting any news to the *anxious parents of* probably abducted kids is not better than nothing.

In Germany it was now coming up to lunchtime, but still nothing new, just confirmation from Ulrike that she was on the case. So we were a rather pensive trio as our taxi made its way through Taipei's evening traffic the short distance to David and Peggy Lim's house .

The entrance gates were suitably impressive as befitted one of Asia's most successful shipping tycoons, or Chinese Asian ,Tai Pans.

As a smart staff member opened the cab doors, David appeared with his wife and  Hiroshi-san hovering at his elbow.

All of course with a questioning look.

At my, 'nothing yet,' he seemed almost to shrink in stature. But he quickly recovered his composure and showed us in, with a quick burst of Chinese, to Peggy and various anxious staff members who were in the hall, obviously passing on my non encouraging message.

I introduced him to Oleg who came up trumps, that's trumps as in trying, horrible circumstances to reassure parents whose kids have been abducted, or still strictly speaking, probably abducted, saying.

"As Daniel just said, I am here representing the UK Security Service and they are aware of the situation. My chief, Miss Stanton,  who is the head of the  service, is fully committed to offer all our resources to help resolve this. "

"Also Daniel and I were in the USA yesterday and had a meeting with President Appleyard to discuss other aspects of ship and trade security. Given that the disappearance of the girls may well be related to your business, whilst we have no news right now, there's a lot of skilled people looking, and more ready to start looking into this." Oleg smiled encouragingly at the three anxious Asian faces, but got little visible reaction.

I reported on the details from Ulrike in Germany, and continued. "Our priority is getting the girls back safely. I'm going to go to Europe tomorrow or early the next day, but I need some facts first. The most likely clues to the originators of all this-that is if the girls have not just set out on an adventure-are here in Asia. Before I leave I also want to check some threats to disrupt shipping here in Asia first, mainly now as they may be related to the situation with the girls."

David said, "I am sure you're all doing whatever is possible for us. I suspect you could all do with a drink."

Whilst one of his staff served us drinks, we discussed various likely reasons, including my view that it was more likely to be a criminal activity, looking for ransom than political gestures, for the abductions.

" But," I said, "We do not know yet 100% that the girls have been abducted. They may have embarked on a stupid teenage adventure. We are really focused on either scenario, and not waiting for any confirmations either way."

After hearing our updates, and  a brief chat, Hiroshi stepped forward to say he was leaving in David's jet to be with his wife in Tokyo, but that he had wanted to see me first. I suggested to him that, "We will co-ordinate all 'real information' through my office especially as Suki speaks Japanese. She is you and your wife's first line of contact at any hour of the day or night."

I warned him," There will be a lot of rumours when the press get to hear about this, and opportunists trying make money from this. "

"Try to avoid talking to the press under any circumstances- whatever they promise. Press speculation really could endanger the girls. Before you go, let me say this again."

"We only know for sure the girls have left the boat. It is very unlikely there's been an accident- we would have heard. We do not know if they have left of their own accord. To meet boys, an adventure, or even to join a 'save the whale' demonstration. There's a lot of feeling about that in colleges in Europe right now."

"If they have gone not of their own free will, again that could be for campaigning or political reasons. Or it could be an abduction for money. But really note this, if it's an abduction, in all cases, it is in the interest of their abductors to keep them safe and well."

With David's wife, we all went outside and with an unusual amount of hugging for Asia, we saw poor Hiroshi into the car.

Before he left he wound down the window down and said. "Getting Tamiko and the girls back is more important than the ships, the business, money or my life."

Toddy leaned down and right into the car window, and said, "We all know that mate. Don't you worry we'll get 'em home, and if they've been buggering about on some girly adventure, causing all this worry, we'll make 'em carry our golf clubs for eighteen holes . On a hot day." Even Hiroshi smiled. A little wanly- but a real smile.

As Squeeze had said one of the world's richest men really got on very well with our Chris, an ex painter and decorator from Fulham, London.

As he was driven out of the gates, we stood in silence for a moment. The cooling G&T was welcome. I liked the Lim's. They had been clients of the man from whom I bought the company but since then we had become friends.  I had watched their children grow and flourish and had checked out every stage of Mays, European College opportunity. Even to her embarrassment, me getting thrown from her horse.

David said." Daniel ,Chris, Oleg . Peggy and I know you are good men. We know you won't rest till you find her, and the other girls as well. I also know you are well connected." He nodded politely at Oleg.  He went on, "I have some connections also, shall we say, not mentioned in our annual report to shareholders. Old school friends from an age when we all, as Chris taught me to say, 'we ducked and dived ' for a living."

I nodded discretely. He continued, "Those old contacts have chosen to go a different route, on occasions on the other side of the law. But they have on occasions protected us from others, not school friends, who wanted to make trouble with the cargo's, at the docks or even cause delays to ship building if we didn't, shall I say *'pay to join their club'.'*"

"Some clubs I joined, carefully, or there will always be 'a new club' to join.' Some others, Daniel you explained that we didn't want to be in a club that would let just anyone in. Right now I can't remember your Groucho Marx club story."

"But we fixed those problems well you and me, and Rewan before you. Never pressured but always giving a little space even for the bad guys to feed their families."

"Later tonight I am having a meeting with some of those 'club organiser's. They now know about the problem regarding May and Tamiko, and one by one they have called. They are family men also, and although they are not the kind we want to do business with or even be close friends with, in this case they are speaking from their hearts "

" They are asking around, very quietly within those who work on the wrong side of the fence to see what they can learn for us."

He sat back looking calm, and as they say about Chinese business men. Inscrutable. 'Inscrutable.' From miss-use in movies and books, the word has become abused and possibly a little insulting, racist even. In reality, some of the world's greatest, 'and therefor inscrutable,' poker players and gamblers are Chinese.

I nodded and said. "Fine David , I trust your judgement."

Which I did. "But please listen to me. I stress again, rescue heroics are not the way forward. Quiet negotiation is the only safe way. We must ensure there's no jumping to stupid heroics, from the security services or your friends. That also applies to my people, no hero's, just careful planning and we pay if needed."

" Another question is if we have to involve the insurance companies. We have to handle them carefully as they tend to be fixated on saving money more than saving lives."

Another silence broken only by the chink of ice in our glasses, the crackle of logs on the fire, and of course a faint sound from the air conditioning.

I said David, "I am sorry to ask this but can you or Peggy think of any business or family reasons why May might want to run off on an adventure?  Also, earlier you mentioned some 'interesting people' Can we be sure they are not involved, you yourself said, they are in their various unsavoury businesses' worldwide. How did they get to find out about May going missing?"

David, all logic and focus as usual, said. "I agree that kidnapping is not unknown to those criminal elements. Actually they only know because, when I got the first call about May going missing from the school principle in Switzerland, I was at a fundraising lunch here in Taipei, for a special school for disadvantaged kids."

"One of those, 'very borderline,' characters, he was actually from my class at school, has a very needy child in that school. He raises a lot of money to assist."

" There are always private discussions with the school board if we should accept his money, but he always comes with perfect paperwork, so I have to say we, 'look the other way', and accept his money. The school and the children need it."

"I was so shocked at the call from Switzerland, that I told him all about it. I think  his unsavoury friends calling in with offers to help, is kind of their way to say thank you for the work we do for that special school."

I reminded David to be sure and stress the need for secrecy with anyone he spoke with.

He asked his wife, "Can you think of any personal reasons why May should run away." His wife, red eyed and fighting hard to control her emotions said, "I really can't. For sure many girls of her age would be 'teen boy crazy' as we say here."

" But as Hiroshi and I were saying, just before all this happened, May and Tamiko's ongoing interest I horses has been wonderful. It's given them time to grow up before they get pressured by their friends, and todays media, to get that 'boy crazy stage'."

"So ,no reason that I know of. The school principle called an hour ago and said that she had spoken with all their friends and none of them could think of any reasons for the girls to run off. The girls are popular at the school, so she thought they were speaking from their hearts, and not hiding anything."

David said, "Should we come to Europe with you?"

My response was. "Not immediately. I think you should stay here for now, there may be shipping or banking decisions to be made. So at the moment no. If this is a planned and targeted crime then the target is you and any demand will come here. What we do need to do right now though is to set up a record and trace system on all your phones."

My phone went again. An e mail from Barry:*BP.Am in contact Gerry McMullen boss of Calvettioni. More follows. End.*

I mouthed 'Nothing,' at the Lims. As they say in the suspense novels,' the minutes seemed like hours.' Well I can tell you they bloody do. Worse even. Suddenly, every time it's a shock, my phone beeped. Msg. This time it was Squeeze. *SQ. Suki reports Mrs. Yamada near hysterics, blames Brigitte for leading the girls astray. Ends."*

I said to David Lim, "I think we should get back to our meeting room at the hotel, this may go on all night. We'll report immediately when we have something factual to say, day or night. "

"Two things though. Can you immediately get in one of your IT people to set up all your phones, house, office, your cell phones to record all calls. Keep them all, every one. We may need to refer to them later."

" One other thing before we go; As you know we had heard some rumours of an attack on shipping or shippers, which was one reason I went to Europe and then to the USA. We don't know is this is it or connected."

"What you may not know is that earlier today four Calvettioni ships suffered a possible attack with four reefers reporting fire at the same moment. Now of course the kidnappings have added a dimension to that."

David said, "I guess that's what my office have been calling about. I've got a new ship blessing and naming tomorrow lunch time , I was thinking of cancelling it."

I immediately stepped in and said: "I think it's better, if you can , that you are seen to go ahead with that in the usual way. It will help steady the situation and if we can avoid press questions about anything it will be good. Maybe we meet at our hotel when you're on your way to the ship dock, if it's at the usual place, I think that works for the route."

David agreed and said. "Yes, I'll carry on with that, maybe we meet at the hotel at say 10.30,"

With handshakes, and even a hug for me from Mrs. Lim,  I squeezed her hand and said. "Don't worry we'll bring May home."

We walked out to car, Mrs. Lim clutching Chris.

In the car, Oleg said, "You know boss I'm not sure about Mr. Lim's dodgy friends."

Chris said, "And I'm not sure about his 'ducking and diving phrase', he learned that from me, and was staring straight at me when he said it. So I'm a bit worried about his 'friends' as well."

Back in the hotel over yet more snacks, we collated any updates. From Barry, only, that he was still having problems getting direct contact with Mr. Calvettioni. It seems Mrs. Calvettioni was becoming more hysterical and he had a couple of his staff arriving at her house in France shortly. Apart from anything else we needed to set up a call record and trace on her various phones.

 Nothing material from  Ulrike, Oleg's office or Paul Isted here in Asia. I felt a sense of unreality and frustration creeping over the team. As Toddy said, "somewhere there must be something useful."

Eventually we crashed out, despite taking into account it had been almost 30 hours since I had left my bed at Fallon Airbase, it wasn't my impression that I got any sleep.

**27. Sunday.June 26th. 6.00 am.Central Taipei.Taiwan:** *One of those long, getting nowhere slowly, frustrating days when even the slightest hum from the aircon drives you crazy.*

Squeeze and some others have a code number for my phone that can over-ride the off button and makes vile wake up sounds if needed. But this morning I was eventually awoken, from my obviously very deep 'couldn't sleep at all,' by Chris hammering on the room door. "Rise and shine boss, cup of Rosy Lee out here."

We assembled for breakfast.

6.am.Taipei.... Midnight in Europe.

From Barry Purchase: *The four Calvettioni freighters on holding positions awaiting arrival within six hours Naval vessels with Hazchem equipment. Some crews evacuated to company ships nearby. Press sniffing. B.P. Ends*

Second mail from Barry. *Still having problems contacting Mr. Calvettioni. Seems Mrs. C. likes a drink or three, and is mid divorce, hence the communication problems. My team there now- and she has a sister who seems a bit more together. Mr. C. on an island somewhere. With someone. B.Ends.*

Squeeze's attention to company overheads in our early days had meant that as breakfast was usually way cheaper outside hotels, we ate out or brazenly brought them in.

But this morning I had drawn the line at Chris being sent on our usual economy food hunt. I'd had more than enough noodles in plastic bags and 7/11 croissants in Taipei and elsewhere in Asia over the years. Also we hadn't really eaten since we had lunch six thousand miles ago with the commander of the Fallon naval base.

So, full on, cooked English, or American as they called it here, breakfasts, set us three up well for the day. With superb timing Paul Isted turned up as we were finishing our eggs and bacon.

We of course offered him some breakfast.

"Not for me thanks boys, bit early for me. But I'll have a mug of tea though. Looks like you've got the real deal here."

Paul was his usual slightly gruff but always beaming self. He said, "Nothing new to report about the 'whole crew' recruiting, having said that, the 'whole crew suggestion' is odd. Every seaman and even the bar girls know the job agents. "

"One other odd thing, there's a mystery about the 'Mama' who told me about the crews getting paid to take time off. She's gone off the radar."

I started to tell him about the probable abductions in Germany, and he stopped me and said, "I got all that updated from Squeeze yesterday. Sounds more like teenage tantrums than criminal, but you never know anything in those cases until the kidnapped or the kidnappers make contact."

"Mind you if it is a kidnap, someone's done their re-search. It's a big attack on a serious chunk of shipping. Maybe that's what we're hearing stories about. Or the four ships with fires."

I told him about the Hazchem warnings slowing down the investigation into those ships. He grunted. I continued, "But you'll like this one. Thanks to your reminder about bars using week numbers, not day and date systems, we managed to reduce the entire alphabetical world of US security to shocked silence."

" The final pay off line of, 'using week numbers, not US style dates, the threat is not for 27th January but July 4th' being the stunner."

His comment. "Daft bastards, and those bars are packed with US Marines, Navy, Air Force personnel."

I told him of our concerns about David Lim's so called 'school friends.'

His response was, that many Asian billionaires of today had quite humble origins. How they got to where they are is not always clear. There are many stories of funny money and political favour. Indeed some of the original entrepreneurial characters quite relished stories of being well 'connected with likely lads.' But these days of course with their companies being stock exchange listed and their sons graduates with MBA's from the best business schools in the world such old matters were best left sleeping.

About David Lim he had never heard anything more than 'the usual stories'.

He concluded, "Mind you if he is still 'well connected,' even if it's purely nostalgia and old contacts, the Taiwanese and Chinese diaspora worldwide is so immense so it may yet be a tool to be used. Could be a bloody useful information source."

After sharing a few more EB teas with us, and having regaled Oleg with scandalous stories of life in Moscow during the cold, war he left, agreeing to meet Chris at ten in the evening to see what they could turn up about our crew hiring mystery man.

Chris and he were old mates.

Paul said finding the face who was offering VLCC crew jobs was like looking for a "virgin in any of those bars." But he and Chris would give it a good shot, even if it meant visiting many of those portside bars. Purely on business you'll understand."

After Paul left, I pondered. Were our client's daughters in real trouble, or were they in a bit of average teenage trouble, listening to music, drinking red wine, and enjoying the attentions of some nice young male friends. With no demands from anyone the current indications were that a student jape was still a possibility.

I said to Oleg. "One minute we're dining with the president of the USA worrying about the safety of the world shipping, and the next we're worrying about the virginity or not of both bar girls and our client's daughters."

"I get that" said Oleg, "and I've been thinking about that also. Not their virginity, but all the time I come back to, is the shipping connection a co-incidence because they are a team of friends, and so they would get into scrapes together ?  Or as you said, is it related to these hi powered tip offs and warnings?"

I agreed, "If it's not Fergal Sharkey and the Undertones with 'Teenage Kicks.' it may be Ella Fitzgerald "This Could be the Start of Something Big.""

Oleg gazed at me open mouthed, "I don't know that music boss. Before my time, but I think I know what you mean."

I retorted, "The Lims will be here in a minute, I wonder if they managed to get any kip?"

Oleg, "If you're going to talk London style ,I'd better spend more time with Chris.  But I'm not sure how to catch up on forty years of old song titles !"

This time there was no reverse thrust airplane engine noise to cover up my F*** Off. Just the sound of the doorbell.'

It was the Lim's. Predictably looking pale and drawn.

Whilst Chris organised tea and water, we got Squeeze in Singapore and Hiroshi and his wife from Tokyo on a conference call, their amplified voices sounding a little echoey and now again the sad sound of Mrs. Yamada sniffing.

I reported. Pausing now and again for Hiroshi to translate for his wife. "Rather as I expected there's been no word from anyone yet. This really just confirms no accidents, and suggests student's playing games. But we are all working as if it is an abduction."

"*We know some stuff,* but not much:"

" What time they had left the ship. They had been seen getting into a taxi. Their bracelets showed they returned but video numbers of returnees don't add up. So we assume they never re-boarded."

"The stables had confirmed to the German police that three girls had been to the stables on a 'usual tour.' They had seen the horses, watched demonstrations of dressage, been to the shop and it was believed they had a Taxi waiting outside for them. They guessed that they had left around 1.30 to 2.00."

" Some security cam footage at the stables confirmed they the only visitors, and indeed they had a taxi waiting outside, but the camera showed no useful detail."

"Then we had a blank and knew nothing until the Computer at the gangplank to the ship checked their numbers in during a rainstorm around 5.00. We don't know where they were what they did – nothing."

In Taipei we heard a flood of Japanese from Mrs. Yamada in Tokyo ---- and eventually Hiroshi saying, "My wife says, we do know somethings because the girls send she some picture on that day."

Chaos broke out with everyone taking at once.

Chris took control. Strong steady voice. "Hiroshi -San send those pictures to me or Daniel. Now please. We will wait."

A few minutes later we were sharing the view of six pictures on my laptop.

1. A selfie picture. Two girls, Brigitte and Tamiko, river, some hills and in the foreground presumably the rail of the boat.

2. The three girls under a sign in old style German. Something something Fahrman. Fields and fences. Presumably the stables.

3 and 4. A couple of selfies of Tamiko and the other two girls with horses in the background.

5. A slight blurred and crooked shot of the girls at a restaurant table.

6. A better straight focused shot. All three girls, Pizza's on the table and a busy street outside. Lots of shopping bags on a spare chair.

Oleg said immediately. "Copy them to me I'll get our people to check them out."

Chris said, "Hang on everyone. What we want to know is who took the group picture at the stables, and who took the picture in the restaurant." This started a discussion guessing that the stables shot was done by the cab driver and the restaurant by a waiter or waitress.

We ran through various logistics, with me suggesting they, "Extended their 'record all phone calls', to include Grand Ma's and others close to the family."

As David and Peggy left to attend the ship naming, Kenji, stressed again, "Getting the girls back is more important than our life, business or any money we have." The Lim's both agreed.

We agreed to meet the Lim's across town in a couple of hours at the naming and blessing ceremony for the ship.

Copies of the pics went to Ulrika, Barry Purchase, my office and Oleg got talking to his photo experts in London. " They should be able to tell us time of day, see what's outside those windows."

We were just starting another conference call with Ulrika, Barry, when Squeeze said, 'it's the The Pizza Real.'

Shocked silence, followed by Chris saying, "Wife. How the F*** d'you know that?"

To which Squeeze replied, "Read the bloody backwards writing in the café window, Di**head."

Whilst order was restored Oleg, laptop working flat out as usual, said. "OK. Ulrika there's a Pizza Real in Mainz, that's not far."

Ulrike, "I'll get down there now."

Barry spoke up. "Dan, nice to hear your multi-talented team in action-before you all rush off, a few words on the ship Hazchem situation. The French Navy are waiting in the Indian ocean near the Calvettioni Eiger for an improvement in the weather to launch one of their helicopters. They have plans to get some samples from some poor 'dope dangling on a rope' in a full Hazchem kit."

"Ditto the US Navy somewhere between Hawaii and L.A. As right we now don't know if there's booby trapped systems on board ,they are going the French route with a heliman on a rope, investigation on Calvettioni Mont Blanc. A British frigate is almost alongside Calvettioni Kilimanjaro between The Canary islands and UK but they've busted their helicopter. I am waiting to hear from them."

"And lastly off Northern Florida the US coastguard are on the scene with Calvettioni Olympus, people there are also talking helicopters with sniffers etc. That's it for now."

Before we closed off the call I asked Barry to check with Mr. and Mrs. Calvettioni to see if they had received any pictures or anything in fact from the girls.

Barry said, "I'll work on that. We at last know Mr. Calvettioni is due back in France today. He was on a Pacific Island somewhere with no airstrip and almost no electrics or phone. Right now he seems more concerned about the boats than his daughter, which is odd. I'm looking into that one as well."

It was soon time to cross town in the Taipei traffic and out to the main dock area for the ship blessing and naming.

Chris and I left Oleg on line in the hotel and the team at their research in about five countries, and right outside the hotel door, soon found the Mercedes that Lim had sent for us.

Our main conversation on the thirty minute drive was about cars. Mercs indeed, and how many Asians found it very difficult to pronounce Mercedes, therefor in most countries out here they are usually referred to as, 'Benz.'

In Thailand they pronounce it Mer-Sadists, which I thought was due to the spares and servicing costs, but it seems that's just the way Thai's read it. With rain and traffic we were a little late when we entered the dock area, and as we did, I got a txt from Ulrika: *Two Girlie Phones just logged on and then off in Venice. Am checking. U.S. Ends*

I told Chris ,and intended to tell the Lim's, but as we entered at the back of a crowded tent over the fourth floor terrace of the dock building we could see the ceremony in full swing.

Massive ship docked just meters away, too big to see the top or either end. Monks, incense, some chanting- live and recorded I think. Prayers, speeches, lots of photos, awards to what looked like workers, managers, shipwrights and lots of suits.

I guess Mayors, bank managers, suppliers, would be customers.

Very much part of the handshake and Asian style bowing line, were some guys in smart Naval style uniforms, some Asian, and an Indian looking gent.

Also several westerners, blue navy jackets, gold braid, white shirts. Caps with discrete gold braid, not weekend boaty type scrambled eggs on the hat. I recognised them.

Yet again my Naval history bug cut in, and I was trying to remember navy talk. Dressed in, 'Number Nines'- or was it 'Number Ones', or was that what Jack Hawkins or David Niven always called their other officers in the black and white movies.

We waited. Champagne was opened. Canapes served. Lots of mingling. Still the sound of drums and the odd waft of incense from down on the dockside. Chris and I stayed discretely at the back.

I watched David Lim, followed politely as is often the Asian way by Peggy his wife. David- full of smiles, sincere handshakes, pat's on the back, 'Job well done' I could almost hear him say.

I muttered to Oleg that you'd never think he had a care in the bloody world. Very professional. Good job we stayed out of sight back here, we might have put him off his stroke.

Eventually the crowd thinned, and Peggy spotted us, and as predicted rushed across to us. Chris slipped an arm through hers. "Nothing very new to tell you. We believe the phones are now in Venice. Our people are there looking into it, but it means very little."

David Lim approached us with two of the westerners , I then realised I had met them a few years back at David's house. Steve Brown and Doug Graham-Smith, his two most senior Captains. Both British, I'd even visited one of them briefly at his house in Windsor just to the west of London.

Chris and I had stopped talking to Mrs. Lim, but she said, "go on, go on, its not much but tell David."

I glanced at the Brit Captains, and David said, "It's OK they're aware of everything, firstly as friends they are staying in our guest house, and secondly as the senior captains in our fleet they need to know."

So I re- capped about Venice and stressed, 'This doesn't mean much'. Not even that the girls are there. My phone rang.

The Lims started to hyperventilate. Chris jumped in quickly. "Venice either means the girls have gone off on a razzle, or can mean someone is holding the girls, or they have just lost their phones. If they have been abducted it will be to collect some money or make a political point. So believe us they won't harm them."

The Lim's went from collapsed panic to collapsed relief.

Mrs. Lim said, "What about poor Hiroshi and Shoko, do they know?" I said, "That was my call, Suki in our office, she's talking to Mr. and Mrs. Yamada."

We continued to fill them in on all we knew. Ulrike had reported that a waitress at the pizzeria remembered the girls from the photo, and also remembered they had so much shopping. Not only that but she remembered the bags. Turned out to be more horse stuff from a shop just around the corner from the pizzeria. "All of this suggests all was normal at least until about 4 in the afternoon when they left the Pizzeria."

"We're now evaluating what we tell the German Police, despite their resources, if this is an abduction don't want heavy booted German Cops crashing around."

I noticed the Brit Captains raising an eyebrow at my Heavy Booted Germans. So I explained that in the stress of ransom payment confrontations, safe recovery of the abductees sometimes got compromised in the heat of any payment/rescue/arrest situation. In our opinion insurance company recovery teams had the reputation of being heavy handed.

"We've noticed that in Somalia." said Steve. At which I had to smile slightly. I declined offers to return to the city with the Lim's and said, "I am still looking for connections to the business out here, but I am pretty sure we'll take your plane to Europe tomorrow unless you need it, in which case we can get one of our own."

David said, "No, take it, We're running the plane's as a business so now we have another one also and with several crews there. So anytime you need, it can be ready in a couple of hours. I'll make sure they realise you have absolute priority. If you want me to come with you..." I stopped him

"No, I want you to hold the fort here. There will be things to be done and keeping the business operating in the usual way stops the, potential for other problems. Also if we get ransom demands you'll need to be here for a while I would think."

I continued, "I am glad you've got Steve and Doug here for a few days. It's good to talk this stuff through."

In the car I remarked to Chris, "I nearly fell into the bloody 'bad people' phrase again. Having dropped him off for his research evening with Paul Isted I returned to the Hotel.

Obviously, as the evening progressed in Taipei towards 8 PM it was still only 2 or 3 in the afternoon in most of Europe. So I planned to spend a long evening on the phones. I realised after a while that Oleg was fading a bit. "You've been on your computer almost non-stop for 24 hours, I think you'd do better if you took a break."

After some protests from him, that he was too 'wired' to sleep, I made a couple of phone calls to Chris and Paul.

Oleg and I went down stairs and with some knowing smiles from the hotel doorman we dispatched him to 'The Lucky Red Lips' bar not far from the shipyard where I had been earlier.

The doorman giving him a couple of address cards for the hotel 'To show Taxi and get you back here.'

I returned upstairs and indeed spent the evening on the phones. Barry, Geoff Barker, Hiroshi, Miss Stanton, Ulrike and several others. In the end around midnight, still early evening in Europe, I too gave up and turned in.

But this time my usual ability to, re charge at any time in any place, let me down and my racing brain kept me awake for almost the whole bloody night.

I flipped channels on the TV. There was a hint on CNN that a container ship was hove too off Florida with unspecified problems, but that only rated a mention as they were presenting live pictures of some 'great white shark' search.

I had flipped more channels, checked my phone and laptops constantly, all in all, a crap way to end one, and start another busy day.

A few hours later Ulrike reported in. She had arrived in Venice. Unfortunately the log on and tracking information from the phone company came delivered as she put it, "by a whole flock of Carabinieri.'

They said the phones were at or near Venice airport. It seems they had been told by their German counterparts that it was likely 'three stupid girls have run off from school. Probably with some boys.' As it happened that quite suited us. Some police awareness and vigilance but not 'gung ho' style.

\*\*\*\*\*\*\*\*\*\*\*

Unbeknown to Ulrika as she reported to me, another German was not far away. He was sitting in a dusty Merc about two k's from where she stood.

The German was tired, having driven pretty nonstop from a riverside boat stop on the river Rhine. Some alpine tunnels, fantastic Italian roads.

Somewhat less than fantastic Italian drivers and a definitely less than fantastic four hours rest in a roadside motel. In a room that smelt of old cigarettes. For a rabid hater of smoking this pissed him off.

What was pissing him off also right now was the discovery that both of the phones into which he had inserted sim card and batteries a few hours earlier now had no power.

More to the point neither did he have the right chargers, and so far he had been to three shops to try and get new ones.

He drove slowly out of the parking lot in search of a big shopping center with he hoped, a choice of Phone shops.

No batteries, meant the tracker trail had gone cold.

## 28. Sunday. June 26th. Morning. The Old Mill In the Sun.

**South Western France:** *Quite nice. But not really their choice for a holiday.*

Even the three girls slept a little easier after Britt-Marie's comment the previous evening that, 'The behaviour of their captors was seemingly quite kind, with their efforts being made to make captivity for the kids and thus them at least bearable'.

Or as bearable as can be when wearing an explosive necklace.

So they breakfasted together, although Anna did have to remind the girls "Eat to stay strong."

The three girls joined Britt and the children in the pool for a game of volleyball. It took their minds of their precarious position, actually fun, boisterous and noisy. So noisy in fact that they didn't hear the arrival of the car outside the gate until, they we're surprised by a shout from one of their captors.

"OK girls, time to send your families some holiday snaps, and later you can call them. I want all the Swedish over here by the big door, and you other three girls we're going to take the picture over there."

The girls came out of the water and grabbed towels.

Britt-Marie grabbed Tamiko's new German stables T shirt and put it on quickly as she started to help the children who were asking many questions.

Tamiko mentioned the shirt and Britt said, "Sorry, grab a clean one of mine from the pile there, I don't really like these guys looking at us when we change. I'll give this one back in a minute."

With encouraging and kind words to the children, their two captors lined up the Swedes against a set of double doors into one of the barns and took a couple of pictures.

They got Brigitte, May and Tamiko at the other end of the complex and photographed them against one of the old stone walls.

The guard they knew as Pete jogged out of the main gates and returned with a bags and cool box. " Here you are girls, fresh croissants and kids, Ice Creams for you."

In the eager chaos of three youngsters grabbing Cornetto's out of the cool box, he spoke quietly to Britt- Marie, handing her a piece of paper as he did so.

" There's some words here that we want you read out later when you call home. I want you to go through this with the other girls. You can use English or Swedish and they can use French, Chinese Japanese, whatever. "

"You can't answer any questions and remember the necklaces. We have people listening to the calls and any clever stuff from you will make some orphans or sad parents."

Britt nodded. Maybe she was getting used to the control by fear.

Pete continued. "Now write down your husbands and your dads numbers including any dialing codes. Get the other three girls to write down their mums numbers."

Britt organised the collection of the numbers and Pete said he'd return in an hour or so to make the calls. Having got the children engrossed in a major Lego construction project the five women went through the script left by Pete, line by line.

**29.Sunday June 26th.7.30 pm.Faro Airport. Algarve. Southern Portugal:**"*We have just landed at Faro, Portugal, where the local time is.*"

Magnus Sorensen, having indeed had a smooth, busy and relatively speedy trip across the Atlantic on a massive cargo ship, noted, as his plane came in to land at the beach side airport of Faro, that the ocean on the Southern Algarve coast was still smooth.

He had to squint a little to see the water, as a big red summer sun was preparing to set over that very sea. Freight congestion had meant that his mighty container ship had to slow a little on it's approach to Rotterdam. To his annoyance, searching online he found the only direct flight from Rotterdam to southern Portugal left at 10 am. Too early for his ship's arrival.

Keen to get away to the beaches, golf course and above all his wife and daughters, he shared an expensive taxi with the ships chief engineer to Schiphol Airport Amsterdam. Magnus just made it in time to get the 5.00 evening Transavia flight to Faro. The ships engineer going to Stockholm, Sweden..

Despite it being an almost three hour flight, he had landed a few minutes early for once, a few minutes after 7.00 pm. He'd gained an hour, as the Portuguese kept their clocks on English time. Some said this was a tradition to annoy the Spanish.

With hand baggage only, carrying his Atlantic Ocean storm wear, he exited through the EC customs channel and in the terminal scanned the faces for his wife. He had sent her a text in good enough time for her to meet the flight.

But there was no familiar welcoming smile. He searched around, tried her cell phone again-- and getting no response assumed the lack of a decent phone signal at his villa meant the message had not got through. Had she been delayed on the road she would have noted his latest call or sent him an sms.

So he joined the taxi queue and gave the driver instructions to drive along the N125 toll road and take an exit right at Alvor into the Monchique hills.

Being high season for tourists and busy with traffic, it was just over an hour later that he paid off the cab and noting his wife's car in the driveway, went around through the side garden gate to the pool area and found :

No one. The remains of some dishes on the table-rather dried up. A plastic bag had blown into the pool otherwise nothing untoward. House all locked up.

Digging deep into his travel bag for some keys he rather assumed that his wife and children were ten minutes down the road at her father's house - where her sister was staying with her kids. Cursing the lack of a phone signal he found the keys to his wife's car and set off to his father in laws.

There he encountered one familiar face at least. The Portuguese housekeeper, Ermalinda. With some difficulty, in a mix of Portuguese, English, signs and mimes he established that 'No, missy Anna and Britt, she and the babies were at his Casa.'

So rejecting offers of Tea, Coffee, beer ,water and a bit pissed off by now he set off back to his house ,but relaxed somewhat when he realised that probably his wife hadn't received his text confirming his arrival.

It was quite dark by the time he returned, and having put on the patio lights, and had a quick shower by the pool ,it wasn't until he sat down with a beer that it occurred to him that Anna's car was at her dads house, Britt's was here at his.

So if the girls had been back at the water slides- how had they got there. It was also late now for them to return, even if they had stopped for food.

It then dawned on him that even if she hadn't received the text, and she wasn't at home she would have had a good phone signal almost everywhere else in the Algarve.

He walked up on to the roof terrace  where sometimes he could get a few bars of a signal. Tried his wife's and her sister's number again. Both had a message in Portuguese presumably stating no connection for now. He was leaning on the terrace wall - happy at least to be in the peace of the Algarve for three weeks vacation when his phone rang.

He snatched it up and said ' Hello darling, where are you."

A somewhat surprised - and slightly blurred (bad signal) male voice said, "It's Jose, I'm just down the road, you have time for a beer?"

Magnus said, "'Yes, yes...come round I'll explain.”

A few minutes later, after friendly handshakes and pats on the back with his great friend Jose Seremenho, Magnus started to explain the situation.

Jose was an Algarvian builder, who long ago had encountered Britt and Anna's father  when he was hired to make  some alterations to his golf course house. The multi billionaire shipping company magnate with a fleet of around 4000 ships had become close friends with the calm reliable Jose-son of a fisherman who's only boat, hardly a ship, was less than 5 meters long.

Not only was Jose good company, and barbecued some mean sardines he was a good and serious builder.  When Magnus joined the family by marriage, it was Jose who built the villa in which they now stood, on a plot of land purchased years before by his wife's father and given to his daughter and Magnus as a wedding present.

"Beer or wine ? " said Magnus. "It's almost nine o'clock so wine is good," said Jose. Magnus found plenty of ice cold Aveleda Vino Verde in the fridge, and they adjourned outside...and after a few enquiries about Jose's new Brazilian wife and child, Magnus started to explain his worries..
"Not met at airport. Not good but possibly because no message received."

"No phone response then and now. Not good."

"No messages or notes. Not good."

"If there had been an accident or emergency one or other of the sisters would surely by now have called. So not so bad."

"Not only that, we know where both cars are so they haven't had a car accident, but they can't be shopping."

Jose agreed, and with some hesitation, looking at his friend with concern said, "I assume everything is ok between you and Britt. I mean....."
..Magnus interrupted and said, "Sure it's never been better, we were both really looking forward to this holiday and time together."

He jumped to his feet, "I know," and ran into the house saying, " I'm going to check the safe box. In a couple of minutes he returned, looking shaken and said, "Their passports aren't there. "

"Although if you drive here you're supposed to carry it, she has a colour photocopy in her bag as she's always scared of losing the actual passport. So all the passports live in the box from the day we arrive until the day we leave. Her jewelry is in the box so we've not had a robbery."

Jose said, "Something's not right. I think we should call the police."

They were both very aware that some years before an English child had gone missing, presumed abducted from an apartment in not so far away Praia da Luz. The Portuguese police had been much criticised, probably somewhat unfairly, for a slow response to the emergency.

Jose said, "OK I'll go down to the corner of the road and call the police in Portemao. You look around for anything worrying."

He was gone for about ten minutes and returned to find Magnus slumped in the chair. " I don't know about clothes and stuff because Britt packed all that, but I can see that the duvet on Liv's bed is not there and nor are her special soft toys, she can never get to sleep without them."

Jose told him the police were on their way.

He omitted the conversation he had, in which the desk duty officer had said, "If I had a 100 euros for every time I turn out my men each time some holidaymaking couple have a domestic argument, I'd be a rich man."

Jose had then spoken to a senior officer with whom he had been to school, and remained friends with over the years at their monthly, 'Friday lunch club' at which fifty or even more sardines were consumed, per person, washed down with copious amounts of wine.

A few minutes later flashing blue lights reflected over the house, and three police officers entered through the side gate to the patio area, where Magnus had now also turned on the lights throughout the villa.

Jose, having made the introductions, had a long conversation with the officers in rapid Portuguese.

After a while the officers said, in not bad English. "At first three questions".

"How long have they been missing?"

"When did you get here, and where have you been?"

"How do you know that they haven't just now returned to your father's house down the hill or even to their home country?".

Magnus gasped at the third question and said, " Maybe I should call Sweden and check- but I need a phone signal".

Jose interjected and said- "Actually it's his wife's father's house. I'll go to Mr. Haeggqvist's house and check. We don't want Ermalinda to collapse with shock."

After a little more Portuguese in which he confirmed that indeed Ermalinda was the same Ermalinda, who had been in their class at school. The policeman said, "Do you mind sir if one of my men takes a look around your house?" Magnus, now in somewhat of a daze, waved him to carry on.

The senior policemen looked at him and said. "And where have you been, and when did you get here."

Magnus ,speaking slowly told him about New York, and mentioned that he had spoken to his wife ten days ago. He'd got in to Rotterdam at around 3 that afternoon and flown from Amsterdam this very evening.

The police man looked sceptical and said," And you and your wife, everything is OK between you? "

Magnus's, "Yes," was listened to and the policemen then went on, "Then why is your wife on holiday then without you?"

His explanation of school holiday schedules, his job responsibilities and the fact that his wife had other family in the Algarve seemed to be accepted.

Anxious to avoid more misunderstandings he fumbled around in his pockets and produced the stub of his boarding card, and also chanced up the receipt from the taxi which had brought him from Faro to the villa.

The officer, having asked one of his men to call the cab driver using the number on the receipt, then said '"Then it is possible that they left here ten days ago. You were on a boat all that time."

Magnus explained that there were many on the boat who could confirm that, but indeed his wife could could have left at any time whilst he was at sea.

The other police man returned and in rapid Portuguese confirmed the taxi journey, and pointed out to his boss that the receipt printout was timed as well as dated. The young policeman who had been searching the villa came out and had some quiet words in Portuguese with his senior.

The senior said to Magnus. "You will be pleased to know we can see no obvious signs of any struggle or disruptions."

Jose returned and said, " No one at the other house except Ermalinda, and I called the Swedish number and your housekeeper answered, and said the girls were in Portugal."

The senior officer said. "OK, it seems that our friend here can make a good account of his position over the past ten days since he last spoke with his wife. But we have no idea of his wife intentions or movements during those ten days that they have been missing."

Jose interrupted, *"Actually it's not ten days they have been missing its five. The two sisters and the children all had food at the other house five days ago.* They had come back from the water park that way, to leave some laundry and collect clean clothes. They came away from that villa loaded food and wine for Magnus's arrival, and with some of Ermalinda's homemade pastal de nata."

Magnus, rushed into the house and said, "The fridges have loads of fresh food in, and some of these," Holding out the familiar Pastel de Nata. 'egg custard cakes.'

The senior policemen looked serious and said, perhaps a touch wearily. "Then as I said, the missing may not be missing, just visiting someone for a few days," and looking at Magnus said, "And do you have any idea whom that may be?"

"No, there's no one." was the almost shouted response.

The policeman sighed and said- "Sir, you were not on holiday with your wife, you were not here during that ten days, you don't really know if much of their clothes are missing as you didn't become involved in the packing. There seems to be a lot you do not know."

"I will put out a call- and alert officers, but with no missing vehicles , a description of two Swedish looking ladies -and three children - blonde  is not much to go on.  It fits thousands on holiday here in Portugal and throughout the Spanish coast. But we will of course do our best duty. You can rely on us, do you have some photos in the house we can have just in case."

He stood as did his colleagues. Magnus was just about to enter the house when he said, "Hang on I may have better than that," and retrieved his phone. "I've got a picture of all of them ten days ago in Portemao that Britt sent to my phone."

He showed around a good bright smiling picture of the two women and three children- sitting at a table with the remains of ice creams, glasses all around. "It must have been taken by a waiter, I know she sent it then because I had it before we sailed out of Newark."

The policeman looked serious. "Perhaps you could blue tooth that to me," said the policeman, and followed up with, " You said Newark. Earlier you told me you were in New York. You have changed the story?"

Magnus explained New York being one side of the Hudson River and the main ports of New Jersey and Newark being on the other.

The policeman nodded. "Good. Now we'll go to Portemao and see just who took that picture, just in case there's someone else involved," and having shaken hands, spoken with Jose, and departed saying. "Contact me immediately you have news."

Magnus slumped in his chair, head in hands, "They don't believe there is a problem."

Jose said, "Actually they are starting to. He will do what he said. That picture was a good idea." Magnus shrugged. Jose went on," Actually Jorge is a very bright guy, he picked up on the New York - Newark point very quickly."

Magnus said, grudgingly, "Well he may be a bright cop but geography's obviously not his strong point. "He sat up abruptly. "The bloody alarm system wasn't on. Britt drives me crazy sometimes, she always sets it even if we're just popping down to village for five minutes. That's very odd."

"I'm going to go down to the other house to use the phone and call old man Haeggqvist and also our security people at the office."
As they locked up the house, he scrawled a note and put it on the kitchen table, 'Am down at your dads house. Magnus 10 pm.xxx.'

In the car he explained to Jose that the call to the security people wasn't to be about the alarm system, but with Charlie's family being well known and wealthy they had a company who kept a watch on family as well as company safety.

This time they accepted Ermalinda's offer of food, despite the late hour she seemed happy to have people to care for.

Magnus managed to get hold of his father in law who was on his plane somewhere over the USA, and making for the Algarve.

His response was a mix of instant concern, tempered with, "Nothing those girls get up to surprises me."

He approved or agreed with Magnus's plan to call the security people. "Try and get hold of that Purchase guy at Matchless, he always seemed like an able captain to me." With a quick, 'keep me informed,' the line was cut.

Smiling at Haeggqvist's nautical reference Magnus searched around in his phone looking for Barry Purchase's number, thinking as he did so, when he gave me that number he told me to put it on quick dial as when I called him it would be in an emergency

Accepting a glass of red wine put into his free hand, Magnus spoke to and then listened to Barry Purchase for some time. "OK, OK, we'll see you then. I'll call the police here, and I'll send you the picture."

He slumped back, this time exhausted more than frustrated. "He thinks it may be serious, so Barry's is going to be here tomorrow as soon as he can."

" It seems that some daughters of some other ship-owners have also gone missing in Germany "

"But he very strongly wants us and the police to keep this quiet."

" The point being the girls are worth millions and if it gets into the press too quick then there will be thousands of opportunist calls from people looking to win the jackpot with a big reward. It will screw up things for the police at this stage."

Jose said. "I get that, stupid opportunists caused a lot of wasted efforts here with the missing girl. I'll call Jorge now and get him round here to explain. I think as it's me, and given the circumstances, he'll understand very well "

As he got on the phone, Ermalinda appeared on the terrace and bustled around laying out plates and things on the table.

Jose put his hand over the mouthpiece of his phone and said to Ermalinda. "You'd better make that table ready for three people, I've got an old admirer of yours coming round in a minute."

**30.Monday June 27th. 5.00 am.Central Taipei.Taiwan:**
*Fans come in various modes. Wild and enthusiastic, as in music or
football crazy, or slow and languid, as in 'Asian tropical cooling'
necessity. Rotating or old style 'punka-flip flap', mode optional.*


Needing sleep belied the concern and urgency and of the situation. I
guess the re-charging factor was useful. Oleg claimed to have banged on
my bedroom door three times before I heard him calling me from the
adjoining room. " Six o'clock, cup of Rosy Grey here boss."

Having corrected his London rhyming slang, I was relieved to find a
large size paper cup full with good EBT and not the dreaded Earl Grey, with
it's taste of bergamot sun cream.

I thanked him for going out to the 7/11 across the street to get it, which
he now knew was our usual company way to save the petty cash.

Oleg, "I didn't go to the 7/11, there's free coffee, tea and muffins in the
lobby, makes it easy for early arrivals and departures. Apart from that, as
Squeeze kept saying, 'keep all the receipts, you can now bill Uncle Sam via
Matchless."

But free tea was better, and it was life saving, or at least kick-starting.
He told me that he had just seen Chris coming in looking, 'interesting.' but
that as he was in the coffee shop, Chris was in the lift before Oleg got there.

We shared out the muffins and croissants.

"Talk of the devil," I said as Chris entered, hair wet from the shower.
"Bloody hair of the dog may be what I need." he said. "That Paul, I don't
know how he does it. I'm getting too old for this."

He turned to Oleg, "After you left, about one, I think that was, we went
onto about another ten bars. I left him to it still plugged into a beer talking
to some old bird who ran a bar near where we started yesterday."

"I guess she'll be the bar boss. 'The Mamasan'," I explained to Oleg.
"Controls everything, the prices, how much they water down the booze, the
girls, everything. They know everything."

"Blimey, thanks Oleg," as Oleg gave him a cup of tea, and told him they
were free down in the lobby. Chris continued. "Well apart from about 50 or
so little Chinese girls and a few 'almost girls' telling me and Oleg, 'They
loved us, most handsome man' in every bar, there's only one thing to
report. Paul found out that one of the Mamasan's did know the face of the
guy who had been talking about hiring people of all skills a few weeks back.
He wasn't a regular but she would know him again."

Chris continued, "I said to Paul, we should put her on a bonus of $1000
if she could let us know when he came in again. Paul said, that wasn't

enough because if her network of bar ladies found him they'd only ask the guy for $1500 not to tell anyone."

"So Paul told her it was a newspaper story, and he'd share the money with her, probably $5000 maybe more, but first he had to talk to the guy to get the story. So if she frightened the guy away they all lost."

Overnight I noted a mail in from Barry in Washington :

*Shipping and freight fires: No traces Hazchem's. But containers not yet opened in case of booby traps. US and other authorities raising the terrorist alert level at all ports, freight terminals, suggesting same for Panama, Suez ,St Lawrence Seaway and similar narrow waterways.*

*Girls missing Germany : Nothing new. BP.ends.*

Chris went off, for a sleep. I ran through our other business with Squeeze. Keeping all the various clients safe happy and informed that they were being cared for. I messaged the Yamada's and Lim's with nothing to report, but didn't really imagine it made them feel cared for.

I then stretched back, and in a kind of blur gazed at the ceiling fan. Fans are a much needed feature in the heat and humidity of Asia, despite modern air con which is what really keeps us cool.

As usual, our hotel room was indeed equipped with fan. In this case a large and impressive, shiny, brass, slow moving, circulating five blader. More for old time Colonial style effect, than cooling, but pleasant all the same.

By 8.00,we'd started at 5.00, I was thinking about coffee. Enter Chris with a selection of exactly that.

Chris was not happy. "I got them from the bloody lobby coffee shop, but then I learned it's only free until 7.30 in the morning. Cost an arm and a leg." Before we could take this 'domestic' conversation further all the phones burst into life pretty much together.

Oleg's: Message. *'London, say trackers turned on and off again in Venice."*

Chris: "It was Paul. One of the Mamasan's says 'The face's telephone number was in Philippines. But no, they don't have it now, as the girl who had it has lost her bloody phone."

Mine was a game changer: *Sms/txt from J & S and SQ. Flash. Just found: Portugal. Sat. 12.00 Midnight. Portemao Police in Algarve report some Swedish girls missing. Families Sorenson / Haeggqvist. They Matchless clients so think unlikely or we would know. We're checking. Repeat Swedish girls gone missing. ends.*

Having shared the news with Chris and Oleg, I was sitting back gazing at the slowly rotating fan. Chris said, "Penny for your thoughts boss."

I responded, "I was looking at the fan and just thinking that it doesn't look like the sh*t has hit it, but I suspect it may have done."

"But Haeggqvist's are Matchless Consulting clients so possibly can't be so, or we would have heard from Barry. We don't want to waste time speculating on a lot of 'what if's? "

"But if there's any truth in the missing Haeggqvist family members, that suggests the three girls in Germany aren't out playing stupid games. That also suggests a coordinated attack on four of the biggest freight and shipping concerns in the world."

Oleg who had been furiously working his laptop said, "I did some research on all this yesterday, and he passed over his lap top for me to read:

*Between them, the Lim's, Yamada's , Calvettioni's and now adding in the Haeggqvist's it's about 53% of world freight by volume. 27% of active refrigerated freight shipping.*

*Almost 2200 ships of all kinds which 900 are active in intercontinental freight, the rest local. Originating and delivery ports 1672, including smaller vessels, with local stuff. Ships mostly hardened against piracy but no armed guards on board as far as we know.*

*Oil and gas transportation not global speciality, but some subsidiary companies doing oil and gas rig support, ferry services etc. So many local contracts for that. Some land transport as back up, also land based facilities companies.*

*BOSN, the Haeggqvist company have a number of leasing agreements with US military. Some dry leases for ship use only by the forces, others are "wet leases' where they are contracted to deliver freight, arms, troops.*

*I am not sure yet about Lim and Yamada freight/ship use breakdown it's less publicised, or not so much in English.*

*It's not easy to get real facts about Calvettioni, but there are a stories out there suggesting they have cash-flow problems. Recently a Cyprus based trading company was apparently buying into the Calvettioni business.*

*The four families privately control the majority of their company shares some in private companies and some quoted on various stock exchanges.*

As I passed the screen back to Oleg he said, "That's it for now."

I reacted: "Okay, lets get that story cleaned up and encoded. If Jacko's rumour from Portugal is right we may need it in a minute."

I leaned back in the chair and studied the fan again, looking for signs of sh*t sticking to it.

I found them about 30 minutes later with a call from Barry Purchase. Barry. "I just spoke to Magnus Sorensen, midnight Portuguese time. He's married to one of Charlie Haeggqvist's daughters. He called our people. "

"It appears his wife, her sister and their three kids have gone missing, not seen for five days. No evidence of any struggles or notes. He called Portuguese police who so far assume it's a domestic family dispute."

" We feel it's likely an abduction, too much of a co-incidence given the German problem. I'm on my way to Portugal ETA Faro, I guess about eight or nine hours."

He went on, "Oh yes, Calvettioni's still being elusive but my people are "on it."

We agreed it really was was simply too much of a coincidence, with the implication of kidnap in Portugal suggesting that also now most likely scenario in Germany, and vice versa. In any event both needed further investigation.

Neither of us liked the sound of the coordinated attacks. He said he'd obviously update me.

I told him I would leave for Europe right now.

"Chris. Get on to Lim's Jet Co office, confirm we do need to be out of here pronto, and someone call Rory MacLeod."

"Oleg, lets encode this as a heads up for:

*DC/OT. Miss Stanton and Dal Booth. CC. BP, SQ.*

*Seems likely major attack on four major shipping lines in progress as family members of four ship owning families reported missing. Now assumed kidnapped in various locations. For safety of abductees, and to keep clear view for investigation keep under wraps as long as possible.*

*Newly reported five young Haeggqvist/Sorenson family members missing from Portugal.*

*Nothing confirmed yet on Lim, Yamada, and Calvettioni family members missing now two days from school cruise in Germany.*

*Obviously given both abductions, Portugal and Germany likely occurred same day that this coordinated attack on major shipping companies. Daniel C. Oleg T.*

I called Suki and asked her to carefully speak to Hiroshi Yamada and I called David Lim, to give them the news about the Haeggqvist girls.

"We have to assume that the disappearance of the Haeggqvist family members, if confirmed is linked to disappearance of the girls. Then we can expect a ransom demand of some kind. May be political may be cash. Barry and I are still leaning towards criminal, but I must make clear that's only a hunch."

David started to say again, "If its money it's not going to be a problem, both Hiroshi and I have access to serious funds. I can....."

I stopped him and said. " David, I respect what you say but right now, as planned yesterday, we're on our way to the airport to back up the people we already have in place in Europe. "

"Chris Todd will stay here and will have back up from my office. So we can talk policy, payment and planning later."

He said he understood.

I went on, "Could you call Hiroshi-san, over the next few hours, or days, when you feel able. You never know what you can find out just talking to each other, and it's good not to be alone on this."

" Send my love to Peggy and tell her, next time she sees me I'll have May with me." I heard a tearful sniff, and realised that Peggy had been sharing the call.

I called Hiroshi and went through exactly the same conversation with him and got very much the same responses.

Checking out took moments, as Chris was staying and we just routed the bills to his room. Oleg and I grabbed a cab from the rank outside. Oleg spent the journey urging our Brit. Dip. to get a move on and get the 'difficult bag' to the general aviation terminal pronto.

It was nearing eleven as we walked into the general aviation terminal and Rory was waiting. He said, "Squeeze called me, I was here checking out paperwork on the old flight. Understand you've got another Gulfstream 650 from the Lim family."

I nodded and said "Where's your kit?"

"All here, "he said , lifting a shoulder bag.

Having found Lim's 'Asia Jet-Works' office, my briefing to the two pilots, both Chinese, produced slightly concerned looks.

"Just aim at Venice Italy , fastest possible route, but it may be Nice or Faro." I looked at Rory, who amended it quickly into Pilot speak. "File a flight plan to Nice. Three PAX. Hand Bags only. One hold bag, certified. We'll update flite plan as needed. The three PAX have UK Passports so no visas needed."

All of which seemed more professionally acceptable.

Having completed flight documents, passport control and the like in double quick time, I sensed the hand of David Lin behind the speedy routine. We signed for the 'difficult bag' as it was loaded on the plane and the door sealed by a rather more smiley Brit. Dip. and unformed Taiwanese police, and were soon climbing into clear sky's out of lunchtime Taipei.

As we settled back into the flight Rory said, "Subject to the usual stuff, should be about a 12 hour flight, we're chasing the sun, so arrival Nice around 5 p.m. this evening." He went on, "I suggest we do actually route to Nice. We're well located there for your European office, also for Portugal and Venice. Even with bloody French bureaucracy, because Nice has loads of general aviation movements it's the easiest place to set up a local chopper or fast jet to be on standby."

Although this plane came complete with a smiley Taiwanese air hostess, Oleg made tea and we sat at the four seater table.

We talked on for several hours, with London, Squeeze, and Barry who was also enplaned somewhere over the Atlantic, aiming at Faro Portugal from Washington DC.

Oleg spoke, "I need to update Miss Stanton we agreed on the following, and also that we'd obviously copy Barry for Dal Booth.

*Attn B. P. Matchless. K.Stanton.Lon. CC S.T. Sing.*

*1. Original ref.: Rumoured crew hiring. Have potential contact. Likely Philippine in Taipei. Expect follow up next days. Not sure link to July 4 threat or new kidnaps.*

*2. No updates on global ship locator system hack.*

*3. Kidnap resume: Those missing:*

*A: Three teenage girls ex school party on Rhine tour boat.*

*i) May Lim. 17. Daughter of David and Peggy Lim. TOPS Shipping of Taipei.*

*ii) Brigitte Calvettioni 16. Daughter of Andre and Mrs. Calvettioni. FIC Shipping of Rotterdam. Euro registry.*

*iii) Tamiko Yamada 17. Daughter of Hiroshi and Shoko Yamada. NIPPON- TOFCO shipping of Tokyo-Yokohama. Japan.*

*B:Two daughters of Charlie Haeggqvist and their three girl children.*

*Ex villa in Monchique. Algarve. Portugal. He founder and majority shareholder BOSN Shipping. Malmo. Sweden.*

*i.) Britt Marie, was Haeggqvist, now -Sorensen 32. Liv Annika 7.*

*ii) Anna Haeggqvist. 34. Lisa 6.*

*Refer to mssg of 23/hrs. for combined corporate and business details. ends.*

After a surprisingly good meal 'Chinese style', with couple of glasses of wine each for Oleg and I, none for Rory, 'Just in case I'm driving this later', the three of us spread out around the 14 seats. As usual I reclined mine to almost flat and as usual at 35,000 feet, and after a crap night before, slept immediately. It was almost four hours later that I roused and noted Oleg and Rory working their laptops at the four seater table.

With a mug of tea from the Taiwanese air hostess, " Mr. Oleg ,he teach me how to make special English tea for you." I joined the guys.

"Nothing majorly new from anyone really, or I would have woken you." said Oleg. "Nothing of import from Ulrike or Purchase's people. Barry's landing at Faro about now. Then its 30 minutes to Mr. Haeggqvist's villa near Vilamoura."

Rory said, "ETA Nice still 5.00 PM. tailwinds helping a little. "

An hour or so later Barry came on the line. "OK, I'm with Magnus Sorenson and also now Charles Haeggqvist. We've checked the Sorenson's villa again. Based on not much more than the fact that the car's there, whilst various items are missing from the villa, including some passports. But valuables and cash all there, so we now convinced abduction and not robbery. They were last seen five days ago by Mr. Haeggqvist's maid, and all seemed normal then."

" Magnus had already called the police who at this time think it's a domestic quarrel between absent husband and holidaying wife. We're letting them think that. Actually the policeman has good handle on the reasons."

All this and other research , meant that for some reason this flight unlike the one to Taipei went quickly ,and in what seemed like no time we were skimming in over the Med into Nice Airport. 5 P.M. Sun thinking about coming down over the sea. Same sun, but slightly different sea.

Helped indeed by it being really well geared for general, read 'private', aviation we sped through the formalities. This time the Brit. Dip. was ready and eager, and possibly more used to to helping with, as Oleg called them 'difficult bags'.

Having been nodded through immigration and into France, there, I was pleased to find Johnnie Wells standing chatting to Sam Barkshire my main man in Europe. 'Car's outside,' leaving Rory to park planes and do pilot stuff, we piled into Sam's car and were on our way, less than ten minutes after touchdown.

"Given the eager gendarmes and French security, I don't know how you always manage to keep the car right outside the terminal," was my opening line to Sam.

Barkshire, in his trademark Cashmere, Riviera glow to his face, grinned and replied, " We always park under a great French airport drop off sign that says 'Kiss and Fly."

" I always tell them, that I need one more kiss and nip inside before they can complain. It always works, although the 50 euro note probably helps a bit as well."

My phone having established it was back in Europe again, rang.

5.30 PM European time. Around midnight in most of Asia.

Squeeze calling. *"Urgent. The Kidnappers have been in contact, and it's criminal for money."*

My response, "We're on the hill road to the office right now, we'll be there in under ten minutes."

**31.  Monday June 27th  Early afternoon. Marrakesh, Morocco, and Venice, Italy:** *Just a one centimeter break in a digital chain.*

In a large and fairly plush hotel in Marrakesh, Morocco, Rashid, one of the original men who had just days before surprised Britt and Anna at home in the Algarve, set out a selection of phones on the desk in his room. Having handed over the two Swedish mums and their three kids to his colleagues, he had driven on to Toulouse Airport to get an Easy Jet flight to Morocco .

On the hotel room desk in Marrakesh , was a new Samsung mobile he had bought in Portugal, and the two phones he had taken from Britt and Anna.

Into his new Samsung he inserted a new mini memory chip and a Moroccan sim card he had also loaded with credits.

He turned it on, allowed it to figure out its new connection and then having called France  and received by return an incoming message giving him Britt's and Anna's contact numbers for their father and Britt's husband.

 The message also had a picture attached which he down loaded on to the mini sim card. Having checked that the picture showed the Swedish women and their three kids, he then copied the photo from the memory chip into the two phones belonging to Britt and Anna.

He checked the incoming message on his own mobile and punched in her husbands phone number into Britt's phone and using it sent the photo to her husbands number, with an sms/txt message: *Soon listen. Do not ask questions. Do not call back  or this phone will finis.*

Using his new Portuguese Samsung, he called the French mobile number which was answered by Pete who was in a quiet room at The Old Mill in France.

"I'm ready I have the Britt lady here. I have told her to read from the paper when you tell her to start."

Rashid put the phone he was using  to call France on to loudspeaker mode. Then he picked up Britt's phone and dialed the Swedish number again. It was answered instantly.

"Wait, listen," he said, holding the two phones near and facing each other but opposite ways up - top to bottom/bottom to top he spoke to Britt and said,  "start now," and with his spare hand draped a towel loosely over the phones to exclude outside noises. In France, mindful of the threat to her children, Britt carried out the instructions carefully, reading in Swedish from Pete's paper on which she had written notes.

Her voice incoming into the loudspeaker on Rashid's phone in Morocco, and then relayed by her own mobile to her husband's phone which happened to be at her fathers house in Portugal.

*" Hello. it's me. Don't speak. I say again don't speak to me, just listen . This call will cut off if you speak. I am OK but as you can see from the picture I have a bomb around my neck. If things go wrong or someone tries to rescue me the bomb will kill me and maybe one of the others. I have been on a plane, boat and many cars. If you do what is asked then we will be released.*

*The people here want 100 London Standard or similar 400 troy oz. bars for each of us. So minimum 1240 kgs each. The gold must be put on 8 standard flight pallets for transportation.*

*You also are to stop all your ships from moving, at sea or in port.*

*You have 24 hours to arrange this stoppage. Any delay or ship movement and in the next pictures we will have fingers missing.*

*I cannot answer questions. No negotiation. No changes. I am being treated very well so far but you must do what they say. Today is Monday. Goodbye."*

As she said goodbye - Rashid hit the off button on her phone.

He repeated the process a few minutes later with Anna calling her father from effectively her own phone, but in reality relayed across the one centimeter to Rashid's phone that then sent the words on the final part of their journey.

The whole process quite time consuming, but should, or rather more likely ,when someone put a trace on the call, the trace would stop there in Morocco and would not automatically be followed back to the real origin in France.

As it happens her father was actually also sitting with Magnus and Jose Seremenho in the study of his villa, overlooking Vilamoura Golf course. Again as Anna stopped speaking Rashid hit the off switch. Job done.

He put Britt and Anna's two phones into a cardboard box with some cheap shirts he had bought somewhat randomly in the local market the day before and went downstairs to check out.

He paid in cash. Not an unusual event in Marrakech.

Having told the receptionist he was going back to Europe, he walked casually into the street.

After making his way out of the crowded alleys of the souk, surrounded by locals pestering to,' carry his box',' buy souvenirs,' 'see the sights.'

When he spoke to them Moroccan Arabic they backed off a little but when he eventually found a taxi they surged in again to open the door for him, hands outstretched for tips.

He went to a main post office.

There he turned on the Swedish phones again and buried them deep into the mailing carton. From his hand baggage he removed a roll of tape, an already written address label, and a universal Post office customs slip, labelled 'personal clothes' NCV. No Commercial Value.

Handing the box over the counter, It was addressed Mr. and Mrs. Beckham. Hotel Guest. C/O The Manager. The Hotel Desert Melody in Algiers. Algeria.

He paid for,' special signed for post' telling the clerk in Arabic, that it was just some favourite old clothes of his mother's she had left behind at his house. "You know how it is when the oldies start to forget things."

The post office clerk agreed, sympathised and after much stamping of papers, sticking of stamps and application of some old fashioned string and sealing wax the package was dispatched. He paid cash and reflected that state owned postal services were still quite good value in many countries.

Back in the souk he bought a complete Arabic robe with head dress 'telling the assistant that he couldn't buy anything like that in Sweden where he lived. I will keep it on as I feel happy again.' He paid cash. He paid cash as well for a cab to the airport, where he had only a short wait before proceeding though security control, where they accepted his head dress without question as they also did on his arrival later that evening southern Morocco.

*******************************

**Meanwhile.. Outskirts of Venice. Italy.**

Whilst Rashid was in the Moroccan post office, near Venice Italy Hans 'the taxi driver,' was at last almost ready to make three similar calls to the numbers he had received for Brigitte, May and Tamiko's families.

He had been delayed finding chargers and then fully charging the phones belonging to the three girls. He was still driving the by now even more dusty German Merc, which luckily had lighter sockets, in the front. and in the rear, so at least he could charge two of the phones at once.

On the outskirts of the city he had pulled into a huge out of town shopping complex just off the autostrada. Assuming security cameras were in use he chose a parking spot in the middle of a mass of cars.

He was pleased to note a variety of international car registration plates around him and figured that he would pass for just another tourist taking a siesta after a long drive.

He sat in the passenger seat of his car and as with others in the hot sun pulled down the main sun shades and hung a towel over his side window.

Retrieving the three girls phones and using them one by and keeping them plugged in to the car charger just in case, he repeated Rashid's call to call system.

That is he copied the downloaded photo of May, Brigitte and Tamiko into each of their phones, sending them with the sms/txt instructing 'no questions etc.' to their parents using the three numbers he had received from Pete and Jack in France.

He then called Pete in France on a new phone he had bought the previous day on the road to Venice.

On getting the I'm ready message, *using Brigitte's phone*, he called Brigitte's mother again and told Brigitte to read the message which she did reasonably clearly between sobs and sniffs, which he could hear on the loudspeaker of *his* phone as he held it close to *Brigitte's phone*.

He cut off the connection, and then repeated the process with Mays phone and then Tamiko's.

*Each time holding them nose to tail close facing his phone with it's slightly muffled weepy incoming call on the loudspeaker picked up on his relayed on the girls phones to their mothers.*

Although it was unlikely that any tracing was already in action he left quickly. He parked his car at the airport and packed the phones into a mailing carton.

From the arrivals terminal, he took an Orange line ferry to the world famous St Marks Square, where he eventually found the post office. Luckily, just before it closed.

It was insanely busy, thronged with tourists and the harassed counter clerk was just happy that his postage box ,now with all three phones inside and turned on, was sealed and addressed. Ready to Go. In fact to go to - to a Mr. and Mrs. Rooney. Guest C/O The Manager at The Magnificent Hotel, Bucharest, Romania.

A little confused he boarded the wrong Vaporetto back to the airport going on the slightly longer Rosso Ferry Line, and thus missed his flight to Copenhagen.

He then discovered that the earliest flight in the morning left from nearby Bologna, not Venice.

Whilst on the boat back to the airport, he had considered tossing the keys to his now abandoned car over the side. Luckily he still had them, and the parking ticket, so he retrieved the car and drove a further three hours, where he stopped overnight in a basic hotel near Bologna Airport.

Across the street from the hotel he enjoyed a decent meal- as the Italians can provide in surprising places- and a good few beers. Whilst enjoying his food he wondered when the phones or trackers would be traced.

He had a very low opinion of Romanians, and fully expected eager postal workers or sticky fingered customs officials to help themselves to a decent collection of two i phones and a late model Samsung galaxy.

After a few more beers he returned to his Bologna hotel room, accompanied by a very friendly lady he had encountered in the bar. Back in the hotel she became extra friendly through that later part of the evening.

By coincidence she turned out to Romanian.

When he woke- alone - in the morning the fact that some of his cash had gone missing in the night didn't do much to improve his opinion of Romanians.

Having now abandoned his car in the airport parking lot, and doing his best to avoid security cameras, as the sun was coming up he caught a flight to Denmark.
*******

Such is the speed of digital communication these days that in each case, almost before the senders had started to pack their phones in their mailing cartons the five calls- apparently from Morocco or Venice had been received by the anxious parents, in Tokyo, Taipei, The Algarve and Grenoble.

Then copied instantly to a security company office in Singapore. And then on instantly to our offices in Vence. France. About 20 kilometers inland from Nice Airport.

## 32. Monday June 27th. 7.00 pm. Offices TrePolPen Security. Vence. Alpes Maritimes. South Eastern France : *"Hello. It's me."*

My European office, which we also operated as a security training school for ships officers, was in an old villa. Located on the outskirts of Vence, about 20 minutes inland from Nice Airport.

Once owned and converted by a Scandinavian dot com' company in the hay day of internet bubbles in the late nineties, I'd acquired it, with help from David Lim, who very kindly had guaranteed my company bank loan with which I had bought it.

With decent internet, meeting rooms and simple, but more than adequate accommodation for 12 scattered around the house and some converted farm buildings around an open courtyard, with a small pool, it was perfect for our needs.

Having grabbed my bag and run from the car, I was hardly in my office chair when it was confirmed that the merde, ordure, shit, call it what you will , had really hit the French fan. I suppose, actually a French fan but probably made in the far-east and likely transported in one of our client ships or containers.

I called Squeeze who gave me the general details and said the incoming calls to the Algarve, Taipei, Tokyo and Grenoble had all come in with about thirty minutes of each other.

Now at least we knew it was neither Swedish marital disputes in Portugal or girls having a lark in Germany.

*It was a kidnapping for cash.*

We put the two pictures up on the system.

One showed the two Swedish ladies and three kids squinting a little against the sunlight standing in front of what looked like an old door. T shirts, shorts, the two older women with what looked like bike locks and thick cables  around their necks.

The three girls were clutching each other in front of an old stone wall. Again what looked like  covered cables  around their necks.

Next we listened to the tapes, which it turned out were in various languages, but general consensus was pretty much all the same.

Copy recs - to *DC/OT/BP. Ex SQ.*

*Hello. it's me. Don't speak. I say again don't speak to me, just listen .*

*This call will cut off if you speak. I am OK but as you can see from the picture I have a bomb around my neck. If things go wrong or someone tries to rescue me the bomb will kill me and  maybe one of the others.*

*I have been on a plane, boat and many cars.*

*If you do what is asked then we will be released.*

*The people here want 100 London Standard or similar Good Delivery Standard 400 troy oz. bars for each of us. So minimum 1240 kgs each.*

*The gold must be put on 8 standard flight pallets for transportation.*

*You also are to stop all your ships from moving, at sea or in port.*

*You have 24 hours to arrange this stoppage. Any delay or ship movement and in the next pictures we will have fingers missing.*

*I cannot answer questions. No negotiation. No changes.*

*I am being treated very well so far but you must do what they say. Today is Monday. Goodbye.*

We agreed to adopt pretty standard kidnap drill.

Squeeze would send us and Barry the check lists, for us all to work our way through, routing answers via Squeeze we were sure we were all singing from the same song sheet.

I sent an sms to Barry. *DC: Assume you talk this through with Haeggqvist and Sorenson. I am calling the Lims and Yamada's. Are you in better contact with Calvettioni yet. ends*

I went to the quiet of my room and had predictably emotional conversation with both sets of parents in Asia. The result.

We could discuss problems of stopping the fleet in an hour or so. There was no question or hesitation from both Lim's and Yamada's. The ransom would be paid, and regardless of cost they would stop their ships.

We assembled in the meeting room, Oleg, Johnnie Wells, and Rory occupied one side of the table. Sam and myself the other.

On the speaker phone; Ulrike still in Venice, Barry Purchase in the guest house at the Haeggqvist Villa in Portugal. Squeeze was online in the Singapore office.

In Taipei Chris Todd was out in a bar with Paul Isted. Possibly his was the winning assignment at that moment.

We pooled what information we knew. Contact made: Monday. Late afternoon Europe time. Midnight or more much of Asia. Contact was: From Anna and Britt Marie's own phones to their father and Magnus.

Also with own phones. Tamiko to her mother, May to her Dad, and Brigitte, we thought to her mother.

In each case a photo sent first with text in English. Then calls in Swedish, and it turned out in Japanese , Taiwanese and French.

Magnus had pointed out that the girls seemed to be reading the words and putting them into their own language. Oleg cut in and said, " Strictly accurately ,their own 'sims' had been used by each, may not actually be their actual phone." We agreed that given that some of the phones had tracking systems that's a possibility.

We had recordings from each of the Lims, Yamada's, Haeggqvist's and Sorenson's.

I said " So the only person we don't know about is Mr. Calvettioni."

Barry. "Now we do know about Mrs. Calvettioni at least. One of our girls, Alice, from our Paris office is with her. We're following up on Mr. C. He's now En-route direct to his operations center in Rotterdam."

I spoke with Barry about accessing help from the NSA or CIA to find out what we could about where the calls originated from and their route to the parents. His response was, "I think Oleg and your people can sort that quite easily. We used to need access to the switching records of the local cell-coms companies, but you can now get a lot of info direct yourselves."

Oleg was waving and mouthing, 'We can do that,'

Barry said. "I suggest we leave the US folk out of this right now because they are not going to like the 'stop your ships.' That suggests there's a danger of them marching in guns blazing.

Stopping or delaying their vital supplies will be their priority, not the safety of our girls."

Barry went away to start both debriefing and re-assuring his clients.

I got Squeeze to patch me through first to Peggy and David Lim and then the Yamada's. The main part of both conversations with Asia was indeed re-assurance, not re-insurance.

"The kidnappers want ransom. They will take care of the girls and in most cases provided no one tries a crazy rescue they will be safe."

The words fell on to pretty disbelieving listeners in both cases, but as ever in these situations as with drowning persons they grasped at straws.

I went on. "The question of the ransom demand. It's a huge amount each." David Lim cut in, "About US $45,000,000," and I could hear Hiroshi agreeing with the figure.

I continued. " As we have discussed before, in these cases the insurers usually want to take over all negotiations. They do have excellent specialist teams. Generally though they will try and delay things, try to get the ransom release price lowered, and at the same time try and find out the location where the girls are being held. That's when I see a risk."

I could also hear what was presumably a mix of Japanese and Taiwanese sniffing and sobbing in the background.

Hiroshi spoke first. "I want to work with everyone on this. I am prepared to pay and do not want my insurers involved if they make even 1% extra risk. I will pay as asked."

In faltering English he continued, "I must put strongly that I will work with David ,and or his people to make sure we succeed together."

I was a little surprised, as usually, such is the difference in Chinese and Japanese culture, David would be the first to respond.

David, for the first time also sounding very emotional said, "I too can pay what is asked, where and when we are told. I am not involving my insurance."

I said, "Give me some time to find out about the Haeggqvist family attitude. Try everything you can not to let this story get out to the media. Do not even tell the school we have contact."

David Lim said, "We understand. My associates that came to see me the other night fully understand. The two English Captains are my most senior Captains, and good family friends since before May was born. They are still here in our guest house and I will take care to warn them, and my staff here to be silent."

Amongst louder Asian background noises both David and Hiroshi thanked me and rang off.

Squeeze came on. "Some things boss. Firstly Paul Isted and Toddy have a lead to follow up in an hour or so."

"Secondly. Although he's Matchless Consulting client it seems we now know that Calvettioni was holed up on a Pacific Island with a girlfriend."

"Thirdly. I've sent you a value chart for the gold."

I suggested Squeeze got some sleep as it was nearing dawn in Singapore and tomorrow would be busy. She said, "Just about to do that, J and S are taking over here. Oh yes they say that those amounts of dosh are more than most insurance companies will cover for individuals. Speak tomorrow."

I studied the value chart and started to worry even more, the values were mind blowing.

*London Standard Good Delivery bar 400 troy ounces.*

**Which is about 12.4 Kilos each...or 1,240 kgs for the 100.**

*That size quite hard to get.*

*Bars vary slightly when cast, which affects price but usual values here. Here todays gold price averaged.*

*12.4  kilo value - £GB     297,000:00   or  $US      458.000:00.*

*124   kilo value - £GB   2,970,000:00   or  $US   4,580,000:00.*

*1240 kilo value - £GB 29,700,000:00   or  $US  45,800,000:00.*

*Total for 8 girls- £GB 237,600,000:00 or  $US 356,000,000,:00.*

*FYI.* **You can get about 1500 Kilos in the back of a pickup truck**. *Ends Squeeze.*

It was now well after midnight French time. The office was littered with coffee cups, empty water bottles and the remnants of pizzas and such.

Barry Purchase came back on. "OK, My office tell me Charlie's family and the grandchildren are insured by Akxiom Remutual".

"This has been a hell of shock for him today, and so I haven't told him yet that the others are prepared to pay and don't wish to claim from insurance, to avoid possible further dangers. Also that at this stage the Asians were keen to work as a team."

"I think he will need time to think, it's a hell of a lot of money , he's got to pay for five people. He did say, 'recovering his daughters and grandchildren was his priority above all and regardless of what the others chose to do'."

Presenting a unified front, we agreed was the strongest strategy. I told Barry what J&S said about insurance not covering those amounts for individuals.

His response, "Hadn't thought of that. I'll check here, but that makes a difference or gives us some answers already."

I mentioned Calvettioni having been away with a girlfriend and Barry's response was, "I'm not surprised, that's what we thought. He's mid divorce with Mrs. C and she keep pressuring us to give her information about him. We're still having problems getting any real answers from him."

Barry continued, "I happened to mention this when Charlie Haeggqvist was in hearing and he said two things."

"One. Calvettioni's in big trouble and tried to sell his business to him a year back. He's so desperate for business he's undercutting everyone."

"Two. He, Haeggqvist is leaving in the morning either to go to his office in Malmo or coming over to you to talk about ransom. In Malmo he needs to talk about stopping the entire fleet. Magnus is going with him."

" He's hoping to stop off and see Cavetti's CEO Gerry McMullen to talk about that and to see what he can find out about generally. I'm going with them. He's been a personal friend of Gerry's for years. I'll let you know when I know."

I told Barry that Lim and Hiroshi-san could access their gold in quick time, and he said he'd, 'introduce that fact with the other points at a 'good moment'. Oleg, Sam, Johnnie and I talked around our table for while but my eyes started to droop.

Johnnie Wells said, "I suggest you two call it day, I'll keep on watch here and call you if needed. But some rest would be good," and with typical Wells understatement said, "Might be a busy day tomorrow."

## 33. Tuesday June 28th.10.30 am.Inbound from Italy. Copenhagen Airport. Denmark: *The loneliness of the long distance abductor.*

Despite, or perhaps because of, his overnight sojourn in Bologna, Hans was in a good mood when he arrived at Kastrup Airport Copenhagen. He'd used the flight time to check out the instructions for his new phones, but still found them a little confusing.

He'd also had time to review some detailed information about BOSN shipping given to him by a Russian a few weeks back when this whole business was being set up. The Russian, apparently an ex employee of the company, had given him the location of, and details about some of the owners residences, not far from their headquarters in Malmo. Sweden.

With those locations in mind, he had researched the name Charlie Haeggqvist and predictably was swamped with shipping and financial news.

Narrowing the search came up with a number of endowed buildings at various Swedish Universities, various wards at a number of hospitals, and a cluster of name checks at some small schools in one area of Malmo's suburbs.

Further investigation of the schools, came up with some local newspaper coverage of various old tennis club tournament results for a Britt Marie and an Anna Haeggqvist.

At Kastrup, steps away from the arrivals door, he found a gaggle of car rental desks, and with his passport, driving licence and credit card was driving away in a nondescript Opel within thirty minutes.

The rental kid, a throwback to student employee car rental cliché's was wearing his Hertz hat a jaunty angle, helpfully suggesting, "Next time book on line, and with all the paperwork in the computer you'd be away in half the time, and probably at half the price."

He tapped Malmo Sweden into the Sat Nav system, 'optional extra 50 Danish Krone, per day' and followed directions towards the still new looking bridge and tunnel over, and indeed under the Oresund Straights.

The rental kid had also queried his renting of the sat nav system, saying, " But surely you have that in your phone sir?"

Hans had not wished to confess he knew that, but, with so many phones, he wasn't too confident about how to operate them. He also worried for Mr. Hertz if all their employees were so keen on saving customers money.

That morning, Romanians were again on his mind. Waiting briefly at the toll booth for the crossing to mainland Sweden he wondered about the mobile phone package he had posted to Bucharest. Where and when in the mysterious labyrinth of old style postal connections would the authorities catch up with them.

Twenty minutes later with virtually no customs or passport checks he was on the outskirts of Malmo. Using the sat nav he quickly found the Baltic and Orient Steam Navigation HQ and took some photos out of the car window. Then aimed for the first of the locations where his research suggested the Haeggqvist clan might live.

There in a leafy suburb there were certainly plenty of expensive looking properties. He quartered the area once and pulled into the parking bay of a small store. Newspapers, cash machine, barbecue fuel, and a hot dog stand which was covered at that time of day.

He went in to ask some questions, but drew a blank as the assistant was Turkish with little or no English and no local knowledge.

But just around the corner however was a small local gas station. Bingo. Perfect result. Having filled the car with gas he went in to pay where the jolly Swedish lady behind the counter was not only local but also very chatty.

Hans started to pick up various other items whilst asking questions. He was he said an employee of Baltic  and was being transferred from Hamburg to head office. He was house hunting and would need local schools for his young family.

In no time he exited the store not only with an armful of chocolate,  a map, the local paper, and a lotto ticket- but also a complete run down on the locations and habits of, 'Your boss Mr. Haeggqvist. Also his son in law, and the fact that the Sorensen children came in the shop regularly. Very polite they were too.'

'Not like some who came in these days.'

Hans also had detailed instructions on where the two primary schools were, and the best of the local schools for older children.

Oh yes and the address of the tennis club.

He spent a few more  hours driving around taking photos. Hot dogs for lunch at a Denmark bound gas station, and was back crossing the Oresund towards Copenhagen by 2 pm.

On the outskirts of the city he spotted a hotel from the road and eventually found his way back to a Crowne Plaza and checked in.  One night, "I'll pay cash," but they needed a card as deposit so he used the same credit card that he had used to rent the car.

He sent a text to the usual French number saying. 'Have got pictures homes and offices, I will choose best for next week if we need them.'

Almost by return he got a text saying,' running late here will have new pics of girls soon, will send to you for re-sending with message in an hour or so.'

\*\*\*\*\*\*\*

Back in France, whilst Hans had been driving around in Sweden, near their homes and schools, for the girls, despite the constant pressure of confinement and the vile necklaces the day passed well enough. Now more confident with the girls, it turned out that the Swedish children spoke English quite well.

For them, getting even more language skills with Japanese and Chinese writing of their names had become a favourite game, helping their concerned mothers keep them out of the sun for at least part of the day.

May and Britt even produced 'Chinese style food' for lunch. The tables decorated by Chinese lanterns made by the children under instruction from Tamiko.

"I guess they're a bit young to understand the difference between Japan and China for now," smiled Tamiko.

It hadn't taken the three girls long the previous day to find the horses. They were standing, looking through a couple of rusted holes in the wire fence around their compound. But the girls, nervous of the necklace bombs held back.

Having gained an OK from their guard they knew as Pete - "All OK girls to feed the horses. Just stay inside the fence."

The horses became eager recipients of sugar, carrots, crisps and more. The girls teaching the Swedish little ones how to hold their hands flat to avoid being bitten.

In his usual good natured way Pete said, "I'm off to the shop again, you'd better put a big bag of carrots on the list if we're gonna feed the bloomin' horses every day....I'll be back soon to take another picture and send another text."

Whilst he was away in the kids usual 'siesta, or rest time out of the sun', Brigitte amused them with her horse drawing skills.

This was a big success and soon she had to complete whole horse families for the kids to colour in.

Britt Marie said, "Now all the horses need to have names."

" Which you children must write on all the pictures," which also kept the kids busy for quite a while.

Brigitte discovered that in the scrumble of drawings and pens on the farmhouse table, she'd got a big blotch of black ink from her felt tip marker pen on the front of one of her spare white T shirts.

One of the kids said, "Look the ink on your shirt is just like the mark on the front of 99's face."

Brigitte, realising there was no way the ink mark would wash out, then drew a horse's face around the ink stain on the shirt front.

Then as the kids looked on, at their insistence, "He must have his name," she wrote—99 AX5CM93 underneath the picture.

Britt- Marie came in and admiring all the pictures and asking each of the children about the names, then asked, "I like the names , but why all the numbers and not a name for the horse drawn on your shirt?"

Brigitte grinned and said, "Well the kids have been naming all their drawings and they insisted."

Britt, *"But why has that one got numbers and letters and not a name?"*

Oh," was the answer, "I was checking the horse's mouths to show the children their teeth, and show them how old they were, and they saw that horse had an id tattoo on the inside of its lip."

"It's the law now in most countries, horses must have a microdot or a tattoo for an ID. It's so vets can know which is which, and if they've been inoculated against bad stuff. Helps stop horse thieves, and the spread of diseases.".

"So that's his number. We call him 99, but Liv demanded I put his 'whole name' on my shirt for fun."

They heard a cheery shout from outside. "Carrot and Ice Cream delivery kids."

Brigitte, grabbed on her newly drawn on T shirt and joined the rest as they all brought the shopping in.

Pete said, "Just before you get your ice creams kids, one more picture please." He lined up the Swedes in the same place, and gave Anna a newspaper to hold up to the camera.

Ditto the three girls, In their case May, held a newspaper to camera.

With his usual warning to the girls and the Swedish ladies, made whilst pointing to his own neck, " Don't forget, no funny business," he left.

It was only a little later in the evening that they looked at the newspapers. One seemed to be in Arabic and the other in what they thought may be Hungarian, then Anna spotted an English language printers address and said, "I think it's Romanian."

Indeed it was, and they were. One Algerian the other Romanian. Dated with the day's date.

Down at the gate house, Pate had picked out a text in English on his Italian phone and forwarded it and the two new photos of the captives with the newspapers to Hans who was waiting in his Copenhagen Hotel.

Just before 4.00 pm with all the new pictures of the girls in his phone, and with a copy text, he grabbed a taxi into the city.

Still with his concern about being traced and sticking to the idea had he'd read somewhere that using busy locations to send messages was less conspicuous he had decided to visit Copenhagen's famous Tivoli Gardens.

The idea had come from a Tivoli brochure he found in his room as he waited. He'd been there once as a kid. So why not have another look. If nothing else, he could look at the girls passing by.

He inserted the various numbers for the Lim's, Yamada's, Haeggqvist's Sorenson's and Calvettioni into one of his new 'pay as you go' phones, copied in the txt and the two photos of the girls.

An hour later he was sitting in a seemingly old brewery in the Tivoli gardens, drinking a cold Faergekroen lager.

Despite being Danish his beer seemed seemed German style and was good. Very good. So good that whilst sending the five messages and photos to the various parents, he had several more.

This time he read the leaflet that came with the beer, and discovered that it was made with German Hops. The beer being a little stronger than he thought, he was very happy about the hops, and in fact all seemed well with the world. For him, at least.

With his phone skills slightly confused by the beer, and the various phones and systems he had encountered in the past few days, he didn't notice that he had also forwarded to each the whole file of his Malmo street pictures as well.

A little later when his phone soon received an incoming txt, actually from Barry Purchase making suggestions, he forwarded the message to a number in France.

He returned to the hotel, with a number of shopping bags, and large stuffed bear that he had won at the Tivoli. In the morning, leaving the rather large bear sitting on his bed as a tip, and now sober but slightly muzzy headed he paid by credit card.

He returned and paid for the rental car-asking and using a different named passport, took a plane to Paris, Orly. After a long wait, and by now more than somewhat weary, he boarded an Air Maroc flight, going South.

## 34. Tuesday June 28th. 6.00 am.TrePolPen Company Office. Vence. Near Nice. France: *A perfect French summer morning, near Vence. Alpes Maritime.*

The sound of chickens and the smell of coffee wafting into my bedroom window at what turned out to be 6 am French time had me confused for a moment...I then realised that for once I was in the same time zone as my priority focus, the kidnapped girls. Or at least I assumed and hoped they were still in my time zone.

Awake and located, a speedy shower and I went out onto the terrace, ready for a coffee infusion myself. Johnnie Wells, "Morning boss. Tea or Coffee? Very quiet overnight, I got some sleep myself."

Oleg, standing ,wearing wet swimming shorts, tucking into about a meter of crusty looking French stick, said, "I know you're a tea man boss but this coffee is great, and so is the bread.."

I helped myself to coffee and explained, the night guardian nips down to the village bakery at about 5 am and gets them fresh for us when we're here.

Johnnie said, "He also nips in to the office about that time to clean up the place. I think we both shit ourselves when he came face to face with me under a blanket on the office couch."

With a cable snaking out of the window, there was a phone on the breakfast table, and its shrill ring shattered the illusion of an idyllic summer morning in the Alpes Maritime. There was of course urgent work to be done, but we all groaned slightly.

But fine. It was Rewan Trelawney, the previous owner of my company. I had called him a few days earlier, before we even knew the disappearances were confirmed kidnaps, so he could cast his mind back in case anything material came up. His immediate suggestion was that he could pop out for a day or so.

When we got the ransom messages yesterday evening I had copied him on them. This morning he was at Gatwick Airport just about to get the plane to Nice. Seems his plan to help had been formulated with a view to coming out to Asia.

This had been not only welcomed by his wife, but also by her carers and doctor who could see the break would help him, but the South of France probably worked better than Asia for all concerned. He said he had been ordered to stay with us as long as was needed and to get some Riviera air and relax a bit. I said we looked forward to seeing him.

Quite how relaxing helping to solve a full on multiple kidnapping with global implications was going to be, remained to be seen. But his arrival would provide a massive boost for the Yamada and Lim families who knew and had trusted him for years.

With second coffees, and in Oleg' case, dry shorts and shirt, we assembled ourselves in the meeting room.

Oleg had some news from London regarding the origins of the ransom calls to their families. The Swedish girls had apparently called from Marrakesh Morocco, and the calls from May Tamiko and Brigitte had originated in Venice Italy, where we had noted some on off tracker activity previously. Both places within quite easy reach of the sites of their abductions, although getting unwilling travelers to Morocco was an interesting one.

It seemed at some time in the past there had been plans and even docks constructed for a Portemao Algarve – Morocco ferry. J & S were looking into it.

Squeeze came on the system. "The Lims and Yamada's were just about to depart to Europe, and their message to me was, 'gold under control'. They were going to Geneva, where David had an office, and I guessed gold connections. I could call them on the plane when I had time or news."

By mid morning we learned that Barry , Magnus and Charlie were on their way to Nice to meet us, Mr. Haeggqvist wanted to speak to us in person.

Of course there would have to be conversations with all the parents about the obvious points, the main one being, 'how do we know they will release the girls?' The short answer to that was of course. 'We do not, and worse still, once the ransom is paid then they really are at maximum risk'.

The secondary obvious question, how and where we were to deliver the ransom had yet to requested or resolved.

Oleg and Johnnie were currently fully occupied tracking intermittent signals from the girls phones. Oleg's quote, " Looking at the overnight track of Britt and Anna's phones if I didn't know better I would think they were on a Moroccan camel trek."….followed up later with, "now they're in bloody Algeria."

Sam Barkshire picked up Charlie Haeggqvist, Magnus and Barry Purchase from the usual 'Kiss and Fly' parking at Nice Airport and delivered them to our Vence office in record time.

Introductions and handshakes all round ,and whilst coffees were being prepared I started to brief Mr. Haeggqvist on the current 'let's pay' attitude of Mays and Tamiko's fathers. He said, "Firstly, please call me Charlie, most of the world does. Secondly I know where they are at on this, I spent most of the flight here talking to them."

I could see Magnus was bursting with a lot questions but he deferred to his father in law who said. "I would like to have a quiet word with just Barry and Daniel and of course you Magnus."

So we moved sat in a secluded shady alcove outside.

Charlie started. "Firstly this is between ourselves. I have thought and talked a lot about the dangers and practicalities of this on the phone with Hiroshi- San and David Lim. I know them both- we have met many times and they are both very correct and both run fine companies. Luckily for us all there's been enough business to keep us all happy over the past decade or so. "

"It's a lot of money that is needed but we can get it together between us. We need to work out delivery and release logistics urgently."

He went on. "But first  Calvettioni. I have learned from an impeccable source that not only is he's broke, but that the company technically is busted."

I interrupted, "Sorry to butt in, Mr. Haeggqvist, it seems he owes various Casinos in Macau tens of millions. He's also got banking problems in Cyprus- partly because of their banking crisis a few  years back but mostly of his own making."

Barry responded.  "So that suggests that the  little shit  could possibly set up an insurance scam with those four ship fires. But would the bastard kidnap his own daughter."

Charlie Haeggqvist smiled in his usual calm assured manner, and said. "Barry in your best American style you have said what we Swede's would perhaps take some time to get round to."

Barry looked a bit embarrassed at his outburst.

But Haeggqvist patted him on the arm and said, "Sometimes both ways are equally appropriate in some circumstances."

" I don't know about the insurance scam, but I do know he can't raise the money.  So very much between ourselves, the Asians and I will have access to what is needed in a couple of days for us and for the Calvettioni's."

"I stress again between us, we can also cover Calvettioni's share, to be sure about the safety of our girls, we don't have much choice in the matter."

" Even sharing the problem with David and Hiroshi  $40 million is a lot extra for us to find. But we have an idea to free one or two of his boats from their 'mortgaged' status by moving those loans to his other boats. We can then buy one or possibly two ships from him, for around $40 million."

"We will give him a genuinely correct fair deal-not take advantage. We can sweeten it by working with him on some future routes. This will help his business and of course the cash flow will fix the ransom. If we find he is too indebted to the bank to even sell a ship, then between you and me we will still find the money. We want no extra risk for our girls."

" I now have one suggestion which I have not yet even discussed with Magnus, and for that I apologise. "

"I suggest we show our good faith by delivering half the ransom, and the kidnappers then release the three girls and my three grandchildren. We will then deliver the rest and they can at that time release my daughters."

Having delivered his words, the last ones somewhat emotionally, he stood and moved over to look out across the hills and red tile rooftops, to the sea. Magnus also looked pretty stricken but managed to say, "That makes good sense."

Just as Charlie re-joined us at the table, Squeeze came on the line from Singapore HQ.

"Sorry to interrupt Boss, but the the guys now say the phones for May and Tamiko have come to rest in Bucharest. We'd been getting blurred signals from various points around Romania from the past day, but now they have stabilised in Bucharest."

" Don't know where yet. I've dispatched Andy Keeling from Milan to see what's what. "

"He'll be there in four hours, and he's got a scanner."

We went in to the office, and having informed all present of the Romanian connection, I asked Oleg for an update on the two Swedish phones but first I made it clear to Charlie and Magnus, "Knowing the location of the phones doesn't mean that's the current location of the girls. We're dealing with some sophisticated people here."

Oleg, "Well it's been too intermittent to home in on but for the last few hours they seem to be in Central Algiers."

In answer to Charlie asking, "What do you mean about intermittent?"

Oleg responded, "Just as with your place in Portugal, it can mean just a big hill not giving clear connection to a phone mast. "

"Or if the phone is in a truck or on a train, really in a metal box, as far as being a phone is concerned, and the signal is not very strong, the signals cut in an out, as they jump away from one mast to another. When they cut out, the hand set then has to find the nearest transmitter /receiver mast and log on and then await recognition. That's when we also get to know where they are. Tracing them used to need help from the local telco's but we can do it ourselves now."

Squeeze said. "I'll dispatch Matt Button to Algiers just in case, he's already in Morocco based on the earlier call."

After brief break for a working lunch on the terrace, Magnus and Charlie went to use one of our rooms to organise gold affairs, and shipping logistics.

Despite it being late in Singapore, Oleg, Johnnie and I spent a lot of time, on line and talking with Jacko and Suki, researching both necklace bombs, and likely timelines and from the limited amount of information that we had, potential hostage locations.

I also got offers of assistance regarding likely necklace systems from Sir Geoffery Barker.

Just as importantly for our team, Squeeze had managed to contact Joel Williams, who ran a team of ex-special forces guys, who specialised in covert and other action. Joel promised to, 'be ready on a plane to London' within the hour.  We had used his company before with, low key but positive results.

Just prior to their 5.00 pm departure to Geneva, Barry and I were just about to resume briefly with Charlie and Magnus when both their phones came to life with incoming messages. Same message to each.

It was the abductors again.

First came six photo's. Two, with their girls holding up a newspaper. Then some houses and what looked like a school.

Charlie and Magnus freaked out,  "Christ, that's my house, and Liv and Annika's school." Then the message:

*Gold in 12.4k bars to be put in eight equal weight cargo nets. Mesh size not more than 5 cms. Load on to 8 flight freight palettes. You deliver by air freight.  Destination West Africa tbc. Be aware any tracking devices will bring bad result. You must note we checking positions your ships. Reg number freight plane and departure airport to this number. Goodbye.*

Of course I had the Lim's and Yamada's on the phone in seconds reporting receipt of the same stuff. I apologised for being brief and said, I have a lot to check right now and will call you back with any news.

We assembled the team on the phone and in the conference room and on line.  Oleg quickly established  this time *all the new calls* with the messages and photos came from Copenhagen area and from one phone. It was not from any of the girl's phones. Which were apparently in Romania and Algeria.

On the other hand in the photos the girls were holding up to date Algerian and Romanian papers (Ulrika recognised the language)

A bluff or a deception ? Probably.

A relay? from Romania and Algiers to Copenhagen. Possibly.

Now we had an idea of the ransom load and destination, Rory was on the case with freight plane charter.

Barry said, "I'll get a 24/7 team at the Swedish places. Immediately."

From the back of the room Mr. Haeggqvist who had been watching and listening said. " Possibly a bit late with the Swedish home security. Maybe I should have accepted that years ago when you suggested it Barry."

" I think all our lives have just taken a nasty change. But please follow up on it all , with whatever it takes." He went on, "Just to finish what we were going to say. These days shipping the gold legally is not easy, especially out of the E.C. But with our Asian friends we have hopefully come up with an answer. We are also going trade some ships with them."

" They are going to trade some route contracts. As private companies those are reasonably private transactions. We don't think they will attract regulatory investigation. As it happens we can even make it all tax neutral for our companies, and at the end of the day we should be able to ship our own money around. All we want is our daughters back."

Again the tough exterior softened and he left the room.

Quickly he re-appeared, back in control. "Let's respond to that text before I go to Geneva. David and Hiroshi will be there soon."

"Gerry McMullen is trying to organise Calvettioni to come there. So we will follow up on his gold situation. You have enough to do here."

We figured out a response, including Charlie's suggestion of stage payments, but also trying not to look like we were making problems.

Having agreed it with Charlie and Magnus, and they said they could agree on behalf of David and Hiroshi.

*SMSD/TXT. All Gold instructions noted. FYI total gold stretches resources of all payers but is available. Real concern new laws mean gold export  problem with Swiss authorities. We are working on this. We  propose two equal shipments.*
*First delivery gets release of the three girls and the three children.*
*The two Swedish ladies to be released following second gold shipment.*
*Ship Control. Stopping ships agreed 100%. But takes time, subject to weather and safety of crews. Note. Stopping is agreed 100% by us. But we do not control ships within  port areas. Response number to us is: XCXXX. Ends*

We agreed the text and sent it from one of Barry's phones.

Conference over we started to sort out various aspects of what was needed. Johnnie Wells speaking to a chum in Copenhagen for some urgent local phone tracking.

Oleg homing down on Romania and Algerian telecoms, Andy Keeling was En route to Bucharest and another of my guys, Matt Button, to Algiers.

I had just started to try and find Rory Macleod around the office somewhere when Squeeze was back on. "J&S say, ship locators starting to indicate many ships slowed or stopping. "

"Just talking to Paul Isted. He says that it's starting to be noticed in the bars where they show the locators on their TV's. His point is. Surely this will let the cat out the bag, and media will wake up shortly and start looking for reasons. Also is it not our priority to avoid global speculation over shipping and commodities ?"

Squeeze continued, "Ref skilled crew being looked for. Paul, now wonders if it's just a local advance payment scam. Usual thing, 'you give me money now ' and I get you big good paid job soon'."

I thanked her for both bits of information, found Barry and grabbed Magnus and Haeggqvist just as they went out of the gate to go to Nice airport. I explained, " Philippine and Taipei girly bars are showing ship locator details, that reveal many ships stopped or stopping."

Magnus said, "If the story is out that quick, that's going to rock the commodity markets a bit as you feared."

My response, "I agree, and that will upset the Yanks, but now my serious main worry is news getting out of the real reason for the stoppage and thus the kidnapping story getting out."

Barry said, "Well I agree about the priority but we'd also better think about dancing with the one that brung us."

This produced questioning looks from the rest of us. Barry continued. " We've been so focused on the safety of the girls that regarding the order to stop the ships, we've focused on the action and logistics of stopping, not the effect. Given our remit from the US we'd better tell them something, to either tune them in ,or put them off the scent."

Haeggqvist said. " That's what Magnus and I have been working on with our people. The ship stop does mean many knock on problems about loading and unloading. Docking availability. Need to cancel thousands of trucks daily coming for just in time pick up's and drop offs. "

"Then of course no supplies means factory closures and empty supermarket shelves very quick. For me, and I think the Lims, Hiroshi, and I imagine Calvettioni, I am sorry but the ships will stop, and the trucks can wait, the girls are the only priority."

My phone buzzed, I glanced at it and said it's Paul Isted in Taipei. "Hang on," and I put the phone onto loudspeaker mode.

Paul said, "I was thinking in the cab about the big picture, and your overall global concerns if shipping stopped. Right now, globally a lot of tabloids and TV are going to have a big day with this, stirring up the shit, or worse exploiting the story of the missing girls in an unhelpful way."

We all murmured agreement, Paul said, "I have one idea that could buy you a couple of days. We've already said we've had a small and controllable incidents on four ships. We've not said much but the story is out there in the eyes of the media people."

" How about if a bunch of owners quickly today issue a very boring press release, to me, that says something like. 'Mindful as ever of safety at sea and the welfare of our crews, customers, and the environment we have ordered some extra but standard safety checks on all our vessels."

They can also witter on, "The maritime industry has made huge advances in cleaner fuels, engine emission efficiency, waste disposal control both out at sea and in inshore waters. We have also made progress with the latest fire control systems. We have instructed our crews to carry out a full audit to make sure that current and future cargo's are fully compliant with all needed standards with the wellbeing of the environment in mind. Bla bla bla.'"

Paul went on," I can get that out as the main part of, ' look lots of ships have slowed down for a few hours, and it's for a good reason."

"If it's boring enough like boring ship owner bullshit usually is, it will get buried on the inside pages at least for a few days. Also makes your boring owners look extra responsible over other ships not stopped."

Charlie Haeggqvist leaned forward and said. "Mr. Isted, it's Charlie Haeggqvist here, one of those very boring ship owners, and that suggestion of yours is genius. Get that story out as soon as you can."

" I will say OK, also for the other boring owners in the problem that we have. Great stuff, and make it as waffle and boring as you like, you can quote me in any useful way. Well done and thank you, I look forward to seeing you again soon."

Paul said. "OK Charlie. Job done, it will go out within an hour." and with a characteristic, "Cheers," he was gone.'

Still chuckling Haeggqvist said, "I'm off to Geneva to meet the other boring owners."

After they'd left, Barry said. "'Well that may be a lucky break as far as the media goes, but for you and me, it's still a problem. When I said about, 'dancing with the one that brung you,' I meant the US and UK Governments who are terrified of any stoppages for any bloody reasons...and as it happens they are paying some of our bills"

"But still when they see it's our clients that have stopped they will go ape shit. They've paid us to dance to their tune, which at least means keeping them informed, so we had better do at least that and very pronto."

Having sent out our, 'everything under control press release,' Barry and I, with the rest of the team worked on through the evening on the kidnap situation, desperately looking for clues of any kind but finding very little of any meaning.

I mentioned my thoughts to Barry, and his response was, "I agree and regarding the US ,when Dal Booth and all those guys have finished digesting what we sent and looked at the shipping screens, then I fear electronic indigestion on a big scale from the US time zones, will hit our phones and e mails. I'm turning mine off for the night."

I did the same, and leaving only a bleary looking Oleg still hunched over his computer, and knowing the office in Singapore were fully occupied searching on line for any clues- no matter how tenuous- I wandered across the courtyard and went to bed.

## 35.Wednesday. June 29th.Too bloody early.TrePolPen office. Vence Near Nice, South of France: *The Germans usually call mobile/cell phones- 'handy's.' Maybe, just may be, this one was.*

The extra loud wake-up tone, triggered by Squeeze caused a serious shock to my system, crashing me from sleep to reality. More from nervous habit than current condition, I was awake in seconds and sitting on the side of my bed. As I groped for the bedside light switch I listened to Squeeze as she repeated her words of one minute before.'

"Wake up boss. 5.00 am your time."

I found the light and asked Squeeze, "What's new?"

Her answer was mixed. "A crop of crap from the USA to you and Barry. Paul's news story about stopping ships is quite big in a lot of media. Quite positive. Both Andy Keeling and Matt Button need to talk, they can't raise Oleg just now."

" Oh yes David, Hiroshi and their wives arrived in Switzerland a while ago. They also gave a lift to the two UK ships captains. I'm not sure of their plans."

I said, " Does Barry know any of this?"

The answer came immediately from both of them at once. A, "Yes." from Barry, and from Squeeze, "Yes, and he wakes up quicker than you do boss."

Barry added, "Actually Squeeze I was already awake and talking to Rory about gold shipments."

I said. " OK 30 minutes, Squeeze you alert the team."

Barry said, "I'll check those mails to see reactions from our friends at Homeland, CIA, the President's office. I'll see you in 30, You kick Oleg on the way, I would imagine he's having a well deserved sleep he looked absolutely shattered last night."

On the way across the courtyard I hammered on Oleg's bedroom door. No response. I tried the handle and luckily he hadn't locked it.

He was seated at the desk, crashed out asleep, dead to the world, head on his arms slumped over his keyboard- headphones on and music still playing quite loudly. No wonder all his alarms had failed.

I shook him awake and stepped back as he jerked to his feet – scattering mice, papers, empty cups in all directions.

As he focused on me and snatched off his headphones, I said, "You needed that sleep, meeting in the ops room in 25."

As I entered the ops room I was surprised to hear the welcome London tones of Chris Todd asking, "Rosy Lea or coffee boss?"

As he rustled up my tea, and I powered up the machines, he told me he'd arrived in Nice late the night before and had made his way up to us by Taxi.

He said, "Unbelievable for me but, David got his plane to drop me off at Nice on their way to Switzerland. Georges' the night guard let me in here, and I figured I'd snooze on the sofa here until morning. What's new?"

I told him that his other half- obviously working Asian office time, which is what enabled us to get some rest in Europe now and again, was currently waking up our world with a lot of calls.

He said, "I just spoke to Paul, he's got a little bit further with his contact in Taipei and is also thinking of going to the Philippines. He's on the case but we figured you were busy enough not to need to know that. He also said, you would probably be happy with today's press coverage. Whatever that means."

As I explained to Chris about the 'stopped ships 'very boring press release, Oleg and Barry arrived, both looking shower splashed and very alert. Chris busied himself with the espresso machine.

Barry, Oleg and I buried our heads into our computers, mine was adding new mail faster than I could read what was already in the queue. Barry's email to Miss Stanton, Dal Booth and various others had, as expected, sparked of an electronic storm.

Barry grinned and said, "Well we both know who's paying the bills right now. Uncle Sam's got a bargain, and he still can't speak Tagalog."

I accepted another big mug of 'Rosy,' from Chris, with some bizarre logic he said, "too early for espresso's, boss."

I wandered outside on to the old terrace and watched the Riviera sun coming up over the old town.

Whoever said, 'a week is a long time in politics,' has never spent a week hoping to rescue innocent kids, and working on saving the world at the same time.

Chris approached, and speaking into his mobile said. "OK honey. Got it." He handed me a big fresh notepad and several pens. " Squeeze said this is what you'd need."

He returned with a bottle of water and said, "I'm going to have a kip and went inside."

I made notes...as Squeeze well knew, I liked a fresh pad of paper when working on a situation report. Having made a list, I took one more deep breath of fresh morning air and went into the conference room

Round the table we had Barry, Oleg, Johnnie Wells, with Chris Todd dozing on the sofa, head under his jacket, "I'm listening boss."

I enquired about Rewan, and Barry said, "He went with Charlie and Magnus yesterday to see the Asians." Which seemed like a good plan to me.

On the line Ulrike Sommer, now back in Germany, Squeeze, J&S in Singapore. We waiting to hear from Andy Keeling in Romania and Matt Button in Algeria.

Barry. "There's a lot of politics that Dan and I need to address about stopping the ships but first we must focus on the girls."

I ran through the list.

" One .Tracking the first phone contacts suggests they, or at least their phones, were in Morocco and Italy."

"Two, the second call suggests or wants to suggest locations changed by showing Romanian and Algerian newspaper front pages. Fresh dated and can see they real papers."

" But those calls to the parents came from one phone, new to us, from Copenhagen. They also included pictures of Haeggqvist properties in Malmo."

Barry said, "Rewan said one thing before he left. 'Was the Copenhagen call and the Swedish office pictures a frightener, or to suggest an inside job?' i.e. someone from within Baltic Shipping."

Barry said. "We have a biggish office in Norway because of their North Sea oil and gas business, so it was easy to send people to Malmo and Copenhagen yesterday. They are reporting to me at nine or sooner."

"So," I said. "In the real world we are not yet any nearer finding the girls. The ransom is ready in a pile somewhere, but we could to with finding them before we pay. Not to save money but just to be sure of getting them back. Alive. Reality is, once we've paid the abductors have no reason not to kill them."

I continued, " Just before we go back through that list in detail the other situations in a nutshell."

" Rumours of complete crew being hired."

"Paul Isted reports it's starting to look like a local advance fees scam, possibly pretending to be Korean to make it sound more attractive."

I asked Barry and Oleg to explain this and pass on to US and UK, as a work in progress.

"B. Current attacks on ships. Hazchem checks have found nothing. Booby traps still real possibility and thus concern. Ships still at sea awaiting answers from various bomb squads."

"The next problem being where they can safely, unload quite a few thousand containers, any one of which could be explosive, without stopping the usual business of a port. "

"Reason for the attack not clear, no claims made. North Korean influences unlikely because they can upset China. Insurance scam we discussed yesterday. Again Barry and Oleg to pass this on."

"Back to Number one priority. The Missing Girls."

" Gold ransom all available. Mr. Haeggqvist , Hiroshi-san and David Lim trying to clear export paperwork with the Swiss authorities. New money laundering regulations apparently make that difficult despite it being in fact their own gold. The Swiss playing strictly by the rules-despite those rules largely bullied into them over the past few years by US anti money laundering laws."

Squeeze cut in. "Magnus just called, wants you and Barry to come to Geneva and see Calvettioni with them this afternoon."

Barry nodded, and I said, "OK, we'll be there, Fix it please ."

Andy Keeling came on the line. "I'm in Bucharest,  I've managed to track the phones to the luggage store room of the Magnificent Hotel here. "

" I suspect they sent here as red herring. Particularly as they are in a postage carton addressed to incoming guests named Mr. and Mrs. Beckham. Very unimaginative, but I don't think them obviously being fans of English football is much of a clue."

"Right now the Concierge won't let me have them, I'm waiting for the manager to arrive, I hope he will allow me to collect the phones.  He's Swedish, so I am going to tread carefully in case there's a connection."

Andy went on. "I've been updating Matt Button in Algiers for the last hour or so. In his case, the Swedish phone signals faded soon after he left Ben Gurion airport. Then they came back with just a burst of life. Batteries fading I guess, but that last burst of life lead him to a small square in the city center."

" I told Matt about the position in Bucharest, and as there's a big hotel on that square in Algiers , he's trying in there, just in case."

Right on cue, Matt Button came on the speaker. "My hand held tracker is getting signals again in the Desert Melody  Hotel lobby, near the luggage store room. "

" The manager is away in France, but the Concierge is just waiting for the night manger to go home, and a $100 bill gets the luggage store room unlocked. I'll report in a few minutes I hope."

I wished him luck.

Ulrike. "Boss, I've been looking at the pictures of the Asia girls and the Swedish lot. There's a couple of things. Firstly the groups are never shown together and it seems from the new photos that they want us to think they're in Algeria and Romania."

" Well. Here in Germany with our big numbers of Turkish immigrants you can get Turkish papers everywhere, I bet it's the same for Romanian. Also I'm sure I've seen Arab papers for sale all over France, Holland and UK, maybe just at airports but it could be getting them is easy."

"Secondly. This is may be more important. In the first picture we got, Britt the Swedish lady is wearing a T shirt with a logo from the German stables where Tamiko and May went."

" I only noticed this just now, because I was looking at Brigitte's shirt in the new pictures and there's a horse on that as well. Obviously hand drawn. When you bring it up on the screen there's some numbers written underneath the horse head picture."

"I'm about ten minutes from those stables and I'm going in and see if they have ever seen the Swedish ladies. You can check that with Magnus. "

"I'm also going to see if they sell or can tell me anything about Brigitte's shirt with the horse drawing on it."

I agreed, all good maybe valuable points ,we'd wait to hear from her.

Oleg had brought the various photos up on the big screen and said, "We really should have noticed her wearing the German shirt before."

I agreed. Oleg went, " I have punched those letters and numbers from Brigitte's shirt into my computer and so far nothing, but maybe Jacko and Suki will find something."

"Already looking into it boss," It was Squeeze, alert as ever.

Then the day got a tiny bit better.

Firstly Matt Button. "I've got the two phones and the batteries are now indeed dead. I've got them in plastics and I'm on the way to the airport. They were posted from Marrakesh central post office on the 27th .They were addressed to a Mr. and Mrs. Rooney. I'm sending you a photo of the labels."

I cut in. " So they were posted on the day we got the first texts and pictures. Hand carry those phones to us here."

Squeeze cut in, " Matt there's no direct Algiers to Nice today. Give me a minute."

Just then more good or at least positive news. Andy Keeling. "Got 'em boss, all three phones. I guess bugger all in the batteries, but I've turned them off and put them in plastic bags".

" Swedish hotel manager here good as gold when I told him it a security matter in UK. They were posted from Venice to here. Addressed to a Mr. and Mrs. Beckham, which given Matt's Mr. and Mrs. Rooney, can't be a co-incidence, and like I said not very imaginative. Can't read the date stamp."

I told him to , "Get them here to us pronto."

Squeeze "Again, Andy no direct flight today Bucharest to Nice. Hold on." Oleg was waving his arms around: I said," Hold on all, Yes Oleg?"

"I suggest we need real specialist phone forensics on those phones, more than we can do here. My people can do that in London. But the first thing they can do for us when they get there , is copy the cards, photos, chips and call details to us online as that's the bit we really want here. "

"I also know there's loads of direct Bucharest London flights everyday as they are always writing about them in the tabloids, saying they are bringing pickpockets to London."

Before I could agree; Squeeze. "Matt can you get to Algiers Ben Gurion airport by eleven-ish?"

With an affirmative answer she then said "Andy, can you get to Bucharest airport by around eleven? " "Can do," he said, " near enough."

"OK," she said, "I'll txt you both booking details your flights. Both leave about 12.20. Luckily you both go to Gatwick."

Andy said, "You want me to come back here boss because we don't know if this a double bluff of some kind and the girls may really be here."

To which I responded. "I don't think so, I can't image anyone is going to come in and claim the phones, but we'll talk it through here whilst you're travelling. Before you leave you might have a quiet word with the Hotel manager if he seems reliable, tell him a little bit about the problem, and ask him to keep his eyes open."

"Well done, Oleg about the forensics, your plan way better.'

The morning remained positive. As Ulrike came back on.

"I'm outside the stables here near Rudesheim, and they say that T Shirt Britt is wearing, is new this season. So that's about a month and they only sell them here at the stables or at shows.  But they haven't been to any shows with that one yet. So it must have been bought here in the past four weeks."

"You need to check with Magnus if Britt's been here in the last month. Seems unlikely, but if she has not been here then, the girls or at least the shirts are or were, all together in one place."

She continued, sounding excited, "Here's something more though, the shirt Brigitte's wearing in the second batch of pictures, with the drawing of the horse on is not  one of theirs from here. "

"Of course it may just be a horse that Brigitte likes, or she bought the shirt somewhere."

"Here's the interesting bit, they say, the number looks like a horse ID number.  Seems all horses in Europe must have microchips and passports which records their inoculations and suchlike to be able to travel.  To encourage chipping or tattooing they can't enter shows without them, even little village horse shows, so most horses, not just the thorobreds are now chipped."

"But bad news is, there's no central index of details, the owner literally gets a card passport that's got the appropriate number on it. When they get medicines or travel details it gets updated, by a vet or a horse transport company."

"But here's the good news. They said that the code numbers are only issued to vets by a national horse society or agriculture department. So it should be possible to check out which vet that number at least went to."

"Luckily the people here have so many equestrian customers around Europe that they can find out some stuff for us. They've made some calls and we're waiting for an answer. Take care though of course it could just be a T shirt she bought in a market.'"

She hesitated, "Oh hang on," we could hear German conversation and at the end lots of 'danke', 'danke's'.

"OK- me again- we now know that number was issued to a vet in somewhere in France."

" They are going to try and get me details. They did stress that if the number was issued a while ago, if alive still, the horse could now be anywhere in the world."

As I thanked her I could hear Oleg muttering, "Or in a hamburger somewhere."

Which made me think of lunch, but nothing to do with the French habit that so appalls the English, that of eating horse meat.

I was hungry, may be too many days just snacking at the desk, may be some kind of relief that maybe, just maybe we're getting somewhere with this tangle of mysteries.

As the last few days had demonstrated we had a great system for feeding the staff in the office. After breakfasts courtesy George the night guardian, we had a housekeeper / cook from the village on call from mid-morning. She also supervised the two cleaning ladies who took care of the rooms.

She was used to our strange hours and provided lunches, which could be for anything between 5 and 15 people. She made sure that she always left a selection of quiches, cold meats, cheeses and her killer 'mousse au chocolat' for those working late. So we never went hungry.

I suggested I was going to take a break for early lunch, and said, "I'm going for some fresh air first. Back in 20 minutes." I needed to 'get out'. I realised that I had not ventured outside the office or the terrace for three days.

I set out, not to eat, but first to run my usual route round the village walls.  It was about a three K run and although usually I did it in the cool of the morning, not in the mid-day heat it still cleared the head.

I observed that French dogs, actually unlike 'mad' Englishmen out in the midday sun, just lolled in the shade, tongues out, and couldn't be arsed to do their usual chase and snap at any passing joggers heels. So I jogged on, but still thinking about bloody phones and German T shirts.

**36.Wednesday June 29th.11.00 am.In the street outside the TrePolPen office Vence. France:** *In the heat, my run took 35 minutes not the usual 20.*

As I jogged nearer the gates of the villa, a taxi had arrived and I could see  Sir Geoffrey Barker and with him Joel Williams settling the cab bill.

I had enough time, whilst recovering my breath, to consider the potential for conversation on their flight from London. Sir Geoffery, regardless of job title, effectively both diplomat and spy, with 40 years experience in almost every corner of the globe.

Joel, about 35 years old. A Brit, but ex French Foreign Legion. Bizarrely at one time the co-operator of a bar in Kabul in war torn Afghanistan, "Check you weapons in here with your coats please."

He was, or rather is, now the very much hands on owner operator of a much in demand 'active service team.' Active service meaning special ops. We had used their services on several occasions, mainly in Africa and in some possible piracy events. I liked Joel's quiet professionalism.

I had alerted him some days before about 'a potential problem, and then updated him about necklace bombs and the rest. He had gone  to the UK and Sir Geoffery had assisted in opening some doors with the latest info about such things opened. Or so I hoped.

Having established that despite it only being 11.30 they were both hungry, it turned out that they'd had had an early start from  Gatwick airport.  I had a quick shower and we grabbed a couple of the office motor scooters, much used in the evenings for collecting pizza's, and rode over to the Colombe d'Or in the next village. Definitely not famous for take away pizza's, but my favourite restaurant and hotel in all the world.

The gardien there greeted me cheerfully. As usual, even at this early for lunch hour, he was busy manning the rope that kept the inevitable crowd of tourists and paparazzi from pushing in to gaze at what the US TV shows call 'The Rich and Famous' dining on the terrace. Or under some of the most famous paintings in the world in the old dining room.

He was not at all thrown by our arrival on scooters and gave the keys to an assistant ,more used to parking Porsches and Range Rovers.

With no reservations, I told the Maitre'd we had to get back to the office and would only be an hour. As he muttered, 'shame for you,' he was beside himself that we may be 'deranged' by the sun as he managed to find us a table on the already busy terrace. Assisted by a willing waitress, he promptly moved a huge umbrella to shade us, completely exposing the couple at the next table who were finishing their coffees.

Our murmured apologies were cheerfully smiled away, as they gathered their belongings and said, "No problem, that was breakfast for us, we're off to the sunbeds by the pool anyway."

I waved away a menu for me and I said. "Hors d'oevre and later a mushroom omelette please." "Make that two," said Joel. "Or even three," said Sir Geoffery, and in his usual joking style said, " That's one for him and him and one for me." His bad attempt at English humour was met with a slight 'sniff' from the waitress. Despite our, 'no wine' we're working', the same lady waitress, said, "It was unthinkable for us not to have at least a glass of 'my usual'."

As we sat sipping the crisp white house wine, Sir Geoffery said, " Sitting here on the best terrace in the world is really not the place to keep on with the 'Sirs" and Misters, please call me Geoff or Geoffery it that works better for you," he smiled and said, "makes me feel more part of the team."

I updated him and Joel on the mornings, 'happenings'. " Some progress at last I think," and as we slowly attacked the selection of fifteen or so hors d'oevre dishes, Sir --sorry - 'Geoff' went first to update me about explosives likely to be in necklace form. Rather off putting when eating, but both had to be done. He spoke quietly, " The advances in technology over the past few years have been amazing. Particularly since 9/11, when with money no problem  the Americans threw everything they had at finding ways of finding and identifying concealed explosives, and finding ways to deal with surprise nasty situations."

"We've looked at these first pictures of the four bombs we can see,  and to be honest have very few clues.  They look like they are made of neoprene-'wet suit' material, the 'pouch on the front, also covered in neoprene- is about the size of a box of matches. "

"The question is, can they be nasty. The answer, I am afraid, is yes, probably. Or rather yes, likely. If the long piece round the neck was explosive 'detonator' cord the results are horrible."

"If the long piece just a strap and the explosive is only in the front part the results may be less nasty. That's provided you could get a Kevlar pad or something between it and the wearer's neck. If you can do that they may possibly stand a chance."

"But the boffs say that det cord would not stand up very well to constant flexing and movement so they says there's a better than 50 - 50 chance the neck strap is indeed not that. But it could part of the electrical system or an aerial, so if its part of the circuit, then cutting it is not good."

Joel then continued. "Checking for explosives. This is the really clever stuff these days. If we can get near. As you know from the use of sniffer dogs, explosive's of all kind give of some kind of clues, mostly fumes that tell what they are."

"In this case, from what we can see of the small pouch at the front of the necklace,  we assume , or even reasonably know it can only be a tiny amount of the bang stuff, so that cuts down the list.  Without going through hours of detail with you, about the only thing we are all agreed on, is that it must be one of about five possible explosives.

Two hard to get, but not discounted ,three easy to make or get."

"The good news is that their scent patterns are all well known. Which helps a bit, and makes detection of even tiny quantities a tad easier."

"Not easy, but better than sniffing for a complete mystery."

"Checking for them. Sniffer dogs are still good but also rats and even bees are the noses of choice these days. The rats are now widely used in Angola and Cambodia, on leashes sniffing out landmines, much quicker than hand clearance."

I said, "But that must use a lot of rats."

Joel responded, "No you twat, they find the explosive, and are too light or non-magnetic to set it off. So they sit up and ask for their  treats, that they've been given in their training every time they find something. The place is marked and the disposal boys do the rest. If a rat does get blown up the handlers go spare. But we're not in Cambodia. Then there's various hand held devices, Flirs is one.  Sophisticated sniffers really. You see them at the airports."

"You also see large boxes, and similar that analyse smells, vapours, even light reflections with various programmed in patterns. That equipment used to be the size of a car, now they're back packable. The programmed in patterns they look for can be drugs or bangs."

He continued, "But of course when you've found it we've  still got to deal with the nasty bit, so we should check what the French and American experience is. They are good at that stuff."

We agreed on the big problem :First locate the girls. With our advance research we would then at least be best prepared to deal with stage two : Get near enough to use the modern equipment.

Which only left, stage three : Deal with it. F***ing carefully. After a few moments silent contemplation, in my case pondering the bizarre  situation, brilliant food and service, on one of the worlds most legendary terraces, but discussing appalling possibilities.

We refused coffees and made our way back to the office.

**36a. Wednesday. June 29th.Windsor. Around 20 miles west of London. England:** *River Thames, Castle, Near Ascot Racecourse, nice open countryside.No wonder the Queen lives there for much of the year.*

On Tuesday, the previous day, both Joanna Brown and her great friend Sue Graham-Smith had been delighted by the news that their husbands were returning a few days early from the Far East.

In neither case, as they were on an open phone line had the husbands explained about May and Tamiko going missing.

Just that they were, 'hitching a lift' on the boss's plane.

The women were together at Joanna's house sipping wine watching the best of Glastonbury on the TV when the call came in. The husbands suggested that as they'd both slept well on the plane and would be at home by mid afternoon maybe they could get together for a Barbecue.

So it was a few hours later that Jo and Sue had to explain, Melissa and Tiggs absence to their husbands. "Before you both go off the deep end- you were out there- we were here, and Michael's at Glasto with his band mates. " The girls are sticking together, and I think half their school mates are there as well".

Doug, raised an eyebrow at, 'Glasto.' and Steve Brown spoke, "I agree with Doug, and I'm sure you went into it, but they're a bit young."

The two mothers looked at each other and Tiggs mother said. "Hold on a minute, we're all in this together."

Before Jo could move she nipped into the living room and came back with the photo of Jo and Steve at the Pink Floyd concert.

"Unless Jo's been lying to me all these years I think this beautiful young lady with that old ruffian is aged 15 years and 8 months in this picture. I rest my case Captain."

Steve and Doug grinned and Steve said," You don't get to be a Captain without learning when it's time to stop engines."

"I guess we're just feeling a bit sensitive because:" and they explained about the missing girls, which of course produced, gasps, hands to mouths, and "oh my gods, poor Shoko and Peggy," and of course, "What's happening now, can the police find them?"

Steve explained the danger inherent in police activity, where despite their concern of course for any kidnapped victims, they naturally tended also to try and apprehend the culprits.

So it was a subdued foursome who ate some good English barbecued sausages and salad, mostly from their garden. As darkness fell they started to discuss the return of the two girls from Glastonbury.

On the TV news they could see the usual pictures of, 'The big clear up,' and heard the usual voice over. "As the last of the 175,000 music loving revelers pack up their tents and go to join the long lines at the stations and bus parks, the big clean up is under way. XYZ tons of rubbish etc."

Now it was the turn of the two husband to be reassuring. "They're not stupid. We would have heard if they had a problem. They'll be here soon."

Ten, eleven then midnight came and went, no ring tones from any of the girls phones. Nothing from brother Michael's phone either, "It's too late now to call any of the other parents."

A call to Glastonbury Police was put through to a weary sounding voice at Bristol Police telecoms HQ. "Sorry madam. No reports of any problems. It's the same each year after Glasto, we have a listing of almost 1000 missing, 'children,'" They heard the almost audible sneer in the voice at the word 'children'.

"There are some late trains still running. We have logged your call. Please advise us when the 'children,' - that tone of voice again - "when 'the children' return home, so that we can then focus on more pressing problems."

They dozed, eventually at 1.30 am Sue and Doug went home , "I'm still on Asia time.....of course we'll call you...you call us at any time of the night."

At 4 am Jo and Steve awoke, startled to find their son Michael, equally startled to find his parents asleep in the living room......"No he hadn't seen his sister or her friends..... Actually not for the whole week end."

"But that's not a worry he and his mates were in the backstage area where most couldn't go, and in the end he could not get backstage passes for them ...but they should not worry, the phones were terrible this year. If they didn't mind he was going to shower and bed for the first time since Thursday."

Wednesday morning, and over early breakfast teas, the vigil started again. By mid morning after another inconsequential call to missing persons 'Bristol', "Well last night we got up to 1340 missing, we're now down to about 240, so it's all fairly normal, for Glastonbury weekend, that is."

Far from being encouraged by the friendly, but weary, police voice the families were seriously concerned. Steve said, "I'm going to call Daniel. It's lunchtime in France now and I think we should let him know just in case.

We've both got quite a high profile here after that TV series on Big Ships-better to be safe than sorry."

Calling the office, they spoke with Squeeze, "Dan will be back in a short while, but tell me all about it as we've got the whole team in France on the line as well as us here in Singapore."

Squeeze listened and said, "Let me talk this through with the team and we'll call you back within 30 minutes."

To the team, kind of cheerful as some progress seemed to be under way, the possibility that we had two more missing girls from a hi-ish profile shipping family was not welcome.

Most of the team had seen the TV series about life aboard a mega ship, or had met the Captains in Singapore at one time or another.

They concluded that even though the Captains were, 'employees-not billionaire owners,' that their high profile from the TV series, may , indeed did, make them potential targets.  Just as Barry said, 'I'll pop down to road and talk to Dan," the phone rang.

With the mood in the office having gone from guarded optimism to gloomy 'god what next,' they watched and waited. Nervously...

**37. Wednesday June 29th. Lunchtime. TrePolPen Security Company offices.Vence. France:** *All a bit of 'un Montagne Russe. 'Which, I am hopefully reliably informed, is, or should be the French slang for, 'Roller Coaster'.*

As Sir Geoffery, Joel and I walked in from our brief lunch, there was a slightly ironic cheer from my team. Johnnie Wells and Oleg also nodding at their UK boss.

"Nice lunch boss?" From Chris.

Also from Chris, "We didn't like to disturb you with the call about the two more missing girls from the shipping business."

That stopped me, "What the fu**?"

And from Barry, "We also figured you could wait to see the picture of kidnapper number one."

Which produced a, "Christ Almighty," from the usually imperturbable Sir Geoffery.

Chris, "It's all OK now boss." He explained about the two girls missing after attending Glastonbury music festival weekend. Their dads, both senior captains with Lims who had having flown to Europe with Chris in the Lim Jet, had called him.

"We know them" I said.

Well Chris went on, "The girls were a day overdue getting back from Glastonbury, and given the situation with May and Tamiko their dads had called in to us. But less than ten minutes later they called again, very embarrassed...... The girls had just walked into their houses. Safe and sound. The delay something to do with, 'staying an extra day at Glastonbury to earn money to pay back a grandmother'. Oh yes, and a useless brother not reading his texts to pass on messages to his parents."

So it stayed being a good day, and with Barry's report it got even better.

Old style detective work in Malmo, as rather suits a nation where old style detectives have become global literary and movie heroes, had also produced useful results.

In remarkably quick time yesterday, a couple of operatives from Matchless Consulting Oslo offices had arrived in Malmo and started to map out and check the area to prepare a comprehensive security upgrade for the Sorenson and Haeggqvist houses.

On a hunch from Rewan Trelawney to use what he called an 'old school style,' investigation, the Matchless team started by discretely chatting to locals, the postman, a couple of workmen cutting grass and suchlike.

Then 'bingo' they also struck really lucky in the little local gas station and general store. The same chatty lady was on duty, and at their questions immediately said, "That's funny you should be asking about all this only yesterday I had a German gent in here asking all the same stuff."

Thirty minutes later not only did they have the number of Hans' car but they had some remarkably clear video shots from the security cams in the shop and outside. Having suggested this was a probably a security matter, some discrete and speedy work with Danish and Swedish police, and the passage of the car both ways through the bridge toll booths was noted.

Establishing where the car and the occupant had been over night was the work of just three hotel visits. Again more video, from the hotel reception. The receptionist recalled the man checking out and noted he must have been to Tivoli as on the previous night video, he was carrying a large bear and other stuff in Tivoli bags. Bingo again, more good quality stills and video.

The trail went cold at the car rental office at Kastrup airport, but copies of Han's driving licence and credit card details were now theirs. The names drew a blank for any outbound flights. Checking the system to find a face using a different name and I.D. would take a time, but they were confident of success.

At this stage Barry had requested from the Danish authorities a 'no news stories/press releases please,' this is an ongoing operation.

Our early lunch, meant that Joel had time to have a quick energetic game of volley ball in the pool with Oleg and Johnnie, whilst I showed Geoffrey Barker some of the background we had for both the kidnapping and the various ship attacks.

He said, "I liked the week numbers used, not dates story that Miss Stanton told me . Good stuff."

I responded, "It was good to do, but we still have nothing whatsoever about what exactly that bloody threat is all about. So it's still a priority."

Squeeze reminded me that an air taxi awaited in Nice to take us to Geneva. Chris drove Geoff, Barry, Joel and myself down to the airport. I had asked Joel to come with Barry and I ,action may be the next phase if we're lucky, so reassuring the parents may be the way forward.

Having left Sir Geoffery in the Easy Jet queue for London, we found the general aviation desk and were taken straight through to a small departures lounge. We talked on as the plane set off on the quick hop to Geneva.

**38. Wednesday June 29th 5.30 pm. Geneva Airport. Switzerland. But in the real world...** *For us arriving at Geneva, the peace and serenity of 'chocolate box' pretty Switzerland belied the turmoil of the unknown.*

*For the Swedish women and children it was ten days since they were kidnapped.*

*For the Asian girls and Brigitte, seven days.*

*For the Parents- an endless nightmare.*

*For us, intent on safe rescue with or without payment of ransom, too bloody long. So long, I wondered if we were starting to grasp at straws and rumour.*

For Geneva, private jets and air taxi's are the norm, so whilst of course quick and queue less the general aviation terminal was much as any other part of the business like airport.

That is, no queues inside, but the usual taxi queue outside, but I guess most private flyers have chauffeurs.

There hadn't been any telecoms on the air taxi, so as we exited the terminal buildings all our phones came to life with calls.

Squeeze's voice, luckily loud above the traffic noise. "I've got some stuff for you lot and it's bloody late here in Singapore."

I listened. " Firstly. We know the exact details of the horse doctor or vet that used that number. It's in Carcassonne. That's an old city Between Toulouse and Montpellier South West France. Closed today now. Opens at 9.00 tomorrow morning. I've sent you sat nav. co-ords. Of course that's not the location of the horse, if it's alive and not Oleg's hamburgers."

"Secondly. The boys are back in London from Algiers and Bucharest. All the girls phones are now at Vauxhall Cross, they are copying data to us and working on them, any and all calls made, received and all that."

"Thirdly. Rory has a freight plane lined up with a 'special crew.' But I need to come up with a $75,000 charter and fuel deposit and a further $18,000 tomorrow to cover crew and machine insurance-not contents insurance ,which we can't get."

I spoke to Barry, who taking my phone said. "Squeeze, bill Matchless Consulting from your Singapore business account for $175,000 general advance on fees and expenses. "

"I'll get it transferred right now. Don't mention planes, or we'll get Swiss style paperwork problems from my office. In a few days bill them for another $100,000." He continued, " Oh yes—we need make sure the Pilots have their Amex Cards pre-loaded with $20,000 each. We don't know where and how many times they may need to re-fuel and Amex works for planes at av-gas suppliers everywhere."

Oleg came up next on my phone. "Interesting, the picture and txt we got yesterday from Copenhagen, *came in to that* phone just a few minutes earlier from somewhere near Toulouse."

Having thanked both Squeeze and Oleg, and come to the front of the taxi queue, we made our way to the hotel where Charlie had based himself. Talking with Joel and Barry on the plane we had agreed that we could pretty much assume that, whilst the message content was important the apparent call-send locations, Algeria, Morocco, Venice and Romania were red herrings to put us off the track.

Thanks to the T shirt clues we were starting feel the girls were all together. In the taxi, we continued. With that phone message to the phone in Copenhagen originating from the South West of France, and the writing on the second T shirt now sending us to a vetinarians office in the same area, may be, just maybe we just had something.

Joel said. "I know that area like the back of my hand, and the stonework behind the girls in those pictures, looks very local. Of course it could be anyone of a million bloody villages but it looks right to me."

He continued, "Also moving eight people with kids around is not that easy. Setting up false trails is likely easier."

We agreed however that we should not read too much into our suppositions, but investigating them was a priority.

Barry suggested, that subject to whatever happened this afternoon, he'd stay in Switzerland working with the ship owners, and as Joel and I spoke French, and Joel knew the area well we would go to Carcassonne together.

Joel's response to that, of, "Well, so far Dan all of the jobs I've done for you, at least this one looks like it's got clean drinking water and soft toilet tissue," had Barry in slight hysterics as we arrived at the hotel.

Earlier we had agreed we needed to know more about Calvettioni' as there were parts of his story that didn't add up, we had planned be quite forceful about his business and debts in Asia, and his reactions to the kidnappings, to gain some reactions from him.

But by the time we walked in obviously a lot of talking had taken place between all of those lined up waiting for us.

Barry introduced Joel and I, to Calvettioni and Gerry McMullen, and Joel to the other ship owners.

As we settled ourselves around a table in a very swish meeting room, David said, "We've mainly kept our conversation to shipping business whilst we waited for you guys . Actually we also talked a bit about the ransom situation, and have something interesting to report on that."

He turned to Calvettioni and said, "May I give the guys a resume of the discussions and the agreement we have penciled in".

Calvettioni nodded and David started.

"We are all very familiar with the ups and downs of business. I often think the bigger you are the wilder the roller coaster ride. "

"Charlie and I have agreed that getting to where we are today has not been a smooth ride, and we three had the big advantage of starting 25 years before our friend Andre here."

Barry glanced at me, I think we could see where this was going, and in the corner of the room slightly behind Calvettioni I could see Gerry McMullen looking fairly relaxed.

David went on, " Many are the times when, without state help from Taiwan's shipbuilding or export promotion boards putting pressure on our bankers that we could have failed "

"I know the same applies to Hiroshi san with his associations in Japan. Of course we were all following this old rogue," he said, indicating Charlie, "he just seem to surf on the crest a wave for year after year."

Charlie smiled and said, "Little do you know David. But for sure I was in the right place at the right time to expand an old established and already very active business"

" Actually we also gained help from yours and the Korean and Japanese shipbuilding boards with soft credit for new ship orders. More to the point we started from a way better point in time than Andre here."

He nodded at Calvettioni.

Calvettioni spoke, in quite accented English. "If I may David, Charlie, Hiroshi.You are very kind – too kind really. We did indeed start at a tough time, taking over, French Island Cargo which quite frankly was a failing 'around the islands' freight shipping company. Of course as is the way when you are young and ambitious, we started without enough funding to hand."

" Despite getting advice of the dangers ahead I went on with my plan, or mostly I just reacted to daily business needs. But always, it seemed, having to take a step to large."

Gerry McMullen, nodded, quite vigorously at that.

"The French Government is all talk, when it comes to business assistance. The 'Made in France' label on a new ship also means 'Made in France, slowly and too bloody expensively,' as Gerry would say. I'm a patriotic Frenchman and Gerry is a brilliant accountant as well as being a genius sea master, but that's the situation, politics rarely really help."

"So what David is very politely leading up to, is that due to combination of circumstances, many of my own making, I totally over reached my business five years ago. This despite Gerry's advice, to which I was too arrogant to listen to properly, and we have never really recovered since."

"It seems that it has taken the disappearance of my daughter to bring me to both my senses and to at last follow advice from Gerry to enter into a full and open meeting with these guys."

Barry said. "On the subject of your daughter, I do have to say that when the kidnap happened you seemed very blasé and relaxed about the matter."

Calvettioni said. "I understand and I regret that picture. I was getting messages when I was on an Island in the Pacific with electricity only for three hours per day."

" But the main reason for my slow response was that I assumed it was yet another kind of play, by her mother and Brigitte."

" My wife and I are separated, divorcing and Brigitte has not taken it well. She has been constantly threatening to run away from the school and home and stuff like that. So when the 'apparent' kidnap happened I jumped to the conclusion it was exactly that."

"At that time apparent was not yet 'confirmed abducted,' I was wrong and I hope I didn't cause you extra problems."

"Additionally my wife, soon to be ex-wife, also doesn't want to speak to me as she doesn't believe I am not worth billions for a divorce settlement."

" It is not helped by the fact that she is such an alcoholic that it's almost impossible to talk properly with her."

Calvettioni seemed a bit over come and went to the side table and busied himself pouring water.

Gerry McMullen said. " Andre's picture is very accurate, including I am sorry to say about the impossibility of communicating with Mrs. Calvettioni." He lightened the mood, "Actually that's the only bit I really blame Andre for, having Mrs. Calvettioni blasting off in my ear is an interesting experience."

Calvettioni now recovered said, laughing, "Yes, sorry about that Gerry, but at least be thankful you weren't married to her."

"Actually," he went on, "of course I hope for her and Brigitte's sake that her mother can get over the alcohol problem. I think that with me not there ,may be that will help. Of course once I realised that Brigitte was truly missing, it's not been easy." He looked grief stricken again, but with a deep breath continued." Where we are now ? I have reached an agreement in principle for David and Charlie, with some private help from Hiroshi,  to assume financial control of my company, F.I.C. "

" I am now understanding at last that I cannot sail the waves solo with my own business. Also having lost the confidence of the banks it will be a pleasure to be able to put my energies to building F.I.C. as part of a new joint company with them."

"Of course their assistance with the ransom money is part of that, but the arrangement is more than very fair. They have not taken advantage of my personal position. Of course they get the company at a low position, but to be honest, for me, the alternative is total bankruptcy of the business. "

"It is not that 'they are the last game in town', luckily for me, and the employees, but also they are the best. It's a dream solution for me that I will have to live up too."

Charlie said, " The possibility to do all this quickly, is helped by my confidence from knowing Gerry for so many years."

Gerry said, " I think that in certain territories, especially in French Africa and other French territories, we , F.I.C. can bring also some benefits to a consortium. I also think that with some territorial shuffling, ship re-registration and the like we can avoid the need for any competition investigation by the EC."

Barry said, " Well all that sounds good and I am sure if all parties are happy..." Calvettioni interrupted, "I am indeed. Of course I was in a weak position financially but this is a practical trading agreement, of the kind we had been seeking. Way better than I could ever have hoped to arrange with a bank, and believe me I have been talking to many banks. Banks only bring money and debt, this brings in real business."

Barry went on. "I am still seeking clues to assist with finding the girls, so I have to ask four key questions and although they are somewhat personal to Mr. Calvettioni, I know that David and Charlie are aware of them."

Calvettioni said, "Exactement, quite, I fully appreciate that. Carry on ask what you need."

Barry said. "OK. This applies to our need to find possible motives or background to the kidnapping.  Firstly we have learned  that you have several gambling debts outstanding in Asia and that certain 'interesting' Chinese groups have been endeavouring to collect on them."

"Secondly, as you know from our conversations last week ,it seemed a little strange that four Calvettioni ships had been attacked out of the many at sea. Now of course the rumours were and indeed are, that this was an inside job, possibly an insurance scam. Or if not, was it related to point one, the Chinese debts."

Calvettioni looked straight at Barry, "and points three and four?"

Barry said. "Hang on- oh yes, three is about raising the ransom, four was quite honestly about what seemed strange at the time your somewhat relaxed attitude to your daughters disappearance, but you've covered them already earlier. Points taken and well understood."

Calvettioni smiled and said, "Barry, I fully understand your professional concern on all of them."

"Regarding the insurance, your point two, nothing set up by us. If anything we are under-insured. Regarding the contents of the boxes I have no idea, that's a freight content owners responsibility. But I can't imagine in the real world anyone could hope to collect on a tricky claim like that."

" Regarding the gambling debt. That was partly true, I explained this to David and Charlie earlier. I was desperate for cash for the business last year, and some Chinese contacts on the mainland arranged a loan for me, to be collected in cash, from a mysterious casino in Macao. So not really a gambling debt but a way of drawing out the cash."

"I did indeed do that, but the loan, and the stupidly high interest I had agreed when desperate, was repaid in full last year also, by the lender buying the a ship from us at well below the market price."

"At the time, I was so embarrassed about that I even tried, unsuccessfully I might add,  to hide it from Captain McMullen. He will confirm to you that we sold a ship to a Chinese company based in Cyprus."

Gerry McMullen nodded as Andre continued,

"Regarding the difficulties in contacting me at the start of all this. To be honest I was taking a few days off with a young lady, and given the negotiating position with my wife's divorce lawyers I was trying to keep that a bit quiet."

Charlie said. " We went through this earlier and Hiroshi-san, David and I are happy now.  Barry?" He looked at Barry quizzically.

 Barry replied. "Well I am not happy."

Looks of shock and concerns from David, Charlie, Hiroshi and especially Calvettioni.

 He grinned. " I am not happy, because whilst I now fully appreciate, and accept all your answers. So that's all fine and well understood. But what makes me unhappy ,is that they completely blow apart Dan's and my three reasons for the attack on the ships. So now we have to start again!"

Smiles all round.  I started, "Now we should focus on the girls, and the ransom." I continued. " First of all Mr. Calvettioni.  Are you totally  aware we are so far taking great care with the kidnap situation to try and avoid too eager law and order organisations putting the girls lives at risk by attempting early rescues."

Calvettioni nodded, "I understand and am 100% with you on that-especially as we as a company had a bad experience with a botched rescue of a pirated crew off Somalia."

I continued. "The Somali hostage recovery problems, seem to be well known in the shipping business. Now I can tell you we have made some small progress in tracing the abductors, or at least the persons sending the messages to us all. "

"We have a positive id that appears genuine, together with stills and video footage of the gentleman who has been sending us the ransom demands."

I nodded at Charlie and Magnus, "The same one who photographed your houses. We also have fingerprints. He may be an abductor, part of the team or just a  messenger. The danger is he could be employed as 'a cut out'. i.e. knowing nothing, no locations nothing, no people ,just paid to receive and send phone numbers. So we have not ,repeat not, made any public appeal with his photo's. Yet. But we are taking active steps to establish where he went after Copenhagen."

"I stress we can do nothing with that information yet, otherwise we may endanger the girls. When we find them we will still have the very   serious problem of the necklace bombs controlling their life- or not."

At that Calvettioni's hand flew to his face and tears came to his eyes, and Charlie Haeggqvist growled, "Just pay the bloody ransom and get them back."

Joel spoke for the first time. "You are right Mr. Haeggqvist, in many ways there are no points to be gained in making delays or trying for deals. But on the other hand, *in reality there is no guarantee, once we have paid, that they will be released.*  In fact there is more danger then, as the girls may have seen or know too much for their own safety."

I said. "We all understand that, but as we all have discussed many times, nothing will happen to them for sure until we pay. The first point I make now is definite. The following is work in progress, but encouraging at each step."

"First of all, this morning, we have retrieved all their personal phones, from Romania and Algiers. They are being forensically checked now in London. We do not think the girls are in, or have been in those places."

"Secondly, thanks to some clues involving horses on T shirts worn by the girls, we think they are being held together. We have now established that one of the T shirts has a horse id code on it issued by a vetinarian in Carcassonne, South West France."

"Joel and I are there early tomorrow morning as soon as they open. Of course it may just be that there's a local T shirt designer there who sells shirts. But a new clue has emerged just now and that is. The phone used to call you yesterday, with text and new photos, called from Copenhagen. But we now know it had been receiving and sending calls to and from South West France."

Joel said, "For what it's worth, and I don't want to build up false hopes, I know the area very well, I lived there for a while. The stonework in those buildings behind the girls pictures looks kind of right for the area."

Joel continued looking very serious, "In a way we are all putting too much hope, thought and interpretation into those pictures, because they are all we have. But Dan I will check all that out first thing tomorrow. "

"Two things is a co-incidence, we have three, 'the origin of the last calls, the photo background, and now the location of the horse doctor,' when considered together are quite positive. "

I said, "But let me say one more thing. Opening up the gates to a flood of global publicity, could help us. More likely on the way to helping us it would bury us in an avalanche of false leads. Some just concerned, but wrong-others malicious. More to the point it is our considered opinion that any such publicity could alarm and panic the abductors, but we need to consider that amongst ourselves. Whilst we make the final plans to pay."

After a flood of questions, Gerry McMullen said. "Gentlemen. That's all good stuff and all understood. ..but Getting back to the ransom. We have a problem getting the gold out of Switzerland."

"Might happen after a month in court, it's our gold after all, but we don't have a month. We have chances to source it in Asia or the Gulf states, but Andre has a suggestion, that could be quick and easy. By chance, I assume, it involves South West France also."

Calvettioni said. "We have discussed earlier before you arrived, that in Marseilles airport there are several large bonded, customs approved, and sealed storage facilities. One belongs to my company and we have operated it for many years. That's usual for the shipping business. Of course we operate it, under strict customs controls."

"Mostly it's full of diamond drill tips and other valuable electronic stuff that's tax free when being shipped in or out. But there's always at least one shipment of gold in there."

" The gold, like the other goods, is not belonging to me or our company. It's mostly incoming from one or more of our clients in Africa. Francophone influence in Africa remains strong, and a lot of our commercial and government business is routed from there.Usually, gold remains there for a while, I know there is some now, when I realised the ransom demand was for gold I checked."

" I am sure the owners of that bullion would be very happy to have the ownership of their Marseille gold moved, with good documentation to Switzerland as its origins are a little cloudy shall we say. Actually, we could probably even make a good deal on that."

"Also in a bonded warehouse at Toulouse airport, which we also operate, there's even more gold."

" The paper work on this is better. There's various shipments our airfreight people shipped in there for one of the governments in West Africa."

" Again they would be happy to have it in Switzerland. I say the ownership paperwork is better, which it is. But now as they are slightly at odds with the French over some human rights issues in their country."

"Nothing to with the gold but political points. Not ownership disputes."

Gerry said, "So, as part of the deal with Andre's company to raise legit paperwork, with some juggling of ship and route ownerships here, we can set up good and legal reasons to properly transfer the ownership of the gold in France to here in Switzerland. Essentially the gold here changes ownership but stays in Switzerland".

" Doing that is easy as it technically isn't yet in French jurisdiction, and the paperwork covering -why- it came to Switzerland will keep the authorities here happy.  We get the gold in Toulouse and Marseille in exchange. That's all without it ever actually physically leaving the country."

"What we choose to do with it then, is our concern. Again with no real permissions needed from France to export it, as being in the bonded warehouse, technically the gold isn't even in France, we can export it again.

"We can TIR transfer the two shipments either Marseilles to Toulouse, or Toulouse to Marseille and airfreight them to wherever the bad guys demand." Barry said, "TIR?"

Gerry explained, "It's a system where customs seal a truck, or the load on a truck if its passing through a country without stopping. This avoids the need for local tax on something just passing through. Its used also if the shipment is between two bonded-that's tax free warehouses."

I said, "Right let's make a timeline on this. Today is Thursday, originally we were supposed to pay the gold by tomorrow, but we already alerted them to a slight problem. "

" If we can message the bad guys that the gold export problem is fixed 100%. Tell them that the shipment is now originating from Marseille airport not Switzerland. We can hopefully ship it anytime from Saturday or

Sunday. This buys us at least 24 hours plus, to try and find the girls before we ship. And to do more checking done about the necklaces."

I looked at Gerry and said, "How quickly can you confirm the gold ?"

Calvettioni answered and said, " Right now. The chance for the African owners to exchange their whole shipments for properly registered London Standard bars in a major Swiss bank will make them very happy, and make me a hero."

"At least in parts of Africa.

"So the gold is all OK now. For me, we can confirm Saturday what suits you. If you 'ave the plane you need. If not, both Toulouse and Marseille get a lot of trans Africa stuff so that will be easy if needed, my office do planes for those airports every day".

I explained we had a plane on stand by, but would keep his offer in mind and that I needed to get to Carcassonne for 9.00 in the morning and started to make plans to get back to the office, and we agreed Barry should stay in Geneva.

As we started to compose a text confirming shipping details of the ransom, Barry's phone, with the number we had used to communicate with the kidnappers, came to life with a series of incoming texts.

He said, " Hang on gents we have a new message from the bad guys, replying to ours of yesterday."

*TXT. No changes to release plan. All at once. We agree inshore ship moves. But all rest of fleets, owned or operated by you must stop where they are. They have remain stop until we collect golds.*

*Note we can repeat set fire on many ships across the various fleets. If this ships all stop not actioned then we will mail you fingers being cut off from the children. Finis.*

After some conversation about the likely nationality of the sender and some discussion about the implications, and origins of the new 'fire threat' we agreed to respond in the way we had just agreed.

*Att . All gold to hand ready to pay in one shipment as required. But Swiss law on gold impossible. Have arranged 100% will be shipped from Marseille France Saturday afternoon. ETD and Plane id number to follow. We are stopping vessels that we can control. Obviously we need destination details and hostage release plans from you. Ends.*

Within minutes of sending the message from Barry's extra phone, his other one rang. "Speak of the devil, It's Dal Booth."

As Barry adjourned to the corner of the room and sat looking out of the window I explained to Hiroshi and Calvettioni that Dal was head of America's CIA and the point man acting for the entire US Government.

I also explained that Barry and I felt that the US and probably the UK were eves-dropping on to all our calls and texts.

After a long and from our end what sounded like a fairly heated conversation, he returned to the table and said. "They've called an emergency meet in one hour at The White House, they are as we thought obviously reading our messages."

"Dal says they are 100% against any stopping of ships, and will likely order US Navy board all vessels and assume command."

Hiroshi and David started to say," but they legally can't do that.

"I agree," said Barry, " but I don't think 'legally' works when, they are defending The Good Old U.S. of A."

Old man Qvist was sitting quietly, eyes closed looking almost asleep. But now he spoke. "Earlier I agreed with the idea to put out our own press release, which we did, and I suspect that bought us 24 hours on this. Right now let's wait and see what the USA say before we do anything else."

"Any plan they have will take time, many days to set up, even if they had this idea before. It's now 9.00 at night here, late in most of Asia and morning on the East Coast of the USA. So we aren't going to hear much for a few hours." Charlie continued. "I suggest we eat. As ever the Viking rule is 'stay strong for the fight', so we can plan whilst we eat."

I said, "Before we eat, I think I'll call Chris to take the car out early tomorrow he can get to Montpellier Airport, which is a good way towards Carcassonne, where we have the lead about the horse. Joel and I'll get an air taxi out of here early and meet Chris there".

David interrupted and said, " Use our Asia Jet-Works plane, we came in on that last night. I'll tell them to be ready at 6.30 am for a short local to?" he looked at me. "Montpellier," I said. "Just near Marseille, but Marseille has horrible morning traffic." I could see Calvettioni nodding.

All was fixed with a couple of calls, and as we left the room I said, "I just realised, where's Rewan ?"

David said, " He's being chaperone and tour guide for Peggy and Shoko. They don't really need him for guiding but he's a good reassurance for them both. But I will call him and see if we can rescue him from yakkety women and get him to come and eat with us."

Whilst we waited for the elevator, we discussed David's learning of English from Chris Todd. 'Yakkety Yak Women,' didn't sound like it came from a language school in Taipei.

**39.Wednesday. June 29th.9.00 pm.Sun setting behind the mountains. A lakeside Hotel. Geneva. Switzerland:** *'Well we may be traditionally and peacefully neutral, but we sure as hell aren't neutered.'*

So much of life in Switzerland, does actually confirm the cliché of all that is usually seen as Swiss . Not the same exotic and mysterious cliché's as Shanghai, but clichéd none the less. So, as has been said too many times, Chocolate box pretty, and like the best of their watches, organised, discrete, well run. And, of course it was just that, as we took our places in the alcove to the hotel's main dining room.

Round the extended oval table, Hiroshi, David, Charlie, Magnus, Gerry, Andre, Barry, Joel, Rewan and myself. A flood of people arriving un-booked didn't cause a ripple with the restaurant manager. Tables and chairs were re-arranged, cushions were plumped, napkins flapped into place, chair backs straightened and water, still or sparkling, of course proffered. All without even being requested. All very Swiss.

The Maître d'. "Bonsoir, welcome. We have our full menu, we also have our special late supper menu here. Of course if you require anything in addition I can speak with the kitchen."

Classy professional, and at first sight a very normal and calm gathering. For those around the table it was not, repeat definitely not, situation normal.

For some, their constant nagging, gut wrenching concern about their wives, children, grandchildren. For Barry and I, wrestling with, it seemed, some progress, but generally so far an unsatisfactory search for facts.

Light meals were ordered, wine mostly declined or accepted in moderation, and a subdued conversation continued. The key points being - we had made progress with the ransom, with some luck we had found some detail on a kidnapper or at least a kidnappers messenger.

I explained that, we worked a lot with Joel when we needed operatives with police or military experience. Joel explained, "Right now there's ten of my people keeping an eye on some mega yachts at a show near Bordeaux. They were used to this kind of hostage activity in various locations around the world."

Joel said, "I have discussed with Dan that there is only one priority here and it's not the safety of the ransom, it's the safety of the women and children. I fully understand that."

"My guys have almost all got kids, not many current wives though. But in a way, their relationship with their kids is their only personal emotional attachment to any kind of home situation, so that makes them even more understanding of the need for great care."

He added, "Mind you I wouldn't fancy being a kidnapper with that lot around once we get the kids and women away."

We updated Rewan on the payment to be made Saturday or Sunday. With him saying, "That's all good and understood, but push them for a release scenario. They'd expect it."

We then explained to him, and a little more to Joel, how the kidnappers had created a secondary but very serious problem for us by insisting that all ships stop until the ransom had been shipped and received. The question was, why?

To put pressure on us ? Likely.

To make a political or other protest gesture ? No links or claims so far. With his many years of counter espionage experience, Geoffery Barker had suggested a few days back, that possibly this could have started as a political or a protest operation, and then been hi-jacked by the organisers, or 'mere operatives' who saw an opportunity to enrich them selves.

But so far no signs of, who or why?

Rewan nodded as Barry repeated what he had explained to the rest of us earlier. The facts that the USA and some other governments, fearing empty supermarket shelves could quickly cause serious trouble on their own streets, would view any such a major stoppage of their vital supply ships as an act of terrorism if not war.

Our problem: "For them the parlous position of the girls would become an unfortunate side issue to the defence of their nations supply chain. For us, that likely reaction was obviously more than concerning."

"So their threat to invoke the use of their Navy to take over all stopped ships was real," Gerry McMullen said, "if logistically difficult."

The others nodded, and a long and serious discussion continued for almost three hours- well into coffees and Swiss chocolates.

The sound of Barry's phone startled us. "Dal, That'll be Dal," he said. We listened to one side of another obviously difficult conversation. At the end, " OK I've understood that. I will get back to you."

He returned to the table, looking grim. "As we expected or feared, they want the ships moving again immediately. For exactly the reasons we know. In fact under some order or another, defence of the nation or something, they are issuing legal papers giving them the right to temporarily take control of all ships in US, and more surprisingly in international waters."

" They instruct you all, to allow the US Navy to come aboard and take control of your ships. They of course understand our position with the hostages and wish us well, and if there's anything they can do etc. They have ordered Dan and I to facilitate this action. Which you can be assured, Dan and I will ignore. Your girls are our only priority."

I nodded in agreement.

Long silence and grim faces around the table. Various suggestions are made, including putting out another press release which could act has a diversion.

Magnus said, "given that we are hopefully just two or three days away from paying the money and hopefully retrieving the girls, maybe we can argue for time".

Hiroshi said, " I fear that the Japanese Government will agree with the Americans, they can exert a lot of pressure."

David agreed and said. "Right I now, I see I have a message just into my office requesting me to go immediately to see the American Ambassador in Taipei. "

"Things are moving quickly, they have obviously had a plan in place in case something like this happened."

Oleg called and said. " Boss I'm sorry, it looks like I'm being recalled to London for an urgent briefing. Apparently there's a British Cabinet meeting at 9 tomorrow to consider the position of the British merchant fleet."

Gerry McMullen snorted at that.

Silence fell with concern etched on all faces.

Charlie Haeggqvist called the waiter over and asked for a small Calvados, which arrived very pronto. I assumed we were the only customers in the restaurant, it now being midnight.

He stood up and said. "Captain McMullen made an interesting suggestion to me earlier."

"Hiroshi-San how many ships do you control?" Hiroshi said," All types including support vessels, harbour tugs and that?"

"Yes all," asked Charlie.

Hiroshi "360."

"David you?"

"Well including our oil support vessels, safety patrol ships and some of the drilling rigs, some island ferries, as well as the ocean freight business it's about 450."

Andre ?..."With our subsidiaries we have 220 ocean going and about 200 mainly inshore, Pacific Islands and even in African Rivers."

Charlie said. "Well not wishing to be clever, but with our freight business, oil support, port and local supply. Surveying, oil rigs and over 30 deep sea rescue and fire control vessels."

" Oh yes we keep some harbours and rivers free of ice. We also have ferries and hospital ships around the islands of all Scandinavia."

" I think it's over 975 vessels."

Magnus said, "Actually just over 1200."

We all looked at Charlie.

He downed his Calvados in one and said.

"I am going to order all my vessels to immediately return to their home ports for more safety checks. I'm doing this in order ensure the safety of the crews. "

"Each and every one, regardless of where in the world they are, or how long it takes. Only when we are sure of their condition we will then be able to re-start supply of goods to the USA."

He nodded at David, Hiroshi and Andre. " My suggestion or request is that you gentlemen, if you feel you can, you do the same. That action, when we tell the Americans our intention, will I suspect make them think a bit and possibly step back."

" Especially when we say, 'resuming normal service may take a month or two, especially if anything happens to our families'. When of course we will be again unable to work for quite a while."

He went on, "I would imagine that the only vessels of ours that I cannot commit are some on long term charter to the US forces and in reality we will not stop our fire, rescue or hospital services. Although we can threaten to do so.  I think Gerry and Magnus can give you more detail on my behalf."

Gerry stood and said. "Charlie, old friend, we have talked socially over the years about port and country of ship registration. "

"I suspect that the British Cabinet tomorrow will find their fleet is these days only a few old coasters and ferries and not much more. "

Hiroshi and David had been talking together and David raised a hand, and then spoke. "We are with you, and we feel as you say in English, there is safety in numbers."

Andre, said, with a smile, "Well I'm either with you, or if the deal I made earlier with Charlie for my company is already started, I'll do what the boss says." Despite the seriousness of the situation, there were some real chuckles and some , 'Well said, Andre's.'

Gerry said, "There is indeed safety in numbers, and well done all." He went on, "Barry and Dan are you employed by the US and UK governments?"

Barry said, "I know the paperwork very well. We are not employed we are consultant advisors."

Gerry said. "Well then they can hardly give either of you orders, except to consult and behave legally, or terminate your services. But we should try to ensure that our move with the ships re-routing threat must not reflect badly on you guys."

"I suggest that you urgently contact those for whom you consult and say the following..... 'You have heard what they have demanded and instructed."

" Sadly despite your best efforts, you passed on the message from the US in exact detail to David, Charlie, Hiroshi and Andre and they have requested you reply with the following '."

Gerry dug out a piece of paper from his inside pocket and saying, "Charlie and I had an overall plan in case there were moves from various countries, this is just my notes and slightly making up suggested wording as I go along. If we agree then we need to go through it in detail," he read aloud:

*"From Barry Purchase and Daniel Craig.:*

*We have made every effort to ensure that the various merchant fleets referred to in our conversations, cede control to and allow immediate access to the US Navy.*

*We pass on a formal response from the companies and for an on behalf of the company principals: Charlie Haeggqvist. Andre Calvettioni, David Lim, Hiroshi Yamada.*

*" We appreciate the offer from the USA to employ the respected skill and might of the entire US Navy over the next many months to take over some or all of our More than 2000 ships in a similar number of locations worldwide.*

*This including freighters, oil tankers, hospital ships, ferries, rig and island support and supply ships, fire and safety vessels owned and controlled by us.*

*At this difficult time for the US, despite your kind offer, rather than trouble the US Navy, we, as the owners of these vessels, are soon to be issuing orders for our entire fleets to return to their home ports or ports of registration for further more detailed safety checks.*

*This is for the possible safety and welfare of the crews.*

*It will also preserve our position for the future provision of our usual standards of service to you and other customers, when we resume our usual schedules as soon as possible.*

*We hope to resume usual service in several month's, provided nothing untoward happens to our missing family members.*

*Of course in the interest of customers, safety of oil rigs and their operating crews, and the doctors, nurses and patients using our island and rural areas transport services we suggest the following.*

*Health, Fire , Rescue and safety cover : We will continue to provide cover for the next seven days from Saturday July 2. to enable the US Navy to take over responsibility for and operation of all such specialist services.*

*We note we provide 170 Doctors, 2870 Fire and rescue personnel and so on in 704 locations.*

*Until 24.00 hours GMT Saturday our fleets will remain stopped whilst we plan their return to their home ports.*

*After then we will, as required by international convention be issuing a formal notice regarding all this as 'Notices to mariners, customers and crews' In addition as many of our customers are not in the marine trades we will at the same time issue press release to all media.*

*For the avoidance of doubt be aware that Saturday July 2 is Week 26. Day 6. Ends."*

A stunned silence fell around the table.

It was Hiroshi, usually with the mildest manner and the least English, responded first. He rushed to the bar and returned with 10 shots of Calvados. Beaming he stood and said.

"I cannot and best not, as a Japanese comment on this situation of utmost resistance to the Americans. But Mr. Gerry and Mr. Charlie I salute you on the bravery of this action that will I think wake them up in Washington, London and elsewhere."

"So I toast the historical moment of, 'A declaration of shipping independence and disobedience,' from little Sweden to the might of the USA. *'Kampai!'*...or maybe, my Swedish history is not too clear, but perhaps it should be, *'Vikings forever'.*"

Despite the ultimate seriousness of the situation that brought more smiles to all concerned, partly because it was the mild and usually quiet Hiroshi who had originated it.

We raised our glasses. Everyone started to talk at once, after a while Gerry raised a hand and said, "Look its 1.00 am. Dan, what time are you and Joel flying this morning. You need to focus on searching for the girls."

I said, "We fly at at 6.30."

Gerry continued. "If you agree with the general feel of our approach why don't you and Joel get some shut eye, and the guys, with Barry and I will work on the message which we will send to the US within the hour."

I said. "That's cool. Send a copy of the reply to Miss Stanton, Geoff Barker, Squeeze, and Oleg."

As we left, Charlie was explaining that, he and Gerry had, on the golf course over the years, "Discussed many times, their almost monopoly position with some parts of their businesses, and how not to abuse their strength. So for now it was a simple a matter of reversing the situation."

Barry said, "Make sure you turn your phone off Dan, and don't sleep with it under your pillow, once Dal and the Five Stars get that declaration, I mean suggestion, the air waves and e mails will implode."

**40. Thursday June 30th.07.30 am. Inbound. Montpellier Airport. Southern France:** *How they sought some good news, or actually any news, from Vence to Aix En Provence - or actually, Carcassonne.*

Chris well knew the fifteen minute drive from our office down the Var Valley to join the French toll road auto-route system near Nice Airport and Cagnes Sur Mer.

From there his sat. nav. suggested just over three hours to do the 300 kilometers west to Montpellier. He had left at about 4.30 and was waiting outside the main terminal at Montpellier when Joel and I exited at 7.30. No private aviation facilities there, at least not at this time of day.

I said, "We need to press on it's about another 150 kliks I think."

Joel said, "I've got an 'on official business' paper here from the French police from something I was doing last month, so go for it. It could still work if we get stopped."

I first met Joel when he was recommended to me by the previous owner of the my company. He'd used him to follow up on some apparent gun running taking place in the middle of a properly legitimate cargo shipment of engine parts.

The ship owners and their freight agents, and the recipient of the goods, were genuinely not involved. Despite the old joke amongst African freight pilots, both airborne and maritime that suggests, 'If it just says engine parts, it's dead cert it will also fire a bullet or a rocket.'

In this case the main Renault dealers in South America were certainly not expecting anything except genuine Renault bits from France.

I said to Joel, "Weren't the North Koreans involved in that hooky cargo you intercepted."

Joel grinned and said. "Yes. But they had such dodgy paperwork that the Panama Canal people picked it up and made a simple search. I think the paperwork was so bad that their reps didn't dare look the other way even when given a few thousand dollars to do so. Helped a bit that we'd also mentioned a reward or finders fee-in cash."

At well over the speed limit and listening to Joel's stories - despite having two security professionals in the car- none of us noticed the blue flashing lights behind us for a while. When we stopped we wound down the windows and put our hands in full view, actually, not really the requested thing in France, but habit for us.

With a touch of his cap ,a business like 'traffic cop' started the usual, "Are you aware how fast you were going etc."

Joel let him say his bit and said-in French, "May I have a private word and show you this," and proffered a paper that he had tucked in the sun visor above his head.

He opened the car door and stepped out, I noticed that the second 'flic' stayed admirably placed and very alert. Good training in France these days went through my mind, and these days they need it.

Three minutes later, we were on our way.

Joel, "They've even radioed ahead to the next patrol to tell them we're on our way, and they are very excited to be 'super discrete.'"

Chris said, "How come your French is so bloody good?"

"Well," said Joel, "When I was in my late teens I was a bit of a scallywag around Manchester where I grew up. Nothing too bad, just stupid behaviour, dodgy motorbike racing on the motorway and the bike, which I'd actually paid for 100% properly from a main motorbike dealer, turned out to be nicked."

" Also some usual kids stuff, dope smoking which they were being quite strict about that week. So I did get nicked, several times. I got off with several official cautions."

"I wanted to go in the Army, you know SAS and all that. But all my mates suggested to me, that my problems with the law would  go against me. As it happens, now I know that's bloody incorrect, or they wouldn't have any Scousers or Scots in the British army. At least that's what they say in Manchester."

"I was also having a bit of girlfriend trouble. So prat that I am I joined the French Foreign Legion. I did the initial five years and then I copped a bullet in my gut. We were in Cameroon then.

The army medic and the hospital was great, but some nasty tropical infection wiped me out for a long while."

"I could have gone back on duty, but only doing office type stuff didn't really seem fun. I'd also had enough of Africa so I was invalided out. I get a good pension though, got a medal as well, so I guess I did my bit."

Chris said, "I noticed that hole shaped scar in your gut yesterday when we played volleyball in the pool. I assumed it was something you were built with to let out that crap beer you have in Manchester out before it kills you."

"Moving on," I interjected, "moving on  before this gets nasty. Today. It seems a bit far fetched to be chasing after a horse whose number is on a T shirt worn by one of the girls. We don't know why.

According to her dad, it's not her horse, she has all the ones she's ever owned at their farm near Grenoble."

"The shirt looks hand drawn, Andre said she can draw, at least she can draw horses because she always does, but he doesn't have a clue about her style. Of course it's probably a hi bloody fashion T shirt by someone famous fashion icon."

" So far fetched? Yes. But it's something- or almost the only thing we've got except for some clues from the guy near Copenhagen and Hamburg."

Joel. "I've been on several of these rescue and recovery jobs, and to be honest they are not usually great. But let's assume that somehow, sometime, somewhere we get enough to pin down the location of the girls. Before or after the money is paid. But I don't like those, necklace bombs."

"Despite what Geoffrey Barker and I got from the experts in the UK they're a new one on me."

" Pretty much the only real info I could find about them was some blokey in Australia claimed to have put one round some kidnap or extortion victim's neck. I don't know what happened except it wasn't the real thing."

"We have to assume these ones are the real deal, and that they have remote controls, or worse time switches that go off if not re-set all the time. F****ing unknown nightmare."

" But what I do know though, is after we pay, we can't trust the bad guys to become good guys and let the girls go. Why should they, surely by then the girls will have seen and heard too much. We could try the old one of offering extra dosh if they do the good thing. But I doubt they would fall for that."

"So regardless of when or where we find them we're going have to deal with those F**** necklaces."

We drove on in silence.

Chris asked Joel, "What did you tell those cops, there was a lot of saluting when they left?"

Joel answered, quick as a flash. "I noticed the PM of France is at the airbus factory in Toulouse this weekend. Well you know he is supposed to be a big party guy...I told them you were his new short time ladyboy and I was delivering you for a dodgy weekend with him in Toulouse."

I refereed. Again. "Sorry Chris, I think that beats the drain plug for Manchester ale."

Now the auto-route was featuring lots of blue signs and even more brown ones with pictures of Castles and the like on them.

And then Carcassonne.

Well before 9.00 . Bloody good time. Well done Joel.

---

Indeed, as we neared the city we could see some pretty impressive castle stuff on a hill ahead, but before we got any nearer the sat nav directed us to a modern looking industrial estate.

There, with pictures of a whole menagerie of animals was, '*Animal Hospiteaux. Specialties les Chiens and les Chevaux.*'

We pulled into the parking, and Joel said, "It's not 9.00 yet, but the doors are wide open."

We left Chris aiming for a Café across the street, and Joel and I went in to the animal docs. Big smiles. The plan was to try and find out any useful information and then Joel would do his, 'please keep this to your self bit.'

We expected all sorts of complications but we were in and out in ten minutes....with what seemed to be interesting stuff.

Yes, 99 AX5CM93 was one of their allocated numbers. A quick tap on their computer produced a print out with all the medical and ownership details.

"Why do you want to know?"

I suggested that, "I was thinking of buying the horse", and then apologised for my bad French that meant I had said, "We didn't know where they were," we meant, "How were they health wise, not, 'where were they?"

"They would be good to buy." said the vet, and of course he would be happy to give them updated check up. "I saw them about three months ago to up date their various inoculations'."

" To be honest ,an owner who will use them will be good for the horses, all they do is roam around that big estate  They need proper care, some shoes and contact with humans they are getting quite wild."

He continued. "I don't know why I still deal with that owner, she still owes us for last year's work. It costs more to send out the bills, but I can't let the horses get sick. Not only that, but each time I go there it takes the gardien about thirty minutes to find' the 'orses. They let them go all over their land."

He went on, "Did I say, they will need shoes before you ride them, I can put you in touch with my son. Il fait des fers a cheval. How you say?... 'Il est un un forgeron'...he is a blacksmith."

I thanked him for all the info, and making sure I had the printout of the details in my hand said, "I apologise again for my bad French, all we have to do now is to try and find our way back to see the horses one more time."

I was hoping of course he would tell us where they were, unfortunately he focused on being polite about my French!

"Au contraire, Monsieur has excellent French." ... and so with lots of thanks we started to exit.. telling him, 'we would be in contact next month when we came down from London to organise our house. And yes the new check up sounded good.'

'At that time would pay any old bills, after all the inoculations were indeed important as he said.

It was complicated with a holiday home  to find good vets and we were happy he was so well recommended.'

I tried again, "As I said, the only problem we have is finding the field where they are again- we keep getting lost everywhere we go."

"Zut," said the vet, obviously now very keen to gain some new clients. "Zut, O.K. let me give you the co-ordinates of the horse field and maybe the nav sat, she will take you back a quick way."

"But remember this is to the horses field, not to the owner she, 'as an apartment in Narbonne with her sister."

With more handshakes all round we left.

Joel put his head back in the door and said something in rapid French to the vet, who rushed to door and shook Joel's hand again.'

We found Chris still vainly dunking his tea bag in a mug of tea. "Bloody French, why don't they get tea."

But the coffee and the croissants were great.

I asked Joel what he had said, "Oh I told him that you, 'the boss,' were very keen,' but the amount we were offering was, 'top wack' so he shouldn't say anything to the owner in case she put the price up."

"I also said, I'd be taking care of things here for you, when you were back in England, and not to worry I'd also make sure his son got the horse shoeing job as well.' Seemed to go down well."

" At least we now know that's a real horse number, the animal is still alive, and he also said the horse was born locally. So unless it's a pure coincidence with the number, whoever designed the T shirt, has to have seen it. But who?"

Less than an hour later we were on some very rural side roads, surrounded by vineyards and farm land and apparently nearing the field where the horses lived, or so, as the vet had put it, 'le nav sat,' 'she told us'.....

At an old stone gate house, the sat nav showed 'destination'. We kept moving.  Opposite the gate house there was a massive field of vines stretching as far as we could see. On the same side of the house it looked like grassland, quite high and not cut. So we figured the horses were on our left. The same side as the house.

Joel said, "Take a left and a left, that should take us round the land,. surely the horses can't be loose to cross the road on their own."

We drove for almost a kilo and found a small track, possibly a road, possibly a farm track to the left.

Joel said. "Let me out I'll go on foot."

He continued. "I think it's not good for the car to be seen round here too much just in case. You never see people in the country, but there always eyes everywhere."

"Look on the map, there's a river down there go and park and have picnic or something, I'll find you there."

"Look touristy." He looked at Chris, "or act like he's the Prime Minister of France."

Before Chris could respond Joel went on, " Or if you want mark the place on the Sat Nav, go and get touristy stuff at that gas station back near Carcassonne. But don't go in any local village shop."

Taking a bottle of water, and his usual camo jacket he left. .

The river turned out to be a few hundred yards further down the lane, and was actually quite touristy with a parking place and a couple of picnic tables.

We continued on, crossing over a canal bridge, and after about ten kilos we were in a smallish town, but big enough for a couple of tourists to be quite usual, not noticed as strangers. Several 'super Marché's' and then quite a large gas station.

We stocked up with water, some good looking cheese, bread and charcuterie. The gas station even sold fishing rods.

Despite a slight moment of nerves when the lady said we needed, 'un licence de pecheur,' for the canal or the river it turned out just to be a cash transaction. No id. required.  It even came with a sticky back licence to put in the window of the car.

Thirty minutes later we were parked. I was on the phone to the office and Chris fishing.

After about an hour, an incoming txt from Joel. 'Found the horses, F***ker bit me when I tried to find the right one and find  the tattoo the vet told us about. And he ate my apple.'

Then a call. " I can see a collection of houses.  Maybe a big farm, I think that gate house may be their way in. I'm trying to get near without anyone seeing me but the bloody horses keep following me."

Chris said. "I think we're not doing this fishing thing right, I'm a townie but should we be using worms as bait – not French bread."

I suggested he tried a bit of cheese, and carried on with my laptop.

Two hours passed and then, jogging down the road.

Joel. Big big smile.

"Gottem, boss, we've f***ing got them."

Chris and I just stood there open mouthed, as he repeated,

" I could kiss that f***ing horse.  I've seen all of them except one of the small kids."

" Both horses suddenly legged it across this big open field towards those buildings.  So I snuck round the side in the hedge and after about 300 yards there's a bunch of girls and kids feeding the horses."

"I used my binoculars because didn't want to get too close. One of the girls is even wearing the German shirt, but the older girls have got those necklaces on. The two little kids I saw haven't."

I grabbed my phone, and said, "I need to report to the parents." but Joel grabbed my arm and said. "Hold and wait. Let's get out of here, we could be under observation. Like I said there's always someone watching or listening in the country side. If those guys are professional, phone scanners are cheap as frites here".

Found......By chance, a lucky break?

Who cared. Found was found.

The road ahead seemed a bit misty, until I realised it was just my eyes. The elation then tempered with thoughts of how to deal with the bloody necklaces.

But, as Joel inimitably said, "We've F***ing got 'em." Almost.

## 41. Thursday June 30th. 4.00 pm. TrePolPen.S.Co. Office

**Vence. France.** *Miles of smiles.*

By the time Chris and I arrived back in Vence at about five o'clock in the evening, elation had turned to practical concern.

But the team had achieved a lot. Joel was staying in the area near the now found girls and calling in reinforcements.

With him we had gone back to nearby Carcassonne, where he picked up a rental car. He was getting back to the site, within the hour. With Bordeaux just a few hours away and some of his team all there available and ready to go, he was confident of getting some 24/7 back up cover- very carefully- actually before I got back to Vence.

"We can't risk losing them now for Christs sake." was the agreed sentiment.

I had waited till we were near Marseilles on our return before speaking to the parents, telling them the good news.

Tears from all, I have to say me included. Again.

"I know this is fantastic news, but tell no one. Not even the grandparents. This is the most dangerous time." Also continue on working with Barry, Squeeze and Rory on paying the ransom. But we still need the exact delivery destination for the flight plan, fuel load etc."

Walking in the office the atmosphere was electric, utilising our satnav info and descriptions with the office team we quickly established the exact location of where we had been.

We now had military grade maps and Google Earth pictures of amazing quality. These included good photos of the buildings, showing the layout around a pool, and a long driveway to the gate house or cottage on the road.

We quickly established that the place was an old farm- then recording studio- and that it had been for sale or let for several years until taken off the market about three months earlier.

The owner seemed to be the widow of the original owner- and she indeed lived in an apartment in Narbonne, about an hour away.

After and hour or so, Joel called us back.

He reported, " We're on the case with a 24/7 watch, taking care not to be noticed."

" One of my guys, is right by the farm buildings, I'm back in Castries at this moment getting some kit together. We don't know how many bad guys there are, if they have dogs, where there's cameras or sensors."

He said , "I'm going to install a watcher with lots of serious fishing kit, down by the river that borders the land, just along from where we had parked. He can see the back of the farm and very importantly, the lane between the gatehouse and the main farm where the girls seem to live very well from there."

" I'm giving the bloke a bike with carriers, a sleeping bag, fishing and cooking stuff, and so he at least looks like a slightly off the wall solo tourist."

"We also urgently need to install a camera sending live pictures of the farm exit. I can get that done - but again we don't know how or what sophisticated electronics they've got there so I think we'll have to use the telecoms cables to bring us the pictures. I'm already using four operatives with various vehicles so we can discretely follow anyone who exits the farm."

I said, "We're on our own now, let's keep the uniformed flatfoots out, to be safe."

Joel said, "I agree up to a point. As we discussed in the car on the way to Carcassonne, I had the ten guys near Bordeaux guarding some superyachts at that tradeshow. I've pulled eight of them out, and they are getting on with business around the farm area already".

" Before the yacht contract they had been in Iraq for months taking perimeter care of an oil refinery, so they welcomed the job at first. Now though they're very happy for the change, it seems anything is better than seabird shit bombs day and night."

"They are English, South Africa and actually two are Swedish. All ex legion and all were based at Legion HQ in Castelnaudary for two years when they joined. So they know the area and the language. They've got a variety of cars and vans, all with fairly local numbers so they look local."

" Although the locals are used to Legion types around here ,I'll keep them out of the village and the local shops, just in case."

"I've got my dad doing the watching and fishing bit. He was well connected with the SAS when I was a kid - but stays fit and we can trust him 100%. He's been in Bordeaux watching the watchers. I use him quite a lot - no one really suspects an old blokey so much. His French isn't great but with bike, sleeping bag food and fishing kit it'll work. He's also brought up my old Citroen 2cv van.That looks local to say the least."

" Tonight or early tomorrow we'll fix the cameras."

"Every one is hanging well back, and no hero moves, we don't know yet about those f***ing necklaces. The more I see the more I worry".

He continued, "Going back to what you said about, 'uniformed flatfoots'."

" I know what you mean, but we need help with those necklaces and maybe more. So I'm going to the Foreign Legion barracks at Castelnaudary. The current commander was a trainer there when I was a squaddie ten years ago. I know him well, and the fact that we're on his doorstep is the first bit of luck we've had."

" I know your office is getting advice from specialists and bomb disposal worldwide, but I want to talk to him as well about those necklaces. The legion are well equipped, very experienced with a lot of special forces stuff in Africa so they know street stuff from that."

"Not only that but they are also used to having to make stuff up themselves, to fix local problems, or find  out answers, miles from help in remote locations so they may have some thoughts. If I know them they certainly won't be sharing what they know with any poncy politico's in Paris."

Chris said, "And what about your day job Joel, or a bit of fishing, you've got time on your hands ?"

With several good lucks everyone started in their allocated tasks.

A few minutes later Joel called back and said, "I forgot, we need a base or we'll be living out of the cars."

" There's a million vacation villas around here, use google earth and street view to try for something with bugger all neighbours, and parking hidden from the road. But not nearer than say 15k from the target."

I wandered out on to the terrace and sitting at a table, gazing at the darkening view and called Barry in Geneva.

Having updated him about Joel's work and plans, I said. "Can you get Magnus over towards Carcassonne because we may need him there to help the kids ? "

"But I want him to keep a low profile, the bad guys seem to know a lot, and that could include his face. Also given how visible the Asian parents are, and how small the area is I suggest they stay in Switzerland for now. David can keep his plane on standby for quick parent action when needed."

Barry reflected, "I agree about visibility and all that that. Regarding the, as Hiroshi has named it, 'Sweden's declaration of Naval  disobedience,' on the mighty US Navy , the results so far are a stunned silence."

" That could be good news if they are simply outmaneuvered and having to think. More likely it could be very bad news, as I am sure Dal and the other spooks are now throwing all they've got at finding the girls. Like you I still fear anything more than, a 'softly softly' approach."

I said. " I've got Joel calling I'll get back to you."

Joel asked, "Could join me at the legion base in Castelnaudary tomorrow morning?"

My response, "Of course, no problem, and I am trying to get Magnus over there in case we need communication with the Swedish women, or to deal with the kids.".

Before I turned in for what was going to be a short night Squeeze called and said, "Too late tonight in Europe to organise a rental house near Carcassonne, but we're on the case on line. I think we've got a couple we can go for early tomorrow."

" One good thing, next week there's some kind of air traffic controllers strike in Spain, so we can use that as an excuse to a rental agency why we have a last minute booking. Change of plans due to Spain and such."

I then remembered Oleg was expected to have returned to London. On enquiring I got a great answer, "Can't fly boss, got a sick note for an ear infection. And I got a nice email from Miss Stanton saying she hoped I'd be better soon."

He told me there was still nothing much turning up on the girls phones. They had found that the picture of the girls, in each of the phones, was not taken on the phone, but copied into the memory chip from somewhere. It was the only item on a new chip.

The 'real' pictures taken on the phones, were lot of river and horse pictures in Germany, but no taxis or other people.  Ditto the Swedish ladies, loads of kids, pools, water slides, beaches but nothing useful.

Apparently London were scanning all the pictures with some kind of face recognition system for people in the background, but nothing much known or even expected.

That was it. I would have expected to sleep easier, knowing we had at least located the girls, but it was not the case.

Turning on my phone, to check for any updates I received a message from Barry. " *Flight destination Noukachott Mauretania...just south of Morocco. Rory aware and works for plane we have.'*

With yet another factor to consider sleep became even more elusive.

**42. Friday July 1st. Good and early. With positive news, perceptions of early starts change. Montpellier Airport. Again. Waiting for inbound:** *If the necklaces had been designed to control by fear, the effect was more wide spread than the than the kidnappers probably assumed. Or may be they had been planning for all contingencies...*

At 4 AM after a few hour's sleep. Or not. Chris set off again towards Carcassonne, this time with Oleg and I as passengers. Based on instructions from Barry sent overnight, he was aiming again to Montpellier airport, this time to collect Magnus.

Barry also sent me another overnight email, slightly encouraging. 'Yanks backed down. Kind of. . In as much as doing nothing yet re their Navy taking control all ships. But they not happy, and I assume they now sniffing around kidnap problem'.

As we exited Montpellier Airport, Magnus was quite understandably, nonstop asking about his family. " 'What had we seen? Did they look good? Were there armed guards? Did the kids look happy, any signs of violence?'

My response was genuine, reliving Joel's first brief view and more through the day that, and, "surprisingly they just look like they are on holiday".

I stressed, "All very encouraging, but of course the pressure on Britt and Anna and of course the Asian girls must be immense. That's why we have to be very careful when revealing our presence."

As we re-joined the auto-route I called Joel.

Having established where I was he said. "Right. Listen up boss, in about 100 kliks. Junction 25 on the A61 AutoRoute. Exit there."

" Right by the junction there's an airstrip. Posters for sightseeing flights and I think a flying school and parachute club .We meet there. Wait for me. He continued. "I just spoke to Squeeze and she's waiting on confirmation about two houses for you to look at. So if Toddy and Oleg go and deal with that, Magnus you and I can nip over to the Legion base and talk tactics and necklaces."

I answered, "Sounds good to me, I'll be there in less than an hour". but I think he was gone already.

Having found the place, we had just parked, when a very basic Army chopper arrived. The pilot delighted in landing about 20 meters from our car, which sent Oleg and Toddy diving back into the car to escape the dust.

Joel jumped out and said, " Mark this in all your sat nav favourites, you might have to come and pick us up here later."

Magnus and I clambered aboard, and as we left, the chopper still with its doors open, the pilot, wearing goggles gestured at us to shade our eyes and we were up through and soon above a serious cloud of dust.

Joel was shouting to Magnus that, "His dad had seen the kids and women that morning from a distance, and through his telephoto lens, and all looked OK."

After 20 or so minutes of flying, following the line of a big canal, we landed on the militarily manicured grounds of the Legion base. Waiting there, was an officer and what looked like a small military welcoming escort. Lots of salutes and feet stamping.

We shook hands with the Commanding Officer, 'Call me Francois.' He turned out to be French but having been brought up in Mauritius, spoke great English, actually with a slight South African accent.

The men waiting were his most experienced snatch and rescue squad and some bomb disposal experts. Just a few steps and we were comfortably sitting in a conference room.

Coffee, water, tea, croissants, all offered. All, except water declined.

Before I could much more than confirm to Joel that the delivery of the ransom was now set for Saturday night, the C.O. said, "If we may proceed as we need to make plans."

"Firstly," he continued, "I am very aware that caution not valour or rash stupidity is the absolute priority here."

"Secondly and obviously, as you will imagine before I make any moves of any kind in this country I should of course get the OK from Paris. But in this case, I am satisfied that the matter is of the utmost security and urgence, leaving no time to refer. Up to a point that is. A point which I will explain in a moment."

"Thirdly. The Legion has a history of never abandoning its people and I am satisfied that Joel needs our assistance."

" I can also say," With a smile at Joel and one of his men, "As I said I am also concerned about an unknown threat so near to our base here. So as far as Paris is concerned we proceed, as required. As I say up to a point. Without some serious permissions, our assistance is legally limited to emergency logistics, but I think you will find we take a very broad view of that term. But note this. Paris or no Paris. We can, I hope, help with the humanitarian need of a rescue for those endangered children. But we cannot knowingly assists with the payment of any ransom, which is outside any legality here from France."

He turned to Magnus, " I understand you are the father of some of the victims, you 'ave my sympathy, not an easy situation. But if the circumstances are as Joel and his spotter think, then I have a feeling we will be able to help."

Sounded encouraging to me. Magnus looked slightly less stricken than he had been.

The C.O. went on to Magnus. " But I want to talk operational matters and realities with Daniel and Joel, and some of the options, activities and results and dangers may not be pleasant to your ears. My suggestion is you let one of my guys show you around the base there's some interesting history to be seen, whilst we work on this. After we have a plan we will inform you of the best hope and worst hope situation."

Magnus said. "I would rather stay, I'll sit over there. Do not feel you have hold back in anything you say, if it's too much for me I'll take a walk outside. You have a job to do and obviously you know your stuff."

He continued, "I should tell you just before you start, Charlie Haeggqvist the Swedish Girls father, and also the three fathers of the other three girls, Taiwanese, Japanese and French are aware of the neck bombs. So originally they wanted to pay the ransom, and not attempt any rescue.....but now they understand the reality is, that the chances of the girls being released un-harmed after the money is paid are almost nothing. They will have seen or heard too much."

"So any rescue attempts by you or any team approved by Barry Purchase and Daniel here, is 100% approved by all of us, and we are aware of the dangers. Please carry on."

The C.O. said. "I salute you sir, and the positions are as you say. Many of the officers here are also family men. The Legion has a long and glorious history of individuals pulled together into a team and the Legion becomes their new family."

" Mostly this is true, but many of us older men who have served our time around the world- now reside here and are instructors and planners, and we are hence, many family men. Now we have two families. The Legion and our own, so we well understand your anguish."

"O.K. The first problem is of course the necklaces."  He put several photo's of the women up on screen. Obviously taken that morning by Joel's father, long lens effect, blurred fence, and usually with a horse in the frame as well.

Francois said , "Joel's father, by the way ,whom I know very well  and respect for being professional, says the women seem to come out of a door at the back of the farm building with food for the horse. I think it may be a kitchen door. The kids come down the side where the fence is lower."

"These necklaces are very new to us. We can see the size exactly, and unfortunately we know of plenty of explosives of that size that can cause horrible damage if ignited. "

"Having said that, it also seems from other observations that the ladies swim in the necklaces, and we assume they must wear them all the time."

"We need to get some hand held explosive detecting devices on or near them. If we are that near, we also want to rub an alcohol soaked cotton on them as it could provide us with more technical clues."

" I am sure you've seen both the sniffers and the swabs at most airports. They are more accurate back up checks if something else has alerted standard security."

"From the three necklaces where we have several images it appears they are reasonably loose around the throat.

" So I am fairly confident we could take apart some bullet resistant vests, and insert some of the Kevlar pieces between the necklace and the neck coming high up round the chin, ears , and back of the head."

" Maybe we do this in several pieces that will be easier to slide into place. It will be like a high necked woollen roll neck shirt."

"If this collar of Kevlar is angled out it should  protect the face and head, Separately a body vest will protect the body and arms. Essentially it allows, encourages even, any blast from the small pouch on the front to go away from the victim. It's not guaranteed for sure, but is better."

"That's good news. But what we don't know is if there is also explosive in the neck piece going round the back of the neck. If so it is new to us. Standard det cord explosive, would produce a decapitating effect, but det cord would not survive wearing, bending etc."

None of us dared look at Magnus during the 'decapitating effect' part of the speech.

Gesturing at some of this men, he continued, "If you agree, and of course we need to make more detailed plans, but if you agree we get started with the utmost 'urgence' to take apart some flak jackets, what you call bullet proof vests, and make some collar pieces, they will start on that right now." The CO went on. "Based on discussions with Joel overnight and today we could be basically ready and equipped from say four hours from now."

" I suggest we install a well hidden team on the spot to move in immediately in case there are bad moves from the captors. Please be sure to understand this is only just in case things suddenly look really threatening to the girls, and the captors are not waiting for any payment that might happen."

With the 'payment' words, he smiled encouragingly.

"So any early intervention will have risks  as we will not have any knowledge or the idea what is in the necklaces. For that we must first get near enough to check them. So I stress again, any interception action is guaranteed only if we observe the bad guys immediately endangering the girls or kids ."

"I understand that they insist you ship the ransom on tomorrow night."

" So our priority is the sooner we can get near to swab, sniff and possibly electronically check and may be even neutralise those necklaces the better. Yet again, no early heroics, you have my guarantee."

Joel said, "I agree 100% we need to get to touch those bloody necklaces, and near that kitchen door is ideal. Its well concealed from the lane."

" But I am seriously concerned that if a couple of us in camo and face paint step out of the bushes in daylight or at night, either of the women or the girls could freak out. Noisy hysterics would not help. They must be pretty edgy after all this time."

We all sat silent for a while and then Magnus spoke. "If I may make a suggestion. Sometimes in the village in Portugal, we make a treasure hunt. A looking and finding game for the kids. They draw some small Swedish Blue and Yellow flags on paper and I write clues on them...which they have to find. And the clues of course usually bring them to some ice creams. If we made a couple of Swedish flags and put them on the fence maybe the mothers would see them."

Joel smiled, "I like that, and  if you just write in Swedish the word, 'secret, say nothing, I am near, ' on the back and maybe put a  special nickname for you or your wife,  it could make her think. "

"If it looks a bit like a kid did it then if for some reason the kidnappers find it then they'll hopefully assume it's a kids game."

 Francois said, "That could be really good, it's a small risk but close checking the necklaces is vital." He looked at me and said. "Time to decide. May we proceed?"

I said, "I very much appreciate and accept your plan 100%," I glanced at Magnus and he said," Absolutely, and fully understood your information about the risks. But for all of us, please carry on."

I continued. "I need to have a conversation with the fathers to make sure they fully understand. But, please note, it is just to inform them. On my say so and also on their behalf, we proceed with your plans as soon as possible".

The commander spoke, rising to his feet. "May I suggest gentlemen, we have a quick lunch and talk some more at the same time, and then we can get you helicoptered back to the pick-up point."

" We do fly over the farm where the captives are held, but they are always used to very many air movements every day around here. But the pilot will video downwards on every trip. "

"My people are even now packing up some more kit and then Joel, myself and some of our people will go discretely to the Old Moulin."

He looked at Magnus. "I applaud your fortitude, and I hope we can and have given you some confidence."

We ran through the plans again over lunch or more correctly what ever the French word is for, 'brunch', in a canteen full of fit looking legionnaires. A kids colouring set having been found somewhere on the base, quite what they thought of Magnus busy drawing and colouring little Swedish flags I am not sure.

But the comment from him was interesting.

He said: " I really am as confident as I could wish to be. Part of my job is to judge our Ships Captains as people sometimes. They have very stressful jobs. So I know a little bit about studying people in command. Joel and Francois I am very happy we are in your good hands."

Whilst we were eating I called Chris Todd about a pick up.

In his usual laconic tones he replied. "I know where to go, just look for the dust cloud. It's only about 25 minutes from here if I don't get lost."

I told him I'll be there in about 40 minutes.

Magnus and I were shown to a smaller and even more basic Army chopper which delivered us to the dusty airstrip.

The pilot delighted in landing again about 20 meters from the only car on the site, which again sent Toddy diving back into the car to escape the dust.

When we could speak, he inimitably said, "I would have thought I should have learned about the bloody dust."

He went on, "We've got to pick Oleg up from a big hypermarket on the way back," which we did, loading a two trolley's full of supplies into the back of the car.

Chris explained. "We took the first villa we saw, as it was fine, and very much ready to rent. Back at the rental agency office they said they'd had several new bookings and some from people cancelling because of the strike in Spain, so they were cool, and understood why it was urgent."

" Happy for the extra business I think."

"Because it was last minute they doubled the security deposit, which I can understand, but once the credit cards and cash were cleared they gave us the keys, and sent us back to the villa with a team of ladies doing cleaning and making up beds."

The ladies were still there when we arrived back. "

"Us having carried bag after bag of supermarket supplies into a large and typical holiday villa, that smelled strongly of floor cleaner, we tipped and thanked the ladies who had prepared it so quickly. Magnus and I had a swim in the pool to freshen up.

In the cool of the living room, Chris and Oleg had started to shuffle tables and chairs to give us a working area.

They were busy setting up a selection of electrical extension leads and unpacking a serious supply of pads, paper and suchlike.

The largest scale Michelin map they could find was taped over a picture.

"Big improvement on the art, I can tell you," said Chris, "It's a painting of some black lady with no clothes, but a lot of fruit on her head."

"Bit of luck with the villa. It's English owned but the owners go back to the UK this month for Wimbledon and Henley. Unless we ask there's no cleaners due back here for two weeks, just some pool service blokey once a week." said Oleg.

" So I've marked the target on the map, and with those net curtains I don't think the pool guys can see what we're doing."

Oleg said, "I'll have wi fi working in a minute, better than using each of your phones, I think we'll get stronger connection connected to my dongle and then sharing with the Wi-Fi. "

"It's amazing, you can get everything in French super stores."

Chris had announced that he was making an, ' All day breakfast,' as it was now 3 in the afternoon and he'd had nothing all day.

Thirty minutes later I looked from setting up from my laptop to see Chris with large tray piled with French bread and all the usual breakfast stuff, he was in very 'Chris' mode. "Looks like you can get everything in France, but not sodding bacon. I've been through Oleg's shopping and used these packets of stuff called 'poitrene fume,' and 'lardons,'."

"Looks like bacon bits, smells like bacon, cooks like bacon and bloody tastes like bacon, so why don't the difficult bastards call it bloody bacon."

Despite having eaten at the legion HQ, as ever the smell of bacon, sorry poitrene, is irresistible.

We set to  the fantastic French bread with considerable enthusiasm. With Oleg commenting, "My 'translate' app  on the phone says 'poitrine also means big breasted'."

Fortunately before the conversation degenerated further, as promised by Oleg, my laptop came to life.

Oleg then instructing me with new passwords and suchlike. " Wi-Fi is good and reasonably encrypted. ....shouldn't be leaking too far."

Minutes later I had a lot of mail to read. First from Joel. "All captives look OK."

Squeeze came on, with, news of 'other business':

Paul Isted was there in the Singapore office, "Seems he want's to talk to a couple of financial journos here, but without alerting them to something."

"J &S say the spikes in US security traffic had to be seen to be believed last two nights. But they don't know what it was about."

Which raised a wan smile from me.

Squeeze went on. "Some concern where to dock the four attacked ships. Needs big lifters for the containers. I'll keep you informed on that. Barry's, on an Easy Jet to Toulouse. Picking up a rental car. He with you in about two hours."

I signed off from Squeeze with. "By the way Toddy, will make someone a great wife one day, makes great breakfast, but seems obsessed with large smoky breasts."

To which her response was, "That's all those red light bar visits with Paul Isted. Mind you from what they say the only ones with large breasts in those bars are the lady boys. So take care boss."

Rory called me. "Freight Plane all under control. It comes in to Marseille mid morning tomorrow . Will need a four hour turnaround."

*"The gold at Marseilles and from Toulouse is already packed and is ready to go. We have here, the four pallets of gold from this customs store. The gold from Toulouse on the other four will be shipped to Marseille this evening.* They have a regular road shipments several times a week".

"It's all on four Pallets as ordered with Tarps double no tamper plastic shrink wrapped over the gold in the usual way, and then in 5cm mesh cargo nets on flight pallets."

"Actually how it is packed is the standard way, best to avoid sticky fingers with the cargo handlers and aircrews. Calvettioni's people are doing the paper work for both loads."

He continued." The flight time to Noukachott is about 5 or 6 hours depending air traffic control routing "'

I thanked him, and he added. "The extra guys from Joel's squad are here now, and shacked up in the airport hotel. Quite how the hell he's done it I don't know but Calvettioni's got them customs cleared already, so they go straight on the plane. Helps a bit with their, 'sports equipment'."

Which made me both smile, and make a concerned note for future security activity. The sports equipment being guns and ammo.

I wandered outside and found that the hot Languedoc sun had gone round enough to allow a pergola and some vines to shade the outside table and chairs.

I checked the time and to my shock it was only 5 pm. A lot had been done in 12 hours.

The pool looked very inviting, but Squeeze came on the line again, saying Paul Isted was on the line for me.

"Dan, nice office you've got here, and great tea Mrs. Todd makes, mind you I miss Chris he's a good bar companion…. a babe magnet, keeps the good time girls away from me," I could hear Squeeze give a loud snort.

Paul continued. " Anyways. Ship problems new and old. I filed some boring news pieces as agreed, and it worked, but to be honest so far as usual  most media more interested in explosions and big ships, than reasons. Mind you'll they'll wake up soon to that end of the story."

"Regarding the possible reasons for your kidnappers demanding the ships stop. I came here to Singapore, to see a few mates, mostly financial hacks. You know the types, Bloomberg, WSJ, FT, CNBC, and the like."

" I'm not revealing any sources but they all agree that several punters, and they use that word to indicate 'gamblers ' more than market investors. Several punters have some seriously big and exposed  'positions' on commodities and general freight related futures. When they say big they mean billions of dollars."

"They say big money has come from the USA, which doesn't surprise them. But some really big money has also been put up from Asia. It's laid off on various UK, US and European markets but its origins are likely Japan."

"All this could indicate advance knowledge of the current attacks on those four ships, or more to come. A lot of ships stopping could swing the markets. With insider trading and the like being very detectable these days, it could also indicate, like that Texan you mentioned to me, someone just trusting and gambling that rumour will move the markets."

He continued, "Oh yes, Singapore is so highly regulated, that despite the Chinese gambling influences, here they are usually wary of too much speculation in the markets. "

"Regarding the crew hiring story. Someone is still trawling around in Cebu and Manila looking to hire. I still suspect it's a scam, with North Korea being mentioned to make it sound good."

I asked Paul, "Going back to the fire attacks, given the ongoing rumours, what about any likely Korean input into the ship fires deliberately manipulating speculation about world freight markets."

His response. "I wouldn't have thought they can rustle up the huge investment dosh needed to gamble like that. So my guess would be, no North Koreans, and of course they don't dare to seriously piss off the Chinese."

He concluded, "Bloody Squeeze has got me on a 09.30 flight tomorrow morning back to Manila." And he was gone.

I sat back and decided that the pool looked seriously refreshing again, whilst I was doing a few laps Magnus and Chris joined me. Thanks to Oleg's good stocking up ,we were able to agree that we'd eat at the villa that evening so we could quietly go through the next few days.

Magnus. "I was just thinking, you guys, are under a lot of pressure. But you keep some normality's and jokes in your conversations and daily life."

" It doesn't mean you're not taking everything that matters seriously, but I think that really helps you do well with the stress."

" We used to have problems with the masters of our ships if they became too isolated. They would be at sea for months on end. That's very stressful, even with the latest equipment docking a ship 300 meters long that takes a long time to stop even if it's going at walking pace."

" With the newer ships we now make the officers mess a better environment and make it the only place where there's e mail connection to try and cut down on the isolation factor. We encourage the masters not to isolate themselves."

"The results have been impressive, in crew satisfaction, accident rate, and in the health of the older officers."

Chris to me. "Older officers, That'll be you then boss."

**43. Friday July 1st. 5.00 p.m. horses field near Carcassonne. South West France.** *So near and yet....*

Around the same time that I was swimming, Joel and Francois with others of his team were concealed about 50 meters from the old farmstead. They were waiting for dusk, to try and make an approach to the women, and get close to the necklaces.

They had taped a small hand drawn Swedish flag on the wire outside what we had figured was a kitchen window.

Not finding any radio, or microwave signals, no trip wires, no sign of any cameras, or new wires between the Farmhouse and the Gatehouse they had concluded that the bad guys were relying on the fear of the necklaces to keep the girls under control.

Francois had set up a patrolling system on the lanes using his guys all on bikes. In the months around the Tour de France the whole of France is full of guys in Lycra riding everywhere, so no one was going to notice them. A few changes of head gear and shirts now and again helped.

Joel's remaining guys were there with various cars at each end of the D road leading to the gatehouse and farm to follow if anyone exited by car.

The cameras and watchers in the surrounding lanes reported the return of one of the guards with, what Joel's dad, who was between the Gatehouse and the Farm House said was a whole lot of shopping. The women, girls and kids all apparently helping with the unloading.

Joel's dad's text. *Both men now back in Gatehouse. I have good sight of track Gatehouse to Farm. ends*

Less than ten minutes later, it was still not at all dark when the back door of the Farm building unexpectedly opened and Britt stepped out, obviously with an arm full of vegetables for the horses.

They saw her notice the Swedish flag and take it off the fence. Having studied it she just stood there. Presumably shocked.

Although their plan had been to make contact after dark, with a nod from Francois, Joel called out. " Britt, It's all OK now. Magnus knows you here. But keep silent now. Stay quiet please."

Britt's hands flew to her face. Joel and Francois stood, and with fingers to their lips approached.

Joel quickly said. "Magnus says hello. Sorry about our face paint. Listen to me. Magnus is about five kilometers away but we can do nothing until we fix your necklaces."

In tears her hands flew to her neck, and she looked about to collapse. Joel continued..."look I have a message for you from Magnus on my phone."

He held his phone up to the wire and played a short video clip with some Swedish and hopefully calming words from Magnus.

Now very tearful, one hand to mouth and the other holding the fence to steady her self, and looking on the verge of complete collapse.

Joel again, 'We understand this is a shock, but we're going to get you and the kids out of here very soon...but listen to me. First we've got to find out more about those necklaces."

Francois spoke. "Be sure Madam we will soon rescue you all, but first we must sort out the necklaces. Please, please, right now, tell no one about us."

Britt, obviously in shock and in tears as the pent up emotion of the last ten days was released, at least nodded.

Joel went on. " Listen carefully. We will be here, very near. When the kids are asleep, and you are sure the guards are not around, come out here again to talk some more. Do not tell the others. Only a few more hours, we promise. But we must first fix the neck bombs."

Britt just stood there, still frozen, obviously stunned, shocked, fearful.

Joel pushed. "Do you understand?"

Francois decided to be tough. "Please Madam, I know this is a shock But it is good shock I promise, For your children do what we say...then we will later make it all OK for you and them. First we have to deal with your necklaces to be safe for all."

" Try to be normal in there."

Britt said. "OK. OK. I can do that. I come out after the children are sleeping. I understand, I really do. But can't you take us out now, please, please."

Reaching through the wire to hold her arm, Joel said, " Hang in there a little bit, we need to find out more about the necklaces to remove any risk. "

"So just a few more hours. Maybe one more night. But we don't want any risks for you or the children."

He nodded at Francoise- "These guys know what they're doing and your Dad, Magnus and all the other parents are aware that it will be a little time to make those neck things safe."

Britt, had noticeably calmed, and breathing in a less panicked way said, "I get it I really do. I will come out later when the kids, are asleep. Don't worry I understand." ...and clutching the note she went back into the house. Joel and Francoise having retreated into the darkening field, were both optimistic and realistic.

Francoise, 'Môn Deiu , that was near I thought she was going to scream or drop to the ground...she's a strong lady."

Joel nodded and said, " Maternal instinct I guess. Lets hope her sister will be the same."

A couple of hours later, sun down but still not very dark, Britt came out of the door. Peering into the darkness. Joel called out softly. "We are here and we are coming to the fence now .There are a few more of us now."

Britt, "The kids are just about asleep. The girls have gone to their little house to look at a dvd. I know you said tell no one but I had to talk to my sister she will come out in a minute."

Francois said. "I have expected that quite well. Listen we don't know how much time we have undisturbed here so let me focus on the necklace."

" I need to check it. Do not worry, we know what we are doing. Please come close as you can to the fence."

Britt pointed and said "Look, a bit down there hidden by the by the bush there's quite a hole in the wire, that's where the smaller kids were feeding the horses."

She moved along as did and Francois with a quiet "merde," as he stepped in some horse dung said, "Much easier. Now let me scan the necklace. It will not trigger anything. We know this stuff, it's what we do."

He produced what looked like a largish TV remote or old style mobile phone, and said, "This sniffs explosive, let me run it around the necklace."

After a minute he said, "and its showing nothing. But now we try a more detailed test."

 He reached into his pocket and pulled out a handful of plastic tubes and carefully extracting a stick with a cotton swab on the end from several of them he ran them over the necklace and the another over the cord around Britt's neck and inserted them back into the tubes.

With almost no sound, some of his team had come near. These guys fully armed. Francois, handed some of the used test swabs in their tubes, to one of his men, who ran back, keeping close to the hedgerow.

With a slight start to all of us Anna appeared in the door- finger to her lips. "All sleeping."

Francois said, "Business first Madame. We are of course planning to rescue you very soon, but we think it is safer to try and test these necklaces carefully first. "

"So you have to stay a few more hours, maybe even until tomorrow night about this time. But I can tell you this place is surrounded and my men are ready to move in instantly if there are signs of any troubles."

"But first I want to check your necklace for explosive traces," and he went through the routine again.  He sent another of his men back with the sample swabs,  "We have to test them quickly, but so far we find nothing."

Anna said, "Is that good then."

Francois, " I have to tell you true. Yes in a way, but to be sure we don't know if constant swimming and sun tan cream can affect the readings. So we still assume we have a nasty problem, but we know how to fix this for you."

He continued, "Please tell me what happened when they fitted the necklace. Remember all you can."

Anna spoke. "They fitted them when we were in Portugal, just by clipping them round our necks. "

"But when we had just arrived here one of the guards, who now seems always very kind to the kids made a game of it for them. He had some melons on the wall over there and got the kids to stand back telling them it was fruit fireworks. "

"He pushed a remote and they exploded. He told us it was what would happen if we tried to get away or to take them off. I don't think the kids understood the English but they liked the melon mess."

"OK. OK." Francois continued, calm voiced, "Think very carefully Madame, did he put a necklace on to the melon or was it set up ready ?"

The girls looked at each other and Anna said, "No he went over to the melons first but he didn't have anything in his hands. So I guess it was set up ready."

" They are always telling us that the bombs in here," she touched her throat, "are safe. Even if we bang them or the kids pull them. We just must not go outside the fence wire."

Britt, "I remember they said they were used to, 'trigger' I think he said to make bombs go off late after they had hit the ground."

" He was telling us not to worry too much about them. But they always remind us about the danger also, and to stay near the house."

"The guy who brings the food shopping he wears the exploder thing round his neck, the thing that made the melons explode. It looks like what we open the garage door with from the car at home."

Francois . "OK . I want to check where those melons exploded. "

Francois started picking bits of stuff from the ground and putting them in plastic bags . Having done that he said. " This is the plan. It may change, but this is what I what I want to achieve. I am sorry, but whilst we make everything safe for you and the others, including the children you will have to wait one more day. Try to be normal."

" Tomorrow, I hope at this time, but listen to me. It may be later, much later in the night. We will have your Magnus coming to take the kids from you at this back door."

"We will cut the fence. Only when I tell you, note that, I stress, only when I tell you, one of you is to bring the three kids out to Magnus. The others then quietly go and get May, Brigitte and Tamiko. "

"We want to get the kids away from your necklaces quickly."

The women looked at each other, and reached out to touch hands. Francois said. "I know, I understand but this is real. So please listen to me...and of course we will tell you again exactly what and when to do things tomorrow."

Anna said. "Of course of course."

Francois continued. "Whilst Magnus, with my guys assisting, get the kids away, silently we hope, my team will come in through the wire, to help you and the girls into bullet proof bomb vests. "

"This the most important part. The vital and first part is that under the necklace, right round, we slide separate six pieces, like high collars, I think you call them turtles or roll necks?"

Both women nodded, and he continued. "They will be high, not comfortable but are needed for a short time. Also we will have goggles for you. Once we have you in the collars and vests we will take away the necklaces from your body."

He paused. "When that is done we will be deal with the guards."

Anna, "Will you kill them?"

Francois brushing the dirt from his knees said, a little sharply "I hope not we, need information from them. Are you concerned for them?"

Britt and Anna glanced at each other and said. "No no. We were talking the other night about, I think they call it, 'Stockholm syndrome ' where captives get to like their captors, and we said we could understand it."

"That's right" said Francois, "It happened during a long bank hostage siege in Stockholm. It is much studied and written about."

"Listen to me", Francois spoke, and his voice hardened, "Remember this is to save your children from some very evil people. And you all probably know too much for them to keep being nice. That's why my people are all around here now hidden. Just in case they change in the way they are."

"But, please try try to act as you were, just one more day, that will give us time to be better prepared and safer for you and the kids."

Anna said, " I can tell you, we don't worry about the guards, I think I was really meaning about if the kids get to see something terrible. And anyway we're from Malmo."

Anna heard call of 'mama' from inside the house and made to go inside.

Francois , "We will speak tomorrow night. Do not keep looking over the fence for us. We will be right here but we're watching and ready to act."

" Be careful how you speak about this. We only assume there no microphones inside this house with the bad guys listening, but we are not sure, neither are we yet 100% about the necklaces, but we will fix them be assured. Bon Soir."

He said , "Oh yes, I can't give you a mobile phone, in case they have a scanner, that detects it. Be strong ladies, only another day. Oh yes again. Magnus and your papa send their Love." Britt went in and he retreated, but leaving a couple of team members concealed nearby.

Just over a kilometer away after crossing the small river, he came to the banks of the Canal Du Midi. Base camp, a bunch of guys fishing, a barbecue, lot's of coloured plastic kayaks tied up. All looking very usual here at summer weekends. Good cover.

In the back of a truck with more kayaks on the roof some worried faces bent over a machine. Looked like big photocopier in a flight case, it was sniffer that can detect the most minute traces of almost anything it's told to look for. You get them at airports now.

The machine operator, presumably a soldier but in this case in bright orange track suit said. "There's no trace any known explosive. That should make us smile, but now we know about them being worn swimming, with suntan cream we're very nervous. I never hear of this machine not sniffing out something, but then again I don't think daily swimming, sun tan oil and much shampoo has been much tested."

"Check these." Francois handed over the plastic bag of bits he had scrabbled up from the ground at the melon site.

In less than two minutes, the operator said, "Lots of reactions on everything. I would almost guarantee it was standard slow det cord that had been used."

Joel's, "Oh F***. I was hoping for more of nothing," was tempered by Francois. "Look we know that it cannot be det cord in the necklaces, it's too unstable, and given how the necklaces are deployed it simply would have broken down or gone off long ago."

" So I am inclined to think that the necklaces are a bluff, but with some easy to get det cord used on the melons as a frightener. But we keep to assume the worst danger, just in case."

Francoise ,having given a series of orders to his team, they climbed into Joel's old Citroen van and drove along the canal path until a bridge, where he could join the lane.

Then stopping only to pick up Joel's dad who was waiting by the little river crossing, Joel called us, "We're coming to the villa. Have made contact. All good."

It was nearing eleven when he arrived .

Having dispatched Joel's dad for a shower, him having been lurking in the bushes for a few days, I introduced Francois to Barry who had also just arrived.

Francois, shook hands, but before talking to Barry, went and spoke quietly with Magnus, who quite understandably became very emotional, they wandered over to the far side of the pool.

"Where's Oleg and Chris?" asked Joel.

" Gone in search of food," I said. "When we got your call it seemed like a good plan."

Having listened to the de-brief ,as a somewhat refreshed Joel's dad joined us, a car pulled into the driveway and Oleg and Chris appeared laden with pizza boxes, pasta, salads.

We told Oleg to forget plates, but Chris who seemed to be chief cook and host, found wine glasses and cutlery.

As we ate, Chris. " I say it again, these Bloody Frogs , they do know their food, this is just from the campsite pizzeria down the road. But they all looks and tastes as good as anything in Singapore."

The commander said, "Chris. Us *French* we do know our food. "

"But it seems to me that I might have to recruit you into Legion serving under me that I may find a way to stop us being, ' Bloody Frogs.'

Chis grinned and said, "Sorry mate...or do I mean, Sir."

Francois continued, "Of course we can still be ' Bloody Frogs' when it comes to the Rugby."

I told Francois, "That's lost on Chris, he's a football man. Fulham at that." "Man and boy, a Fulham fan." said Chris.

Silence fell as the eight of us tucked into Pizza, salads and wine. Francois saying, "Just the one small glass, I am very much on call".

He spoke. "We still know there is a big risk with the necklaces, and possible remote control. I can understand that you are ready to 'pay' the ransom so to make no problems."

" I am thinking that, if you make the ransom flight departure tomorrow afternoon, we should move to free the hostages in the five hour window when it gets a little dark, between the kidnappers knowing we have departed the gold and it arriving in the designation. "

"So that is only if there is no risk, before it is handed over. So soon after dark tomorrow. They'll be safe till at least then."

"Of course if we see anything bad starting earlier then we can move first, but I don't like the sound of the guard man wearing a trigger for the girls necklaces around his own neck."

The commander, having made a call said. "OK, long days coming, I'm going back to Castelnaudary. Joel, tomorrow you bring the Citroen down to the Canal I'll see you there at nine. And Magnus, Joel will come and get you at about three tomorrow afternoon."

He stood and a said, "Thanks for the great Frog pizzas Chris."

He went on. "By the way, isn't Fulham near that really famous team Chelsea." and he walked down the lane as a motorbike rolled into view, taking a spare helmet from the driver, he sat on the back and was gone.

Chris paused in helping clear the rubbish away into bin bags, "I guess I asked for that. Bloody Chelsea, Cheeky sod."

Magnus said he had better report in to Charlie and the others, and I asked him to call Calvettioni.

The rest of us shared a few more glasses of wine and then having found spare bedding, sunbed mattresses and the like, we all, I think, slept.

At The Old Mill, predictably, Britt and Anna whispered and hardly slept.

**44. Friday July 1st. 8.00 pm. On the Canal du Midi. Just south of Toulouse. About 125 K from Carcassonne:** *The Accidental Millionaires. Part two.*

Andy Allister and Faye-Lin, his Vietnamese lady, had for almost five years now been operating their luxury holiday barge, The Lady Faye, up and down the glorious waters of, as it said in their brochure, 'The peaceful tree lined, but sun dappled waters of the Canal Du Midi.'

Mainly cruising between the Mediterranean at Sete and Castelnaudary about 30 kilometers short of Toulouse.

On occasions they ventured further into the Canal Lateral a La Garonne. There having joined the Garonne and Gironde rivers they somewhat reluctantly went on all the way to Bordeaux.

In recent years their fleet had grown to include a second boat, The Lady Mali. She was operated by their Portuguese boat builder, and now friend Carlos, and his wife Maria. Both boats were near as dammit booked solid for the six month season.

Down the canal, near the Camargue, the old boatyard where they had found and restored the old barges was very different from the day Andy first set foot in it six years earlier.

There were now two bungalows behind the yard, home to the Portuguese and their families, and the shell of another home, on the banks of the canal, not yet completed, but destined to be Andy and Faye-Lin's.

They had embarked into a staged payments plan, to buy the land and the boatyard business, such as it was, from their old Landlord Jean – Baptiste. As word had spread about the new professionalism of the yard it became busier and busier. They were even now agents for a UK tour company, and operated ten rental boats for them in the season, maintaining them in the winter.

Back at the boat yard, holiday makers arriving to pick up their rental boats seemed to enjoy their, mostly one sided conversations, with old J-P as he sat in the sun, Gitane as ever, hanging from his lip, as he watched their attempts to learn the rudiments of navigation in the sheltered and safe waters of the canal.

In reality J-P had never really got to grips with the trend to 'Bain Plastique,' as he called the modern family cruisers of today. Although he had to admit they worked well. It was only when both, Miss Mali and The Lady Faye, were moored alongside each other, that he really saw what he liked. Sure, they had old black steel hulls, scuffed and scraped with the marks of a hundred lock encounters, the boats, after all at 30 meters long were the maximum size able to fit in Paul Riquet's 500 year old locks.

But on deck. Scrubbed teak , gleaming brass cleats and lamps, coiled ropes, flowers in boxes on the top deck- and on the wheelhouse and galley roof a well-used and well-tended herb garden for the kitchen. Cream or dark green sunshades, chairs and loungers.

J-P liked that, and the boatyard crew, mostly college students with a dream summer job, were happy to acknowledge his watchful eye, and when no one was watching, to sneak him a snifter of local red wine.

On this particular Friday on the first day of July, only the Lady Mali was at the boatyard as Andy and Mai in the Lady Faye ,were more than   200 km to the north west, just south of the industrial city of Toulouse.

They had just completed a weeks charter based in and around Bordeaux. In addition to the interesting navigational challenges that a slightly salty tidal river with constantly changing sand bars offered it was also quite busy.

As they made their way back upstream, to Castelnaudary, much boat cleaning was in progress.

They had passed through the evil looking  graffitti'd  urban walls of the Toulouse section of the canal and were about ten kilometers further on. Andy was thinking how he preferred the more rural areas of the Canal. Where they were, for some distance the canal ran within view of, or at least sound of, the S3 main AutoRoute out of Toulouse. The AutoRoute engineers  having largely followed the line of the old canal as it worked its way across the country, and on some rare occasions, the busy, noisy road running just meters away from the usually peaceful canal.

French AutoRoute's have the usual huge gas stations equipped with shops cafes restaurant and in many cases motels.

But with distances in France being quite long- every 30 k or so they also have a series of very basic rest stops- or 'Aires'. Named after the district or region. The only facilities at 'Aires,' being parking places, for a quick 'rest.' Usually a few picnic tables and a basic toilet block. Also, as many have observed, a lot of dog shit.

Despite hating the 24/7 noise of the big road, and the slightly shady people who seemed to lurk around in most of the 'Aires', he had this time stopped the Lady Faye right on the concrete steps down to the water at such an 'Aire.'

He had good reason. The advantage of this one, the inappropriately named 'Aire de Repose de Renneville, ' was that it had serious range of garbage bins  within a few steps of the canal path mooring. His priority was to get rid of a weeks accumulated empty bottles and  cruise rubbish to those bins.

On his first trip to the bins, he had wondered why there were none of the usual cars or trucks with sleeping drivers in them. Then he observed a line of 'no entry traffic cones,' across the only entrance from the busy main road.

He assumed that a closure for maintenance, was also the reason for there being two palettes with tarps over them on the ground, around which he had to manoeuver his trash barrow.

On his third trip, having decided that the closure might provide Faye and himself with a quieter night, he was little surprised to see a flatbed truck and a pickup truck pull up to the cones, and then a figure dragging the cones to one side and replacing them when the two vehicles had entered.

Andy figured that his dislike of 'dodgy characters' was just about to be tested, and of which he wanted no part.

He stepped back behind the rubbish bins and called out to Faye, "Maybe dodgy people out here, lock the doors. I'm waiting till they have gone."

Remaining concealed, but unable to resist looking , Andy observed the flatbed truck, having lowered it's legs, using its hoist to quickly unload two of four wrapped pallets from the back of the truck.

Then just as swiftly replaced them with the two from the ground that Andy had steered his trash barrow around. French voices, "Where's the f-ing knife, and the super glue."

Andy could hear grunting and, peering round the end of the 'Aire' building, he could see some work in progress on the back of the flatbed. Then legs up, the flatbed was gone, taking the un-coned off exit road back onto the main road.

"Six minutes, not bad, now quick let's get this stuff into the pickup, I've cut the tarps." Andy could see the pickup driver and his mate picking up bricks and loading them carefully onto the pickup.

The constant throb of tyres and flash of headlights continued but suddenly the French voice again, " Merde. Look blue lights, it's the police , let's get out of here."

Andy couldn't see round the building, but he could see blue flashing lights reflected in the windows of the pickup and his barge. With a splash of gravel, the pickup pulled rapidly out of the Aire parking, up the exit road and was gone.

He leaned round the building and saw that a police van was actually now backing away up the entrance road to the Aire. He guessed the police had seen it empty of parked vehicle's and assumed that maintenance was forthcoming, either that or they had seen the swift exit of the pick up.

The words, "All clear," were hardly out of his mouth when Faye- lin rocketed out of the bushes near the boat and said, "Are you OK honey?"

She was brandishing a large heavy steel mooring pin.

"Sure," he said, "But some funny business going on here though. Someone dumped a load of this, whatever it is ,and two guys started to load it into a pickup truck. Drugs I guess."

"We'll keep out of this, and move the boat now."

Faye-Lin said, "Hang on-let me look, give me the torch."

She squatted down and lifted one, or tried to lift, one of the bricks off the palette with its sliced open tarp.

"This isn't drugs. It's a metal brick. Very heavy though."

Andy crouched down and saw some dull goldish coloured bars with various markings on. None made sense.

He lifted one, "That's about 10k,or maybe a bit more," he said. He then spotted a sign that said, 'cscscsomething'. He couldn't read the first bit but the words, 'state bullion mint. 999.99% Standard Pure,' were very clear.

"Christ honey, I think it's bloody gold, or looks like it. If it is I wonder what its worth."

Faye- lin said, "We Vietnamese always know the daily price of gold and 10 kilos is worth at least $400,000 US."

Andy said, "You're kidding, you know you always get the decimal point wrong."

Faye -Lin, standing, hands on hips, "I don't get the value mixed up with gold my little, round eyed beloved. Look there's at least 100 gold bars here – that's over 40 million dollars. If there's the same under the other tarp that's a lot."

Andy said, "Well whoever legged it when they saw the Police is going to be back bloody quick, so let's get out of here."

Faye practical as ever, "If it's been stolen there will be a reward. Let's call the police."

Andy, " Sure, I can see them believing we just happened to be here, and found millions by the bloody road side. No way, lets go. For all we know the police are in on this, and you and I have seen too bloody much. We'll end up in the bottom of the canal."

Faye-lin "OK then lets hide it, and when we know who it belongs to, let's talk to them."

Andy. "Hide it where ? Not on the bloody boat."

Faye-lin said, "Look we've got the barrow, lets drop it in the canal. We know where it is and a diver could get it back one day. We're doing our duty to hide it from the bad guys."

Somewhat unwillingly, but it did kind of make sense.

Most of Faye Lins plans usually made sense, and any kind of reward would be good. So he,  Andy agreed.

In thirty minutes of frantic and strenuous activity they shifted 156 gold bars.

Most they dropped, straight in the canal between the boat and the edge. They wrapped a couple in the tarps and dropped them over board on the far side of the boat.

Andy chucked the palettes behind the rubbish bins, saying as he did so, " There must be big footie or rugby on TV because there's no fishermen about." Later a quick glance at their TV, showed  France and the New Zealand All Blacks Rugby, live from Paris, with two of the Toulouse team in the French fifteen. New Zealand won.

Fearing the return of the men, they quickly unhitched the boat, and got under way. After a bend in the canal they were lost to sight of anyone pulling into the Aire. After a few hundred meters they approached a lock. The Ecluse de Renneville.

"We could go through ourselves but we never usually do that at night. So I think we'll anchor midstream, that way no one can come aboard. Madame Eclusier, will see we're waiting when she opens up at seven in the morning."

When he was satisfied the anchor had taken hold, he came back to their wheelhouse and found Mai lin had produced some cheese, figs, and some tarte tatin from the larder.

With a glass or two of wine their hearts calmed. Later that night as Andy got into bed he stubbed his toe on something . Faye said, "Sorry honey I kept two of the bricks, just in case."

Before he could reply she had snuggled up to him in the bed and then squeaking said, " Ouch, shit that's where I put the other one."

Andy said.  "That's really not good. What if the police find them on the boat?"

"No." she said, "That's where you are wrong. If the Police come and do find these few kilos, which they can have back, but if they get nasty then they won't learn from us where is the rest. If they don't believe us ,well they lose."

Andy. "That's nearly 100 million dollars."

"I know sweetie that's nice. Goodnight." The unusual events of the night made sleep hard to find, and despite being convinced he hadn't slept for a moment Andy suddenly started: opened his eyes. Broad daylight. He leapt out of bed as Faye- lin started the engine.

His beloved's greeting to him for the day. "Look, the lock's open, and the coffee's ready. Do the lock carefully I'm not making you another cup."

Between the next few locks, after a long discussion they decided that, 'what's done is done', and to wait until they saw something on TV or in the media about the gold.

A reward sounded good, and it was very unlikely anyone would find the bulk of the gold sunk into the mud at the bottom of the canal.

Andy saying, " There must be a lot of people looking for this stuff...police, the pissed off robbers and  surely the customers the gold was going to."

Faye-Lin weighed one of the bars on the scales in one of the guest cabin shower rooms, and bounced up on deck telling Andy -"it's 12 and a bit kilos, so that's worth even more."

Not wishing to compromise the situation by losing either of the two ingots Faye-lin had stashed on board, they put the gold in a plastic bags, and having levered off the top of their waste water-toilet waste storage tank they dropped the two bags in.

"It'll be easy to get them out one day. We can flush the tanks first with fresh water as we do when we empty them anyway and hook them out with a boathook..."

For several days they bought a selection of newspapers, listened to the news on radio, watched TV but heard no mention of any gold.

They decided to wait, although Andy tended to think about their possible secret fortune every time he used the toilet.

**45.Saturday July 2nd.06.30 am.A Vacation Villa Carcassonne. South West France. Sun coming up. The start of a very long day, a night and another day:** *Armies may, 'march on their stomachs', but they survive and win on planning. Planning is good. Unknown, is not good.*

There was no avoiding the tension, as, sitting our by the pool, before he went to check in with Francois, Joel, his dad and I had an early morning coffee, and 'kind of,' enjoyed bacon sandwiches from Chris.

The sandwiches were welcome, and good, but the nerves were not. Planning, surprise, training, technical expertise, professionalism, now we needed all of them and more. I hoped we wouldn't need marksmanship or other combat skills.

We ran through everything we could think of to ensure the day went off as safely as possible. 'Planning is good'. 'Unknown is not good', is the age old military maxim.

And 'bloody necklaces' as Joel always referred to them, were very much in the unknown department.

My nerves were not much steadied by Joel telling me of an encounter had had late one night in his bar in Kabul, Afghanistan, in which another old military maxim had come up.

'The element of surprise-keeps you alive'.

He had observed a pretty miserable guy sitting alone at the bar, obviously doing his best to drown his sorrows. A not uncommon sight in that long time combat arena.

Eventually the guy, stood, hurled his beer bottle at the TV screen and stormed out.

Joel, who had observed extreme reactions to the, 'wrong refereeing,' decisions during televised football matches, was a tad shocked as the TV was showing an old, and very innocuous UK game show called Surprise ! Surprise!

Catching up with the guy, at their secure entry/exit gate, to ensure his departing customer had at least, as was the rule, safe transport home, Joel had said, "Hang on pal, any problem I can help you with?"

I could see what was coming as Joel continued, "The guy's bleary eyed response. 'Ta mate. Not this time. Bad week. We were the ones surprised-not doing the surprising'."

Joel's point, to me was, that as well as planning, surprise was a key part of what we needed. He went off in the old Citroen van,taking his dad to resume the watch on the old farm. As I pondered the world of special forces, my phone buzzed. David, calling. I assumed from Geneva.

"Just to confirm as agreed we're all making our way to Toulouse in a few hours, should be there about eight tonight. We've got some security taking us straight from the planes into a side door of a hotel, keeping out of sight-just in case."

The reason for keeping them on the plane or out of sight , being that the various individuals had reasonably well known faces, and we, as Joel had stressed again and again, wanted to keep the element of surprise on our side.

The parents had helicopters on standby to bring them to the Legion base if things went to plan, and hopefully not to have to fly to nearby hospitals, if things didn't go to plan.

Barry and I worked our way through the various plans endlessly during a long morning.

At around 11 Barry's phone received an incoming message with likely flight times to the ransom destination.

After a somewhat subdued brunch, Joel returned and drove Magnus and I to the bridge over the canal where you could usually access the towpath.

There a Gendarme moved a plastic roadworks barrier. 'Attention, fermé . Travaux routiers,' and let us through.

Just a few hundred meters down the path quite a team had assembled, some now wearing or carrying full camo, body armour, some with the protective padding extending down their legs.

I noticed several with Tasers.

Francois seeing me looking said, "They can disable someone ,but we have known trigger fingers to jerk as they get the electric shock."

I confirmed, the ransom payment leaves at three this afternoon and it should be about a six hour flight.

Francois said. "About an hour ago, Madam Britt came out of the kitchen door with some horse food. She told us that, the man they call Pete had told her the money was being paid today. He also said they would be free in the next few days, and that he would bring them back Pizzas when he came back with the shopping. She said he 'seemed quite normal'."

"Some of my team are still in place right by the fence just in case there's any changes in circumstances there. We are also ready now here, but we still wait for tonight because we still don't know 100% about the explosive pouch on the front of the necklace. "

"I still want to go slow and careful with them,  and may need quite some time to do that. So we want to be sure we are not interrupted by the captors. It will also be better if the kids are out of the way as well."

" Daniel, when we are at the farm, I know you are keen, but we have more training for this than you, so I want you to stay well back, and out of sight.  Only when we have the captives outside the fence can you reveal your self to the Asian girls who of course know you well."

Obviously I not only agreed with the commander but could appreciate the reasons.

Joel said, "Waiting around is shit, and makes you really jumpy. Why don't we try those kayaks to pass some time."

So incongruously ,we, Magnus, Joel and I paddled along the canal- away from the farm- almost reaching the next lock.

On occasions having to pull over to allow boats filled with happy holidaymakers to pass by. Joel called out. "If only they knew!"

Even Magnus smiled as he said,  "I know what you mean."

**************

## 46. Saturday July 2nd. 2.00 pm Saturday afternoon. Marseilles. Marignane Airport. Freight area : *One of the most evocative, and almost forgotten movie themes of all times is 'Borsalino'. A great movie, set in the intrigue of of the criminal underworld of Marseille.*

A selection of planes lined up, marked with the usual familiar names, and  a number with lesser known logos from a variety of African countries. Many of them from former French colonies, which, together with its geographical location was one reason Marseilles Airport was so busy.

Rory and Oleg were accompanying the ransom gold on it's flight to Africa, and were watching whilst a team of loaders maneuvered  the last of the eight palettes in to the hold of the plane.

Rory, having recently had conversations about the cliché's and intrigues of Shanghai, was considering that Marseilles, with it's docks and shady history, maybe qualified as an European equivalent.

As well as the 8000 kilos gold bullion, we boarded a 'cargo protection squad.' Francois, both thinking of potential reactions from his Paris HQ and wanted, for the rescue attempt to rely mainly on his Legion team who had months, if not years of training and experience working together. So Joel had assigned to us six of his guys, keeping just two, who spoke Swedish back with him.

Fit looking in nondescript clothing. Mostly they appeared to be a sports team as they were all carrying sports bags.

With documents signed off, doors closed. At three local time, the pilot requested permission to take off from the control tower, and was given prompt priority. Rory wondered if the influence of local business operator Andre Calvettioni was behind the quick queue jump.

Rory, not the pilot for once, was sitting in the extra 'jump seat' on the flight deck, and smiled as the pilot, said, "Not often we get to fly a nice new 737-700 cargo version into Mauretania, but Noukachott, is quite a modern airport."

After some weather and route checking, Pilot Frank announced that the flight should take just over 5 hours. "We're only carrying under half our load capacity and ATC have given us a pretty direct route."

As he turned off the seat belts sign, he said, " Let's hope the folks at Noukachott have paid the electric bill so we get some landing lights."

Oleg joined them in the cockpit, and with the pilot's help sent a message to Barry to be relayed to the abductors: *Departed MRS. Est. Arr NKC 9.00 pm local. End*

As they settled down for the flight Oleg learned that, Frank had, been in flying college with Rory.

So once they had reached their cruising altitude and Frank started complaining about the balance of the load, there was a good bit of banter between the two.

Frank complaining, "Those bloody cargo loaders, we're stupidly unbalanced, way heavy in back. Makes this thing fly like a pig."

Rory to Oleg, "Of course, if he knew what all those buttons and stuff did he could fix it, he's from the propeller age you know."

Frank, having reminded Rory that both of them had in fact learned to fly on prop planes, reassured Oleg. "There's no safety issue, just one of fuel economy and thus range. What we got ,is what we got."

He handed the controls to the co-pilot, and with a, "Don't start making trouble for him now Rory, come with me I'm going to search for sandwiches and coffee."

Behind the cockpit there was the usual layout of toilet and galley, and then an open area right to the back of the plane. Looking back past the lashed down pallets they could see the protection team using some of the twelve available seats that had been left in place.

Frank, filling jugs with tea and coffee said, "No trolley dollies on this one then." Oleg looked puzzled. Rory, laughed and said, "You see he's showing his great age again, That's what we used to call Air Hostesses."

Having also found the supply of chilled water bottles and good looking sandwiches, they made their way around the pallets to the rear and shared out the supplies with the protection team.

The crew call button 'binged,' and Frank made his way forward.

Oleg and Rory briefed the team, whilst they ate. "About the delivery of the ransom shipment. What the bad guys don't know is, *we have found the abducted girls.* The rescue squad should be going in when it gets a little darker, but there's delays and booby trapped explosives involved to be sorted."

"This where we're at:

A. If we hear nothing, we just deliver the ransom pronto, and get out and away."

"B. If we get the 'rescue complete' message before, repeat before we have unloaded the ransom then we get away quick and go home."

"C. If the ransom has been unloaded, *and then the hostages freed message comes through.* We see if there's any way we can re-claim the ransom if it's obviously nearby. But only if the hostages have been released."

"D. We must not endanger the captives . This gold is here to be paid. There's no bonus, I repeat no bonus in stopping the payment going through. The only bonus is when the girls are away and safe."

Frank returned. "I have news of a re-route. Message from Barry. New orders from the abductors, now going to Dahkla, and it's an hour nearer. We've got landing permission."

Which produced from the protection squad a few, "Where the F***s that?"

Before Frank could answer Oleg said. "Bizarrely, I've been there, twice. "

"It's in a massive inlet on the coast, technically it's part of Western Sahara, but the Moroccans have been 'taking care,' of it for a while. Actually it was a French or Spanish colony and then Moroccan and then the independence claims started."

"Lots of nasty border disputes dragging on, ending with the creation of the worlds longest minefield, right through the desert keeping the bad guys out, or  the sides apart. "

"The UN peacekeepers and other countries want the Moroccans to withdraw, but now there's rumours of oil offshore, so they are dragging their heels about leaving."

Frank said, "Christ, just what I wanted, another war zone."

Oleg stopped him and said. "No its not really, not where were going anyway. The airport's modern. There's hotels, the tourists  are mostly surfers and windsurfers, which is why I went there. Not much of a port but there's a big fishing fleet based there. There's a Moroccan navy base of some kind there also."

Marcus the leader of the protection squad said,  "Actually I've been there once, also windsurfing. Quite a lot of locals speak Spanish as they have had jobs there, or deal with Spanish fishing boats."

As they chatted, Oleg established that the protection squad, was Marcus who was Spanish, Piet a South African, Jonny a Nigerian whom the others seemed to call Bad luck, and three English, Mike, Martin, and Gary.

"We've got all bases covered here mate," said one of the English guys, and nodding at the Nigerian, "Bad Luck's already got his night time camo on." Oleg could tell from the good natured insults that this was squad who had worked together a lot, and trusted each other implicitly.

A voice on the PA, "More messages here, and one hour to landing."
****************

## 47. Saturday July 2nd. Dusk .On the banks of the Canal du Midi, a few hundred meters from the Old Mill in the Sun :

*TXT.From. Oleg: Departed MRS. Est. Arr NKC with Gold 9.00 pm local.*

Coming back we pulled the kayaks on to the canal bank by the truck, and got confirmation their freight plane had departed on time. Someone had lit a barbecue. With Francois, saying to Magnus, "Please eat sir. Even just a little of the couscous to keep up your equilibrium, my men nearer the farm have rations also."

About an hour later, two dramas. The abductors had changed the destination of the gold flight. We were now aware the flight would be a little quicker. That was not a problem for us, but then suddenly we did have a real problem.

Both abductors drove up to the house in one of the cars. They got out and unloaded something from the car, and started to walk in.

Ready for sudden changes, Francois's men got ready for urgent action, but stayed back. We still couldn't be sure about the bloody necklaces. Joel's dad. "I have perfect view two targets. Carrying boxes. They not repeat not appear armed. One in jeans and one in usual shorts and T shirt, not much room to conceal weapon."

They walked into the farmyard, where it turned out the boxes contained Pizzas. Having dropped them off one guy took the car back to the gatehouse, but the other guy sat down at the outside table. With a small parabolic mike we could just about hear the conversation. Seemed friendly enough. "Sorry it's late girls but we were waiting for a message." Having shared Pizza's with the children, who then went into the house to presumably watch a video. The abductor now known as Pete, explained. "Now in the next few days you are going to be released."

Britt. "You are not joking?"

Pete, "No hundred percent, couple of days you'll all be out of here.But there's one problem. For me and Jack this has been a job. We've been paid by the day, and as long as no harm came to you we get a bonus. So we've tried our best.  I've got kids as well so I hope yours have done OK here."

"Just so you know, we were paid to lock all of you in that big meeting room over there.  But as I say now we have a problem and that is you all know what we look like." At these words Francois, obviously unsure of what was coming next, make some signals to his men.

The guy continued. "So I want you to look at these."

Apparently using his phone he showed them the pictures of their houses in Sweden, the kids school and obviously some that we had not seen.

Britt, sounding tearful "That's Papas house, look that's Grandma in the garden."

Pete said, "Right now, they also have pictures of your house and stuff in Tokyo and Taipei and the rest. Maybe your Ma and Pa maybe grandma, your sisters, brothers. I don't know. But a lot of pictures."

We could hear what presumably was May or Tamiko talking and crying.

" So Listen. I know it's tough but it's very simple. *You all forget what we look like.* Completely forget. Never give any clues about us to family, friends police or anyone. Its not going to be easy for you. But listen to this."

"As time passes you will make mistakes, let out information, but believe me, there's bad people out there with long memories. They now have a lot of, money and they don't want to lose it."

" You can't live all the rest of your life looking over your shoulder, or expecting your kids, sisters, parents all your family to do the same. So you forget what we look like. You can explain the problem to your Dads and they will tell you what to do. I guarantee they will tell you to say nothing to anyone. I can also guarantee that then you'll never see us again."

Britt said. "We understand that. It won't be easy I guess, but actually you have been very nice to the kids, and us, and we thank you for that."

Pete's  phone obviously made a noise which our microphone aimed at the table picked up. He said. "I'm going to walk back to the gate house, Cheer up, all of you, you'll be free to go in a couple of days."

Britt obviously indicated the necklaces. "Yep, we'll turn them off at that time. Meantime take care with them, Goodnight, and don't forget, you never met me." Joel's dad in a whisper reported Pete's seemingly endless, slow walk back up the lane, and his arrival at the gatehouse.

Francoise, now in full camo kit, said, " Dan, you stay back here. Joel, Magnus come in closer to the fence with me please. We will check, but the time is come now I think."

*****************

## 48. Saturday July 2nd. Evening.Boeing 737. SF Freighter. Over North Africa, landing ETA- 9.00 pm Dahkla. Western Sahara: *Globally, at any one time, 1,037, 021 people are allegedly waiting for the pizza man.*

Oleg and Rory returned to the cockpit area where Frank relayed some bad news from Barry. Not terrible but not helpful. All rescue moves were on hold. It seems that one of the bad guys was at that moment with the girls talking to them.

So their instructions were: *BP: Continue with delivery, but try slowish unload. Not saving ransom, but abductor tactics unclear right now. Barry. End.*

At Dahkla, Frank took a couple of extra circuits, telling the tower "wheels down light not engaged, just checking." Having gone round once again and taken a one minute detour out over the sea we were on last finals. Oleg and Rory strapped them selves into the rear facing 'stewardesses' seats on the out side of the galley wall.

Pilot Frank, "Landing, Obviously seat belts on." He let the plane run right to the end, of what the dials told Rory, 'was an almost 10,000 feet/3000mtrs runway'.

Whilst Frank muttered, "Can't waste much more time without looking stupid." Rory said, " I'll go down and ask some questions about refueling. You stay here, " he gestured at Frank, "in case we need a quick exit."

After some further discussions about fuel requirements, and reminding the 'sports team' in the rear to make sure their weapons were well out of sight in their bags, he pushed the button and lowered the air-stairs.

Quickly exiting down them with Oleg, before several smart looking uniformed gents could ascend.

Rory, very English style, " Evening , sorry about the delay, new plane and all that, just checking out the systems."

Discussions on the tarmac were as ever, shouted a little, as Frank had kept the APU power unit in the tail running.

One of the officials on the tarmac said. "Please come with me, your delivery customer inside."

Rory stayed to supervise the re-fuel and the unload, and Oleg followed in to the building where several locals awaited. Two in uniform.

"Customs," said his guide from the tarmac, and the uniforms nodded in a friendly way. Another with a clipboard, "Health and Quarantine."

He had a question. "Any livestock or plantings ?"

Oleg could answer that one. "No none at all."

H and Q was obviously keen to be at home or elsewhere, so having got Oleg to sign about five copies of a form, he gave him two of them, shook hands and left saying, "Thanks you, Mr. Sir."

The customs guys said, "No drug or alcohols?"

"No." said Oleg, resisting the temptation to add, "not this time sadly."

More forms, signed, stamped and some handed back.

The Customs guys said. "We check with goods receiver when unload. But for us OK." and they wandered away.

Oleg's guide showed him to a seat by the window and said. "Please wait, a few minutes." Looking out he could see Frank and Rory standing by a half opened cargo door, with Frank hurtling up and down the air-stairs a few times. Obviously still wasting time. He fidgeted with his phone, not really expecting much, when it suddenly came to life and connected to a service. A logo in the corner Tele-Maroccom, or something similar.

He was sitting there thinking about Maroccom being a great phone service name when a message came in :

*BP. All still on hold here. Captor's brought pizzas and bloody sitting eating with girls. But proceed unload. Possibly captors being informed or waiting for delivery news. So rpt proceed delivery. Ends'*

Oleg looked out of the window and seeing the cargo door was now shut, gave him a start, fearing the unload had been completed.

Then he realised there were still four of the empty cargo dollies there. Frank was standing there whilst a modern looking fuel truck pumped whatever was needed into the plane.

"'Sir", the word made him jump, focusing on his phone and with plane and air-con sounds, he hadn't heard his guide approach.

"Unload must stop while they re-fuel. Your delivery customers just finishing through there with customs on the first four of the load. Not wait long now." He indicated through the window to what looked like a pretty standard customs area.

Oleg could see the four palettes on the dollies behind a small tractor, near the customs inspection counter. He could also see two people in there with the Customs men. One was Arabic looking and the other a westerner.

It took Oleg a couple of shocked seconds to be sure. He looked and then really looked again. The westerner standing there was the same man that he had seen on the video from the Swedish Gas station near the Sorenson's house. Stills of whom, from the hotel reception and the Tivoli in Denmark, he had punched up onto the office screen.

He was 100% sure, and not only that but the guy was still wearing the same baseball hat he had on in the pictures from Sweden and Denmark.

## 49. Saturday July 2nd. Around 10 pm.Behind Le Vieux Moulin au Soleil.Between Carcassonne and Toulouse.France.

*There may well be, more relaxing ways to spend a Saturday night.*

By the back door from the farm kitchen the fence wire had already been cut, and five of the legion bomb squad in very full body armour were hiding behind some bushes.

Francois slipped through the hole and standing outside the back door, tapped on the glass.

Britt opened the door and whispered, " The girls are still by the pool, but the kids are in their room."

Francois said, " I realise now you must tell the girls not to be frightened when we come in, and to keep quiet and do what we say."

Britt said, " Now?"

Francois nodded, "Take your time, be patient this is nearly over."

At a signal from Francois, Magnus slipped though the hole in the wire and the door and hugged his wife and sister in law who was now also standing there.

Then Britt went through to the pool area first and spoke to the three girls, followed by Francois. "Do not be alarmed, your parents have sent us here to take away those neck things. "

"But wait here , stand still whilst we get the children away, then we have help you with the necklaces, and with special clothes for you."

He asked Joel's dad, " Lane still clear?" and when he got the response ,"All clear," Francois said, "OK go get the children."

Anna and Britt re- appeared carrying three sleepy kids and talking to them in Swedish, later we learned it was about 'a secret game to surprise grandad. Surprisingly unprotestingly, all three were gathered up by Magnus who exited quickly.

As he went through the now well opened gap in the fence one of the kids started to get upset, but one of Joel's team pushed forward also talking Swedish.  Liv let go her dad in shock and allowed herself to be carried fast across the field,  chasing after her sister and father.

Francois. "OK all of you. Don't be nervous I have people here to fix everything. Do what my men tell you. "

"Quick, careful but silent."

Immediately the body armoured team rushed in, each gently grabbed one girl and helped them to the edge of the pool.

There, separated as much as possible from each other, the team first pushed six pieces of high Kevlar collar under each necklace.

Saying as they did so, "I know this not comfortable but is not for long."

They inserted the girls arms into sleeves of a 'backwards facing jacket, pushed goggles on to their faces and then waited. Having checked and positioned the high Kevlar collars as much as they could between the pouches on the front of the necklaces and the girls bodies, on an order, in a coordinated movement they cut the necklaces at the back and flipped them the pool, and pulled the girls away from the pool side at the same time.

Apparently there was a slim chance, that the water might absorb any blast, or stop shrapnel flying around.

In the event there was no explosion.

The girls started to struggle, but were told in a mixture of English and French 'Arret' stop' wait'.

Then at helped by the legionnaires moving fast despite their bulky bomb squad clothes they were rushed round the side of the building and across the field.

Once they were all clear of the building, and free of necklaces at last, all pretence at quiet was dropped.

As I ran forward, two medevac helicopters clattered in from, I don't know where, and landed in the field between the girls and the farm building. "To shield them from any shots". I learned later.

I heard flash bangs and the like coming from the gatehouse.

Then only, then, were the girls allowed to take off their body armour.

Tears, hugs for all, including for me as of course May had known me for since she was a baby and Tamiko for not much less. Britt and Anna clutching a tearful Magnus and a scurry of kids.

Doctors and paramedics seemed keen to hustle the abductees away from us but were told in various languages 'we're fine, we're fine.'

Francois appealed for help. 'Girls, ladies, just to be safe and sure, let's allow this medic team to take us all to our base and I promise you within minutes all your parents will be there also.

May said, "You mean they are here in Europe,"

"Very much so," I said, "and your Mama and Papa Tamiko, and your Papa Brigitte. If anyone will needs the doctors it will be them I think after all the strain of the last ten days."

Britt and Anna, with Magnus and the kids were helped into the largest chopper and it departed. Joel and the three girls into the other.

I made the best call of my life. " All well all safe all good. No hospital needed, See you at Castelnaudary base."

Having made sure that Barry was relaying the news also to Oleg and Rory, I made my way to the gatehouse. There I found a rather grim faced Francois, talking to two gendarmes.

"No one here. Zero. Lots of papers, phones and stuff but no people."
"How can it be?" His radio squawked and he stepped away to listen .
"OK get looking, they not go far."

Then to me "It seems they were always leaving today, but they went on bikes. Bikes! We had set up to count cars in and out, not bloody bikes. I am an imbecile."

I said, "I don't think so. I have never seen such bravery as you and your bomb disposal people showed working at close touch to the explosives." The gendarmes were talking on their on their phones and radios very animatedly.

Francois said, "I pity any cyclists between here and Paris, they're all going to have to identify themselves. By the way, I had to have two Gendarmes here as of course I don't have any powers to detain people in France." I nodded, "Of course.".

"OK." said Francois, " This is now a crime scene so let's get out of here and back to base."

Just about ten minutes later the now very familiar chopper dropped us on the parade ground at The Legion base. As we landed, I reflected.

*There are absolutely no more rewarding ways to spend a Saturday night.*

        \*\*\*\*\*\*\*\*\*\*\*\*\*\*\*\*

## 50. Saturday. July 2nd. 10.00 pm. Airside. Dahkla Airport. Western Sahara : *Surfing was not why he was here this time, but maybe, ducking and diving could deliver a result.*

Oleg sat and started to think. Some gold here, on the ground, some on the plane. A chance to get one of the kidnappers. His thought interrupted by a txt/sms from *Barry. BP: Captor departed. We going in now. Barry.*

Oleg could not stop himself, and nervously started to pace up and down.

The wait seemed like hours, but in less than ten minutes his phone again. *BP:Flash. All safe mums, girls ,kids clear. All safe. Barry ends.*

The welcome relief that flooded over Oleg was palpable. He then considered the position of the guy he recognised ,whom he could see pacing about using a  phone.

Oleg said to his guide, who was hovering, looking nervous, "Can you tell me why we wait?"

"Certainly sir, just for the other four packages. The first ones are cleared to go into town now."

As he spoke Oleg could see Rory, in Pilot shirt, walking across the tarmac with Marcus and four of Joel's guys. Bags in hand. The tarmac guide opened the door for them and started to ask a question.

Rory said, " Toilet not work on plane," which produced a laugh from the guide and pointing to a sign for toilets. Two of the guys, keeping up the pretence, went through the doors at least.

Rory, huge grin opened his mouth, but before he could speak Oleg said, " I know, great news."

Rory. "We don't know what the full SP is here, who is paid off by the bad guys or what. We've got to get out of here, with the gold we've still got."

"Right now they want Frank to move and unload the rest later, as there's an Air Maroc flight coming in, and this is the only ramp with working ground power, so it's a great moment for us to up and away."

Oleg told Rory and Marcus he'd identified the recipient for the cargo as one of the bad guys they had in the videos and stills from Sweden.

"If we move quick, before he learns we freed the girls, may be I can get that gold back somehow. Or even grab the guy."

Frank came to the door and said, "All fueled and ready to go."

Rory, "Good because getting out of here quick is good. I think it's better to go with four pallets and leave the rest than try and retrieve them and then lose the lot. But Oleg just wants to check something in the terminal."

"Quick, would suit the airport," said Frank, "They want us to move, right now. I can park where we won't need a pushback truck, should we decide to quick exit. "

"I have noticed that the Air Force planes on the other side of the airport are all lashed down, covers on. It would take them a while to get moving, and Spanish Gran Canary is less than an hour away. If someone's going to be angry with me I'd rather it was there, than here."

Oleg said. "OK Move where ever they tell you, and give me and the guys a little time. Any signs of trouble just go, leave us here."

Marcus said, "Oleg, I think we can risk 15 mins max, then we pull out. Gold or no bloody gold. Guy or no guy."

Frank and Rory left, Rory saying, "15 minutes no more."

Having seen Oleg finish his conversations with Frank and Rory, his 'Arab customer' exited the Customs office and walked towards him. Checking his phone. Oleg noted nervously.

Hand out stretched. "Mr. Barry?"

The Arab's question threw Oleg off guard. Then realising they had used Barry's name in the various txt exchanges. "No, my names Oleg, Barry's in Europe."

He continued. "You speak English?"

"Sure, I do, my name is Rashid and I used to live in Wembley," adding with a grin, "Where the football comes from. You should have eight palettes ready for me. There seems to be a delay."

"No," said Oleg, "just the cargo door electrics, and refueling , they've nearly fixed it. But now they want us move the plane for a while."

As Oleg moved to an alcove near some soft drink machines and sat on a chair. Rashid asked, "You have four more pallets for me? Yes?"

"Sure," said Oleg, and noted that two of Marcus's team were behind Rashid. The other watching the surroundings. Oleg tried a bluff, "I thought I had to hand over the goods to two people."

Rashid said," Yes Mr. Hans, is here, but he just get a phone call and say he must run outside speak to the boss. Tell me to bring everything through to him."

Oleg, hoping that Marcus and his guys would pick up the hint at his change of style, hardened his tone."*OK Mr. Rashid, here's the story. The girls and children in France are safe and rescued.*"

Rashid went as if to stand and was promptly pushed back into a seat. Bad Luck swiftly removed Rashid's  phone and said, "Guns or knives, my friend?" Rashid said nothing. Bravado or shock, not sure.

Marcus said. "You want this the easy way or the other? We don't like people who kidnap kids."

Rashid mumbled, and allowed himself to dragged to his feet and very firmly frisked.

"Clean."  As he was dropped back into his chair, he said, "I am not kidnapping anyone. I work only with shipment here."

Oleg shook his head and said. "I don't believe I heard that. We know a lot. You work with Mr. Hans, His face is on  photos from Hamburg to Sweden last week. At a gas station in Malmo. "

"Maybe he didn't tell you yet that he won a teddy bear in Copenhagen Tivoli last week."

Marcus had been thumbing through Rashid phone, He held up a photo on it to Rashid face and said. "This looks like you and your family. A selfie, even has Wembley in the distance."

Rashid nodded, and started to look tearful.

Marcus continued. "Looking at this picture, there's a nice lady and little girl in this picture. Maybe Hans got the teddy bear for her. But I guess it doesn't matter, because when you and your family comes out of various prisons she will be too old for teddy bears."

" And with what I know about women's prisons she'll be too old for much. " Marcus continued. "Of course I understand that they kill people here for many crimes. Especially here in the special control region.  So I can hand you over to my local colleagues. I don't think they like people who commit crimes against kids, especially not when we tell them a few nasty stories. So Rashid, I think now, if you want to stay alive, you can help us."

He paused, and could see Rashid struggling.

Oleg, thinking quickly, said. "If you prefer, not to help us, we will just leave you here. Of course first we'll tell your boss ,that we gave you all eight palettes  and you've stolen four of them. So then you have real problems, I'm not sure which is then best for you, the police or your bosses. You won't stand a chance."

Marcus said. "My advice would be help us, if you ever want to see your kid again, we're the only people who can help you stay alive ."

Rashid was by now, shaking, shallow breathing and almost vomiting again. "I'll do it. I'll do it."

Oleg said. "Where's the cargo going to tonight?" and got a surprising answer, which on later reflection he didn't quite understand.  Rashid. "I have trucks outside ,they take down to the fish dock, then they float them onto a boat."

Oleg said." OK, Let's get the first four palettes back out on to the plane, and we can take you back to Wembley if you want."

Rashid looked alarmed and said. "We can't do that, we pay the customs import people here already. We tell them the import is diving weights.  If we want to take out back to the plane will be different customs men's, export ones, they will look inside. They know what gold look like. Then we all in big shit."

Marcus said. "Hold on. Oleg can I have a word please?"

Taking Oleg to one side he said, "Just to check we're handling this right. Are you authorised or trained for any of this."

Oleg said, "No I'm just winging it really, although I have been here before."

Marcus said. "Sure you've been here before, so have I, but not like this. Right.  Authorisation is not my problem, and you have a good idea, up to a point.  But I am trained for this stuff. So are my guys and we are with you 100%, but we need to check some things first. Especially if we can't take the bloody gold back to the plane- which sounds like a genuine problem to me."

"So, one. How many people is this guy with tonight ? Here and outside with the trucks whatever."

" Then, two. What's the plan for delivery, when and where?"

Oleg started to speak. "but....." Marcus raised a hand and said, "In a word Oleg, shut up. For now."

" Whoever is expecting delivery, may well be just outside those doors. They are expecting $350 million of gold on 8 pallets. So apart from being a tad disappointed that they've been short delivered. It's quite likely they will be so pissed off that they shoot the messenger or at least the delivery man."

" It's very likely they can see the plane only unloaded 4 pallets through the fence. So they may already be pissed off and only waiting to see if the rest is coming. Like chummy here asked-where's the rest?"

"Whatever the answers are for all those questions, once we've sorted those minor matter out. How the hell do we get out of here, without spending five  years in a Moroccan shit hole before the UK powers that be get us out? That's if they bother."

Oleg said. "Got it. 100%. And thank you."

Marcus went on. "But, I do agree leaving a few hundred million dollars of gold behind is not too clever. We've just got to build a plan, if there is one to be had."

He turned to Rashid. "Don't forget we know all about Wembley."

"We know about France, our girls, your girls, teddy bears and all. So I suggest you just do what we all need. How many people outside and do they know what we were expected to unload?"

Rashid, sniveling and breathing heavily. "There's five trucks out there with drivers, they all friends from my brother. They think we're collecting dive equipment to go to the docks, same we tell the customs. And now Mr. Hans say he wait there ."

Marcus said, "OK, let's see if we can exit towards the trucks, if there's a problem, we forget the gold and do a runner back to the plane. They've only got pistols as far as I can see, and they will be surprised as hell. " Oleg finished the sentence, " And  if we do get outside then we make plan B."

The whole team walked through into the freight hall, Sweating.  Marcus, standing very close to Rashid who had also become very sweaty.

We all sweated even more, when one of the uniformed Customs guys asked questions.

Some more Arabic from Rashid, and surprisingly then a question to Oleg in English. " Says eight but only four here."

Oleg smiled a lot and said, "Bloody bosses ,they give the wrong stuff. Tomorrow they bring four more, we pay you again."

Nodding at Rashid, "I go and tell his boss outside, and very bad. More bad I miss the football on TV tonight."

Tension diverted, English and Spanish Soccer  as ever the magic calming agent, although possibly helped by the thought of a second pay day for the customs guys.

After some discussions involving of course all the usual subjects, Manchester United, Leicester, Barcelona, Real Madrid, Rooney, Beckham, hands were shaken. Oleg and Marcus palming $100 bills into the many eager hands of the customs and freight men, and they were all waved through.

Followed by the tractor smoking slightly as it pulled four pallet trailers, and the almost smoking ,and nearly hysterical Rashid with his no less nervous new best friends. Who stood very close to him at all time.

Outside. No sign of Hans. In fact no sign of anyone.

The airport concourse was deserted, except for a few hopeful taxis. Presumably waiting for the last incoming flight.

Rashid waved the slow pulling tractor over to some trucks parked at the back of the parking area.

Oleg said to Marcus, "Let's get him to call Hans." Handing Rashid his phone, they held close, whilst he called. No answers.

He tried again. Rashid, "Him not answer me."

Marcus said to Rashid. " Now no boss here. I think we take the four pallets back inside and put it back on the plane again?"

Rashid said, "You can, if you want, *but I really did tell you true*. Mr. Hans he pay the customs guy to let it through, and did tell them it's dive equipment. If we go back in they will for sure open and see what it is. That's really not good for you, or me. Near here in Mauretania is many small gold mines so they know gold here when they see it."

Marcus said. "Oleg. I think Mr. Rashid here, to save his own skin has spoken some wise words. Regardless of how much Hans paid the customs guys, it's nothing compared to the value of what we've got here. Lets get out of here, lie up somewhere and, like you said make a plan B. As Oleg nodded in mute agreement Marcus continued. "Rashid. Good.  Keep two trucks , pay the rest. You have money?"

Rashid nodded and produced a wad of dollars and went to speak with the drivers. Two of Marcus' men standing close.

Marcus continued, "Oleg, if your phone's till working, tell Rory to report what we're doing, tell Frank to get away, pronto."

Shortly after they heard and then saw their ride home taking off, with $US 160 million of gold still on board.

The two trucks they had kept, were just smallish flatbeds, used for shifting cars or freight.  They had  small hoists on them, and with considerable lurching creaking and shoving from the team they were loaded, two pallets on each truck.

Oleg, having tipped the tractor guy, who seemed more than happy, found Marcus having a conversation in Spanish with the two truck drivers.

He reported to Oleg. "They say about twenty minutes back, there was a westerner who came out of the terminal and got into a white Toyota Amazon and drove off."

" The guy says, he only noticed because the guy was running, and foreigners don't run in this heat."

"He also says, he and the other drivers, have no idea where we're going, they just know someone who knows Rashid's brother, who paid them to come here. Which can be quite good, looks as if Rashid's not telling porkies," Marcus continued, "Right, what worries me is that maybe Hans has gone for reinforcements , so lets get out of here pronto, split up between the trucks."

" I'll go in the truck with Rashid, we go along a bit towards the fish dock, find a quietish place and make a plan."

### 51.Castelnaudary France. Saturday/Sunday. Around midnight July 2nd. Very early on the 3rd. Tears on the parade ground:

*No words can describe.....*

As the engine of our chopper shut down, and just the swoosh of the rotors slowing for about a minute it was calm.

Then from a distance and suddenly with us the peace was shattered by the noisy arrival of two more helicopters, rather plusher style.

As soon as the rotors had slowed, the doors opened from which hurtled Charlie Haeggqvist and his wife, then Andre on his own helping David and Hiroshi and their wives down the steps.

On the parade ground landing place and then in the mess hall there were floods of tears, and a lot of breath stopping hugging.

Those least emotional were the three young Swedish girls, who were sitting on the floor with Magnus, Joel and one of Joel's guys still in camo kit.

"Hi Grandad, Grandma. Hey mum can we go with these guys and look at the soldiers stuff, they say ,they've got a real assault course with lights and they say we can go on it."

Britt and Anna looked concerned, and Francois who had been watching all this said, "It's good to let them be kids, you've kept the strain from them and I think of all of you they will be the ones best able to cope and carry on normally."

" Mind you I assume normal is not every day they get to ride in helicopters at night with a bunch of camoe'd soldiers. They will be fine with my guys." So taking a very happy Magnus with them, the three ,with Joel and his guy, exited the room.

Without the need, for a while at least, of not letting the kids see how upset they were, then the real tears flowed. From all of us.

Champagne was brought in and opened, coffees were delivered and mostly ignored, whilst I explained to Charlie what at happened at the Farm, in particular about the bravery of the bomb disposal squad.

Charlie said, "Can we thank them."

To which the commander replied, "You are very kind, but that is their skill and their duty."

He then discovered that you don't say no to old man Haeggqvist, and shortly after, some slightly embarrassed looking men now in tracksuits, no face paint were ushered in to receive very sincere and much relieved thanks from all the parents. Translations by Andre who was holding tight to Brigitte, who was talking on the phone in French, presumably to her mother.

With a clatter from another helicopter, Chris Todd and Barry arrived, so the hugging and tears, from all of us , started all over again, on the phone we could hear a party starting in the Singapore office.

Squeeze, "Champagne breakfast here boss, if it wasn't that we don't know where Oleg is I'd close the office this afternoon."

After about an hour as things calmed down, I said. "Well it's now almost two in the morning. I am sorry to push you but we need to make a plan for the next few days. I didn't really dare do that earlier. But I do need to know, as we have to keep an eye on you. We don't have all the bad guys yet."

David and Hiroshi said, "I think we return home to Asia very soon tomorrow. " At which both Tamiko and May said, "Only after we see our horses." Brigitte piped up, "Good plan."

So, somewhat unwillingly, on the part of the parents, a plan was made for the girls to return to the Geneva Hotel for a few days to figure things out. The parents all looked very concerned and nervous, one of the Legion doctors stressing again, "I understand you come from Hong Kong and Korea. So getting back to the home will be good, as it will be very different to here. There could still be many weeks of reactions after the joy of today has gone. For you, as well as the girls, but I am sure you can have local people to help. Please do see them. We know all this kind of thing, and they can help."

David Lim, instantly, on the surface at least, back on his usual good form said quietly to me, nodding at the French doctor. "Medical knowledge excellent, geography, please try harder."

Chris , said to Hiroshi and David. "I've got a feeling that the boss and my missus will want me back in Asia pronto as well. So if I can come with you on one of the plane's that would be good."

Hiroshi said, "One problem Chris."

Everyone stopped. Hiroshi, " Now you and me will have to carry our own golf clubs." Apart from this starting all the tears again, I had a feeling things were already on the mend.

I said, "About the next days and then weeks ahead. This is not going to happen again. It took a lot of planning for the bad guys to know where you were and when they could do what they did. But we need to keep a careful eye on things."

Barry said, "Oleg's going after the rest in Southern Morocco, including the German guy who took the pictures of your houses."

Francois said. " Ladies, gentlemen, I have some experience, once this immediate joy is over, sometime tonight, sometime in the future, a reaction will happen. So please do what our medics said, and get expert help."

I continued. "In Geneva, Barry and I will have a very discrete team to keep close to you 24/7 and when you take the girls to the school to see the horses. Also Rewan's wife is going to spend a week in a nursing home there with her sister, so he will be happy to be around with you all. We can talk about long term plans later."

Re-enter three boisterous kids and a somewhat shattered looking Magnus. Camo smudges on their faces. " Mama, grand mama , you have to come and see what they've got here." " Real soldiers let us climb the wall and do the zip line. Dad couldn't do it. One guy said we could fire some guns but Joel and Lars said it was too dark, and anyway we had to ask you first. Come on ,come on."

It turned out that Lars, was one of Joel's two Swedish employees, ex Legionnaires both. As the mothers, and their grand ma wearily climbed out of their chairs, saying, " But its two in the morning. " One of the Kids said, "Grandma it's not, it's two in the night time, and can we all go to 'Slide and Splash,' tomorrow ?"

This produced some panicked glances between all the Swedes. Joel and his mate ,sensing a need for the adults to speak together, said, "Come on you three. Let's see if we can hide and then your Mama and Grandpa can come and see if they can find you," and then had to run as the kids rushed out of the door.

Britt looked at Anna, "You know, with all that's been going on, and not wishing to dream to much, I hadn't given any thought to what we do next. Returning home to Sweden was first in my mind, but it seems as if the children just viewed all this as part of their holiday. May be we should go back to Portugal."

She looked at Anna, and Anna, at Britt. Britt said, "I think I will be fine, I'm not sure about being at the Portugal house, but I guess if Magnus is there."

Barry cut in. "That's very usual, but in reality you will be nervous where ever you are for a long time. You'll panic when the kids are one minute late from school, or just out of your sight."

He said, "About Portugal, I've got three people in there already now, and it looks to me as if Joel's got a couple of experienced guys, Swedish speaking  who could fit in with the family especially the kids. So they won't even realise that they have close protection. "

"I'm sure we can find accommodation for them very locally and they will set up a 24/7 watch on both houses. The only thing you will need to do, is to at least tell them where you are going each day. After a while you can feel you want more or less protection."

Anna said. "Actually that sounds good to me. I guess we have to fix these demons sometime. So Portugal it is." Britt nodded.

Lars re-appeared and said 'Excuse me, but young people are getting a bit impatient out here." He then, considered who he was talking to and repeated his words in Swedish. All the Swedes went out to find the kids.

Hiroshi and David with Shoko and Peggy temporarily disentangling themselves from Tamiko and May came to Barry and I, Hiroshi saying, "I cannot thank you ever enough for all you did."

David grasped my hand and said, " That goes for us. We can never never forget. We look forward to thanking you properly when we meet at home soon, and not forgetting Oleg and Squeeze and the rest of the team."

I tried to be glib and British, but I had to wipe my eyes a little, "It's a great and happy result. Mind you I wasn't sure when I took this job on that we'd be declaring war on the US Navy."

Barry grinned and said, " Yeah ,we still have to see how that plays out when I get home."

David said. "Barry, I've been thinking about that. Any problems in the US and we'll have jobs for you with us."

"Hang on," I said, " One minute we do a great job, and the next we lose a key client to HIM!" More laughter.

David. " No, No, no, I didn't mean that. May be you guys will work together in future, there's a lot of business out there."

A few hours later at Faro Airport, Portugal as the sun came up inland, holiday makers waiting for their return flights to the cool of Northern Europe, could observe a raggle taggle band of Swedes disembarking from a largish executive jet.

Charlie and Amelie, Magnus, Britt and Anna and three very tired children. Two being carried by a couple of fit looking 'new best friends.'

Having been introduced to the new, 'security guys,' Jose Seremenho, who had come to meet them with several taxis, said to Magnus, "Your villa's all ready. After I woke her up with the good news, Ermalinda never stopped weeping, so I think the floors are well washed."

Negotiations then started with the kids, about the length of sleep required before anyone could even think of going to 'Slide and Splash'.

.....In a rented Villa in South Western France, the fans rotated, empty bottles and glasses littered the table under the pergola. It was a short night, but the occupants slept well. .... Very Well.

\*\*\*\*\*\*\*\*\*\*\*\*\*\*\*\*\*\*\*\*\*\*\*

## 52. Meanwhile: Sunday July 3rd. 1.00 am. All is quiet in Dahkla town. Western Sahara. Dark: *All that glitters.............*

Using a mix of Rashid's Arabic and Marcus's Spanish, they instructed the truck drivers to take them towards the fishing port and find a quiet place to park.

As they left the airport, it became clear to the team on the back of the trucks that there were quite a few well kept Army and Navy buildings around. Presumably well stocked with uniformed personnel.

After a short drive through the still empty streets, the front truck led them between some biggish gates  and round the back of some buildings into a parking lot. Marcus reported, "The driver says it's closed, used to be a fish canning factory."

Marcus took the drivers to one side and gave each, five $100 bills. With some words from Rashid, but mainly with quite good Spanish from the truckies, Marcus's finger on his lips, and a friendly grin was enough. "There's a lot more to come for you every day if you want the work."

The drivers seemed more than keen.

Stepping back to Rashid, "Right." said Marcus. "English this time. What was your plan?  Don't forget, send us bloody  wrong and you and your family will be the big losers."

Rashid's words tumbled out. "With Mr. Hans , I am supposed to go out on the fishing port."

" Not on the end one,  on the side dock, there's a fisherman with a big pile of stuff that I make yesterday with him. When we there we unload the pallets, fix them with what I make yesterday and lower them into the sea using the crane on this truck, and float them out to a big boat."

Marcus pulled Rashid to his feet and said, "How the f*** do you expect me to believe that shit."

Rashid, shaking visibly, said, "Give me my phone, I show you, I not make a call but can show you." Having his phone, and with Marcus poised to snatch it back, Rashid came up with a picture and some English print.

It was an advert from a German yachting magazine for '*Auto-inflate Life Vests. Buoyancy rating 75 kg.each.*'

Rashid said. "Mr. Hans ship these here last week from Germany. I collect them yesterday and put 25 in each one of eight cargo nets, like these."

 He touched one of the pallets. "Today we must fix one net very good onto each pallet and drop them in water. Then the life bag blow up with air when they get wet, and they float Then we get my friend fishing boat pull them out to the big boat."

"We take out to big boat because, if we have big boat come in here on the dock, the soldiers on the dock check everything go on, come off. Always looking for money. They not usually come near fish dock as only small boats there. Smell bad there as well. If they do, only cost small money."

Marcus, looked at Oleg, and said, " Make's sense actually. We used life jackets once to rescue several tons of kit we lost off a river ferry."

Marcus asked Rashid, "Where's the boat?"

Rashid scrolled his phone and said. "Look it's that one, I take this picture yesterday. I've never been on there, but yesterday, they come in and get fuel."

" I meet Mr. Hans at the airport and take him there, he work on that boat before. I think he a diver. He give me money for airport people. The boat wait, is not out in the sea but near inside."

Oleg had been trying to call the office, but couldn't now get a phone signal. Marcus said, "Try this sat phone." Within a minute or two was apparently talking to Miss Stanton.

Marcus, took the two Spanish speaking drivers to one side, and after a lot of hand waving and chat, using the lift on the best of the trucks they unloaded two of the pallets onto the ground.

He sent two of the team with the driver in the empty truck to, "have a sniff around the situation on the fish dock."

Oleg had what seemed to be a fairly one sided conversation. Having completed the call he beckoned Marcus out of Rashid's earshot and said. "Firstly, you were right, about planning the exit route. Seems that this whole area of Western Sahara is still big trouble. "

"After a years of fighting for independence, the UN and The Moroccans with some kind of deal with the Mauritanian's are keeping the peace."

"Now it has got worse again, despite the world telling them to move on through the UN , because of the likelihood of oil, the Moroccans and probably the Mauritanians, aren't moving. So if we get in the shit, there's not many can help us. She's investigating who has good contacts here, but said, 'Don't hold your breath waiting for a pick up flight'."

Marcus said, "Seems to me, that an exit via the airport is a no for many reasons. Not the least of which is our cargo, I'm sure Rashid's right ,once they get a sniff of its value, we're all toast."

"Overland is possible, to the north. Long way, good road but loads of military checkpoints, and we can't be lucky all the time. Again there's the value of the cargo to think of."

" Even then in the north we'd be getting a boat or a plane out of the country from Agadir or Marrakesh. Might be easier than here but I'm not sure, and not with the cargo for sure."

"There's the road round the top of the bay, and then south to the dodgy border to Mauretania. If I remember from what people said then, it can be done, there's five kilometers of no mans land, and those land mines and stuff around."

Marcus continued. "What to do? As you got us in this shit, I think we'll call them Oleg's Plans A and plan B."

"Plan A . Grabbing the kidnappers has evaporated with this Hans having gone missing."

" Unless he's gone to get re-enforcements. Which for that amount of money is the what I would be doing."

"Plan B . Rashid saying they were getting the gold out to that boat, suggests they were going to take it somewhere. From Rashid's picture it looks sea going."

" So I suggest. We take a look at the boat. It may have the kidnappers on it, which would be a bonus, and whilst we hold on to the gold it may be a route out. "

"If the boat's a no go, we dump the gold in the sea, noting the spot, and try our luck overland."

Oleg started to speak, but just then the truck returned.

Martin reporting. "You said have a sniff around, you're not joking, bloody fish stink, I surprised you can't bloody smell it from here ".

"Just as Rashid said. Lot of geezers mending nets, there's piles of shit on the dock, loads of reefer trucks. I guess they're waiting for fishing boats to come and unload."

"I can see that boat, about 150 meters off shore, slightly to the south. Must be it, it's got lights, and paint and that's rare here. Looks like a smart deep sea trawler. Lots of communications kit on top."

Marcus, gathered the guys and explained the options, and the plan. One of the South Africans, Piet, grinned and said, "If there's a real chance the bad guys have re-grouped, I think we need to control that boat before we consider taking the load out there. We'll be low in the water in a slow fishing boat. Sitting ducks. "

Marcus said, "Sure. Agree 100%."

Oleg said, nodding at Rashid, "By the way he's right 25 life jackets each rated for 75 kilos will very easily float 1250 kilos. So 25 jackets on each pallet should be be a goer, they will even float if some jackets fail."

"About getting control of the boat. What about windsurfing out there."

" From first light depending on the wind, this bay will be full of boards of all kinds, right down to the entrance to the open sea at the point. We windsurf out and grab the boat. I can surf OK."

After a few moments thought, Marcus said. "At last, an Oleg plan that could work. In fact it could look better than a fishing boat full of blokes. There's me, Piet and Mica can windsurf well and Martin a bit."

He went on. " When I was here 18 months ago there was a good board shop somewhere in town and a few stalls renting stuff out by the various hotels and beaches. With a handful of cash we should be able to get something."

He checked his watch. "I really want to get moving, I don't trust the opposition not to be re-grouping and come back. "

He continued, "The sunrise prayers will be in a couple of hours, about 5.30 and everyone gets moving just before then. Let's get some rest and I'll see what I can find board wise about 5.00."

Martin said. "I kipped on the plane, you guys, get some shut eye. I'll watch these three. Although I don't think the drivers here are going anywhere, they're up for more dosh, but Rashid I'm not sure."

Rashid, interrupted and said. "Don't forget I speak English. Mister I am not going anywhere, I stay with you and you get us all out of here. My family are in England."

Marcus and Piet left with the empty truck well before the 5.30 call to prayer. They were back within an hour , truck, now piled high with windsurf boards. Sails rolled around masts but flapping wildly.

Not only the boards, but supplies of really good coffees, hot bread and sweet cakes. "The board shop was closed, but a guy on one of the stalls was already washing down sails and stuff. He was dead happy with the weeks rental for four boards. "

" As he assumes we're tourists he also said, with the cross bay morning wind here there's a good café on the beach on the far side of the bay that gets a lot of business. It's in a village called El Argoub."

"He also said, it's really busy with both windsurfers and kite surfers out there in the mornings, and if we have any problems, as only the schools have safety boats, plenty of fishing boats lurk about keeping their eyes open for tip opportunities if they help someone. So it actually all looks quite good for us to blend in and not to be noticed out there on the water."

Marcus said, "The driver says the gatehouse at the fishing pier will be fully manned now, so he says, put two boards on each truck, and you guys sit around on them and this one, and he's sure no one will stop us. They are used to seeing boards and boarders all over town and on all the beaches."

Martin said, "I think surprise for getting on the boat will be the key, Rashid hasn't a clue how many people on that boat. I'd guess at least 8 or 10. Seems to me what you do, is sail around a bit near the boat, and come up on them from the other side when they're looking at Oleg and the guys getting near in the fishing boat."

Piet said," Thanks for nothing Mart, for sure, the wind will co-operate and we'll all leap off the f***ing boards holding our guns in our teeth. You think I'm bloody Jack Sparrow."

Oleg said "Hang on a sec. If when you get out there the boat seems a no go, for any reason, and we do sink the gold somewhere in the middle. Just on the off chance we can come back another day and get it. We can then try that village on the other side for a truck to take us to the Mauretania border. It's at least a couple of hours quicker from over there."

Having managed to re-load the two pallets, despite the weight almost killing the on board hoist, the journey to the fish dock took just a few minutes.

At the entrance, Marcus's driver in the first truck, stopped and leaning down out of the cab had a conversation with a group of soldiers or at least uniformed guards.

With much laughing and gesturing behind. You didn't need Arabic to get the picture. "Crazy foreigners, going out on the water in the sun. Look at them, and they are paying me, so good day. Praise be to Allah."

We were waved through with much waving back from us. Martin muttered to me, "Clever move that, now they won't bother to come out looking at what we're doing."

Weaving around many parked big trucks, some closed with fridges running, others door open obviously waiting to be loaded. Near the outer end of the side jetty following Rashid's instructions we stopped. "

A youngish Arab in shorts, jumped out of a beaten up Land Rover and greeted Rashid, with a fast flow of Arabic, presumably Moroccan. After a few minutes, Rashid explained. "He says in the night time Hans come here, and the boss lady, she's Chinese ,she come from the boat. My friend he listen, but they speak English he think. He not understand but said she shout and angry."

" They go back to the boat. They tell the driver in the big Toyota go somewhere and he drive away, only him."

Oleg said, "Sounds like they got the message about the girls being rescued, or had people looking through the Airport fence like you said and saw us lot. If Hans and her are on that boat we'd better try and get there pronto."

Marcus said. " It's a bit odd the boat's there still if they have decided to make a run for it, and we don't know who's watching us now. So you're right let's go. At least we do look like windsurf party right now."

Whilst the truck guys lowered the four pallets on to the dock side, we investigated the pile of stuff under the tarps. *Brand new, self inflating lifejackets, uninflated but primed to inflate the second they hit water.* Well packed in strong looking cargo nets, seemed to be twenty five in each batch. Plenty of spare rope.

Having lashed the bags of lifejackets to the cargo nets on each pallet containing the heavy gold. Trusting to Oleg's calculations about flotation power we only used four of the available eight nets prepared by Rashid.

Martin said, "I just hope the net bags are big and strong enough when all twenty five of those lifejackets inflate all together when they hit the water. I don't fancy diving in that shit to bring it all up if it sinks."

Piet sent two of his guys to the end of the dock to rig the windsurfers. One of them called back. "Water's cleaner here thank god."

Marcus, told the driver to lower a pallet down into the water.

But after a lot of Spanish, and some translations from Rashid, it seemed this couldn't be done. "The truck she will fall over into water, can only unload very near the truck, not swing it out away from truck."

We all tried shoving the load towards the dock side, but got nowhere. Then the driver, threw down some iron bars or tubes, and with the hoist, raised the pallet a little allowing us to slide the bars underneath. Then with the miracle of rollers and leverage we heaved the load over the side. As it kind of scrabbled slid down the dock wall there was no satisfying splash, just a slurp and it disappeared into the murky water.

Peering down, there was more than enough time for some, D***s B***s, Sh*ts and F***'s in a variety of languages, before ,as all the lifejackets auto-inflated with a quite a force, and the whole bundle surfaced.

With no time to waste they did the same with the other three. One, was easier to move, and floated higher in the water.

Marcus said, " Gary, Jonny, Oleg, get down there with Rashid and the boat guy and get going, it's going to be slow. Oh hang on a minute, "and he grabbed a few of the unused lifejackets and chucked them down in to the boat. He then went to the two drivers and told them. "We come back later. I give you another $500 now. You not tell people about what we do and when I come back I have more work for each of you."

Their enthusiastic reaction with many thanks Arabic style, prompted Bad Luck to say, " Not that it's their party, but it looks like all their Christmases have come at once. Or not if you know what I mean."

With a burst of predictable stinking black diesel smoke, the fishing boat eased away from the dock with almost 5000 kilos of gold bobbing along behind. Ten minutes and we were well clear of the dock and aiming slightly out into the bay towards the boat. Or, now we could appreciate its size, more accurately, the ship.

A few minutes later the four windsurfers shot past, and then circled round a few times. Oleg noticed that the guys sports bags were worn now backpack style, with arms through the handles and asked Gary, "what happens if the guns get wet, do they work."

"Reasonably" was the answer, "the ammos waterproof. We usually put condoms on the end of the barrel which helps, at least until you fire the first shot. We used to call those condoms, terrorist birth control, but I guess that right now boarding a boat we're the terrorists. At least as far as those on board are concerned."

As they were about 100 meters from the boat and suddenly the windsurfers all made a dash for the stern of the now quite large vessel.

Gary, who had binoculars said, "looks like a stern trawl net ramp and some steps." With no sounds of gunfire or similar, Gary instructed Rashid, "Tell him to take us to the back of the ship."

With Piet waving us in, and giving a thumbs up we came alongside, with some difficulty Bad Luck and I jumped on board, Gary saying, "I'll take care here until you are ready.

Lying on the deck, face down, cable ties on their arms: Six people.

Magnus, gun in hand said. "We searched the whole ship and that's the lot, no sign of the other two. Oleg, It's time for you to tell them a kidnap story on behalf of the British Government."

He heaved the various figures around and propped them sitting up against the ships rail. Four Asians and two westerners. "Who speaks English ?

"Five heads nodded.

Oleg, doing his best to look authoritative addressed them, " OK listen up. I work for the UK security services. Some kids and women were kidnapped in Europe. Last night they were all freed and we're here to detain the kidnappers. But if the Chinese lady and the German man are not here it seems they have done a runner."

"That means the Moroccan Police only have you to blame for the terrible crime of kidnapping kids. We understand the sentence they usually give, is the death penalty. But given the state of most prisons here you'll probably welcome death  by then."

"So right now, you've got five minutes to explain who you are."

One of the westerners said, "I'm South African. I don't think we need five minutes. Firstly, she's Japanese not Chinese. If the German guy is the one I think you mean, he's the ex captain of this ship. I never met him till last night."

" This morning early, she emptied the safe, took her bag, and left with the two Russkies, both computer guys, that worked on here and the ex Captain. They left in the rib, to go over there at first light." He gestured in the direction of El Argoub, of windsurfing beach cafe fame.

" Second. Me? I guess like you two, he nodded at Piet and Mica, a couple of months ago I was hired as a freelancer, as Captain of this 'fish survey vessel'"

He heaved himself a little more upright and continued. " You can find the adverts for the job if you look. It's chartered from a pretty standard charter company in Cyprus."

"Thirdly, Kidnapping? New to me, and sounds bad."

"I was hired, because she said she was researching fish stocks. Mind you given all the hours that 'Boris and Brainski' spent with the computers and satellite kit, I suspect what they were trying to catch was data from other ships around here to learn about local oil prospecting chances."

"Fourthly. These guys," He gestured at the others sitting on the deck by him.

" Miguel, the Spanish guy seems to have been with the boat for about a year. He's from Las Palmas and with a lot of Spanish being spoken round here, and in the fishing business I suspect that why he got the job. He's O.K."

"The Two Koreans and two Filipinos. For sure they know nothing. We only picked them up in Las Palmas ten days ago. I found them and hired them from an agency. The others she had were useless. Filipino's are cook and steward. The two Koreans, good engineers, really good."

He looked at Oleg, and then Marcus and the others. "Now having told you all that. F***ing untie me, or get off my ship. I'm hungry."

Marcus said. " Give me a couple of minutes on that. As we don't want to be accused of piracy would you like to volunteer to take us all out of Moroccan waters as soon as we can?"

The South African, " Yes and No.

" Given that the owner's gone as far as I can tell, my answer is. Yes, as away from a Moroccan prison sounds or any kind of grief sounds good. "

"No, whilst I'm tied up."

Marcus started to speak and he heard some shouting from Gary, still in the fishing boat. Marcus looked over the side and said. "Got it. OK."

He said to the still bound tied up South African. "It seems there's a Moroccan Navy boat that's coming into port past us, and there's a lot of eyes looking at us. So how about, until we get to know you, we get you up to the bridge. I keep your legs loosely shackled, but free your arms so we can get out of here."

The Captain grinned and said, "Good by me."

" But you'll need to free the Koreans if we want engines, and the Filipinos if we want food, and Miguel if we want the anchors up and stowed".

Piet started to cut them free and Marcus said, before we go. "Three things."

" One. Do we need a pilot to get us out, or permission to sail.?"

The Captain. "Good point, but no. Not from here, only if we go on the dock."

"Two. What range have we got with the fuel that's on board and where can we go?"

The Captain said, "We bunkered yesterday, so depending on speed and weather almost 3000 kliks. Bit less if we get out of here full tilt as soon as we hit the open sea. The Canary Island are easy to get to , part of your EC market, and," with a nod at Oleg, "I guess friendly to him, if he is what he says. U.K. Security."

Marcus. "Thirdly We've got four loads floating here. We need to pull on board up the trawl ramp."

The Captain, stood up, and said. "Hold on. If that's f***ing drugs I'd rather be taking my chances with the Moroccans as a kidnapper."

Piet said. "Got that, bra. Not drugs, guaranteed. We'll cut into each of the packs when we can get to them and show you. By the way, what's your name? "

The Captain, "It's Leo, and also by the way, there's a Kalashnikov in the wheelhouse. I tell you this because I wonder if those Koreans see me tied up still they will assume we've been pirated and do something to stop the engines or rescue me."

Marcus stepped forward, cut Leo free, and shook him by the hand, and with a nod from Marcus  Piet went and unloaded the Kalashnikov.

Leo, massaging his now untied hands, turned to the Koreans and the other crew, said. "All OK. These good guys now. The boss lady go, so these guys pay all of us now. I am happy they pay me and I pay you 100%. And bonus for all of us when we finish. They come on with guns because they look for the boss lady. But they OK."

Big smiles from the freed Koreans and Filipinos. As ordered, a few minutes later the engines started. It then took about thirty minutes with various winches to heave the palettes on board.

Marcus said to the Captain. "What we hauled on board is the ransom in gold which the Japanese Lady and German were expecting from the kidnapping. There's about $160,000,000."

" Oh yes, Oleg is indeed Brit security. I guess he'll be able to rustle up some official protection and papers for us fairly pronto. We were really hoping to grab the kidnappers."

Leo, whistled and spoke. "For that amount I wouldn't be surprised if they haven't gone far yet and are figuring out how to find it and get it back."

" If she was bringing the old captain back on board with the gold I have nasty feeling that I might have ended at the bottom of the sea. Miguel says he was a nasty bastard.  I tell you what, if we think they may be lurking around here somewhere, why don't I send her a message saying the shipment's on board. What do I do now? "

"If they come out alone you grab 'em...if they come out team handed we'll leave, full speed. If it looks manageable  we'll play it by ear."

Oleg said,  "It sounds brill to me, It's up to Marcus."

At that moment, Gary appeared and said. "Well I have good news,  bad news and stupid news."

"First of all boss, the stupid bit. I've lost Rashid."

" He obviously slipped over the side when I was lashing down the four loads. He had a life jacket on, so I suspect he's on his mates fishing boat now."

Gary said, "I've still got his phone as I didn't trust him, and anyway he was so shit scared about Moroccan Prison I'm sure he's not going to say anything in town. Its pain that we lost him, as I guess he might have had stuff to tell you."

We had a discussion about looking for him, but with no small boat available, the fleeing owner and her team having taken it, we decided against it.

Gary. "More news. The good news is there's three pallets of this," and he heaved a 12 kilo gold bar on the table. Despite having been immersed in sea water it still glowed very gold.

Leo said. "Seen some of that in my time, that's real money."

Gary went on, "Bad news is. The other pallet is full of these." and he dumped a rough and rusty lump of iron on the table. Roughly the same size as the gold bar, but of course about one third as heavy.

"Explains why that lot floated higher out of the water."

Oleg said , "and why the airplane was unbalanced, I think I need to call the office."

Leo and Marcus agreed ." Wait a little till we're out at sea. You really don't know who else is listening here."

Marcus continued, "On the subject of listening, let's see if the Japanese lady over there is checking her phone, and actually as we've got Rashid's phone, we know he called the Hans guy from the dock, so we could send a similar message to that number from Rashid's phone."

Leo sent a text message to the Japanese lady:

*L.Your expected delivery four heavy pallets winched on board from a fishing boat. Please advise what I should* do next. Leo.

To Hans : *Sms. Have four pallets on boat now. I wait you here yes?"*

Whilst we waited Leo gave various instructions and Miguel, with help from Piet got the anchor sorted, and we started to move, very slowly just holding our position against the tide current and the wind.

Leo, "As I said, I'm hungry, seems to me that we should eat whilst we wait."

Watched by Mica, the two Filipinos produced a great looking lunch and laid it out on the deck table. We'd all started early early, now it was only ten in the morning so maybe it was breakfast. Whatever, we were all starving.

Piet was sitting in the deckhouse talking to the Captain. Not surprisingly in the small world of soldiers and sailors for hire they found they had several mutual acquaintances.

Marcus said." I've checked the whole boat again, I've locked the ladies and the Russians cabins as I guess we'll need fingerprints and stuff. There's no phones, computers or anything there that I can see. I guess there's a safe somewhere."

The Captain laughed, and said, " You're sitting on it. It's only got all the boat docs, and the crew papers in it, that's all."

He went on. " Computers, they're all in the deck office. She spent all day and all night in there with Boris or Brainski."

Magnus said, "I think we should only give it another 30 minutes, and then start moving out to sea. I can't imagine she would dare contact the Moroccan Navy but you never know."

Leo said, "On the subject of the Navy, any navy in fact, if you shift your arses, I'll get to the safe and get the log book out. If I record in there that I put out a distress call, electrics all failed, no control , danger of drifting ashore and stuff. Then, there's a reason for me letting you all on here and there's a good reason we're moving off shore, away from danger if the weather changes."

"So if someone comes looking because Mrs. Japan says we've nicked her boat I'm legally safe and so are you lot. That's safe, as in the real world. Not sure about Morocco and around here though."

As Leo dealt with the log, Oleg said, "I'm going to try and check the computer room. I've got to be uber careful, because I can't even turn stuff on, if everything is password protected and I blow it, they could auto delete. "

"But I'll see what I can do."

About thirty minutes later he came rocketing out of the deck house, holding some papers, and said to Magnus. "Now I do need the phone and it's truly urgent, this may save some lives. I need to call now regardless of who is listening."

By mutual agreement, with no response from the Japanese lady or the one we knew as Hans, we gave up on our 'capture the baddies,' plan and with Leo at the wheel we moved, slowly at first, towards the open sea.

Using Magnus's sat-phone, Oleg called the office and Squeeze found me at the villa, clearing up stuff with Barry and planning to drive to the office back in Vence.

Squeeze, "I've got Oleg for you, seems frantic,"

"Hi Dan I'm on a friendly boat. I'll get the skipper to give you our co-ordinates. Speak to Miss Stanton, we could do with an urgent escort or pick up. Two things first. One, minor point , we've got four pallets on the boat but one of them's not gold, just rusty iron. They haven't been out of my sight, so someone's playing games in France."

"Two, main point. Have you got anywhere on the various ship fires, or updates on the threats for tomorrow ."

I responded." Nothing, why?"

Oleg said. "*Right. This needs you to check, quick. I think, the original fire attacks were controlled from Sat phones, connected to the reefer container control and report systems.*"

"The Japanese lady, who probably organised the kidnapping ,has an office on this boat. She was working here with a couple of Russian computer guys. I don't dare turn on their computers, but on her office cabin wall there's a load of yellow 'post it' stickers."

"Some of them have two dates written on them. June 25 and July 4 and with the month written in Russian. Under the dates in biggish letters, again Russian, like it's, ' don't forget!' is the word 'Defrost'."

"On the desk there's a printout of a list of sat phone numbers, with written ship names against them in English. *The first four on the list, are the names of the boats that had the fires.*"

"So my hunch is that, sending a 'defrost' signal, to individual reefers on various ships is somehow triggering some fire bombs, and could do the next lot. "

" Whilst you study the phones, and the codes, at the same time I suggest you need to run a quick check on say two ships from the list as a test.Get them to un-plug a couple of reefers and see what happens."

" If it just 'defrosts' and another fire happens it's easy. If nothing happens then maybe they also need a special code from the sat phone to the reefer phones...or of course I am wrong about it all."

He sat back, looking exhausted.

"Oleg, its Dan, that sounds really possible. Can you email the list of ships and numbers and where are you? "

Oleg said, " I'll figure out a way to e mail you these numbers. Like I said I don't want to kill these computers by turning them on, and so I can't risk the bloody scanner."

Piet, waving his arms at Oleg to get his attention said. "How about photographing the lists with your cell phone, then email the pictures, through the sat phone data port."

Oleg, "Christ, I should have thought of that, I'll do the photos now. Here Dan speak to the skipper about where we are," and made to go in the deck house, but waited till Leo had finished speaking, grabbed the phone and said," Numbers coming in a minute."

" But listen, obviously we are not the only ones with this info, presumably the Japanese Lady or the Russians have got it and could still use it. So we'd better run those tests quick."

"Not only that *but it's the start of July the 4th in Asia in about six hours from now*. I'll send the names and numbers to Squeeze right now."

Piet and Oleg, found a connector and emailed the five page list complete with hand written notes, and added a few pictures of the 'post it' notes. "

"Having transferred the data and explained to Captain Leo, and to Marcus and Piet about some of the background to the shipping threats Oleg said, "Christ, if I'm right, that is a big big fix."

" Mind you, they've got to sort what's Russian, what's English, if they need any other codes and more. I'm going to go and see what else I can figure out but still without turning on their computers in case they self destruct the programs."

Leo said, "Oleg I've got a laptop if it might help, I'll bring it through to the deck office."

Whilst Oleg worked, Rashid's phone came to life with a message, presumably from Hans, saying. *"Am waiting in Al Argoub beach café come and get me. '*

We discussed it, trap or appeal, not sure. We continued on out to sea, but at Magnus's suggestion we sent a response. *"On our way will take a little time. Wait there."*

A couple of hours later a shattered looking Oleg exited the deckhouse office and joined Leo who was looking not very relaxed at the wheel. "I can't figure out any more but I hope they are getting somewhere. I could murder a cup of tea."

He slumped further down in a chair still desperately studying the lists and his notes.

Leo, used the PA and called the galley, then saying, "they're asking green or English Breakfast, Tea."

Oleg, "EBT please, this is very civilised, where are we?"

Sitting up he glanced around, mainly now in open seas, a blur of land astern. Leo said, " It is civilised my friend, and given that it's less than two hours since I told that guy where we are, you have friends in hi places, bra."

Indicating the AIS screen, "look at that, there seems to be several Navy ships on their way to meet us."

He pointed to the screen again, "That looks like a rendezvous with the Royal Navy in an hour or so. Which may be handy as that now looks like someone else's Navy coming up behind. Quite quick."

The unfamiliar sound of Marcus's sat phone surprised them all. Squeeze. "I couldn't get through before, but we got all that stuff a couple of hours back. They think you are on to something honey."

Oleg said, "Can you tell Miss Stanton, to ask the Navy to speed up a bit, we're being chased."

Piet and Marcus gathered behind Leo in the wheelhouse, and he pointed to the radar. Behind them a blip, now nearer and complete with on screen name. Seemed to be Moroccan Navy.

In front of them, about the same distance , two blips, also now with names, seemed to be British as one was called Nelson and the other Cornwall.

Oleg muttered, "Clever that AIS, when it works."

Leo said. "OK. Guys. Just like those shit questions in school."

"The ship behind is about five kliks back and going about 14 knots chasing after us."

"The two in front are about 15 kliks away, but making about 17 knots towards us "

"We're doing 11, away from the ship behind, and towards the ships in front. What happens next?"

Oleg, Piet, Marcus, looked concerned, and started to mutter calculations. Behind them, one of the Filipinos stewards , standing with a tray of EBT said. "Captain Leo, if you don't mind. That's very easy."

The steward continued, " The Moroccans are only gaining at three knots, because we both go same way. That's their 15 minus our 11. "

"But you can add our speed to the The British Navy ship so they are coming towards us speed of 28. That's their 17 plus our 11. So can be good for us. The British will be here first."

Leo said," Fantastic, Pedro. You're right," …

….and looking at us said. "All ships really rely on Filipinos."

Oleg looked up, mug of tea in hand and said. " You don't know how true that is, my friend.

 You just don't know how bloody true that really is."

**53. End September.A standard meeting room, in a business hotel near Toulouse Airport:** *Almost 12 weeks had elapsed since the parents of the two kidnapped Swedish mothers with their three children, and those of three teenage girls, had gathered in this very room to await the outcome of a bid to rescue their kidnapped offspring.*

The successful rescue had probably produced more tears falling onto the hotel carpet in ten minutes, than drinks had been spilt on it, in all its years of existence.

No tears today though. Smiles. Greetings. Handshakes, some hugs and from me a lot of, "Thanks for coming."

Those present: My self, Barry Purchase, Oleg Tverskoy, Dal Booth and Katie Stanton. Charlie Haeggqvist, Magnus Sorensen , David Lim, Hiroshi Yamada and Gerry McMullen with Andre Calvettioni.

A couple of others from the CIA and SIS. Including someone making an official report for the record.

The agenda: A 'de-brief and a 'sign off' for Barry and I from the CIA/SIS investigation into threats to global shipping and trade.

I started. "Thanks again for coming, seemed a good idea to get the business out of the way before most of us adjourn to Castelnaudary. As we've come from all four corners of the globe a quick update."

" Charlie, David, Hiroshi-San and Andre came in this morning from Portugal where the girls and the Swedish families are having a re-union. For your information they are all doing very well, with very few flash backs or bad memories etc."

" With that said, as well as the kidnap we were also dealing with various other aspects of shipping related security, so today is as much about sharing information with our friends as fleet owners, as them as parents."

"Obviously it was mostly  your ships that were affected by the various attacks and threats. Despite us all sharing vital information, some of the actions and conclusions have been confidential as part of ongoing investigations till now, so I hope some of this closes a few books for you also."

"Back in June, with messages from the Chinese security services, personal calls and other high level contacts between the US, Russia, China and others, it appeared that fears of multiple attacks on global shipping were the flavour of the week. Then though, even at that high level ,rumour was king and facts were hard to find."

"Eventually as we all discovered, there were a number of wide ranging cyber attacks on various shipping systems. Suspects and indeed culprits: Many. "

"Rather worryingly, physical attacks-activated, or in the end prevented, by Oleg and the team, did by various means slip through the systems and directly affected 57 ships and delayed hundreds more."

"I can't imagine they will be the last attacks, so we learn and remain vigilant. Dal and Miss Stanton are going to share our review of our small part in all this with the various agencies concerned."

"Let's get the easy ones out of the way first."

"One. Our concern with someone looking to hire a full ships crew with many skills. Primary danger of course a renegade ship blocking a canal or vital waterway."

" Turned out to be a legitimate US/Scandinavian Cruise operator's China based cruise company secretly hiring a complete staff with varied skills for a new island resort."

"The China connection explained Liu Qiang getting wind of it. Case closed. But the potential for this type of 'blockage attack' by say, a hi-jacked vessel is a real future concern."

"Two. Black outs and cyber attacks various ship locator systems. Paying attention to bar girls and lady boys, in the red light bars of Philippines, steered us in the right direction on this, and more to the point about the real dates for the more active threats."

"Dal's people, the NSA and SIS UK and others now believe it to have been yet another cyber activity by North Korea. With the threat date July 4, presumably to annoy the USA at minimal cost."

" Given potential damage to Chinese interests we assume that Liu Qiang's people are also looking into that one. So we doubt it will re-occur from that source at least "

Dal Booth said, "Dan if I may. I've been receiving some rather graphic reports from some of the field operatives we sent to the Philippines to look into the accuracy of the facts coming out of those dockside girly bars."

" Given the lurid detail in the reports, not to mention their expenses claims, I think it best we leave that area of expertise to your people in future."

Whilst I shared in the general laughter, I dared not catch Barry or Miss Stanton's eyes as Dal mentioned the likely adventures of agents gaining their first experience of the red light girly bars of dockside Asia.

I continued. "Three. Filipino crew taking offers of well paid leave, and subsequent container fires. Origin Brazil."

" Initial thoughts that this yet another drug smuggling ploy. Now how ever we believe this could be part of a protection racket linked to the annual rental of thousands of shipping containers at inflated prices. i.e. Rent containers from us ,or you will have problems with your freight. "

" A Japanese organised crime connection to the millions of Japanese living in Sao Paolo seems likely, but not yet proven."

"Four. The New Zealand connection and the triggered fires . All the *sat phone triggered fires*, as opposed to the *crew set ones* from Brazil, were in reefers from the same meat and fish processing plant in New Zealand."

" We have more evidence about a Japanese crime connection link to that factory, but still not to individuals. At least not yet. Obviously we assume they are connected with the South American originated ones, but really is only an assumption, based on the Japanese connections."

"For finding and beating their trigger control system that was igniting the fires. We have to thank quick thinking by Oleg."

"Mind you having said that, I think most of us here would have enjoyed being at Miss Stanton's meeting with Oleg on his return to their London office."

" He was supposed to be on a watching brief, more than active service. Somewhere along the line, with some armed assistance he seized a ship apparently in the name of The Queen."

" That's as in Her Majesty The Queen of England not as far as I know Miss Stanton." Cue, much laughter, especially from Miss Stanton and bright red face from Oleg, who said, "Actually the biggest problem was explaining to the accounts department why we had rented four windsurf boards."

"Then having explained it all , they wanted to know why I hadn't reclaimed the rental deposit back."

I continued. "Luckily for him, at least as far as Miss Stanton's potential wrath was concerned, additionally, the other results he sorted were also great."

" *With the exception of two pallets stolen in an unrelated bullion robbery here in Toulouse, he also got the whole ransom of around 400 million US dollars of gold returned."* I saw some of the 'note takers' look up in shock at the huge sum of money.

"Moving on. The Russian language notes Oleg found and deciphered on the ship he had seized, resulted in us disconnecting the sat phone controlled triggers. They were set to 'switch on' if so ordered, to defrost, in 60 or so containers-all ex that chiller plant in New Zealand, by then scattered around on to 47 ships."

"Oleg's quick work enabled that 'disconnect' to happen about three hours before the July 4 threat date, as noted by all those bar girls, clicked up in Asian time. The key, although, at that time we didn't know why, was keeping the containers frozen."

"Turned out the trigger system was quite simple. Imagine two large ice bricks about a foot apart, with thin bags of reactant chemicals between them. Above and below, bridging the space between the bricks, stiff spiky plastic rods, held in place by very strong elastic bands, stretched open."

*"When de-frosted the ice blocks crumble under the strong elastic tension, which makes the rods snap inwards, and rupture the plastic bags causing the reactant chemicals to auto ignite, or at least react, making firework type smoke."*

" Harmless, but dangerous looking. Simple and bloody effective at causing chaos. The heat of the chemical fire and the fact that there's no metal parts, electrical timers and the like, left few forensic clues. That made it hard to figure out, until we got to some unignited ones."

"Getting information from the Japanese police is never easy, but with pressure on them from Hiroshi-san ,we have learned that this type of 'ice trigger' has been used in the past to contaminate valuable shipments of fish with food colouring thus rendering the fish unsaleable. i.e. Pay us to ship your goods, or else."

" Actually, it now appears they got this trick from Chinese gangs operating at home in China. "

"Until now, whilst Chinese and other crime organisations have spread internationally, very little international crime was Japanese. It now seems that Japanese crime families have started to try the same threat and protection system, to the shipping container business, and that of course has international implications."

" It's an interesting phenomena, as it's a global crime, but without any internet or cyber crime connections.  Local and rather old style actually, but as we have seen worldwide implications."

"The triggers, using sat phones to control-freeze or defrost settings in hundreds of containers, was set up and manipulated by a Russian who is in custody in Las Palmas in the Spanish controlled Canary Islands."

" The Russian has really only said , they were hired by a Japanese woman, to legitimately monitor and control shipping cargoes. "

"That's all he has said, despite some suggestions that he could be charged with attempted manslaughter. He's now got some hot shot lawyers, so there's legal wrangling about the origins or locations of any and all the crime's. We can only await results."

"There are two more airports near the one at Dahkla where our ransom plane actually landed. Both in Mauretania, a very basic one, Naouhadibou just over the border and their main one, Noukachott where we were originally expected to land. They all have daily flights to Las Palmas, which is just offshore in the Spanish Canary islands, so the Spanish found the Russians, or at least one of them quite easily."

"Unlike the Russian, the German involved in the kidnapping is talking a lot. After Oleg's 'borrowed ship' had met up with the Royal Navy, and with permission from Miss Stanton's people, using a Navy RIB, Rigid Inflatable Boat, two of our guys, with Leo the yacht skipper, went back in to Dahkla, or at least to the windsurfing beach on the other side of the bay."

" Their rib covered the distance quickly, and of course just looked like another rescue boat from one of the board sailing schools."

" They found the Hans the German, sitting with Rashid at the beach bar on El Argoub beach. He'd been abandoned, with no money or papers, by the Japanese woman on that beach. She and the Russians had been picked up by a white Toyota, and having said she would be back with help in a few minutes. But actually abandoned Hans there."

" As I said we know one of the Russians got a plane from Nouhadibou, but there's no sign of her and the other one. "

" Sitting for some hours on the beach, and later surprised by our guys, it seemed Rashid had persuaded Hans that British justice might be preferable to Western Saharan. So he came voluntarily."

"Having enjoyed an ocean cruise courtesy of the Royal Navy, they are both enjoying the hospitality of HM Prison service in the UK. Rashid has filled in a bit of detail but was only really being used for his Moroccan connections."

"The talkative German's says he met the Japanese lady when he was teaching diving a couple of years before. They became lovers, which is why he was more than pissed off when she abandoned him on the beach, with her new boyfriend, one of the Russians."

"He says the original idea from the Japanese lady was to extort a ransom for the girls in *online bit coins*. The two Russians had a bit coin trading business and had done some business with her in Japan. She changed from bit coins to gold after some problems with them, bit coins that is, in Japan. We wonder if the bit coin connection, and trying to manipulate the values, was the reason for the strange messages hitting the Japanese media about ship fires, before that actually happened.'"

"The gold ransom delivery location was chosen, because there's various gold mines operating nearby in Mauretania. The plan was to then utilise one of the various local gold smelting operations to re- cast the gold as newly mined. This making it easier to bring into the world of trade."

"So the only other kidnappers we knew much about, were the two Englishmen, men who guarded the girls at the Old Mill. Both were found dead a few weeks later by Gendarmes. They were called by neighbours to a rented apartment near Bordeaux where the bodies were found."

"The cause of death has eventually been traced to an unusual seafood toxin. It seems they had eaten sea food pizzas apparently taken away from a local restaurant. The cutlery, plates and table settings were for three people. The apartment had been been rented some months before by them. The shellfish toxin is still exercising the minds of France's forensic scientists somewhat as it is relatively unknown to them, but it is known to Japanese forensic experts. "

"The local Police have established that someone other than the the dead guys collected the actual Pizza's from the restaurant, so they have it down as an unsolved murder of two individuals. Miss Stanton is going to a meeting in Paris about that next week."

"So, we've accounted for all the workers, but a lot more proof needed to really pin down the ringleaders. Of course the understandable, 'no publicity, ' precludes help from the public, but to be honest I'm with the parents on this. Publicity will only produce copycat dangers."

I put down my i pad with all my notes, and finished up-rather lamely actually, considering the excitements along the route, "So that's it for Barry and I, as consultants to the US, and indirectly to the UK."

Miss Stanton stood up and said. "Before we go to Castelnaudary, I'd like to thank you and Barry, and of course windsurfing Oleg, for your professionalism. Knowing you also had responsibilities to the the children and parents was not easy. But, your local knowledge was invaluable. "

"I hope we can, and also 'don't need ,to work together again if you know what I mean.' Thank you."

"I echo that, one hundred percent." said Dal.

Charlie Haeggqvist said, "I think that David, and the rest of us families will wait with our thanks until tonight and also until our wives have arrived here soon from Faro. In fact, if we want the rest of the day to go well we'd better go to the airport and collect them now. "

As we packed up, Kate Stanton said, "Dal and I have to pop over to Airbus to pay our respects to someone, we'll catch up with you in Castelnaudary shortly."

**54. Castelnaudary. The first of three days at the end of September :** *Both of Andy and Faye-Lin's hotel barges were tied up alongside each other in the Castelnaudary canal basin, a broad expanse of water on the canal near the town center. A good mooring and popular with tourists.*

Neither The Lady Faye nor the Lady Mali were going anywhere for a couple of days as both boats had been booked by Joel, for use as hotels for some kind of re-union weekend associated with a function at the Foreign Legion Base just down the road.

Andy and Carlos were securing gang planks to the shore and between the two boats. Maria and Faye-Lin were decorating an archway over the main gangplank with flowers. This was their usual 'wedding style' boat decoration, but the special guests weren't to know that, and it looked impressive.

They were the ones impressed, when five black Mercedes limos pulled up on the towpath and from them exited a group of men and women. All cheerful, much back slapping and chat. Small manageable hand baggage was unloaded from the cars. As they shared it out, a seriously beaten up old Citroen 2 cv drove up and parked right behind the limos.

Andy groaned inwardly, not a good moment for his old surfing chum Joel to show up for the first time in many months, even if he had got them the booking.

Joel called out. 'Hi Andy, Hi Faye –Lin.

Andy groaned again, and then looked on amazed as the men and women from the limos all put down their luggage and greeted Joel with much back slapping hugs and embraces.

"Follow me, team," and Joel led the visitors on to the top deck of Lady Faye.

"May I introduce my old friend Andy and his wife Faye-Lin, also Captain Carlos and his wife Maria. Andy, most of these chaps are also in the boat business. This is Charlie Haeggqvist and his wife Amelie, Gerry McMullen, David and Peggy Lim, Hiroshi and Shoko Yamada. Andre Calvettioni, Barry Purchase, Magnus Sorenson, and last but not least Oleg Tverskoy and Daniel Craig."

He went on expansively, "Andy and Faye-Lin own and run these lovely boats so any complaints talk to Andy- it will be his fault - as obviously the wonderful Faye-Lin and Maria can do no wrong."

With much laughter and more good natured comments Faye-lin and Maria showed everyone their cabins, as Andy and Joel delivered the bags and Joel called out, " Drinks up top in 30 minutes."

In less than that they were all drinking Kir Royals, 'just a tiny drop of cassis with the Champagne please Andy. Not too sweet.'

As they proposed a toast of welcome, another black merc pulled up and out got a guy and lady. " Shouts of hi Chris, welcome ,and hi Squeeze."

As they boarded the boat both Charlie and Magnus said, "So you're the legendary Squeeze."

"Indeed I am." She went on, "and which one of you miscreants is Oleg. " As they greeted each other I realised that of course back in June, Oleg and I hadn't made it as far as Singapore-kidnapping emergencies had changed our course.

"Is that all of us? " said Charlie.

Barry said, "Not quite, Kate and Dal had to pay that courtesy visit to someone in the city ,but I think I can hear another car."

A Toulouse taxi arrived and out stepped Miss Stanton and Dal Booth. Andy nipped ashore, and sorted out the driver and the bags. Glasses of Kir Royal and introductions were made and delivered as the the two of the most powerful players in the world of national security stepped aboard.

Dal said to Charlie, "Kate and I were just considering if we should have invited our Chiefs of Naval operations, but we decided against it. Might dampen the party somewhat." Much laughter all round.

"What time do we have to be all dressed up and at the legion HQ for dinner?" asked Dal.

Squeeze said, "In about an hour they're coming to pick us up." Most of the guests disappeared down to their cabins to change.

Even Joel, who leapt onto the canal bank and from his car produced 'Le Smoking' as the French call it, and changed his clothes in the wheelhouse. Pretty soon the black mercs returned, a group of remarkably smart guests went ashore.

'Have a good time,' said Faye-Lin.

As they left  Charlie called back to Andy. "Andy, please put some more of that excellent champagne on ice for our return, and make sure that gangplank's good and straight for my friends."

Some hours later a somewhat noisier and even happier set of people tumbled out of the Mercs. 'Merci, merci. To the drivers, and 'OK see you in the morning, demain, then at 10.30.' Andy had spent some time making sure the gangplank was indeed well level and steady, but he still stood there with Joel to ensure the guests made it across safely.

Faye-lin, offered, "Champagne ,coffee,?"

Squeeze and Miss Stanton together, "Yes please, to both."

Followed by Squeeze, " You lot are going to have to excuse me but I'm going to sit here with Kate and take my shoes off they are bloody killing me."

Much laughter, re arranging of chairs and orders for calvados, Coffees. Lots of water and of course Champagne.

Joel ,having assured the guests that, 'they could speak freely in front of Andy, as for many winter seasons they had worked together on various projects. Not only that but he had known Andy almost since they were kids.'

So the guests chatted reasonably freely.

Miss Stanton." You know after the speeches when the Legionnaire's started to sing their traditional songs, I thought I would weep, it was like nothing I ever experienced before."

Magnus said, "I was happy it was just candle light then I can tell you," and all around the deck there were nods of agreement.

Chris said, "Bloody Frogs, they keep doing stuff really well. The grub was good as well."

Magnus with a smile, "Now Chris don't forget when we have dinner tomorrow night with Francois, 'no frogs', you know what happened last time, and we don't want to see you consigned to the desert with Legionnaires hat and pack."

Magnus continued, "You know when we all split up in in June after the rescue," Andy, who was serving Champagne, looked at Magnus with interest.

Magnus continued, "When the kids wanted Brigitte, May and Tamiko to come to Portugal, I don't know whose idea it was to promise them to do it now at the last summer holiday, just before the winter, but it was a good one."

" They've been in contact with each other all through the school time. Now I've got a lot of photos in today, all seems good there, and very non stop. I hope your guys can take the pace. " He nodded at Joel.

Charlie remarked, "The psychologists said that keeping contact with the others was important. To be honest apart from Britt and Anna being a little nervous every time the kids go out, I think my lot are doing fine."

Magnus said, "Well there's messages coming from my kids asking about water parks in Taiwan and Japan, so contact looks well set for some time to come. I'll be back there in Portugal tomorrow to check it all out with them."

Andre said, "When my ex wife went for treatment, which seems to be going well so far, Brigitte and I spent a lot of time together. We went sailing in Mauritius and Reunion, and had a good time. The last five weeks back at college seem fine."

" Oh yes, Barry and Daniel, your security team there are very discrete, and I think have a provided another step in the girls confidence."

David said, " Hiroshi-san and I talked about this on the way here. We think that for May and Tamiko their Asia home for them is so different that any healing is happening well. "

"I wondered when we said about coming back to Europe if they would be concerned but they were just excited to see Britt and Anna again with the kids. It's almost like they have gained some little sisters from all this."

Hiroshi. 'Getting Tamiko's horse over to Japan has kept her busy, but we'll have to move full time to our country house as horses and Tokyo don't mix well. Mind you the cost of air freighting a horse was such that think we should be in the air freight business not shipping."

Dal Booth said, "Talking about shipping , I have something here for you all. " He reached into his pocket and pulled out a note.

"It's from President Appleyard." Now, Andy, standing by the table loaded with drinks, looked totally shocked and even more  bewildered. "This part is typed on White House Paper."

" 'To Barry, Daniel and your team. Well done for a job well carried through, despite you having loyalties to several masters. Thank the Lord for the safe return of those girls and children. On the wider picture, thank you, America is safer because of you both','"

Dal looked up. "He's also written a note on the bottom of that"

"To Charlie Haeggqvist.  I wish you could have been here to see the reactions when your ultimatum arrived. A heroic move for a Swedish Admiral, and all happily without a shot being fired.'

'Please also pass on the thanks of myself and more importantly The American people to all your colleagues and associates, as we appreciate and rely on your ongoing professional service. So thank you all. Barnaby J. Appleyard'.

Charlie said. "Andy, Faye-Lin it's late, would you like a drink, come and join us." Which they did.

Joel said. "I told you, David, Charlie and Hiroshi are also in the boat business." Much laughter and Charlie Haeggqvist said. "Well we may have a few larger ships, but not many of them as pretty and comfortable as these two."

Gerry McMullen cut in, "And not much Champagne on board ours either." Cue yet more laughter. In the silence that followed, I could see a mixed range of emotions on the faces around the tables.

Kate Stanton said. "It was a wonderful idea to thank the Legion in the way you have Mr. Haeggqvist.'

"Charlie," Charlie said, "please Charlie."

"Actually it was my wife Amelie's idea. She was reading about the difficulties experienced by injured military personnel when they return to their home lands. Although not in the services the problems can be the same for those injured in our employ in our ships and yards. "

"We had already set up something similar in Sweden and also in the Philippines, where a lot of our crews come from. I know that Hiroshi and David are doing the same."

Joel said to Andy, who was looking puzzled. "You know the base commander here ?" Andy nodded, " Well he and his Legion specialists helped us and these people earlier this year with a very serious life threatening problem. I can say that much."

"Mr. and Mrs. Haeggqvist amazingly, have bought and donated to the Ex Legionnaires Association the old farm at Le Vieux Moulin au Soleil. It's going to be fitted out with 12 specially designed 'gites' for wounded Legionnaires and their families. Not only that but with the Yamada's and the Lims, they've set up an endowment to cover the running costs for Legionnaire's past and present."

"Tonight's dinner at the base was part of the celebrations. "Tomorrow morning we have to go to the base, in smart kit again, for the official ceremony . Some kind of blessing and tree planting, with the mayor and a minister, and some ambassadors from Paris."

"That's all over by 3.00 in the afternoon. So we'll probably then need a siesta because in the evening we're giving the commander and his wife dinner in town. Cassoulet at last for our guests."

Gerry said, "So, Andy, you'd better make sure that gangplank's all ship shape again for our return." Charlies wife, Amelie said, "and knowing this lot, re-stock the bar."

"It's a good end to a tough problem, but I would really have liked to close it 100%." said Dal. " I just wish we could pin down the real boss or mastermind."

He looked at Charlie, "I fully understand your wish not to get the German guy charged with kidnapping because that will just get a lot of publicity and make for copycat crimes in future."

Magnus cut in, " And not good for the girls to have to give evidence." At the word 'Kidnapping' Andy and Faye-Lin sat up and looked shocked.

Joel looked at me and at Andy and Faye Lin. "May I ?"

I nodded.

Joel explained, "Some more detail for you, back in the summer a gang kidnapped various wives, children and grandchildren from our friends here. A seriously fraught time I can tell you. "

"We eventually rescued them not far from here, with a lot of help from Francois and the legion."

Andy said, " But I haven't seen or heard anything about it."

Old man Quist said, "No that's the lucky part. We've still managed to bury the story. *If the word got out in a big way then the kids would be at risk all over again from copy cats or trouble makers.* As it is ,we've had to change our lives a lot to be safe."

"But, Dal you are right, getting those who planned and financed this would be good. I guess there will be plea bargains to be had when we parents maintain our point of not wanting to publicise the kidnappings."

Miss Stanton said. " We know all there is about the two deceased Brits, also Hans, Rashid and a bit about the two Russians."

" We checked Phone logs, gas station and hypermarket security camera footage from here and from the boat, satellite phone records, various passports. "

"For the Japanese lady. Also nothing. Not even the boat yielded much by the time we got to it."

"Even the fingerprint searches using prints taken from the boat, have drawn a blank internationally. Actually there was nothing on record, no criminal records, apart from driving offenses, and a few bad debts over the years for the Brits. It's the same with the German."

"But I am increasingly, like Dal, thinking that Hans and the two Russians, like Rashid know nothing really material when it comes to a link to the bosses. There's no other clues here, unless you can call this a clue."

She fished in her bag and extracted a photo, "We've all seen this."

It showed one of the English captors, loading shopping from a trolley into a car. He was obviously talking to someone, who was standing back almost to the camera. It was a blurred image of a shoulder and side shot of someone in a hat."

Joel said. "I'm sorry it's not better a better picture, but at that stage we were very frightened of the necklaces, and I was desperate for my guy who was following not to get in too close in case he was spotted."

Miss Stanton said, " Absolutely Joel. Perfect tradecraft. You were right. It's easy to be clever after the event, and your guy being spotted could have put the girls at risk."

I said, "I agree 100%. It's just so bloody frustrating to be so near and yet so far. I think we are all convinced that the guy they met regularly at that shop in Toulouse was giving the orders. Joel's guy even spotted him handing cash over to the Brit. "

"He must have been the guy they phoned. But we don't know anything else. Believe me every security camera from that store has been checked and re checked. In fact I suspect every security cam in France has been checked."

Miss Stanton tossed the picture on to the table.

Unable to resist Andy picked it up, looked-looked again and called Faye-Lin, "Come look at this."

"I'm washing coffee cups ,hang on honey." She came onto the deck wiping her hands.

She glanced at the picture and immediately said, "That's Maruki-san."

Stunned silence, and before anyone could react Andy said, "For sure that's what I thought. I'd recognise that hat anywhere."

Kate Stanton. "How can you tell from the back of the neck and side of the face."

"Easy", Faye-Lin said. "One. Look at the two ear rings. Two under the hat you can see a shadow. You can't really see it, but I know that's a little corner of a tattoo over a scar."

"I know the hat. He never takes it off," and Andy said, "and he's always got that jacket on even on hot days."

Faye Lin, "Andy told me, Maruki wears the jacket because of the long sleeves means he can hide his hand. He's got a finger missing. Andy says that means he's 'bloody Japanese Yakusa, mafia'."

With shocked expression her hand flew to her mouth and looking at Hiroshi and she said, "Ooh, so sorry."

He smiled and said. " Andy's right, old time criminals used to do that with the fingers a lot in Japan. There's various associations, one is called Yakusa. Mafia would be a good equivalent."

Dal to Faye and Andy. "For God's sake, how do you know them."

Andy said. "They booked this boat three years ago for a holiday. There were just the four of them. They booked two weeks, but they only stayed eight days. When they left they said they'd had a wonderful time, although they seemed to spend it all on their laptops and i. Pads."

He continued, "That guy Muraki, his wife she was from Thailand."

"No his wife was from Philippines," said Faye-Lin. "She was very nice. She used to come to the market with me. She told me that Muraki wore the hat and the jacket because he had a lot of tattoos, and scars on his head from street fights when he was younger. Now he was older and his hair was going, they showed a lot, so he wore the hat."

She said, "She said I must never say, but she said that his head looked like a moon map." Faye- Lin laughed a little.

Andy said. "Then there was his sister's boyfriend. He was Russian."

Barry, Dal and Miss Stanton all spoke almost in chorus. "I don't; suppose you have any photos of them do you ?"

" Sure," said Andy, "We keep a scrap book Hang on."

He returned, not only with a scrap book, but a guest registration book, and Faye - Lin suddenly said-hang on, and jumped down the steps, re-appearing moment later with a framed photo.

The picture showed, Andy and Faye-Lin, The four guests, Maruki full face but still with hat, arm round an attractive Asian lady.

"That's in a restaurant in Carcassonne on their last night."

" The next morning I took them to the airport there in my old car, that was before I before I sold it to Joel." He gestured to the rusted old Citroen parked on the grass verge.

"When we came to airport-I was shocked to find they had their own plane. I remember apologising for the car and they laughed and said it was all fun. They showed me around the Jet, They wanted me to help them with the French whilst they ordered fuel."

"I remember Maruki San paid with a Titanium Amex Card. Real metal the first of them I ever saw. Dal and Barry looked at each other. They were very nice. Then, any way."

Faye-Lin said, "Andy and I had only been operating the boat for a few years then and we were very excited about having a customer with a private plane. We'd never seen one before."

Squeeze said, "Well babe, come to Toulouse tomorrow and I'll show you a few more ."

"Actually," said Dal."Tomorrow there will be one less, although mine's on loan from the US air force, I'm due back in the US."

" Now with this new info, we'll find them. Credit cards, exact dates for immigration in a small airport, flight plans, plane ownership or leasing. Given all this we'll have the real details I bet we know more before I'm even back in the USA."

Kate Stanton said, "I agree."

Dal continued, "I want to be sure I supervise this personally. It's international enough for us to act. We can get them for fraud, stock exchange manipulation and with care not have to mention the kidnapping."

" In any event knowing the death sentence still exists in Morocco and indeed Singapore, they'll tell us all we need to know."

"Do you think they were planning this all those years ago," asked Oleg.

"Absolutely not." said Barry. "They would have been more careful about pictures if they had. I bet that this came about, as here is about equidistant from Germany and Portugal. Then of course it helped that they knew the area bit as well."

Andy said. " When they were on the boat they were besotted with buying a vineyard, they went and looked at a few. They kept finding things on line, but I think that was some kind of fashion to do that then not a plan to do something bad."

" I remember them telling me they had invested in a Safari Park in Angola they showed me a lot of animal pictures."

Joel said. " Dal ,we have all worked to keep this whole story under wraps, for the sake of the kids. How can we, or rather you, accuse them without revealing Andy's and Faye-Lin's part in this. We don't want them to have problems in future, or be at any risk."

Andy looked shocked.

Dal said. "I agree. All we needed was a name and now I've got four names that I suspect are real. I'm not even going to take the pictures with me, although you could keep them safe just in case we can't find Yakusa boy very easily."

Miss Stanton said, "Dal's right of course, with the names and their old credit card details, Andy said they booked online, and paid for jet fuel with his card we'll get them, most likely in hours."

Dal lifted his glass, and said, "I am sure I am not jumping the gun, but I will be shocked if that's not the last parts of the puzzle in place. Well done all."

Miss Stanton added, Especially Faye-Lin and Andy, it's a big co-incidence, for sure, but not an impossible or crazy as this is where the kidnapped were held."

As glasses were raised, Dal said, "Barry, I hear Matchless Consulting are losing you.?"

Barry replied, " Well yes and no. I am joining forces with Dan. But Matchless Consulting are happy.  I'm mainly handling personal and family security, including the expanded coverage we now need for the Haeggqvist, and Sorenson families. "

" Matchless Consulting are keeping BOSN Shipping, With Baltics shipping's huge fleet  and global reach it needs a large organisation so for Matchless."

" Business, works better for them than  personal. I am going to oversee them now for and on behalf of Baltic."

Dal continued. " Oleg, If there's no truth in the rumour Miss Stanton fired you for windsurfing on duty, and that's why you're joining Dan's company."

He paused as we chuckled, and continued, " Or is it that just one night with Chris and Paul Isted was not enough in those red light bars ?"

All of which required considerable spluttering from Oleg, and further explanations for Andy and Faye-Lin, and provoked another round of raised glasses.

Having asked Andy to fix a taxi to Toulouse for very early in the morning, Dal joined the general drift down to the cabins.

Joel and Andy spent a little time talking quietly on deck as Joel explained a little about the various people.

It was 2 am by the time the boats had quietened. Just the sound of the water lapping on the hulls.

**55. Castelnaudary. A second nice September morning:** *By 8.30 on a bright and sunny morning, the smell of coffee permeated even the sleepiest of cabins.*

Early risers making their way up to top deck, found, under the awning, a table 'seriously laden' with fresh croissants, breads, brioche, fruits ,jams and all you needed for a light or hearty breakfast, French style. With Carlos and Maria producing coffees on demand and offering eggs or more.

"French style breakfast is fine today," said Chris," with both lunch and dinner scheduled today, this is good."

Squeeze "And I bet you've forgotten the French for big smokey breasts or whatever it was."

Andy said, ' Andre, Dal and Magnus left this morning at 7.30. They shared a cab and they were really happy because, rather than have to do two commercial flights back to all the kids in Portugal, Dal said he'd drop him off at Faro on his way to the USA."

A little later as they trooped out to the awaiting Mercs, Charlie said, "Andy please, can you and Faye-Lin join us for dinner tonight. I know you know the Commander and anyway after your help last night you're fully in the team."

With bands playing, speeches, prayers, and dignitaries aplenty the morning at the Legion HQ went well, or as Charlie Haeggqvist put it. 'despite the speeches."

After another spectacular lunch, their guests returned to the boats. For most a siesta was very much needed. Kate Stanton reporting to Andy, " Three cheers from 300 soldiers, with hats then thrown in the air was almost as moving as last nights traditional Legion singing."

Andy had fired up their extra, on shore generator, to provide siesta time and all night air con for his guests without the need to run the boat's engines.

Around six when drinks were scheduled, he was a bit surprised to find Charlie Haeggqvist on the canal bank discussing the finer points of diesel generators, in Portuguese, with Carlos.

"I didn't know you spoke Portuguese," he said somewhat lamely, but also speaking Portuguese.

Charlie smiled, "Why not, I've had a house there for 25 years, and come to that I didn't know you spoke Portuguese either."

Andy explained that he had lived for some years in Praia Da Luz, about which Charlie said, "A very nice place about half an hour along the coast from me."

They then both reminisced about the sadly long gone Rocha Negra beach restaurant, and that café by the parking, you know the one. ' The Habana' that's it, used to be called the 'International'. Good coffee.

Other discussions followed about Sardines versus 'Carapau' or small mackerel, and the best time of year to eat them, and rather more seriously about stupid euro regulations hurting small business in one of Europe's smaller but most pleasant countries.

Their old Citroen van trundled smokily along the canal path and parked under the trees. Joel exited as did a stunningly beautiful girl.

As he came aboard he said," This is my wife Betts."

Handshakes kisses all round and extra friendly greeting from Andy and Faye Lin who obviously knew Joel's wife  very well.

Faye- Lin called, "If you have a moment Andy, Mr. Haeggqvist , everyone. I  think it's about time to walk into town."

When they arrived at the restaurant, Covered in signs, 'Traditionnel Recépés Anciennes. Prix de 1953' no less. They were greeted ouside by Commandant Francois with his wife.

As they entered Joel called out. " Sit where you like, no more speeches and formality tonight thank goodness."

So they arranged themselves around two long tables. Red checked napkins, fresh bread, mustard, some butter, cornichons and olives as only the French can do. Also with, most importantly, earthenware jugs of red wine.

Charlie called to Andy, "Come and sit with us with your wife." Andy and Faye Lin were actually a bit nervous, Joel having explained quietly to them the previous night that three of the guests were certainly in the top 100 wealthiest men in the world, with many thousand ships, not boats, owned between them. But Charlie and Amelie were great company.

Also on their table Joel, Betts, Francois and his wife. She was Mauritian so also spoke excellent English, and Gerry McMullen.

Joel stood and said, "I know the boss, or one of them," he bowed to Charlie ,Hiroshi and David  and their wives, "The boss said no speeches but it seems to me that for the benefit of our visitors- here for the first time, we should perhaps ask someone to explain the origins of cassoulet."

He looked at the commandant, "You are our guest, but for the last time tonight please be our guide."

Much applause and Francois stood. "Firstly when I stand ,it is usually to propose a toast, so", raising his glass of red, he said, " Santé, and welcome again."

"Simply put, true Cassoulet is a tradition from Castelnaudary. It is a dish slow cooked in an earthenware pot in the oven. It has confit , that's joints of salted duck or goose previously cooked at low temperature in their own fat or oil. That brings out the flavours, and preserves them. So the confit, with good sausage, some belly of pork is cooked long and slow with haricots blanc, white beans, in a tomato based sauce. Please enjoy it."

" Oh yes, beware eating too much bread with it, as I always do." and his wife added, "and then you complain all the night that you ate too much."

"Bon appetite."

Much raising of glasses again. Waiters and waitresses brought the bubbling dishes to the tables. "Attention. Chaud , tres chaud, very 'ot' ."

I heard Chris say, "She's not joking about 'ot, look at that still bubbling."

The conversation slowed and dropped to a murmur.

After a while it was Chris who spoke first. "Commander, this is brilliant, you Frogs have done it again. Brilliant."

Francois raised a glass to Chris, and said, "Merci Monsieur Chris. I notice your French speaking is coming along well, you say 'ot, just like we do."

Much laughter, particularly from Squeeze.

Francoise, " Chris would you like to know the result of this afternoons football match."

Chris, "Blimey, for sure I would."

Francoise, " Well I can tell you about Chelsea"..... the commander paused, and went on "but sadly the French TV no longer show us the lower down teams like....Fulham."

Head in hands from Chris, with a, "You win!" to the commandant, cheers and laughs from all.

Charlie Haeggqvist stood, glass in hand. "I know the real boss, Francois, said no more speeches, so I am not going to make one."

Amelie, in a not low voice, "I fear you are." More laughs.

Charlie grinned and said, "Actually ,if I stand and speak briefly, may be the food will go down a little and I will find room for more of this wonderful feast."

He went on. "You know, only now do I think I really know this whole drama is over, closed. Of course it was the worst thing that ever happened to me and to all of us as families. But now looking around, at you good people and new friends, *something good has come out of it.*"

"I don't mean new business, that has happened by surprise, I don't mean the cost to us in cash terms, that is what it is. The change in lifestyle had probably to come anyway."

He paused and looked thoughtful, and then continued, in a lower voice, very emotionally charged. " But the real thing was seeing everyone here work together, getting behind Daniel and Barry with a dedication that is humbling."

"As was," he glanced at the commander," Your men at risk to their lives. And then minutes later seeing the kids bouncing around as if nothing had occurred. I am speaking for David ,Hiroshi, Peggy, Shoko, not forgetting Andre and I am sure Brigitte's mother , myself and Amelie, and our children. Family matters most. Thank you."

Everyone stood and toasted....and a good few napkins seemed to be needed to dry some tears.

After quite a long pause after which the buzz of conversation started to resume Miss Stanton stood, tapped a knife on a wine glass and spoke. Quietly. " I won't repeat what has already been expressed, more eloquently than I could ever hope to do. Dal and I both wish, as did the President in his note, to thank Barry and David for their professionalism. Also to Oleg and some of the others not here tonight. Sir Geoffery, Johnnie Wells and our back room teams. So I raise a glass to them."

We murmured and raised our glasses.

Miss Stanton continued. I am sorry to lose Oleg to the private sector, and I won't embarrass him again by suggesting that it may be the fringe benefits that have attracted him"....she paused and went on, sweetly.."

"Not that I am aware, if fringes are currently in fashion in the Red Lips or Moonlite Bars of Asia."...serious laugh from all.

Still sweetly, she went on," Finally, Daniel. I am not angered by you stealing one of my best operatives, but I do hope you will be paying him as the highest paid private security consultant on the planet."

" After all he did foil, what google tells me, would have been the world's biggest ever gold robbery."

As the laughter and the applause died away , I heard the commanders wife say to him, "Did they ever get the guys that lifted the gold here?"

I heard the commander say. "Well, as Andre will confirm it was nothing to do with the kidnap or ship plot. Just a three local Toulouse villains taking an advantage of an opportunity they had been waiting and planning for."

" It seems that gold was transferred most weeks between Toulouse and other bullion stores. It was just coincidence that they exercised their plan on our shipment. After Oleg's discovery of the missing load, and them then checking the plane when it got back to Marseilles, it was clear that two palettes had been substituted for pig iron. "

"The police got the robbers within a day or so. They obviously knew who the driver of the truck was, and they worked from there very quickly."

"Shows you how stupid they were , they still had the gold in the garage of their apartment. Or a rather they had forty ingots. They said they had 'lost the rest'. I am sure  they will remember where the missing ones are when they come to court. In the meantime there's a reward out there for the rest, just in case."

The commanders wife, not a soul of discretion said, "Presumably they were insured."

Charlie said, "Yes it was, thanks to Andre's good business sense, the two storage depots had regular insurance. That's where the reward will come from, and we lost nothing except some legal fees."

Andy said. "Can I ask where and when this gold went missing?".

I said, "Friday July 1st In the early evening. Between Toulouse and Marseille airports."

Faye-Lin said, "And there's a real reward out for it."

Andy glared at her, but she went on. "Then I think that we can help you with that."

The Commander who had already heard about the previous nights revelations said, "Not more clients of your sweet bateaux, cherie."

Which got him a glare from his wife.

"No," said Faye- Lin, "Andy and I found the gold, and were frightened of what might happen to it, and then to us ,so we hid it."

Andy took over, "Actually we found it by accident, and were frightened of what was obviously some bad guys coming back, so we hid it and then ran away ourselves."

" We've been watching the local paper and the TV to see if someone comes up as having lost it."

Faye Lin. "Actually, I have been making Andy wait, so that we could get a reward. In my country rewards always help."

The commander, obviously a little exasperated by what he assumed was too much alcohol talking said. "What make you think that it is still where you hid it. You cannot have moved it far, it is about 2000 kilo's."

Faye Lin said, "I know it's heavy because I moved half of it myself, but  I don't think anyone will have found it."

" Because it's at the bottom of the canal."

Uproar.

**56. September. The third morning in Castelnaudary Probably: That's as in: Probably the third. Probably Castelnaudary. Probably morning:**

*The party, increasingly rowdy, had continued on the boats late into the night.*

Andy surfaced when his alarm went off, Late. For once he saw the small form of Faye-lin still in bed- moaning hang overly under the covers. He could hear sounds of movement outside.

On deck, a miracle.

 Glasses, bottles debris cleared away, the only sign of a very wild night, a large pile of black plastic sacks piled by the parking place for the company van, and from both boats the smell of coffee. On his deck, chairs and table ready, awning open and juice and glasses at the ready.

Maria appeared, he took the proffered coffee and sank into a chair.

His main memory, was he and Faye Lin being asked again and again, "But why didn't you say something."

In the end Charlie Haeggqvist, raising his hand and saying to the excited throng. "They didn't say because of the reward, which I think was an excellent idea for them."

" They also didn't try and walk away with the gold which would have been bad. They were careful, waiting for a sensible opportunity with the real owners, and they didn't know who to talk to until tonight."

Slowly, guests surfaced from both boats, Maria bustling around.

"I'm sorry, I'm sorry," she kept saying, "I don't know where the croissants and the breads are, they should be back by now. When they all left at seven this morning they said they would go to the boulangerie on the way back."

Amelie came up on deck, "Where's Charlie?"

Maria, "The older gentleman went with the army people and Carlos."

By now it was almost nine thirty and Andy was talking about nipping up to the boulangerie on his bike to get some supplies.

Then, the sound of an army truck, followed by the old company van, Oleg and Joel, jumping out with armfuls of French bread and paper bags.

Charlie Haeggqvist beaming, and the commander supervising a team of soldiers dumping a pile of canvas bags by the gangplank.

The commander and Charlie went and spoke to the driver and the men, and with a mix of salutes and handshakes, the soldiers departed.

Charlie said, "Great, coffee, breakfast. Just what we need, eh Francois."

"Indeed, mon ami."

"Nothing like a swim in a canal to freshen you up."

Amelie, " Charlie , stop being totally stupid, anyone can see you haven't been swimming."

Francois, " Madame, with every respect, at 'the boss's' age and corporate position  he has people to swim for him. As actually do I. For me  it is a privilege of rank.'"

Big laughs, especially from Amelie who was now sitting with Charlie.

Francois looked around. "Well done Andy and well done Faye- lin, and before you all explode- we have the gold"

" Exactly where you said.  Well we have 154. The bad guys were found with 40, that leaves 6."

" He looked at Andy, "We found all those 154 right by the wall between the two mooring posts."

Faye-lin said, "The should be another two a little more out in the middle of the canal, we took the tarp that was wrapped round them and chucked it off the outside of the boat away from the bank."

" We wanted to hide it from the bad guys and used the gold to sink it. We couldn't throw them far they are heavy, as you said last night."

Francois said, "Unless there's some lucky anglers with exceptionally heavy fishing line I am sure they are there. I'll get the guys to look there later."

Miss Stanton said, "I tried to say last night, surely the police are going to go mad. It's now an official gendarmerie/police affair here, and they even have the perpetrators of the crime in custody. "

"They will never believe the 'well we happened to be there,' story, and they will hustle and harry Andy and Faye-Lin for years. Especially as we have already embarrassed them about their inability to find our Yakusa man, or the cause of the two deaths in Bordeaux."

Charlie said, "I guess we can't ask them to withdraw charges as we now have the goods back."

"But you don't," said Miss Stanton. "Some of the gold is in police custody and some is missing."

Gerry McMullen said. "I have some experience of audits. So we embarrass ourselves instead, and say to the cops, 'oops you remember that gold bullion robbery'.  We re-checked the figures in Africa, and they worried us, remember also that's where the gold was signed out for, and the police know that is where the goods were going".

"So we've done an audit  re-counted the gold, and we're only missing 40 and you have them from the bad guys. Well done Police. Brilliant job you can close the book, which if I know most police departments they will be pleased to do."

Francoise said, " I think that will work well."

Followed by Katie Stanton saying "Gerry I think you have great criminal mind. That'll work."

Charlie said. "Commander could you get someone to securely- at our risk- deliver those bags either to the safe store in Toulouse or Marseilles. I think the insurance company needs them back."

Barry had gone to the end of the gangplank, and was studying his phone intently.  He returned and said. "OK everyone listen up, I have  interesting information from Dal Booth. They have indeed apprehended the Japanese guy, our Yakusa man with his wife and his sister .

They were at San Francisco airport getting a plane for the Philippines. They are holding him as he was found with several passports.

His Philipino wife is telling all, and that's before she's even been offered any kind of deal."

"She says, her Japanese husband, his sister and her new Russian boyfriend came up with the kidnap plan.  She says, the idea to kidnap the Swedes came from the Japanese lady's boyfriend who lived for five years in Malmo."

" The sister came up with the information about Tamiko and her European school from a newspaper story about Japanese kids learning abroad. Snatching the other two girls was an accident and not in the plan."

"Dal says. 'That sounds like all the loose ends tied up'."

David and Charlie who had been listening intently both agreed.

But then Hiroshi started to say, "I am very ashamed as a Japanese person that my people can do this, and that the idea came through a story on Tamiko."

Charlie stood, and said. "Hiroshi-San , with respect, enough blaming the Japanese. There's Russians,  Germans, English in there as well. Maybe Chinese and Koreans."

"Your fleet has suffered internationally for years, as have ours with crimes from all those mentioned above. *So I really don't think it's a Japanese disgrace.............and who knows, may be the next bad guy will be Swedish......here's some surprisingly bad old boys out there.......but* that's what Barry and Daniel are there for."

Hiroshi,translating quietly for his wife Shoko,  looked less mortified. Slightly. Very slightly.

As they relaxed over more coffees in the now warming up morning Miss Stanton said, "It seems to me that we need Faye-Lin to come and join me in the service. Initiative, language skills, bravery under unusual conditions, quick thinking and not afraid to get her hands dirty."

The commander said, "Then you're competing with me. I think we need her in the legion."

Miss Stanton cut in quickly, "But you have never had women in the Legion. So I win."

"Well actually," said the commander, " You are only partly correct. *There has been one women legionnaire, and not only that, but she was actually British. Her name was Susan Travers. She lived in Paris until about 2004. I think she was 95 years old then.*"

" For her service to her adopted country she was awarded many medals. She held the National Legion d'Honnuer. The Medaille Militaire, The Croix de Guerre....but her main pride was the little Red and Blue ribbon of the French Foreign Legion."

"Amongst other later exploits she was most regarded for her bravery in the second world war. She was assigned as a military driver, not an official soldier. But she had nerves of steel avoiding minefields and enemy attacks that the Legionnaires nick named her 'Le Miss'. "

"In just one episode under severe fire in she was responsible for guiding the escape of 2500 French soldiers who were besieged in Bir Hakeim Libya." He paused, somewhat emotionally, and looked at his audience of spellbound listeners.

Joel said. "For once that's a bit of history that I knew. From my time in the legion and also from the book about the amazing lady. The book's called, 'Tomorrow to be Brave'."

Miss Stanton, said. "That'll be the next book on my shopping list for sure."

As travel plans were made two Mercs arrived, and Hiroshi and David said. " This time, they are for us, we've got a long flight back to Asia. First we go to Portugal to collect Tamiko and May.

David continued, " Thank you again for everything. Thank you for a fantastic time- and to the Commander - I could say that the Castelnaudary Cassoulet was the hi light of the trip, but actually of course in reality it was meeting your team again."

"Miss Stanton thank you for your understanding and sometimes looking the other way. "

"Chris we see you on the golf course , if Squeeze lets you out. "

"Oleg we see you soon, good luck working with Daniel, and the same to you Barry".

"Finally ,Andy and Faye - Lin thank you for everything we have loved your boats. Hiroshi and I were saying that a fleet of two seems a fine size. May be he and I are getting old. My hope is that when you come to Asia-you can bring Joel as well. I have a feeling that with your share of the gold reward that you so deserve, you can all make some travels now."

They left, with much waving, and some bowing from Hiroshi and Shoko.

Gerry McMullen was still sitting with Charlie, saying. " Charlie, hang on. The bad guys took 40. There's two still in the river, we've got 154, and Andy and Mai Lin have two hidden in the bad water tanks on here. There's still two missing."

Charlie said. "Faye-Lin are you sure you have just two ingots?"

" Yes," she said, "they are in the cess pit toilet tanks-shall we get them out for you to check?"

Charlie raised his hand and laughed. "No, no. You have earned every cent of the good reward that will be paid to you from the insurers. "

*"Keep quiet about those two, they can be an 'extra bonus' for you to please share with Joel and his men.* We will all keep quiet about them. I think, the insurance company can think they, and any others not found are lost in the canal. I'm not being too hard on the insurance company but you, in returning all that gold that you did have saved them many many millions."

Gerry was sitting there still looking baffled when Charlie and Amelie's car turned up. Andy and Joel helped carry their bags out to car.

Fond farewells, particularly from Charlie and Amelie to Joel and Francois.

They were just about to drive off when, Carlos ran ashore and calling to Charlie, said, in Portuguese," Hang on senhor, esqueceu-se daqueles tijolos do rio. Eles estão por baixo do assento na van, quer que os ponha noutro lado ? "

" Ah, sim ", disse Charlie," Obrigado Carlos, pode colocá-los na parte de trás do carro,mais uma vez obrigado"

Carlos retrived something muddy looking from under the seat of the van and put it in the trunk of Charlies car.

Charlie looking across at me said with a smile, " Mesmo que o nosso negócio,seja feito a tempo".

And with waves, blown kisses and many more smiles, they were gone. Possibly the broadest smile was from Andy.

After all, he did speak Portuguese. "No tempo certo" indeed.

*......I'll just repeat that in English.....*

They were just about to drive off when, Carlos ran ashore and calling to Charlie,said, *In Portuguese*," Hang on senhor, you forgot a couple of those bricks from the river. They are still under the seat in the old van. Shall I get them and put them with your stuff ? "

" Oh great." said Charlie. " Thank you Carlos, lucky you remembered. If you could get them and put them in the back of the car that would be appreciated."

Carlos retrieved something muddy looking from under the seat of the van and put it in the trunk of Charlies car.

Charlie looking across at me said with a smile, " That was lucky you remembered, and we got everything sorted out .Just in time." ........and with waves, blown kisses and many more smiles, they were gone.

Possibly the broadest smile was from Andy. After all, he did speak Portuguese. "No tempo certo" indeed, *"Just in time."*

*Generally speaking this is a work of fiction,*
*but I should confirm that the overall potential danger*
*referred to in the plot, reflects rather accurately*
*a serious and real problem facing our world today.*

***Should you wish to learn more about the background and ongoing affairs of those involved herein, then check out the following web sites and their various social network pages.***

www.LazyDaysAfloat.com
*More about The Lady Faye and Lady Mali and luxury boating holidays on the French Canals.*

www.TrePolPenGlobal.com & www.MatchlessSecurity.com
*Maritime Security Specialists & Personal Security Consultants. Current activity and further adventures from Dan, Barry, Oleg and the team.*

www.MsssChina.com
*The very unofficial face of State Security..
we'll bring you all we can.*

www.BOSNShipping.com
*Baltic & Orient Steam Navigation Co.*

www.LIMTOPS.com
*Taiwan Ocean Pacific Shipping.*

www.NIPPONTOFCO.com
*Nippon Tokyo Ocean Freight Co.*

www.FrenchIslandCargo.com
French Island Cargo Company.

www.HotelDesertMelody.com
*Old Style Luxury in Algiers.*

www.HotelMagnificent.info
*Heritage and Tradition in Bucharest*

# Also by Harry Buckle. Sometimes Music Is My Only Friend.

This very *funny but true* story, follows the author, then with the pen name 'Pete Lennon,' from his years as being the '60's most read pop guru in *'Jackie'*, then the UK's biggest selling pop magazine. Then, under his real name, starting his own music company, and somewhat to his surprise, bringing you a hundred or so Top of the Pops hits.

"You'd think being a music journalist was safe enough, except for predatory female fans, but *I hadn't really expected the US Airforce to drop four H Bombs on me.* Real ones."

Then he found *himself reluctantly working with both the British and Russian Secret Services,* and interrogated in Moscow about what he had been doing at No. 10 Downing Street. "It seems to us you are seeking to destabilise your rulers with naked pictures of Harold Wilson. No ?"

With many of those hits coming from Depeche Mode, Yazoo, Alison Moyet, Erasure and others, confirmed the old music industry saying 'Happy to be Part of the Industry of Human Happiness' - but then sitting watching national TV news in the USA and discovering *I was apparently working with the Mafia* was a bit of a reality check".

You want to know who was to blame for 'Agadoo', 'Yviva Espana', ' The Birdie Song' and some others, likely starting the whole ' dad dancing at weddings' phenomena : 'Sometimes Music is My only Friend' reveals all this and more.
  *The book is an easy read roller coaster of a story, very much a celebration of the world that created the backdrop for the highly successful, 'Jackie the Musical'. With some fine (and funny ) recollections of life as it then developed.*

## 'Sometimes Music is My only Friend'. By Harry Buckle.

Paperback..ISBN: 978-0-9935576-0-6: Kindle e book. ISBN  978-0-9935576-1-3
Published by MarosaJokato Media            c) MarosaJokato. 2016.

### Sometimes Music is My Only Friend...by Harry Buckle.

*A fascinating look behind the scenes, the shows, the music, the business and the stars, bringing you,. All the Hits and More.*
*\*\*Oh Grandma you didn't? Did you ?\*\**

This scurrilous- but- benign journey from the sixties, through those heady days and following years, follows the author while his music companies were *bringing you parts of the soundtrack to your life.*

An easy reading, but factual , roller coaster ride through the real world of Pop and a Passion for music. Navigating the dangerous worlds of Predatory Pubescent Teenagers, Lords and Ladies, Kings and Gangsters, Winning big on the Miss World Contest, Chart fixing payola and The Mafia.

*Also revealed here for the first time, his chaotic and unwilling contributions to Britain's MI6 and Russia's KGB. "Obviously, although I had met Ian Fleming, I was hardly 007. Sending the KGB in Moscow off to search for deep meanings behind the lyrics of the Wurzels, 'I Got a Brand New Combine Harvester,' 'Looking back, I guess that was a bit flaky!"*
<u>*Depending on your decade. Remember, or try to imagine.*</u>
*How did they survive? With No Facebook, No Twitter, No What's App. No mobile phone!...Well, they struggled through, in a world of Mini Skirts and Hot Pants, Loons and Flares, Babychams and Biba, Discs and eventually Disco and Dad Dancing.*

*Despite this being a very funny book, the reality behind the title, Sometimes Music Is My Only Friend, touches the truth for many in this modern age.*

### Some recommended reads on the sea and shipping.

*Well, Rick Stein studied English at Oxford, and is prone to introducing, and indeed quoting some literary gems whilst standing on exotic shores. Joseph Conrad seems to be one of his favorites.*
*Conrad was rather forced in me at school, I gave some of his works another go recently and now 'get 'what I had missed at school.*

*So thanks Rick, for the reading recipe, and indeed to you, David Pritchard and Chris Denham for the inspiration*
*for the start of this book.*

*More recently: Rose George's: Deep Sea and Foreign Going, Maria Stahl's: Time Zones, Containers and Three Meals a Day, and Horatio Clare's: Down to the Sea in Ships.*
*Each provide their authors take on the real world of container ships and shipping.*

### But for gripping inspiration and graphic reality:

### Eric Newby's 1956 book: The Last Grain Race..

*Outward bound from Belfast to Australia on the steel hulled four masted sailing ship, Moshulu, they took the route around the Cape of Good Hope, (Turn left at the bottom of Africa).*

*Leaving Australia on the 11 of March 1939, laden with corn, sailing towards a world where the war clouds are gathering, through some real storms round Cape Horn. (Turn left at South America)*

*Having passed the Falkland Islands - they eventually make it back to 'Queenstown' in Ireland on June 10th. 91 days from Australia.*

*Have they won the 'the last grain race?'*
*Don't just look on line!*
*Read the book it's wonderful- and by a writer I could never even dream to emulate.*

*Queenstown, on the South coast of Ireland, in County Cork is of course the harbour from which on the 11 of April 1912 'The Titanic' set sail on it's tragic voyage....but that's another story altogether.*

### Harry Buckle. May 2016. Cornwall and the The Spicelands.

16732720R00194

Printed in Great Britain
by Amazon